CW00858585

DEAD AGAIN: WILL SOMEONE KILL TO KEEP THEIR SECRET?

GEORGIE HARVEY AND JOHN FRANKLIN
BOOK 2

SANDI WALLACE

PRAISE FOR SANDI WALACE'S
DEAD AGAIN

'A gem of a book. Not only is there a gripping storyline in *Dead Again* but also an emotional depth not always found in the crime genre.'

J.M. PEACE, SERVING POLICE OFFICER AND AUTHOR OF *THE TWISTED KNOT*

'*Dead Again* cuts to the chase with edgy, suspense-laden drama that exposes the dark secrets of a town shattered by loss. Once again, award-winning writer Sandi Wallace delivers a punchy read, cementing her place in Australian crime writing.'

MONIQUE MULLIGAN, REVIEWER, PUBLISHER, AND AUTHOR

'*Dead Again* is one of the new crop of Aussie crime stories that hopefully turn the world from Scandi Noir to Aussie Noir; family tensions and despair on a background of a harsh land and climate, and Wallace adds her sprinkle of romance.'

ANNE BUIST, AUTHOR OF *DANGEROUS TO KNOW*

'Sandi Wallace brings to life the complexities of a small town coming to grips with disaster, throws in a mystery that could shatter them all, and gifts us a determined and beautifully reckless heroine.'

'Ghosts from a past, their footprints left in the ashes of a devastated town. Sandi Wallace has mastered rural crime, and in *Dead Again*, does not disappoint.'

'*Dead Again* is a gripping twist on the bushfire threat all Australians live with.'

ALSO BY SANDI WALLACE

Georgie Harvey and John Franklin series

Tell Me Why

Dead Again

Into the Fog

Black Cloud

Short story collections

On the Job

Award-winning short stories

'Sweet Baby Dies' (*Scarlet Stiletto: The Eleventh Cut* – 2019)

'Fire on the Hill' (*Scarlet Stiletto: The Tenth Cut* – 2018)

'Busted' (*Scarlet Stiletto: The Eighth Cut* – 2016)

'Ball and Chain' (*Scarlet Stiletto: The Sixth Cut* – 2014)

'Silk Versus Sierra' (*Scarlet Stiletto: The Fifth Cut* – 2013)

Non-fiction

Writing the Dream (contributing author)

To Heather and Peter,
for everything you did raising this little bookworm
who dreamed of being a writer.

NEARLY THREE WEEKS TO CHRISTMAS

CHAPTER ONE

I NEVER IMAGINED KNOWING A KILLER, LET ALONE becoming one.

He lay on the floor facing the light streaming through the broken window. Not that the moon kept him awake; even if it had been pitch black, falling asleep would be a struggle. And he'd soon be woken by nightmares.

I hate myself.

He chewed the inside of his cheek. The metallic warmth of blood on his tongue didn't still the gnawing; a manifestation of self-loathing.

The voices in the other room grew rowdier. A bottle smashed. Somebody swore and laughed.

Same shit, different day.

He rolled onto his side and hitched the scratchy blanket closer. His stomach convulsed. He gasped and turned onto his back again.

Some days, his stomach merely churned and burned, protesting even the birdlike amounts he ate. Others, he cramped and vomited bloody bile. He suspected a stomach ulcer but couldn't see a doctor and didn't care, because he deserved it.

I deserve much worse.

A groan. He tensed and listened. Before long came another. He crept across the room and crouched next to his mate. He palmed his brow. Poor bugger was burning up. The man poured water onto a rag and held it to the clammy forehead.

The kid gripped his wrist. Eyes open wide.

'It's okay, bud.'

'Hungry,' his mate whispered.

'Only got cold baked beans. Okay?'

He forked beans into the younger one's mouth. His buddy ate five forkfuls before falling back onto the bag that acted as his pillow. He shuddered and fell asleep.

The man watched him for a while in the moonlight.

We'll have to move on from here.

The ones they'd hooked up with at this squat were hardened crims and risk-takers for the sake of it. They'd bring trouble on him and the kid sooner or later. They'd split tomorrow, he decided. Find a place quieter and warmer. The broken window and half-rotted timber floorboards in this room were making his mate worse, although his buddy enjoyed a few good days among the bad ones.

He propped against the dank plaster wall and contemplated his half-dead existence. Here but not where he wanted to be. Not dead but not living either. He didn't have any tears left. Sometimes he tried to cry, wanted to cry, but couldn't squeeze anything out. Happiness... gone. The only things that mattered now: not getting caught and looking after his mate.

He thought about *that moment, that day* constantly, the relative flicker in time in which he decided to take someone's life. Not just anybody. No, somebody he should have nurtured and protected against bastards like him.

He added his blanket atop his buddy's and cocooned the slim form. The kid stirred.

'My head hurts.'

The man went to his backpack again and retrieved a packet of paracetamol. He tossed it aside with a sheet of empty blisters. A further dig in his bag uncovered a stray tablet. He picked off bits of fluff and fed it to his mate.

'It's all I've got. We'll have to get some more stuff tomorrow, bud. And we'll find us a new place to stay, too. We've got to get away from those rowdy buggers.'

His buddy nodded. He gave a weak smile and gripped his hand. 'You'll see. I'll be sweet tomorrow.' He drifted into an uneasy slumber.

The man sipped water and his guts blazed.

No point trying to sleep.

He hugged his stomach and replayed what he'd done *that day* – as he would every day for the rest of his miserable life.

His reasons didn't justify his actions.

What made me this monster, the scum of the earth?

He couldn't blame a dysfunctional childhood, lack of education, being unloved or unsuccessful.

All me. All my fault.

CHAPTER TWO

GEORGIE RUBBED HER ARMS, TRYING TO GET WARM.

Coming back's a bitch.

She lowered her gaze. It'd started drizzling a short while ago. Soft, persistent droplets blurred the inscription. She knelt and trailed her fingertips over the grooves of the epitaph engraved into marble. Her heart twisted with each word. She teared up.

She lost track of time. She might've been there ten minutes or thirty. When she rose, tangled wet hair draped her collarbone, and her joints were stiff.

Her whispered 'I gave my evidence at the committal hearing' was muffled by the breeze. Louder, she said, 'Why couldn't that have been enough?'

A cockatoo screeched as if jeering her.

'Did I really have to come back?'

Abergeldie, Daylesford, and these graves...she'd revisited them all, but it left her feeling caught in no-man's land, not quite belonging anywhere, not sure how to move forward.

She ran her eyes over the modern headstones at her feet,

the old part of the Daylesford Cemetery, then the adjoining farms.

Why the hell am I back here? Because my counsellor suggested these tasks, allegedly as sum parts of 'closure'. Empty and over-exercised, that word.

•And, it's not working so far.

Georgie turned slowly towards cypress pines that swayed as the wind sighed through their waterlogged branches. She faced the direction of the Wombat Arms Hotel, but couldn't see it from here. In the backdrop, Wombat Hill looked bleak in the misty rain.

At first, it had struck her as unchanged, except that properties were lush and green, following the glut of rain through winter to now, summer.

Aside from that, what's different?

Me. Maybe eight months is too soon to revisit a war zone.

She shuffled to her car. The black duco of the 1984 Alfa Spider blended into the shadows of the pine hedge. She felt heavy in her boots, weighed down by the past.

She slipped into the car telling herself, *One last visit with my old friend Pam, and then I'm done with Daylesford.* But pulling the door closed brought it back. That less than two hours ago, she'd drawn aside coloured plastic door strips, ready to step into a café, and brushed someone's hand as they came from inside.

'Georgie? What are you doing here?'

Same bass voice. Possibly the same well-worn Levis and plain black T-shirt she'd first seen him wearing at the Wombat Arms earlier this year.

Her heart had done a weird beat, and pinned by the intensity of his gaze, she'd frozen. A blush had crept over his skin, and she'd wondered how he felt about seeing her.

She and John Franklin had a lot of history from back in

autumn, when she was last in Daylesford to check on the welfare of her neighbour's friend. Much of that history was unhappy, and she'd worked hard over recent months to forget him, but her body had betrayed her the instant he said her name. They'd been close enough that she could smell his sweet yet masculine aftershave. Her pulse thudding in her ears, palms clammy, she'd thought, *Bloody hell, he looks good.*

Georgie's gut had then cramped with conflicted emotions. Guilt was topmost, as she'd blocked the image of her boyfriend AJ's face.

Franklin had been at the hearing in Melbourne, too, but she'd avoided him. That hadn't stopped his stare boring into her whenever they passed in the Magistrates' Court lobby or hallways, or her covert glances. But at the café, she couldn't dodge him. Truthfully, she hadn't wanted to.

'Can I get you a coffee?' Franklin had jiggled his takeaway beaker.

'Have a catch up?' After a glance at the moody sky, he'd pointed to an outside table. 'The rain should hold off.'

She'd struggled to reply but taken a seat. They'd talked, drank coffees, and she'd smoked, before killing the conversation.

His eyes had stayed in the forefront of her mind as she'd walked away. They hadn't masked either what he wanted or his hurt. Her apology had burned in her ears.

'I'm sorry' doesn't make it better, for him or me.

CHAPTER THREE

'ARE YOU OKAY, LOVE?'

Georgie gasped and jumped. Hot liquid rushed over her hand, and she righted her mug, wiped her hand on her jeans. She shrugged free of her daydream to find a woman leaning towards her. She wore a crisp white apron over street clothes and had an air force-style envelope cap perched on her mop of brown hair. Georgie recalled she'd been served by her earlier from behind the bakery counter.

'You look like shit.' The woman smiled, revealing buck-teeth which strangely suited her, and her eyes crinkled, taking the edge off her words.

Georgie returned the smile, hoping the bakery assistant would leave it at that, relieved when she flapped her dishcloth and re-entered the building.

Alone again with her coffee, her thoughts reverted to Bullock, a tiny hamlet at the base of Mount Starke in Victoria's north central district. She had no recollection of travelling here, of passing through places like the rambling outer suburb of Lilydale and the vineyards and farms in the

Yarra Valley or navigating the constant S-curves of the Black Spur ascending the Great Dividing Range. And she'd taken the turnoff to this town in the same automatic state.

Her mind had been full of other things.

This assignment came through last night, and as her first rural-based story for the magazine, it raked up events she still hadn't put behind her, as yesterday had proven. Even in bed, Georgie couldn't switch off the memories replayed in an erratic home movie, and she'd moved to the sofa so not to disturb AJ. Her cat, Phoebe, had followed her and nested purring against her chest. It was sweet but didn't lull her to sleep.

Georgie sipped her coffee. It had cooled, but the strong caffeine grounded her. She scanned the street, her editor's instructions echoing in her mind.

A very special story – no pressure or anything.

She tried to see the town of Bullock objectively. Hard because she'd been here before. *Gut feel of this place?* She picked up her pen, rested the nib on her notepad. *First impressions?*

As if in answer, clouds that had threatened since her arrival burst. Water pummelled the perspex roof above her and ricocheted off bitumen that steamed with the almost tropical downpour.

Georgie considered the structures nearby. Signs of rebuilding were significantly less than she'd expected given it was two years on. Portables here and there accommodated struggling businesses; one with the original picket fence marking the front boundary, another sitting beside the large, charcoaled stump of a gumtree.

Water dripped from the verandah roof onto Georgie's notepad.

Where are the animals and birds?

She couldn't remember seeing any since she'd pulled into town. Equally hauntingly, several of the original landmark signposts remained. Warped, scorched, and missing a couple of planks, they pointed to ghosts of guest houses, an antique centre, a plant nursery and the ravaged mountain. Those signs were so evocative that Georgie expected smoke to fill her nostrils.

But that wasn't the story she'd come to get.

'What day is it, love?'

Georgie turned towards the voice, skimming over a woman in a wheelchair to take in an old man wearing black Adidas tracksuit pants with red stripes, a lemon polo shirt and runners, which clashed with his snowy hair and wrinkled face yet fit with his lean and spry build.

'He's always forgetting,' a boy clad in baker's whites commented with a laugh. He lugged a sack from the van out front and jumped rivulets of water running too fast for the drains.

The old man chuckled. 'It's true.' He tapped his skull. 'Sharp as a tack, except I can't remember short-term things. Couldn't tell you what I watched on television last night or what day of the week it is to save my life. But you could fill a set of encyclopaedias with what I recall of Australian and British history.'

That must suck.

Georgie said aloud, 'It's Thursday.'

'Much obliged,' the old man replied. He offered his right hand and shook Georgie's, smiling warmly. 'Norman Poole and this is my child bride, Dawn.'

His wife had to be eighty or thereabouts, too, but in contrast to Norman's contemporary attire wore a drab, old-fashioned floral housecoat that pulled over a plump body and exposed dimply freckled arms. *Child bride,* good to see he hadn't lost his sense of humour with his short-term memory.

The same couldn't be said for Dawn Poole. She sat rigid in her wheelchair without acknowledging her husband's introduction or Georgie's reply and outstretched hand.

Georgie dropped her hand, unsure if the slight was personal.

Norman patted his wife's arm. 'C'mon, MG. Let's get you home.' With a nodded farewell, he raised the golf umbrella attached to her wheelchair, then ambled away.

Alone again, Georgie wondered where the nickname MG came from. As she lifted her coffee mug, a movement caught her eye. A lone sparrow flitted from paver to paver near her table.

'There you go, sweetie.' She dropped crumbs from her plate near the little bird. 'Glad to see you're not all gone.' She smiled, spirits boosted.

But soon she forgot the odd, old couple and the sparrow, lost in dark thoughts filled with bushfires and her assignment.

———

Georgie entered the cavernous tin-walled building as a telephone rang. A woman behind the information desk was the only person in sight and gave a small smile in greeting, then picked up the receiver, allowing Georgie to browse freely.

Tourism featured in the nearest nook. Bullock used to boast an array of hospitality and seasonal ventures, but it had so little to offer now: one brewery, a yabby farm, basic caravan park, and garden mosaic workshop. 'Wanted' flyers seeking help revegetating the historic waterfalls and promos for Alexandra, Healesville and the Yarra Glen winery region outnumbered local attractions and filled the next row of the brochure display.

'Kelly! 'ello!' a man called.

Georgie turned to the entranceway and took in the speaker's long legs, broad shoulders, brown hair in a medium-length shag over a high forehead and equally stretched face. He looked as eccentric as old Mr Poole, and she hid a smile, thinking of the colour these characters would add to her feature.

'Want something from the store?'

The woman—*Kelly*—covered the mouthpiece of her phone and replied, 'The newspaper would be good. Cheers, Clive.'

He left. Kelly continued her hushed conversation. And Georgie couldn't ignore the main display in the info centre any longer, although she felt repelled by it too.

She moved hesitantly to the centre of the room until directly in front of a miniature scale village on stilts. She bent to examine each component inside the glass case.

There was the bakery, unscathed by the fire, flanked by a row of anonymous structures (unbuilt and unlet, she guessed). She easily recognised the new hostel, positioned across from the rebuilt motel. Not far up, a ski hire business was detailed right down to tiny tyre chains framing the pole sign on the kerb, then yet more unbuilt shops. Next, she inspected a cluster opposite the info centre: the general store with licensed GPO, Teddy Bears Picnic (odds-on a gift shop with lots of bears) and a small library. Adjacent to the info centre were a petrol station and police station on respective sides.

Colourful plastic buildings, fake water and grass, and masses of pygmy people. The proposed Bullock reconstruction offered promise and revealed desperation at the same time. It was trying too hard. And it brought home to Georgie as a city-dweller that the devastation two years ago went deeper than charred hillsides and ruined houses.

Her eyes found the historic hotel and caravan park at the end of the shopping strip. Only the bitumen road and fifty metres between them. One untouched, the other had burned to the ground and since been recreated. She shuddered and repositioned to take in the modules behind the main street.

The sports precinct, primary school and attached kindergarten were all impressive. Off from the town centre were two sprawling properties labelled 'minimum four-star guest house/conference centre'.

'Can I help you?'

Georgie jumped; she'd missed Kelly's approach. She turned the movement into a gesture at the model. 'How important are these four-star businesses to the Bullock reconstruction?'

The slender woman shrugged and threaded a ballpoint pen into her wispy bun. 'We used to have five major accommodation venues, and they pulled most of the tourists to the town. Couples on romantic getaways and corporates well exceeded our snow tourists.'

She spoke knowledgeably, inside her comfort-zone. Georgie nodded, encouraging her to continue.

'We need two guest houses to commit to rebuilding to move on to the next stage of the works. Council, government and other businesses are all holding back until then. But while it's crucial for two to get on board without further delay, it'll take four or more for the town to become viable.'

Kelly used her thumb to wipe a smudge off the glass case. Her mouth tightened, making Georgie assess the odds that four luxury facilities would gamble again on this high-risk bushfire region. She wanted to believe it'd happen but thought, *Poor to none.*

She thanked Kelly and moved into the other nook, which housed a historical society display. The exhibits were overshadowed by a notice soliciting donations of photographs, documents or relics relating to the Bullock heritage before the fire.

Kelly's voice startled her again. 'What's your interest? Miss, err–?'

'Georgie Harvey.' She passed over a business card, although she'd intended to stay under the radar a little longer if possible, scoping the town at arm's length before starting interviews. 'I'm researching a feature story to mark the two-year anniversary of Red Victoria.'

The other woman's face shut down. Clearly, this wasn't going to be easy, and Georgie had to win her trust. 'Do you live locally?'

Kelly scrunched Georgie's card in her hand and nodded. 'And you lived here before the bushfire too?'

Kelly jerked her head again in reply, then corrected, '*Wildfire.*'

'Sorry?'

'Bushfires; they happen every year. No doubt about it, they destroy, can be hard to contain and can kill. But what we had that day right across Victoria were *wildfires.*'

She made the word *wildfires* sound sinister, and Georgie's gut flipped in response.

'Speed, height, intensity, spread and spotting distance. They were unstoppable.' Kelly squared her shoulders and stepped backwards.

Georgie had lost her. She scrambled for something to rescue the interview. She guessed Kelly was in her early thirties, so they were similar in age but not lifestyle. Yet two things generally dissolved barriers: food and drink.

'Could I buy you a coffee?'

Kelly flicked the edge of Georgie's card. She hissed, 'My pain's private, not for the entertainment of the champagne set in Melbourne.'

Georgie bristled, embarrassment and pride in competition. '*Champagne Musings* is a monthly magazine with national distribution.' Because it had such a bloody stupid name, she added her rehearsed blurb, 'We cover life, culture, politics and style, and feature some hard-hitting journalism.'

'Sorry.' Kelly stretched the word sarcastically. 'My pain's not for the national *hard-hitting* champagne set.'

Georgie counted to ten to defuse the emotion, then drew Kelly's gaze. 'I'm sorry if it feels intrusive, but people need to know. It's my job to educate and enlighten as much as to entertain.'

While the woman processed her comment, Georgie studied her face. Care lines that hadn't shown minutes ago aged her well beyond her years.

'Well, I'm sorry too.' Kelly pointed a long finger to her forehead. 'I see pictures that are from a horror movie. I hear the roar of flames that's something like ten freight trains bearing down.' She frowned heavily. 'It's impossible to describe. It's a unique sound. Terrifying. And I hear the death screams of humans and animals.' Hoarsely, she added, 'Ever heard that?'

Not trusting her voice, Georgie shook her head.

'I feel the ghosts of my friends. This is stuff that I wouldn't believe if it hadn't happened to me. It keeps me awake at night.' She rolled her eyes. 'Hour upon hour, every single night. And the *smells*...' Kelly shuddered.

It felt cruel to want more, but Georgie hung on each word.

'How can your readers understand when it sounds so unreal, so melodramatic? But it's my living reality. And that of my neighbours – those who lived.'

Georgie felt hot behind the eyes. She squeezed Kelly's arm and received a wan smile. 'Can I ask one more thing for now?'

At Kelly's nod, Georgie said, 'Why did you return after the fire?'

'Because it's home.' The words hung for a long moment, then Kelly added, 'And because no matter where I am, the nightmares are always there.'

———

Georgie left the info centre and slid into the Spider, turned over the motor, but just stared through the windscreen at the feeble sun peeking from behind the clouds.

This assignment's going to be a bitch.

Eventually, she shook off her inertia and pulled the car into the adjacent petrol station. An easel promised full driveway service, so she stayed in the convertible, feeling like an idiot as time ticked by. After two or three minutes, she filled the tank herself and skirted drying puddles to enter the shipping container-turned-shop to pay.

Someone brushed past and hurried behind the counter, muttering, 'Sorry!'

Georgie did a double-take. She blurted, 'Do you work here too?'

Kelly laughed grimly. 'Nah. The guy who normally works at the servo is having one of his bad days.'

CHAPTER FOUR

'It's always the bloody way,' Franklin grumbled.

'How's that?'

'Look forward to a quiet one at the pub and a pair of jokers have to spoil it.' He set his half-full pot on the table and scanned until he spotted the culprits. So far, they were merely heckling.

'Drink up.' His mate nudged Franklin's beer closer. 'They'll be right.'

'Maybe.' Franklin took another draught but kept a watch on the two blueing men.

'We'd play better next year if you make a comeback. Can we talk you into it?'

Quietly flattered to be begged out of retirement, Franklin knew it reflected more upon the piss-poor talent on the senior footy team than his skills. 'Nuh, I'll stick with coaching. The old knee has a hard enough time keeping up with the little tackers.'

'Any future AFL stars coming through?'

Franklin chuckled. 'Mate, you always ask me that. It's off-season and all. Do you really think our

Daylesford Under 15s will spawn the next Matty Richardson?'

———

Georgie lay on the bed after phoning AJ. Although exhausted from lack of sleep the night before and the intense afternoon, it would be a mistake to try to sleep now because her mind was in overdrive. But for once what happened in autumn, and other recurring worries, didn't figure. They'd been sidelined by this new assignment.

She replayed Kelly's interview in her mind. The photos she'd taken around town afterwards were on a repeating slideshow on her computer but already burned into her memory. And she couldn't shake the hostility she'd encountered at the pub tonight.

After ordering a counter meal, she'd tried to chat with the publican. He'd stared her down. His 'That'll be all, then' hadn't been a question, and he'd moved off to huddle with a couple of guys who intermittently turned to look at her.

She'd managed about a quarter of her veal parma when one of the men peeled away from the group. He'd strutted towards Georgie and sat on the stool next to hers.

Without introduction, he'd said, 'Instead of writing some poncy story, why don't you do something useful?' He'd jabbed a stumpy finger at the counter, making Georgie's cutlery rattle against her plate. 'Like find the murdering bastard that did this.' He'd waved around the virtually empty bar, probably meaning the whole town.

He'd abruptly risen, overturning his stool. 'Print that and I'll shoot you.'

His raw hurt had ruined her appetite. She'd felt the men talking about her as she left the pub.

Georgie stared at her photo slideshow. She wouldn't have a problem finding a story. Everyone here carried a tragic story. The tricky bit was finding the right one. And people who would go on record.

———

Franklin abandoned his beer as the volume of the troublemakers elevated.

'I'll have you!'

'Yeah, well, come on!'

Shorty shoved Lanky. Lanky had a good three inches on him in height, but Shorty's stout build propelled him into the bar.

Franklin rose as Lanky retaliated with a cruel verbal jab. 'What would Monica think?'

'Leave me wife out of this!'

One of Franklin's companions moaned. 'You're off duty. Let them sort it.'

Franklin threw back, 'A cop's never off duty,' as he closed the gap to the bar.

He set his shoulders, angled his body in between the men and pried them apart. It worked a treat; they had no leverage to strike him or each other. 'Cut it out, fellas.'

Shorty said, 'Mind your own business. This is between me and that prick.'

The bloke swatted Franklin's hands away. He had sodden rings under his arms and whiffed a bit. *Might be a stress-sweater.*

Franklin gave him a hard look. Shorty was familiar, a local, although not on their books as far as he knew. Not a habitual hothead then, unless he generally did it behind closed doors.

'It is my business. Senior Constable Franklin.' He flipped his badge. 'What's the problem here?'

'It's private,' Shorty retorted, folding his arms.

Lanky smirked, and Franklin decided the fellow's attitude matched his slick shirt. He needed to be knocked down a peg or two. 'Names?'

'Don't think we have to tell you that.' Lanky hooked his thumbs through his belt loops.

I should've let Shorty land a knockout punch.

'You're disturbing the peace, and Manny here could have you up on charges.'

The barman dipped his head once.

Shorty said, 'Neil Hudson.'

Lanky gave a deep sigh. 'Marc Jones.' He held out his hand to shake. Franklin ignored it.

The mob gathered and jostled for prime position. One knucklehead yelled, 'Who'yer backing, boys? Five bucks on your favourite.'

'Get back to your drinks, people,' Franklin called, keeping one eye on the original troublemakers.

The crowd inched back. Not far enough for his liking.

He asked Hudson, 'What's this about?'

'It's between me, him and me wife.'

'Well, you blokes sort it out peacefully or I'll be down on you like a tonne of bricks.'

Lanky sniggered.

Franklin pinned him with a glare. 'What's your problem, Jones?'

'That's funny considering he,' Jones pointed at the other fellow, 'is a brickie.'

Onlookers booed or chuckled, depending on which corner they were in, and Jones laughed, egging them on further.

'And what's funny about that?' Hudson shot back, attempting to grab his adversary.

'Righto, settle or we'll take this to the station.' Franklin eyed the two rivals. No way he'd let them out on the street together. 'One of you has to leave. And one stays until I say differently.'

He shook his head at background grumbles from the spectators who wanted blood sport, countered by a sprinkle of applause.

It didn't surprise him at all that Jones said, 'Why should I go?'

Hudson re-folded his arms.

'Decide who or I will. One of you goes. Now!'

'All right. All right. I'll go,' Jones said. 'She'll be gagging for it again anyway!' He grabbed his own groin and bucked.

Hudson's punch almost connected. Franklin shoved him against the bar. Even if Jones deserved it, he couldn't let it happen.

'Keep that up and I'll take you both in.'

They dropped their fists but kept bitching under their breaths.

'Okay, people,' Franklin shooed the crowd, 'the show's over. Move away.'

He waited for the throng to disperse and warned in a low voice, 'Jones, get out of here. Both of you, remember you're on notice. Any sniff of trouble, whether I'm on or off duty, and I will take great pleasure in slapping you with charges and then into a cell. You got that?'

CHAPTER FIVE

'THIS IS HOPELESS.' GEORGIE ROLLED OUT OF BED AND took a shower. She stayed under the needlepoints of hot water until it turned cold.

Her head ached. Two days in a row of shitty sleep would mess with anyone. But she'd had the best nights' sleep in eight months last week and dared to hope that insomnia was finally behind her. Last night proved that was not the case.

She took a cup of instant coffee outside and curled into the green plastic chair under the verandah, knees tucked against her chest. She drank the bitter coffee, lit a cigarette and took a long drag, feeling an answering kick of energy.

Georgie got to the end of her smoke and stared as the paper burned towards the filter. Although this summer was unusually wet and green, and they'd just had the wettest winter and spring in years, it only took a discarded ciggie, freak wind gust and some dry material to start a fire. In overkill, she crushed the butt into the sand-filled tub and checked it was out before digging it in deep.

She went inside and cranked her laptop, but her WiFi

wasn't talking. She then tried both the verandah and leaning on the Spider's bonnet for wireless access, without luck, and left the motel to walk the streets of Bullock.

The stories she'd heard yesterday—particularly from Kelly at the info centre—made her notice much more than she had the previous day.

There was an oversupply of vacant blocks. New builds were few and far between. A handful of plots bore freshly poured concrete slabs and pristine materials sat alongside, ready for the next stage. One place had its frame up, but the timber had greyed and warped, and grass runners crept over the slab and wound up the posts. The site looked forlorn. Perhaps the owners had run out of money. Or lost the heart to rebuild.

Most shocking were the neighbouring properties with foundations, charred chimneys, buckled water tanks and scorched debris, seemingly abandoned since the fire or a cursory clean-up afterwards.

Georgie stared at one of these until she imagined how the home used to look and visualised a station wagon in front of the garage and kids with their dog in the garden on a hot summer's day. She turned away when that picture morphed into a prematurely dark and smoky sky.

From there, it seemed safer to peer inside the few businesses, including the library.

Still an hour to kill until opening time.

At least the bakery is open.

———

Outside the bakery, Georgie sat slumped on the same bench as yesterday, a fresh bread roll and mug of steaming, black, unsweetened coffee her breakfast. Unlike the instant one earlier, the coffee was aromatic and perfectly made. Soon, the caffeine performed its magic mellowing thing. She tore off a chunk of warm bread and let it go sticky on her tongue, then grabbed up her mobile when it rang, smiling broadly when she saw the caller's name.

'Bron!'

'*Guess what, Georgie Girl?*' Her best friend laughed and raced on. '*The Woomballano has invited me to exhibit.*'

Georgie whistled. The gallery was one of Melbourne's best and featured only notable Australian female artists. The invitation was a huge deal. 'Congrats, that's –'

Her friend cut in excitedly. '*They emailed ten minutes ago, Jo's so proud, I can't believe it! I've already got these ideas; Jo thinks they'll be good, but she's my partner, she's going to say that. I want your honest opinion, GG.*'

From overexcited, run-on sentences, Bron dropped into an almost-whisper as she described a new series of pastels on the theme Belonging.

'*And I think I'll add one oil,*' she mused. '*Something completely different to the rest of the collection.*'

Georgie looked around the almost-deserted town. 'You could call it "On the outer".'

Bron went silent, and Georgie thought she hated the idea. Then she said, '*That's perfect,*' and laughed. The sound mimicked the flute that Bron played beautifully and made Georgie's muscles even more pliable than the coffee and nicotine had managed.

'*You're a keeper, GG!*'

Georgie replied dryly, 'Phew,' and Bron said, '*Must fly. This collection isn't going to paint itself!*'

Then her friend was gone, and Georgie picked up her mug just as she heard, 'What day is it, love?'

She grinned, turning to face the old couple. 'Friday.'

'Oh, look, Dawn. It's that lovely girl from the other day. Er, what's-her-name?'

'Georgie, Mr Poole.'

'I retired from teaching a decade ago and left *Mr Poole* in the classroom. Norman is fine. And Dawn.'

Georgie said hello to the old lady. Dawn turned her eyes, but she didn't speak and kept her expression sombre.

'Out for a walk again?'

'Uh-huh. That's the highlight of our days, isn't it, darl?' Norman glanced at his wife, who made no sign she'd heard or understood him.

Today Norman wore blue denim jeans, runners and a T-shirt with the *Just do it* logo. His wife's dress matched yesterday's, except it had blue flowers rather than pink ones, along with a yellow stain front and centre – *egg for brekkie?*

'Dawn doesn't enjoy travelling in the car anymore. And she's stuck in this thing,' he tapped the wheelchair backrest, 'so I walk and she rides as we circuit the town after breakfast and lunch and before dinner every day. Rain, hail, shine or snow.' Norman smoothed a wrinkled hand over his crown, adding, 'Or squalls.'

The humid wind had teased the couple's hair into bouffants, but at least they'd managed their course between showers.

'Would you like a cuppa?' Georgie offered.

'Oh, no, we just finished one.' Nonetheless, Norman manoeuvred the wheelchair around the table and sat opposite. 'We could stop for a natter, though.' He chuckled as if it'd be the highlight of his day, supposing he remembered it later.

Georgie's eyebrows pinched together. Norman had struck her as a sweetie straightaway. But she was on a job, and it'd be remiss to leave him off her interview list.

As she considered her approach, he brought it to a head. 'And what brings such a lovely lassie to our humble town?'

You old flirt.

Georgie smiled, though she cringed inwardly. Given the adverse reactions from Kelly at the info centre and the men at the pub last night, she hoped Norman still thought well of her after this.

'I'm writing a feature story to mark the two-year anniversary of Red Victoria.'

A long uncomfortable pause followed.

'Oh,' Norman eventually muttered.

Dawn shifted in her wheelchair.

Another hiatus and the old man added, 'Terrible thing. Terrible thing.'

My assignment or the fires?

Dawn's fingers gripped the arms on her chair.

So, she understands some of what goes on.

'Terrible thing,' the retired teacher repeated. 'If they catch the murdering fire-raiser, they ought to string him up on a tree and burn him to death.'

Georgie had heard it before. The court of public opinion held that arson was attempted murder or actual murder depending on fatalities. And she agreed with that. It was the *eye for an eye, life for a life* sentiment that stuck in her throat.

'That's fair,' Norman argued. 'He lit the fire aware it'd take human lives, arguably intending it. Why should he be spared the same fate?'

'What if he's mentally ill?' she countered.

Dawn emitted a low hum. It made the bread roll in Georgie's stomach sit heavy.

The old man rubbed his wife's arm and shot back, 'He'd want to be. You couldn't be sane and live with yourself...*having done that*. It doesn't mean he shouldn't be held to pay, though.'

'Yes, I get that.' Georgie nodded. Mental illness didn't excuse arson. And for the victims, their families and the public, the offenders needed to be held accountable, punished or at the very least prevented from repeating the atrocity.

Norman gulped a breath. Angst still filled his eyes. 'He killed forty-six of our friends and neighbours.'

A horrific number out of a town of about six hundred.

'But the human cost is more than that.' The old man grabbed Georgie's hands over the table. She squeezed back, to show she felt for him. 'Don't you see? It's more than those who died plus the number who ended up in hospital with physical injuries.'

He dropped one hand to smack the wheel of Dawn's chair. 'It's also those who'll never be well again, here,' he touched his chest, 'and here,' he rapped his temple.

Just as her heart had gone out to Kelly, sympathy and sadness for Norman and Dawn flooded through Georgie.

Norman's expression turned from pained to incensed. 'What's worse is not knowing who the bastard is. Perhaps he lives here in town, is someone we see all the time.'

Georgie anticipated his next words.

'What if he's someone we call a friend?'

TWO WEEKS TO CHRISTMAS

CHAPTER SIX

HE HADN'T WANTED ANYTHING MORE TO DO WITH THE other three. But they needed him and the kid as lookouts and promised there was money in it for everyone. At least a few hundred. And they needed food, painkillers, other stuff. But it boiled down to the fact that he was too scared to say no to the others.

So he stood out the front and the kid took the rear. Watching out for trouble, while the others went into the building.

His stomach played up as time went on. It seemed to be taking forever, and he hated hearing things smash inside and loud laughter like they were having a ball wrecking things.

He went inside to check if they were nearly done, and they'd trashed the place. Same as they'd done to their latest squat – it used to be someone's home; now it was a rubbish tip. And someone cared about this place too; it was their business, their lifeblood.

It wasn't supposed to be like this. He tried to tidy up some of the broken glass and Stevo smacked him away. Told him to go back outside. Pull his head in.

He did, reminding himself that he'd have money for what the kid needed. And when he heard a cheer go up, he figured they'd found a lot more than they'd expected.

But back at the squat, he and the kid got twenty bucks each. Like that was going to go far. The others reckoned they'd only found a hundred bucks and split it equally, but he didn't believe it. He didn't trust them. And he didn't like what they'd done.

———

Georgie's foot and shoulder blades rested against the wall as she pulled on a cigarette. She flipped her left wrist and snorted. Even eight months on, she occasionally fell into right-side dominant habits of expecting her watch to be on her left.

She revolved her left hand and examined the palm, an action she generally avoided. But today she wanted to look at the angry seam from heel to the index finger and watch the nerves quiver. If she fucked up this assignment and couldn't find the story Sheridan wanted, she'd take one thing away from it already. Compared with some people's lot, her attack in March and injuries were nothing.

Georgie lowered her hand and snuck another glance at

the little girl who also waited at the library. In profile, she was a pretty redheaded pre-schooler who dimpled as she giggled at whatever her mum just said. But when she turned to gaze at Georgie, the other side of her face was fire-scarred. And yet she smiled brightly.

As Georgie opened her mouth to converse with the mum-and-daughter pair, Kelly's friend from the info centre—*Clive*—arrived with a hearty greeting and unlocked the door. Apparently, he was the Bullock librarian.

———

'Are you moping again?' Constable Scott Hart slapped Franklin's shoulder en route to his desk.

Franklin's face heated, but he ignored the jibe. Then he heard their other mate, Mick Sprague, snigger and couldn't help taking the bait. 'Shut up, Slam.'

The bastard laughed harder.

The front door squealed. As Harty was prepping for a court attendance and Slam was about to go off shift, Franklin rose.

Harty just wouldn't let it go. 'So Georgie Harvey's not the one.'

Franklin threw a balled-up scrap of paper at the back of his neck. The other two kept carrying on as he sauntered down the cramped hallway. He tossed over his shoulder, 'Shut up.'

He rounded the corner, caught a glimpse of a blue monkey suit and remembered that Constable-fast-track-wanker-Wells had finally fast-tracked his way back to Melbourne, with his replacement due today.

Franklin said, 'G'day, mate.' Then he viewed the

newcomer properly. *Shit.* 'Ah, sorry, g'day, ah, pal, buddy.' Rattled, his face heated again.

The female officer grinned and held out a hand. 'Sam Tesorino, probationary constable. I'm starting my on-the-job training here today?'

'John Franklin, senior connie.'

They shook.

Sam stared up at him, and he clocked her at about five-foot-one. Her uniform was so new that the blue and white chequered band on her cap glowed, reflecting a bright smile and big, round brown eyes.

First post after graduating; she seemed so young and far too pretty and small to be a real cop. She made him feel big and awkward and very old-school.

———

'So, that's our grand station, Sam.' Franklin gestured the newbie to a seat at the lunchroom table. 'Tea, coffee? How do you take it?'

Sam jumped to her feet. 'I'll do it, sir.'

'Sit. You'll get enough practice.' He waved her down.

'Oh, if you're sure? Coffee, white with none, please.'

While he prepared their coffees, Franklin saw her squirm on the seat and pluck at the laminate table edge. Her dark blue sleeves dropped halfway over her hands. They were tiny hands and it was hard to imagine them wielding a pistol or baton. She'd definitely stand out in their crew of tall, broad, blokey-blokes.

Once he sat opposite, she turned the full force of her smile on him again.

'You're somewhat of a hero at the academy, sir.'

'Drop the sir. We keep it relaxed among ourselves

unless the big knobs are down or you're in trouble. Call me Franklin.'

'Okay.' Sam drew out the word, showing doubt. 'Well, our firearms instructor is an old friend of yours?'

'Old Divola? Is he still scaring the crap out of you recruits?'

'Yeah.' She made it two syllables, a definite yes.

'He's a good bloke underneath.' Franklin smiled. They'd shared some good times.

Sam said, 'We had worse than him. Anyway, he told us all about your recent stalker and multiple-murder cases?'

Wide eyes and question marks at the end of her statements. Franklin saw he'd have to knock the awe out of her and more confidence in or she'd be easy prey on the street.

'You saved three lives –'

He cut her off. 'Don't believe everything you hear, Sam. Just doing my job.'

'Oh, I don't think so, sir, ah, Franklin. You earned a Valour Award.'

Uncomfortable, he replied, 'Me, Harty, the rest of the crew, the sarge—and *you*—same circumstances, I'm sure we'd all do the same thing.'

The sharp scrape of his chair leg signalled an end to the discussion. 'Right, let's see what happened overnight.'

————

Most of the families had dispersed after kids' story time, although the redhead and her mum lingered in the children's book area. When Georgie rose, she was immediately pushed back to the chair from behind.

'Leave the little one alone.' The librarian, Clive,

dropped onto the adjacent seat. 'She and her mum have had enough to bear.'

Georgie's ears burned in a mix of embarrassment and annoyance. Then she considered his body language. He had more to say. She itched for the voice recorder in her bag but held still.

'So, Georgie Harvey, from some fancy-dancy magazine. My chum Kelly from across the road told me you're here to pick off our scabs.'

A turned-down mouth didn't mask the crow's feet creasing with dry humour.

Even so, Georgie's stomach clenched. She fixed him with an intense look. 'I'm not here to hurt anyone or set back their healing.'

Wide-gazed, Clive said, 'But surely you realise that an outsider looking in, asking questions, dredging up the past, could well have that effect?'

Flustered, Georgie had no answer. She thought about Kelly's comments yesterday. 'I get that you feel you're being hung out on the clothesline for public entertainment. I promise you that I'm going to manage this sensitively and write a feature that'll do your community proud.'

Clive scratched the stubble above his lip.

'I believe that you believe that. But I have a terrible feeling that your best intentions will play out wrong.'

Dread banded Georgie's chest.

What if he's right?

He touched his upper lip again. 'Even so, you're here, you've a story to write.' He quit rubbing. With the same finger, he tapped his cheek and nodded in time.

'You won't be writing this, though.' He dropped into his story-teller voice on low volume. 'Mum over there,' he inclined his head, 'was at a weekend work conference. Dad, the girl and her older twin brothers were home when the fire-front ripped through. Those two are the only survivors of that family. And God knows how many times the little one has nearly died since. Mum will never forgive herself for letting down the family, though truth be told, what could she have done if she'd been home? You'd understand, she'd fight like a fox to shield her one remaining child from any more pain than what she's been through and what she'll go through yet with that scarring?'

Georgie blinked.

Clive took it as agreement.

'If you promise to leave the little one and her mum in peace, I'll be your guinea pig. Fire away.'

CHAPTER SEVEN

'GRAB YOUR GEAR, SAM. FIRST JOB.' FRANKLIN swooped up cap and folder, grabbed keys off the board and held the door for the young officer.

Inside the marked four-wheel drive, he explained, 'We've got a callout to an overnight incident at a warehouse.'

He zipped the truck through the Burke Square roundabout and nosed up Albert Street.

'Vandalism and burglary. Vics are a well-liked local couple. Angelo and Maria Galassi.'

He hooked the wide bend and indicated left into Spa Drive. 'The business is called Magical Mineral Springs Party Hire.'

'Ahh, is that it?' Sam pointed to a musk-stick pink and white striped building.

Franklin patrolled by or dropped in at the place regularly but saw it through her eyes as she said, 'It looks good enough to eat, doesn't it?'

He pulled up out front and agreed, 'Like you could pick lollies off the wall.'

As they unbuckled, he checked, 'Got your gloves handy?'

Sam nodded, tugging them from a pouch on her equipment belt. She snapped them on, and he judged she didn't need to be told to preserve the scene. It was a promising start.

Soon as they jumped out of the truck, a male and a female rushed from a door painted smartie blue. The olive-skinned, middle-aged bloke wore a black suit with a snowy white shirt, tie and rosebud on his lapel, all very formal for a Friday morning. The blonde woman, roughly eight to ten years younger, was also overdressed in a full-skirted white satin dress.

They were just like dolls off the top of a wedding cake, except for their bright yellow gloves.

Franklin greeted Angelo and Maria and introduced Sam, and both had their hands pumped by the couple.

Maria hung onto Sam's hand. '*Sei Italiana, vero?*' She gestured at herself, her husband and Sam, beaming as if the copper was a new member of their club.

Franklin gathered she'd asked something like *Are you Italian?* Tesorino for a surname was a good giveaway, as was Sam's complexion.

'*Sì.*' Sam nodded.

'Good girl,' Maria said in English, then switched back to Italian. The three conversed for a few minutes, sobering when Sam pointed at Franklin.

Angelo said, 'We came in this morning to finish the last-minute arrangements for a lunchtime wedding. Luckily, most of it we delivered yesterday. We were to pick up a few extras and drive on to Glenlyon. But we found this mess!' He flung his arms wide and teared up.

Poor bugger. Franklin looked at Maria, giving Angelo a moment to compose himself.

'Our beautiful kids' party stuff is all over the floor,' she said. 'It's all dirty, but not too much's broken.'

'But they ruined our embroidered tablecloths –'

'Ruined.'

'Hold on.' Franklin held up a hand. 'Let's start with the basics. How did they gain entry?'

'The louvre window above the toilet at the back of the building is smashed,' Maria replied. 'It looks as if they came in there. But the back door's wide open, so they probably unlocked it from inside and walked out.' She whacked her palm to forehead.

'No alarm system?'

'We didn't think we needed one – this is Daylesford, not Melbourne.' Angelo shrugged his shoulders up to his ears. 'Everyone knows us. We do all their parties.'

Franklin gave his back a sympathetic pat. 'Have you touched anything?'

'The front door,' the bloke confessed. 'Only because we didn't know anything was wrong then.'

'Anything else?'

'A bit,' Maria admitted.

Franklin groaned inwardly.

'But not until we were wearing these.'

She and her husband lifted their yellow hands.

He noted that the fingers of the rubber gloves were diamond cut, so with luck, they hadn't touched too much, as the patterning could obscure offender fingerprints. Still, not bad for civvies. They'd shown some nous.

'Right. Better show us.'

Maria and Angelo preceded the police officers. Inside the warehouse, they inspected the graffiti and damage.

Franklin lifted his head and inhaled. He didn't detect anything apart from the odour of fresh paint.

'Sam, can you take preliminary notes?' He tossed his mobile phone to her, adding, 'Take a few snaps for now too. Depending on the extent of things, we'll need to call in the crime scene crew.'

As she dug into her pockets for pad and pen, Franklin queried, 'Is there more?'

'Yes!' Maria pulled him outside the gaping rear doorway and pointed.

Profanities, graphics, and tags—a couple familiar to Franklin and others he didn't recognise—defiled virtually the entire wall.

Sam whistled softly. She gazed around, with her face wrinkled, then back to the graffiti. 'That's a lot of graffiti. It'd have taken ages. But there's no one overlooking this factory, no neighbours to worry about, no direct street lighting, so no need to rush.'

Franklin hiked his eyebrows. Her logic was spot on. 'Yep.'

They skirted the building, keeping a good distance from potential evidence. As Sam noted, the private position played into the crooks' hands. Even late morning on a Friday, he could only hear distant traffic on the highway and reverse beeps from a truck a few doors up.

Franklin squatted beside glass fragments and scanned the area. The concreting stopped at the back door. Overnight rain plus bare ground...*Bingo bango, we have a stamp pad.* Was that a footprint? He squinted. *Yep.*

Sam crouched next to him. 'Good footprint. I'll find something to cover it with, boss.'

He smiled. Sam was proving to be quick and intelligent. And the deferential title kind of pleased him too.

Boss, huh. How will Lunny like that?

He asked the couple, 'Anything else?'

'Yes, they broke into the till and safe. They stole our float and some savings.'

It said much about the Galassis that money figured last.

'How much did they take?'

Angelo fluttered a hand. 'Give or take, eighteen hundred.'

Franklin raised a brow. 'Do you usually have so much cash around?'

Maria erupted into tears with a loud cry. 'Never!'

CHAPTER EIGHT

All quiet in the library. And once Clive Norling offered himself up as Georgie's guinea pig, he turned from sceptical to obliging.

The librarian pulled volumes of books and folders off the shelves, downloaded information from various sites and piled it upon Georgie, accompanied by a patter of local narrative. But she sensed he wasn't ready to talk about his Red Victoria experience. Not yet.

'Your editor didn't give you much of a brief.'

'Uh-huh. She does that with special features. Says it gives us room to find our full potential. Either that or plenty of rope to hang ourselves.'

He guffawed.

They spent the next few minutes lost in separate thoughts. He proffered a tin of butterscotch and they sucked on lollies, their silence unbroken.

Georgie kept brooding over the Pooles, scatty Norman and his disabled wife. Had he meant her mind or heart was shattered in the fire? Maybe that was her angle there. *Nah, not quite right.*

She murmured, 'Should I focus on the arson angle?'

'Hasn't that been done?'

'Hmm.' She smiled wryly. 'Well, I'd have to scoop the police and everyone else and nail the offender for it to be a fresh story.'

'Good luck.'

They contemplated quietly again until Clive's voice startled her. 'I'd enjoy seeing you nail the offender.'

Georgie thought he mocked her and bristled.

'No, I really would like to see that. We need for justice to be served.'

It was a recurring theme already and something Georgie thought belonged in her story, although on the periphery. 'What does that mean to you?' She glued her eyes on his face, watching and listening for nuances.

He twisted his lip, thinking.

'A conviction, imprisonment, I suppose.' He puffed out his chest. 'We Welshmen are legendary for being stoic. So I have to uphold the reputation.'

His smile didn't convince Georgie.

'After the judgment comes down, I'll get blind drunk and finally cry for my best chum who died in the fire. *Really* cry for him. And for the other friends we lost.'

How devastating that he hadn't cried yet for his close mate; that his grieving process stayed suspended until the courts sentenced the arsonist. Stuck for a response, Georgie didn't speak.

Clive sighed and seemed to drift into his thoughts.

A few minutes later, he said, 'I remember being huddled with other people on the oval. But do you know, to this day, I don't recall getting in my car and driving there.' He joined eyes with Georgie. 'I must've gotten through by a hair's breadth before the fire-front.'

Georgie breathed shallowly as if normal breaths would intrude.

'We spent the night scared the wind would change again, bringing the fire back to finish what it'd started. We were cut off and stranded, but we were the lucky ones. A few of us went back to our places the next morning. We had to dodge police and emergency workers. There was debris all over the roads. Couldn't get through by car, so we walked.'

He hung his head, silent for a few minutes.

'It was disturbing enough that trees were still alight, charcoal and ash covered everything, and green gardens were black. Then I got to my place and it hadn't been touched.' He shook his head, as if still amazed. 'With the library gone, so was my job. But I had my car and my home. I was grateful but racked with guilt. Do you get what I mean?'

Georgie nodded.

'Why was I so lucky? My fridge and freezer were packed with food, but with no power, I had to chuck out most of the meat and perishables. I lived out of my pantry and what could be spared from supply runs coming from nearby towns, with no electricity, water or phone for weeks. I was *still* luckier than most. Many of the survivors camped on the oval because they'd lost everything but the clothes on their backs.' Clive shut his eyes.

Georgie touched his hand lightly. 'Can I get you a glass of water? Or a cuppa?'

'Thanks, but I'm okay.' He cleared his throat. 'Would your scoop on the offender count as a feature?'

She adjusted to the sudden change of subject. 'No. Any news story has a short shelf life. I'd have to sell it to a daily and write a different one for the mag.'

Clive offered Georgie another lolly. She shook her head. He stuck one on his tongue, clicking it against his teeth. 'How did you get into this caper?'

'You really don't want to know.' It was a convoluted story.

'It might give us an idea for your article.'

He'd just opened himself up to her, laying bare his memories. He seemed to be grasping for a safer subject. The least she could do was give a bit of herself.

'Okay, well, I dabbled with the idea of being a teacher, to follow in Dad's footsteps like my sister did.' Georgie grimaced. 'But I was crap at maths—which was Dad's forte —and couldn't see myself teaching. So I followed my heart and took a job at the local paper.'

'And you graduated from the local rag to your current gig?'

She rolled her eyes. 'No. The job lasted six months and turned me off studying journalism – I thought for life. I did seasonal work with two school mates next. That was fun, but the following year, reality bit. My best friend went to uni to do her fine arts degree, the other travelled Greece with his family, and I found a steady job and worked myself up the ranks.'

'Yeah?'

'Umm. Met my boyfriend while working at a legal firm. He's one of the good things that came out of that job.' Georgie paused, reminded of those early, easy days with AJ. Clive waited for more, so she added, 'Hated wearing skirts and pantihose, sucking up to the boss and making him cups of coffee. It wasn't me.'

He chuckled. 'What next?'

She gave a laugh-snort. 'I did a full circle, went back to school to take a writing course, then picked up some crumbs, editing and stodgy stuff at the start. Then earlier this year I became involved in a missing person—*persons* —case.'

He cocked his head. 'Did you help find them?'

Her jaw tightened. 'Yeah.'

Clive caught her left hand and turned it scar-side up. 'Is that connected?'

She nodded but deflected. 'The publicity and my personal account got me the magazine gig. I jump at the features but also have to write a society column.' She faked a yawn. 'Still, it's an improvement on cranking out occupational health and safety copy.'

He lifted a palm and commented, 'I think our journey's always for a reason.' At Georgie's frown, he added, 'Nothing, not even the OH&S work, will have been a waste. You'll see.'

He drummed his fingers. 'The question is what part of that journey is going to be your story in Bullock?'

She pulled another face. He'd lost her.

Clive slapped the bench. Georgie jumped.

He leaned forward, cupped his mouth and whispered, 'You know, we have our own missing person case.'

————

In the muster room, Franklin removed his cap and threw it on the shelf above his desk while ruffling his sandy-coloured hair. He hated hats with a vengeance, not because of hat-hair; he didn't have enough to mess up. Nup, they made his head too hot and looked wanky.

He couldn't figure how Sam remained fresh, her uniform immaculate and eyes wide and bright, when halfway through their shift he felt tired and crumpled.

Maybe I am getting old, as Kat says.

Franklin pictured his daughter and smiled. She was nearly sixteen going on twenty-six, rebellious and boy-crazy. Half the time she drove him crazy. The other half he loved her so hard it hurt. God, in two years she might be thinking about leaving home, even moving to the city to go to uni. She'd be dating, legally able to drink, and bloody hell, driving. Where do the years go?

'Something funny happen on patrol?' Harty asked.

'Nuh, all quiet out there. Just thinking Kat'll be getting her learner's soon. Can't wait to start teaching her to drive. All those hours of fun, fun, fun.'

The friends laughed.

Harty explained for Sam's benefit, 'Kat's his daughter, and her mum's not on the scene.'

To put it politely.

'So it's all up to him.' Harty then launched into station gossip, punctuated by his mate's contributions and Sam's questions. Franklin was relieved to be out of the spotlight.

'Don't let these fellas lead you astray, Constable Tesorino.'

All three swivelled toward the speaker in the doorway.

'Sergeant Tim Lunny. Welcome aboard,' their boss said. He juggled a World's Greatest Grandpa mug and yellow manila file, to shake hands. 'Guess what?'

Lunny had been Franklin's boss and buddy for years. Lean, fit and healthy, only the soft white hair square cut over his pale eyebrows gave away his age. With the excited air of a kid in a lolly shop, he plonked down mug and file, and flicked an imaginary rod.

'You're looking at the new secretary of the Police Angling Club.'

Harty and Franklin cheered and Sam gave a light clap.

The team shifted to the lunchroom, toasted Lunny with cuppas and debriefed the Galassi case.

'You've notified the crime scene desk?' Lunny checked, between sips.

'Yep. They're bogged down but hope to get to the address later today. They'll give me a bell with an ETA so we can let the Galassis know. A relo's minding the place while they do their wedding party, seeing as the building's not secure.'

'All right. Well, when crime scene arrives from Ballarat, I want you on site, John.'

Harty drew back, clearly surprised. Franklin wasn't expecting it either. They didn't handhold CSOs at a factory break-in except for on a very slow day.

Lunny asked, 'Have you got onto the detectives?'

'Uh-huh. They want it because of the burglary aspect; especially given the connection to other goings-on we've had here lately. Though of course the suits "are very busy in the crime investigation unit,"' Franklin made air quotes, 'and based out in Bacchus Marsh, so they may need to utilise our "local level input" in the matter.'

Lunny cleared his throat coarsely. 'The Ds want my team to do all the pleb work so they can take the glory?' He didn't wait for an answer. 'Well, anything extra you can clock up with the Ds and CSOs will help towards DTS.'

Sam straightened. 'Oh. When are you doing detective training school?'

Franklin shrugged. 'Whenever it comes up. I hopefully.'

She seemed about to say something, before changing her mind. He wondered if the hungry look on her face was because she had years to go before her chance to join the suits came up.

Harty returned to the original conversation. 'So, Maria Galassi withdrew fifteen hundred dollars yesterday?'

'Yep. It's taken since their honeymoon six years ago to convince Angelo to have another holiday. She gets the cruise deposit out of savings and *poof*, it's gone. Poor things.'

'Same day. Coincidence or not?' Sam mused, toying with her mug.

'Hard to tell,' Franklin admitted. 'Could be. The warehouse isn't alarmed. And as you pointed out, it's not overlooked. It's the perfect situ for someone to take their time and graffiti away to their heart's content.'

'And snagging the cash was a big bonus,' Harty suggested.

'Hmm.' Franklin nodded. 'I guess anyone would expect a stash in a factory, although a party hire business would do more plastic than cash sales, wouldn't it?'

Harty and Lunny agreed. Sam pulled a thoughtful expression.

After a pause, Franklin added, 'So, the graffiti?'

Sam opened one of the images on Franklin's phone and they took turns to examine it.

He pointed to the top-left corner. 'Seen that tag before?'

'Nuh,' the sarge and Harty replied together. Then both said, 'Jinx!'

Sam flicked to another image and sounded confident, saying, 'Check this one. It looks like someone tried to clean up.'

Franklin raised his eyebrows. He'd missed it. 'It does. Good call, Sam.'

'So, we have *another* case with aspects that crossover, albeit not a direct match for MO. What are we dealing with?' Lunny pressed. 'Kids? Druggies? Squatters? Same perps or several groups? A spate, on *my* patch. We've got to stamp it out.'

The sergeant stared at his team. 'Better us than the Bacchus Marsh boys.'

He clicked his fingers. 'Pronto.'

CHAPTER NINE

FRANKLIN CAUGHT HIMSELF BROODING ABOUT GEORGIE and shook his head. 'Bloody hell. You're becoming a mopey bastard.'

Annoyed with himself, he picked up the newspaper and discarded it again, having read the interesting bits earlier. Twitchy, restless, he jiggled his feet, then jumped up and paced. He tried to blame his restlessness on the three months until footy returned, and tucked into an afternoon meal to cover lunch and tea for something to do.

Overfull now, he hit the shed for a weights workout and good long run on the treadmill. Lots of cardio kept his muscles lean, not bulky and slow, and the jog cleared his head.

Yesterday had been a good day in the job. He got a buzz from tucking a newbie under his wing if they gave and earned his respect, and Sam appeared intelligent and keen, unlike Constable Wells, who she'd replaced. Oh, Wells proved clever, or more accurately cunning, but he'd respected no one under sergeant level, if that. There was definitely no love lost between him and that wanker.

Franklin hacked out a cough and slowed to a fast walk. *Bloody smokes*. It didn't stop him craving a ciggie, but he was trying to quit. Again.

He drew a ragged breath and cranked the machine to a steady trot, focused on breathing. Then his mind drifted back to yesterday.

He'd enjoyed helping the Ballarat crew process the crime scene. The footprint he'd spotted was a beauty. Apart from those belonging to the vics, they'd scored dozens of partial fingerprints and one full, clear, handprint on the rear door – they could be very lucky and find a match on record. They'd bagged micro-evidence from shoes and several cigarette butts.

'Ah, shit.'

Franklin hit stop on the treadie and grabbed his watch from the bench.

'How could I forget?'

With scarcely enough leeway before his shift, he chucked on his spare uniform and hustled to his SS Commodore.

Minutes later, a small woman with a young boy perched on her hip answered Franklin's rap at the front door. She took in his uniform in a wide-eyed glance and burst into tears. The startled toddler joined her bawling.

'I knew this would happen. I told him,' she mumbled, clutching her forehead.

The penny dropped. He tried to butt in, 'Ma'am –'

'Not getting younger. More stress, less sleep.' She jiggled the infant and plonked him at her feet so that she could cover her face with both hands.

'Please –'

'All these meetings, driving into town six days a week –'

Franklin spoke over the top of her, loud and slow. 'Ma'am, I'm not here about your partner. I'm sure he's fine.'

He backed up and pointed to the nature strip.

'I'm here to have a quick look at your Mitsubishi Lancer, if it's still for sale. I've driven past and seen it out front. It could be a good first car for my daughter.'

She lunged and slapped his bare forearm, then squealed a laugh, picking up her child.

His skin still burning from the swat, she showed him the car.

———

Georgie straddled AJ, her hands either side of his head on the pillow. Both were naked and tangled in the sheets, softly illuminated by chinks from the streetlight. She watched his face and arched as they moved in sync. The moment was so perfect; she let out a small gasp.

He paused. 'Am I hurting you?'

Her healing injuries were always there, lurking in the shadows. But her breath hadn't caught through pain.

She pulled him tight. 'No, babe. It's good.'

Georgie kissed him, nipped his lip and channelled emotion into abandon, driving both wild. They made love until shaky and glossed in perspiration, and AJ cried out and shuddered.

Still panting, they rolled sideways. Her legs circled his thighs and their foreheads touched. They didn't speak.

Eventually, her bottom leg grew numb and they shifted, yet stayed entwined. Georgie sighed, enjoying the drowsy afterglow. But she could sense AJ thinking.

'I'm glad you didn't go back to Bullock this weekend.'

'Me too. And Mol would say "me three" if she could, wouldn't you, girl?'

At their bedroom doorway, the golden retriever heard her nickname and thumped her tail on the floorboards.

AJ stroked Georgie's arm, murmuring, 'Were you upset before?'

'No.' She smiled. 'It just hit me that we had a *really* good day today and the beach was great, wasn't it?'

As soon as they'd reached the sand, Molly had bolted and dived into the cold water. They'd spent ages throwing a piece of driftwood for her to retrieve and later stuffed themselves with fish and chips as they watched the sun go down.

It was a special day in its simplicity. *Too rare, lately.* Georgie changed the subject. 'This bushfire gig is tough. The writer part of me is in its element. I've got my teeth into the research and interviews, trying to understand what people went through during the fires and since. I've learned so much about it already.'

AJ watched her face as she searched for an example.

'For instance, because of the speed and intensity of the firestorm—and I can spout off all the stats on speed, temperature and everything—most of the casualties either died or came away with relatively minor burns...anything in between the extremes was rare. That's all very fascinating on an intellectual level. But on the flipside, I feel ghoulish.'

'You're doing your job.'

'But –'

'Listen, George.' AJ pinched her lips together. 'Sometimes I have to bring actions or fight cases for my clients that I don't agree with morally, but providing it's within the law, I'm bound to represent them to my best capability. That's what you're doing here.'

Georgie wriggled to free her lips. 'I don't think it's the same thing. But either way, it still doesn't feel *good* to see a little girl disfigured by burns and think of her as a *subject, repulsive* and *fascinating* in the space of seconds.'

AJ's stare was intense. 'But you can help people. Like you told me when you took this assignment, your story can make the rest of us understand and sympathise with what the victims are still going through, and it might be a good reminder of lessons learned the hard way so the same mistakes are not repeated.' After a pause, he added, 'And more importantly, it might even help the victims cope better.'

They transferred to lie facing the ceiling.

Georgie's thoughts were chaotic and raw. They jumped between Kelly at the info centre and then her standing in at the servo, the little redhead and mum left on their own, Clive in the library, and the almost comical yet sorrowful old couple.

After several minutes, she said, 'I'm not sure they want sympathy.' Sadness waved over her naked body, chilling her skin into goosebumps. She hugged her arms to her chest.

AJ propped on an elbow, gazing at her a while, before saying, 'So, another missing person case?'

Georgie couldn't read his undertone but needed to lighten the conversation, for her own sake. 'You wouldn't believe it.' She forced a chuckle. 'One minute, Clive was all excited and announced, "We have our own missing person case." Then he shied off, saying, "But I have to talk to Ally first." As I asked who Ally is, a bunch of senior citzs waltzed in for their noon natter.'

AJ cracked up.

Georgie talked over him. 'Bloody hell, kids singing and shouting in the morning and the oldies having their turn at lunchtime. It's debatable who made more noise.' She laughed. It'd been nice to see a light side to the scarred town.

'And then?'

'Clive still wouldn't talk about Ally without clearing it with her first. So I headed back.' She grimaced. 'I have lead-time left on this Bullock story. If Sheridan likes it, she'll be happy so long as I file my copy at the start of next month. But if she hates it, I'm dead. Anyway, what's a few days' delay? The story will still be there.' Georgie bit her bottom lip. 'I hope. I guess that depends on whatever this Ally person says to Clive.'

With a sigh, she closed her eyes. Her reflections returned to Bullock.

'And Daylesford?' AJ glided his fingertips along her forearm. 'You haven't told me about that trip yet.'

He didn't always grasp when to back off. She fidgeted with her pillow, edging over on the bed.

What to tell him? That the word Daylesford flashed up unwanted images?

Franklin at the café, gazing at her with emotion deeper than lust. His expression turning to a wince as she'd squeezed his hand over the table, saying, *I came back to put it all behind me, one way or another*. Then a flare of naked pain in his eyes before he'd covered them, as she admitted, *There's too many bad memories here*. He'd begged, *Don't say it*. But still, she'd thrust the knife in. *I can't come again. Not for a very long time. If ever*. Her *I'm sorry* was all but the last thing they'd said to each other.

Right thing to do.

She curled sideways and pushed her butt out. AJ moved in to spoon.

'I don't want to talk about Daylesford. Not yet.'

She pretended to fall asleep, with AJ stroking her spine.

Georgie lay motionless, silent. Minutes, hours, she couldn't see the clock to know how long. But it was enough time to drench her pillow with tears.

CHAPTER TEN

'A MIT-SU-BISHI?' MICK SPRAGUE MOCKED A JAPANESE accent.

Scott Hart blushed, glanced around the pub and elbowed his mate, whose pot sloshed. 'Slam!'

'Watch it, Harty!' Slam licked his beer coated fingers and chuckled. 'But a Lancer? Are you serious?'

Franklin shrugged. 'Maybe, we haven't test-driven it yet. Everything high-powered's off the list; no way I'm giving my daughter the keys to a lethal weapon. This is four-cylinder and four-door, so there's less chance of her getting stuck if she's in an impact. Airbags are okay considering it's not brand new and –'

'Yeah, but what *colour* is it?' Slam asked, affecting a girlie voice.

'Obligatory red.'

They laughed.

'Kat's happy with the spoiler, scoop, alloys and sunroof.'

'But can it take her iPod?' Harty cut in. 'That'd be the clincher, right?'

Franklin nodded. 'In Kat's view, yeah. In my perfect

world, her car wouldn't have a radio, CD, iPod or anything that could distract. In fact, she'd be driving a pillow-wrapped artillery tank.'

They chuckled and clanked glasses, probably each picturing Kat in her tank. In Franklin's image, she was also cloaked in a fire suit and full helmet. But with six kids under twenty-five dying on Australian roads each week, safety trounced style for Kat's car – at least in his qualified opinion.

Franklin slugged his beer and gazed around Burke's Hotel. He flicked over familiar faces and settled deeper onto his stool.

What could top a night off with my mates? Oh, yeah, that most of the tourists have gone home to the concrete jungle.

Without giving reason, he raised another toast and his mates happily clashed pots. Although only on their first round, the three were mellow.

'Hey, boys, can we join you?'

Slam jumped up and moved his stool to make space. Harty blushed deeper than before – the sensitive new-age guy of the trio, he was also in a long-term relationship and tended to be uneasy amid a group of other women. Franklin shrugged; he'd been in the mood for a boys' night.

Talitha edged closer and said, 'Haven't seen you lately.'

'I've been around.'

She recoiled, stung.

Don't be a grumpy bastard with her, Franklin. She's a bit intense but still a mate.

And so he played nice and they all chatted. More locals wandered in. The noise level grew. Somebody put music on the jukebox: rock, good old stuff. In between the group banter and general noise, Talitha yakked happily, mostly on the subject of bands they both dug and he knew she'd shoot pool if he asked. She wasn't bad looking either, in a girl-next-door way.

A few rounds later, Franklin felt a tentative hand on his knee.

He dropped a sideways peek. Yep, it belonged to Talitha.

Crap.

Stock-still, he pretended to ignore it. But a bit later, her hand grew heavier.

Awkward.

Franklin tried to catch Slam's eye, but the other girls held his attention. He searched for Harty and clocked him throwing darts.

The moment Talitha glanced away, he called, 'What's that, mate?'

He shot an apologetic, 'Sorry, Talitha. It's Harty…' and hurried across the room.

Harty saw him gesture and approach. He cocked his head with a puzzled frown.

CHAPTER ELEVEN

HE AND THE KID HAD FOUND A NEW PLACE. A SHED behind the old derelict church, where Luke had squatted when he first hit the street. It was close to the police station, though, so they couldn't stay long.

Before they'd left the old squat, he'd waited until the others were out and taken a few things. Nothing they'd miss. A bit of food. A couple of joints, which would do for the kid until he could get paracetamol.

The new place seemed okay, apart from being close to the cops. It was warmer than the old squat, and the best thing was that they didn't have to share it.

A drop of water on his neck made him look up. Next thing, the roof was leaking like a sieve. No wonder there were a few metal buckets scattered around the place.

'Grab your stuff, bud. That corner looks dry.'

They moved, listening to the rain hitting the tin roof above them. It sounded like it'd set in. The kid started shivering and not even their two blankets made a difference.

He needed to do something, so he pulled a couple of wooden shelves off the wall, snapped them into bits and built a fire in one of the buckets. They were out of matches, so he had to use his lighter to get it going. It didn't throw off much heat, so he wrapped his jacket around the kid, and at least his teeth stopped chattering after a while.

He rubbed his thumb over his lighter, feeling the familiar grooves and watching his young mate, thinking about *that day*.

———

They went via Stanley Street, and nearing the Smiths Creek cul-de-sac on Crow Street, Franklin flicked on strobes and siren.

They weren't strictly necessary, but bells and whistles gave the troublemakers a heads-up, even a chance to get away. Preferable to walking unannounced into a potentially explosive situation.

The witness had reported shattering glass, not sure whether from a bottle or window. He'd also mentioned loud, hostile voices, a string of curses, followed by a rock or brick hurled at the solitary street lamp up that end of Crow, which took out the lighting.

The concerned fellow told the D24 operator drugs or alcohol could be a factor. He didn't name names, either his own or the feuding men's. They assumed him to be a close, if not immediate, neighbour. He knew too much and didn't want to say.

'This it, Sam?'

She re-checked the address, replied 'Yep' and braced as Franklin braked alongside a grey picket fence.

He scanned the modest weatherboard home painted similarly, taking in the lawn in front, a couple of shrubs but no real garden. Little cover for anyone lurking. Good.

In the single carport, a white ute and champagne Camry sedan sat nose-to-tail. The tipping trailer in front of the carport, kitted out with ride-on, hand mower and other gizmos, was signed with 'Mr Garden: mowing, tree lopping, weeding, planting and all odd jobs'. The vehicles were a problem, providing too many shadows and hiding spots, so they'd give them a wide berth.

Franklin left headlights and strobes on to counteract the darkness.

'Grab the big flashy.'

Sam passed it over and they alighted. Even from the road, they could hear shouting inside the cottage.

Franklin gave the probationary officer a few words of wisdom and she nodded. They were on the same page.

They approached the front door together. Franklin's nerves buzzed as he sized-up the situation. He glanced to Sam and saw her tense up. Good. No cop could afford to be blasé about domestics.

On the verandah, they stepped over a pile of amber glass and small puddle. In the shine of the flashlight, they identified the glass as a broken beer bottle, which, although smashed, seemed all accounted for, thank Christ. Glassings were too common these days. Usually spontaneous and bloody nasty.

'Open up! Police!'

Franklin rapped on the weatherboards and started the mental count. Ten and he'd try the handle and force the door if necessary.

When he reached five, the shouting inside paused.

'They heard you, boss,' Sam whispered.

Then the voices resumed at reduced volume.

Franklin opened the security screen and reached for the main doorknob. 'Police. We've had a report of a disturbance. Open up.'

He felt Sam stiffen and peripherally noted hands suspended over her duty belt.

Good. Not trigger happy but prepared.

In the split-second he touched the knob, the door swung and he faced the wanker from the pub last week.

Lanky. Marc Jones. Here we go.

Jones threw up his hands. 'Ah, piss off.'

'Language, sonny.'

Okay, the prick wasn't young enough to be his son, but about a decade and a badge between them allowed Franklin to pull seniority. He did a quick head-to-toe. No sign of a weapon but definite alcohol loading.

He pushed through, forcing Jones up the hallway, and Sam trailed. They herded the man towards the racket.

By the sounds of it, at least another male and a tearful female were involved.

Jones preceded them into the kitchen and pulled a tinnie from the fridge. 'Want one?' He offered it to Franklin, then laughed. 'No, I guess you can't, 'cos you're on duty.'

He popped the can as he moved to lean against the

bench top. His bearing seemed relaxed and smug as he skolled his beer but Franklin saw him keep tabs on the others, who'd fallen silent when they entered.

A woman stood in front of a long pine table littered at one end with the detritus of two meals. Plates and cutlery with scraps and smears of fat and sauce, several crushed beer cans, a green bottle and half-empty glass of white wine.

Franklin skimmed back to the woman. Petite, a little mousey looking, he guessed she fell close to his own age, mid-to-late thirties.

Then he realised he knew her. *Monica McKinnon. Well, that was her name back then.* She was one of his ex-wife's old girlfriends. One of the nice ones. She used to have an energy that filled the room and had plans to be a horticulturist. Now, she looked like a washed-out version of that girl.

He greeted her and she dropped her eyes to the floor.

Of the same era, Shorty from the pub—*Hudson*, Franklin drew a blank on his first name—hovered near the stove. His eyes were bloodshot and dark rimmed.

Hudson, Monica and Jones formed a right-angled triangle.

The love triangle. I hate domestics.

Franklin folded his arms and signalled for Sam to lead.

'We received a report of a disturbance at this address.' She wiped her palms on uniform pants, glanced over and received his discreet thumbs-up.

'Why don't we sit down together and have a chat about what's going on here?'

Not bad, Sam. Not sure it's gonna work, but keep going.

Hudson yelled, 'Pig's arse. I'm not sitting down with *him*.' He pointed at Jones and hoicked. Monica glared and he swallowed his spit.

Franklin blinked slowly, remembering. N*eil Hudson, that's the bloke's name. Brickie by trade, according to Jones.*

'We can do this the easy way, sit down and have a chat here, as the constable suggested. Or we can do it at the station. Your choice.'

He scrutinised the threesome, now recalling what Hudson had said at the pub. *It's between me, him and me wife.*

With excessive grumbles from the men, Monica and Jones took seats where they'd eaten dinner, while the overweight brickie staggered across the floor and perched ramrod at the opposite end of the table. Franklin and Sam continued to stand, gaining the power hand.

The woman focused on her clasped fingers. She worried a quick on her left thumb. Jones leaned back, balancing his chair on its rear legs, and threw a casual arm along Monica's shoulders, marking his territory. She cut eyes to her wineglass, picked it up with a shaky hand, drained it and resumed worrying the thumbnail hanger. Jones squeezed her arm. She didn't resist.

Hudson slumped into his seat, defeated.

Franklin read the story and felt sorry for the jilted hubby. Women probably considered lean, young Jones attractive. He was a player and a charmer, no doubt. But Monica would learn the hard way a bloke like that doesn't aim for keeps.

Yep, he felt sorry for Neil Hudson all right, but they still had a job to do.

———

Back at the station, set to a quiet concert of police radio chatter, Franklin helped Sam wade through the reports pertaining to the neighbours' spat, generating more crap for a poor civvy in Melbourne to plug into LEAP. Or as he'd explained it to the newbie, 'Passing on the pain of the mountain of useless paperwork we accumulate every shift to be entered into the black hole of a central database designed to frustrate cops state-wide.'

Their admin in Sam's hands now, he propped boots on the desk, drummed the fingernails of one hand and plucked at his pants knee with the other.

He sat that way for a long stretch. Midnight approached, so their twilight shift was almost finished. They'd caught no new business since the Crow Street callout, and if this kept up, they'd get away on time.

Sam swotted over the reports. He sat, plucked and drummed. Intermittently, he scratched his chin or answered a question, all the while thinking.

Franklin's eyes narrowed and he quit fidgeting. He reached for his daybook, his private log on matters. He jotted names and addresses, not that he would forget them, but because it formed a reminder to keep a regular eye on the Hudsons and Jones.

Maybe he'd do a drive-by on his rest day tomorrow or the next.

He had a gut feeling this love triangle could turn real ugly.

CHAPTER TWELVE

GEORGIE NOSED THE SPIDER INTO A PARKING SPACE. There were plenty of them. Bullock was even quieter than the previous week. Not one person walked the footpath. She counted five cars on the main drag. Eyes squinting into the sun, she spied a few more near the pub at the other end of the street.

It couldn't be a sharper contrast to her home base in Richmond. There, even arterials were narrow and congested, while there were many one-way and no-through roads that barely accommodated a family sedan, and all were permit parking for residents only or steeply metered. Her world comprised everything from glam to grunge. Nightclubs, brothels, factory outlets, juxtaposed with shiny showrooms and offices. Concrete high-rise housing commission flats, posh townhouses and long narrow cottages. Ultra-ugly, mega-modern and period architecture side by side. Everyone hurried, everywhere. Noise clamoured 24-7 via trams, trains, trucks, tooting cars, music of all types, accents of all origin, laughter, arguments, haggling, begging. And this eclectic cultural fusion was set to equally diverse odours and aromas.

And Georgie loved it. Give her that any time over the country.

She secured the soft-top and locked the Spider, stroking the black duco on the car's nose as she moved around it. During the beating she'd copped in Castlemaine last March she, the human pinball, had shattered the side mirror, dented the driver's door, and dimpled and grazed the front guard. Only a few tiny battle scars remained thanks to painstaking restoration work, far less than those worn by its owner.

As she stepped away from the convertible, Georgie zeroed in on her meeting with Clive. Finally, she'd extract the lowdown on this elusive Ally and Bullock's supposed missing person.

———

The librarian leaned his elbows on the counter and steepled his fingers. Then he tucked them under his nose and breathed audibly.

Georgie touched his arm lightly. 'You called me, Clive. You wanted to talk.'

He blinked twice.

'Surely right, Georgie. I'm simply thinking of where to begin.'

She gave him space.

He nodded, blew out a sigh. 'Our missing man is my chum, Warren Goyne.'

Georgie's eyes widened. How could he be so matter-of-fact?

'The person I mentioned to you, Ally, is Warren's

daughter.'

He held up a finger, pausing the conversation, and scanned the library. Apparently content they'd be uninterrupted, he beckoned Georgie closer.

When he didn't speak, she asked, 'How are your missing friend and his daughter relevant to Red Victoria?'

'Not interested in an exposé on a family dealing with the loss of a loved one?'

That wasn't enough in itself. Every person in Bullock had lost people they'd cared for. 'Of course, but –'

'How they deal with it if they haven't been able to bury their loved one?'

She saw where he was going and her pulse thudded.

Clive struck the bench, allowing his hand to bounce up by a foot.

It reminded Georgie of a librarian at her primary school. He'd read to the class from a fat tome. At a juicy part in the hobbit adventure, *slam* went his hand and the kids had jolted, startled.

The teacher had worn the faintest of smirks, as Clive did now.

She waited.

'How they deal with it if they haven't been able to bury their loved one because there is no body?'

Georgie recoiled, stung by déjà vu.

She flashed back to an emerald green meadow. To where she stood among marble headstones, some with pristine flower arrangements, while others had broken or empty vases or nothing at all. Nearby were much older iron and stone graves and a few grassy knolls, unmarked.

She pictured Franklin, face strained, his hazel eyes stripped of their yellow and green glints, uniformed, standing taller than many of the other mourners, her mind jumping to the connection between them and the one kiss that should never have happened that she'd *almost* blocked from her mind. Until a week ago.

The events back then had been sparked by a farmer who was missing, presumed dead, and his wife, who couldn't live without answers. All of it would be best forgotten, but that had proven to be impossible.

That was Daylesford. This was Bullock. But once again she had a story of a family aching for a body to bury. Surely, that's where any parallels ended?

Pull yourself together, Harvey. She watched Clive and wondered how he could apparently enjoy spinning the tale and winding her in, with his friends at the nub. He took stoic Welshman to a whole new level and beat her at her own game of *bluff and bravado* hands down.

Georgie laid a palm flat on the counter. 'You have my attention. Now tell me how this mysterious death fits my feature?'

Clive waved in a swirling gesture. 'Your article could focus on a family...'

He paused, popped a butterscotch in his mouth, crunched and offered the tin. She gave a headshake, anxious for him to continue.

'Where was I? That's right, so your article could focus on a family who is dealing with the death of their loved one when one of the fires on Red Victoria obliterated every trace of that person.'

Georgie frowned lightly. 'But that's not a missing person case, Clive.'

His expression turned sombre. 'Where there's smoke, there's fire. Where there's doubt, there's dumb hope.'

Georgie finger-raked her wavy hair and a tangle of strands came out with roots intact. Her eyes drilled into the brunette wisps with a hint of chestnut, but her thoughts flicked to her editor, Sheridan Judd.

This could be the emotive feature story her editor dreamed of publishing.

———

Franklin geared down the Kawasaki Ninja as he cornered into the low end of Crow Street. He slowed to a stop outside Marc Jones's house and checked for signs of occupation. Negative for the conservative Camry, but Lanky's ute and trailer were home.

He turned off the bike, leaned onto one leather-booted foot and pulled off his helmet. Motionless, he listened, dissecting each sound. Distant traffic, birdsong, but all quiet at Lanky's place.

Drops of rain ricocheted off his leathers, spurring him to check next door while rueing the proximity of his love triangle players. If Shorty lived on the other side of town instead of adjacent to his rival, he and Monica might still be together, and Franklin wouldn't have to babysit the three neighbours.

The Hudsons' cottage was of the same era and a similar style but painted cream on its weatherboards with deep green trims per the trend of ten or so years ago. The driveway led to a double garage with haphazard stacks of bricks against the walls. Apart from that, the garden carried a woman's touch. Maybe the roses and marigolds were all Monica had to show for her horticultural dreams.

Despite the neat garden, the property had a slightly unkempt appearance, and he also sensed it was deserted. Neil Hudson's truck could be in the shed, but Franklin guessed the brickie's day wasn't yet over. Or he'd be found in one of the pubs – hopefully well away from his wife and her lover.

Franklin returned to his bike and fired her up. With a twist of the throttle, he pulled away from the gravel verge. Then he glimpsed two male figures on the road ahead and jerked to a halt.

A once-over confirmed neither was Hudson or Jones. These were an older bloke and kid, and Franklin's gut didn't like it.

He squinted hard and relaxed a little after he realised the kid had to be early twenties, not the teens he'd originally suspected. Of course, an older fellow with a teenager wouldn't have necessarily meant he was a paedo or a crook. But although they both bore shaved heads, this twosome didn't jump out as father and son. And something he couldn't pinpoint continued to irk him.

Then he caught the kid's eye and recognised *the look*. He'd been clocked as a cop despite his motorbike garb. The dodgy glance and duck of the head were giveaways that the kid had been in trouble with the law.

A vague bell rang in Franklin's mind – he'd seen the kid before but couldn't recall in what capacity. As Kat's dad or as the local copper? Because the kid had been in strife or as part of small-town life?

The kid turtled his chin into the collar of his windcheater, but Franklin had memorised his features: approximately 180cm tall, underweight bordering on malnourished, fair hair clipped with number one, Caucasian, with pale, yellow-tinged skin indicating he could be ill.

The bloke with him was in his fifties with a long skinny face, mo and beard. Before Franklin could gather a better description, the bloke dropped his hand on the kid's neck, said something and they scuttled away towards the creek.

Franklin filed their images into his memory bank. Tomorrow he'd check how he'd previously encountered the kid and if they had any flags for the older bloke.

––––––

Georgie had seen the bus arrive and a bunch of high school kids alight. But strict to Clive's instructions, she stayed put. While rain pattered on the perspex roof, the buck-toothed bakery assistant reached for Georgie's mug.

'Finished your coffee, love?'

'Yeah, ta.'

'We're closing up but no harm done if you want to stay awhile.'

Georgie nodded her thanks and lit another cigarette, jigging her right leg. She inhaled the tangy smoke and blew rings.

The glowing tip encroached on the filter, and she did another time check. She mashed the butt as Clive emerged from the library and joined him.

'We're meeting Ally and her mum. But remember what I said the other day: Ally is your story.'

'Sure, thanks, Clive. I appreciate all this.'

He gave her a tight smile. 'We'll walk, it's not far.'

Georgie shrugged agreement, repeating, 'Sure.'

They were similar height and fell into a fast, synchronised stride. She'd had ample time to think, and one question topped her list.

'Clive.' She halted and touched his arm, causing him to stop and face her. 'Warren Goyne is the best mate you haven't grieved for, isn't he?'

She saw a wash of pain, and just as quickly, he recovered and weighed his response.

Finally, he answered, 'Yes.'

'I'm so sorry.'

Clive nodded. Georgie sensed that he needed space and silently took in the surroundings as they walked on.

Soon they turned into a bluestone-coloured, patterned concrete driveway. Halfway along, they stepped through the immature garden—tufts of various grasses and succulents—on large sandstone pavers that led to a new house.

They stood before a detached cottage, a contemporary relative of those common to Richmond. Its cricket bat front door under a sloping verandah contrasted with its asymmetrical front façade and parallel long slit windows. Set back was a garage with a panelled door. The rendered brick home had lots of square lines, in sandstone, taupe, plum and charcoal tones, and Georgie approved its blend of heritage and current trends.

To her surprise, the bakery assistant who'd cleared her mug fifteen minutes ago opened the front door.

The woman laughed. 'Ah, so it is you. I racked my brain after our chat with Clive and figured it had to be you.'

Georgie cocked her head.

'With your eyes darting all over the place, scribbling lots of notes, chugging on the ciggies and coffee like there's no tomorrow, you certainly come across as a writer, love.'

Georgie chuckled, a bit stunned, while Clive made the introductions, adding, 'Deb, are you and Ally sure about this?'

Deb Goyne twisted her bright red lipstick-slashed mouth sideways.

Georgie held her breath, hearing a drum roll inside her mind.

Please don't change your mind.

She didn't, and minutes later, Georgie sat opposite Deb's daughter, watching the teen push away a brown strand that tickled her nose. Smudged pouches ringed her dark chocolate eyes. Frown lines that no sixteen-year-old should possess angled from each eyebrow diagonally up a high, bare forehead.

'You know how they say, "such and such is the life of the party"?' the teen said.

Georgie nodded and sipped her juice.

'Well, Dad was, no question.'

Ally sat forward, leaned on her elbows and smiled. The creases on her forehead were still there but less pronounced.

Georgie willed her to talk freely. She deliberately ignored the digital recorder between them on the outdoor table and tried not to fidget. Then she caught herself staring at the teen, which would do little to relax her, and turned her eyes away.

From the al fresco area where she and Ally sat, Georgie could see Deb and Clive chatting in the family room. In hair colour, eyes, nose and mouth, mother and daughter bore a strong resemblance. But Ally countered her mother's mop-cut with centre-parted straight hair worn to her collarbones; she was tall and lean, her mum short and round; the girl sad and studious, the woman loud and brash.

Looking back at Ally, she noticed her fiddle with the charm on a delicate silver chain circling her neck, rolling it side to side.

'Did your dad give you that?' Georgie hazarded.

Ally froze, then sighed. 'Yes. For my fourteenth birthday.'

She angled the charm so Georgie could see a tiny mouse with outsized ears and wearing bulky boxing gloves.

'Cute.'

'Dad wanted me to stand up for myself and what I think is right. Not sure if he was also making a statement about the ears.' Ally drew back her hair to reveal large ears. She smiled and reverted to silence.

Georgie chewed the inside of her lip, thinking. It was important to cultivate Ally's trust early with safe subjects and gentle handling. So she asked, 'Do you enjoy school?'

'Yeah, I do. Other kids call me lame, but I don't care, they're just haters. Clare always said...oh, never mind.'

The teen waved, then looked lost in thought. Painful thought. Georgie kicked herself for misjudging what was an innocuous topic. The best way to avoid a minefield of painful triggers was to get Ally rolling and let her take the conversation where she was comfortable. Later, she could probe harder and pick up threads.

Easier said than done, because they spent the next minutes in awkward silence until Georgie broke it. 'Why Healesville? It's a fair hike.'

'Our population's too small for our own high school. Most of us bus to Healesville.'

'With all the stop-starts, it must take a good hour. Does it get you down?' Georgie sounded incredulous. Used to inner-city centrality, she couldn't stand a commute of more than twenty minutes when it was a five-days-a-week thing.

'Nuh.' Ally laughed. 'I read or something.'

'What, you don't chat with your mates or send messages?'

Ally shook her head. 'I'm okay on my own, mostly. I read, listen to music, play games.'

Georgie felt a twinge of concern that the teenager was too much of a loner. Ally seemed fine with it, though, and actually looked fairly relaxed at the moment, possibly ready to switch subjects to Warren.

'Are you okay to talk about your dad again?'

To her shock, Ally pressed away from the table and stalked into the house.

Georgie tracked her movements, noting Deb and Clive do likewise as Ally crossed the living room and darted up the hallway.

Still stunned, sixty seconds later they all watched her backtrack.

She thrust a piece of paper at Georgie.

'There. That's my dad.'

Georgie took the thick sheet and examined a portrait of a man with Ally's ears, cropped curly light brown hair, metal-framed glasses, wearing a blue, open-collar, short-sleeved shirt. The laughing man had three distinct chins and numerous upward-turned crow's feet which highlighted his shining eyes.

'Did you draw this?'

'Yeah.'

'It's amazingly detailed.'

Ally shrugged modestly. 'The fire destroyed everything in the old house. We didn't have any photos. And I missed Dad so much. So I sketched his picture, as best I could, the way I remember him.'

Her eyes held a shine like her dad's, but with tears, not laughter. Georgie squeezed her hand.

'I'm so scared I'll forget what he looked like,' Ally whispered. 'But when I'm in bed, in my dreams, it can be like he's right there with me. Do you understand what I mean?'

Georgie's heart ached for her. 'Yes. My dad died when I was a kid.'

'How old were you?'

'Eleven.' Eighteen years ago and Georgie still missed her dad like crazy. Still hated the cancer that had taken him.

Ally grasped her fingers tighter. 'Then you know.'

Georgie paused, taking care with her answer. 'Better than most people, yeah. But I'm not going to lie to you or patronise you and say I know exactly how you feel.'

Ally nodded, then gazed away.

Georgie hadn't been conscious of the sounds around them before. High-pitched frog calls masked the drone of Clive and Deb's conversation. Nearby, a ball bounced on a driveway and thudded against hoop and backboard at regular intervals. She counted the bangs and waited. However Ally wanted to play it was fine by her. Even if it was to change the subject or stop for today, Georgie wouldn't push.

Eventually, the teen spoke. 'If I try really hard, I can smell him. He used to wear a yummy aftershave. It smelt like cuddles.'

Ally suddenly seemed very young and vulnerable. Georgie scooted close and gave her a hug.

Several minutes later, Deb interrupted.

'How does a barbecue grab you, girls? Clive's cooking.'

'You will stay, won't you?' Ally switched on puppy dog eyes.

'That'd be great.' And Georgie meant it.

CHAPTER THIRTEEN

HIS BUDDY FELT WELL YESTERDAY AND HAD PACED THE confines of the squat until they both went nuts. He'd kept opening the door and peeking outside while he scratched at his skin and scuffed the soles of his shoes on the floor, singing the same lines of a song repetitively. Occasionally, he'd knocked his head against a wall, not hard, just demonstrating his boredom. He hated their enforced nocturnal lifestyle, having to be active after dusk like rats.

In all honesty, he wouldn't have chosen the kid as his pretend son or companion in his old life. But his buddy was his only friend and needed him. At least he was helping someone. It didn't balance up with what he'd lost, but he only had himself to blame.

So eventually, the kid won, like he often did. But he'd only agreed to them going out if they were cautious. They couldn't draw attention to themselves. Unless it was unavoidable, they couldn't talk to anyone. Had to wonder if the angst was worth it, but he guessed it was because it made Luke happy for a little while, although the kid often took a turn for the worse after their outings.

But then the worst thing happened. They'd bumped into a cop. He wasn't in uniform, but it was written all over him, and Luke had confirmed it.

They'd gotten away, but he felt worried. How much longer could they stay on the run?

———

'Fucking useless prick arsehole.' Franklin slammed his folder onto the desk.

'That good, huh?' Harty smiled sympathetically.

'Cops like that give the rest of us a bad name.'

'How so?'

'Fucking cold as Antarctica, the arsehole had poor Maria Galassi in tears. Mr-fucking-iceberg-*Defective* blamed her for being quote "too conspicuous in the bank, which enticed the thieves to the warehouse" unquote, and then for storing the stash in the most obvious of places. Bloody hell.'

'Did he come up with anything you and Sam missed?'

Franklin snorted. 'Yeah, right. Took him almost a week to pull his finger out and get to the scene. Then *bang*,' he fired a finger pistol, 'he's in and out, already back in Bacchus

Marsh by now. Meanwhile, he's upset the vics and laid out a list of instructions for us.'

'Does it make you want to stay in uniform after all?'

Harty and Franklin swivelled to the doorway. Sam leaned against the frame, arms crossed, appearing casual but a blind man could see the answer she wanted.

'What are you doing here? It's your day off.'

She bobbed her head in reply to Harty. She plonked onto a vacant chair and rotated full swing.

'I don't know anyone but you guys yet, besides the customers we've dealt with this week. Couldn't be bothered driving to Melbourne for a single rest day and haven't a clue what's worth seeing here.'

Sam wore her hair free of its usual tight bun or braid. Franklin was surprised at its length. It fell around her shoulders and set off her olive skin, highlighting a pixie face. He'd noticed Sam's good looks before, but that big grin with the tiny beauty spot near her left nostril was all the better without the prim pale blue uniform.

Back off. Sam's a no-fly zone.

She stared at him. 'You didn't answer. About staying in uniform.'

'Nuh.' He shook his head. 'But it makes me determined to be a good detective, nothing like that prick today.'

She deflated, then recovered with another grin. 'So, what can I help with while I'm here?'

'Time to initiate Sam into the joys of the vehicle portfolio?' Harty's eyes twinkled.

Each of the Daylesford officers held a specific area of responsibility to help the station run – and keep Lunny sane. They juggled these roles with their general duties and handling files for other branches or the Bacchus Marsh detectives. Franklin tended the social club and youth liaison; the latter which often involved hours of his spare time but gave him a big kick. Consistent with his organised personality, Harty wanted to hang onto the station portfolio, which included bail reports, station cameras, logs and rosters but couldn't wait to handball the police vehicles. Rumour had it quad bikes would be in operation within the year, and Slam kept pestering Lunny to requisition one. Meanwhile their vehicles quota consisted of a permanent four-wheel drive, fleet of pushbikes, new patrol car and the odd loaner from other stations. Sam's first portfolio involved lots of elbow grease.

'It's her day off, Harty.'

Franklin frowned at the young proby. 'Sam, go home or shopping or visit the Convent Gallery. In the nicest possible way, fuck off out of here.'

———

Georgie stopped at the foot of the sweeping driveway. Arched stone pillars stood sentinel to an abandoned guest house. Nobody was in sight, and she took the punt that they wouldn't mind anyway and crunched along the gravel, picking her way around potholes.

Soon, she caught a glimpse of stone and concrete foundations fenced off by cyclone wire. A few steps on, she realised the extent of the destruction and felt shattered. She'd had no idea that the historic manor had been annihilated, although given how much of Bullock had been lost, she should've expected it.

She'd stayed at the guest house with AJ for their first anniversary of moving in together at Richmond. Georgie squeezed her eyes shut for a moment, concentrating. When she reopened them, she visualised the 1920s building as they'd first seen it: a grand structure of stone and timber in Tudor style set among English gardens. Wowed by the majestic entrance, wide foyer, enormous fireplaces, full-sized billiard tables and comfortable scroll-armed sofas, they'd also been spoilt by à la carte dinners and cooked breakfasts, and a spa in their bedroom with a view of the mountain. It cost a fortune for a weekend package, but they'd loved it.

Now, all that remained was the building footprint. *Too sad.*

Georgie moved on, following the driveway until she reached the remnants of the rose garden. She hugged her arms against her body. She and AJ had admired the masses of colourful, fragrant blooms on their anniversary weekend. It was there that they'd agreed to come back one day.

Her eyes stung as she reminisced. How many of the staff had died in the fire? How many guests? How many people other than she and AJ had lost a special place and whose memories would blur with the passing of each year? Would it ever be rebuilt, and could it be anywhere near as good?

A few minutes later, Georgie retraced her steps to the road, pocketing her mobile. She and AJ were one-all on the phone tag tally today. She'd try him again later.

She veered right, to continue her stroll through town. It began to drizzle, yet felt warm and sticky, and two weeks into the season, she decided she was over the summer.

A 'Hello!' startled her. She twisted towards the now-familiar voice as he added, 'Hello! Wait!'

Norman Poole jogged up, puffing a bit but not badly for his age.

'Hello, er...' He checked a notepad and stuffed it back

into his pocket. 'Georgie?' When she smiled and nodded, he continued, 'We saw you out the window and thought you might fancy a cuppa. We have one with a slice of date loaf for morning tea at eleven. Care to join us?'

'You saw me?'

'We live over there.'

He pointed to the block opposite. On it, a tiny plain building, much like a granny flat, perched on a manicured lawn with white-pebbled pathways and not one tree, shrub or plant in the yard.

Grim place. It might suit Norman's taciturn wife, but not the sweet old guy.

'Sure, Norman. A cuppa would be nice, thanks.'

She followed him into the Pooles' little house while ruffling some of the moisture out of her hair. It was frizzing already when she settled on the sofa and accepted a mug of coffee.

Between sips, Georgie told the couple that she might have found the focus for her feature: the Goyne family. As she filled them in, she realised that the usual thrill of visualising the germ of a story was subdued, tainted by what she'd seen and heard since taking this assignment and her emotional exploration across the road.

'And what were you doing over there?' Norman asked.

So she repeated herself. And so did he.

Consequently, for a third time, she retold it, fighting a wicked temptation to suggest Norman record it all in his notebook.

On each retelling, his eyes crinkled when she recounted staying in the guest house with AJ. He wore a soft smile and sighed.

'Isn't that lovely, darl?' he commented to Dawn.

'Yes, dear, you said that before.'

Georgie shot a stunned glance at the woman. Alert and coherent; married attitude in that sentence too. Until this moment, she'd been unresponsive except for clenching her wheelchair arms, humming or picking at her morning tea.

Norman said, 'Oh, ha ha.'

The couple chuckled.

The old guy interpreted Georgie's puzzled expression. 'She doesn't like our walks. But it's preferable to being left at home alone, so she tolerates them.' He shook his head. 'With ill grace, it must be said.'

Dawn poked out her tongue and Georgie laughed.

'I've told her over and over that she's giving people the impression she's deaf, dumb and mute by acting up, but she won't listen to me. It's her silent protest.'

His wife pouted. 'Well, if you were stuck in this thing –'

'You don't have to be stuck in the wheelchair.'

Dawn grumbled something.

'If you did your physio –'

'It hurts.'

Norman said, 'I know. But if you want to get mobile again –'

'Don't care.'

'There you go then,' he replied mildly. 'That's why this time next year I'll still be pushing you around town three times a day, MG.'

MG again. What's it stand for?

He spotted Georgie's puckered brow. 'MG is my Misery Guts.'

With that, he leaned to plant a squeaky kiss on his wife's cheek. She inclined her head to receive it, smiling.

They fell into silence. Georgie glanced over the open-plan living area. From her position on the sofa, she could see the dining nook, kitchen, through to the laundry, and looking the other way, down a short hallway that probably led to the bathroom and sleeping quarters. The house appeared clean and tidy, aside from surface clutter of reading glasses, newspapers and novels in their library jackets. But it lacked a lived-in atmosphere, same as the exterior of the property. No photos, very few knickknacks or ornaments, giving a sense of temporariness.

And providing nothing to inspire conversation.

The man gazed expectantly, and his wife picked at crumbs on her chest. Georgie took a breath. Clueless about where to take the conversation, she decided to stick with the current topic. 'So, how long have you been in the wheelchair, Dawn?'

Wrong question.

Dawn didn't answer or move except for her eyes slitting. After the couple's bantering about Dawn's wheelchair and physio, Georgie never expected this reaction. She shut up, scared that whatever she said—even saying sorry—would aggravate matters.

She wondered if she'd just fucked everything up with the Pooles and she'd be kicked out.

'Another cuppa?' Norman leapt to his feet. 'Lassie? Darl?' He fussed with cups and plates and whistled out the side of his mouth, then flicked the kettle on.

The old man faced the women. He looked from Georgie to Dawn and back to Georgie, then said, 'She took a fall escaping the fire and broke her hip. Lucky for us, we were avid bushwalkers and kayakers. Back then, she was a slip of a thing and I was fit and strong.' He mimed a scooping action. 'I picked her up and ran with her to the oval.'

He stopped.

In a soft voice, Georgie prompted, 'And then?'

'Dawn got shipped off to the hospital and fell into depression. After an operation on the hip that failed, she went into respite while we organised temporary shelter. She's refused more ops, just as she's refused to get active, watch what she eats and do her physio.'

Half-turning so Dawn couldn't see, Norman pulled a sad face and tapped his temple, mouthing, *It's all up here.*

He went on, 'So, near on two years she's been in that contraption.'

'I'm sorry to –'

'Don't be. She could help herself and be much better off. So I refuse to let her wallow. Don't pander to her.'

Georgie gave Dawn a sympathetic glance. Until her own experience with chronic pain, she'd never considered how insidious it was, and substantial weight gain would only compound the problems. 'But –'

Norman held up a palm. 'Nope. There's no point feeling sorry for ourselves. We're lucky to be alive and well overall.'

'We may have survived,' Dawn cut in, 'but we're not lucky to be alive.'

Georgie looked at her. She didn't think she'd ever forget the torment in her eyes.

'Now, darl.'

'No, Norman, let me talk for a change.' Dawn angled to address Georgie. 'This numbness isn't living. Being chained to this chair isn't being alive. We survived, but we lost our way of life when we lost our home, our special things, like my teapot collection and Norman's books and our photos.'

A lump filled the back of Georgie's throat at Dawn's bleakness. And she could tell she hadn't finished.

'We may as well have died too when we lost our town and our babies and too many friends.'

Internally echoing *babies?* Georgie's head throbbed. 'Your babies? Grand-babies?'

'She means our Snoopy and Charlie Brown.'

She couldn't have heard right. 'Sorry?'

'Snoopy, the little Jack Russell who spent most of his life terrorised by Charlie Brown, our half-Siamese cat. We couldn't find them. They died in the fire.'

'Oh, I'm sorry.'

The words strangled around the lump in her throat. Pets were family too. Georgie couldn't imagine abandoning Molly and Phoebe to a traumatic death.

'There you go again being sorry.' Norman tried to smile but fell a long way short. 'The *other* babies were our adopted family. We couldn't have children of our own and would've had six by choice. So we adopted families in town or they adopted us. However you look at it, five special couples and a score of little ones used to fill our home. And we all considered ourselves an extended family.'

Georgie sensed Dawn crying and reached for her hand. They watched Norman.

His face took a faraway expression and softened into a real smile for a flicker. 'We told the little ones they could name the pets, but Snoopy and Charlie Brown were compromises on Scooby-Doo and Shaggy. I refused to stand at the door and holler out those.'

'And...' Georgie faltered. 'And the families?'

'A few of them moved away. They lost their possessions, their homes and businesses, everything, in the blaze.'

Norman tilted his head and shook it, repeating, '*Everything.*' He sighed. The sound quivered.

They were silent for two, maybe three minutes. The only sound was the hum of the fridge in the kitchen.

Norman's voice rasped when he spoke again. 'One whole family was killed.' He balled his hands and stared at them. Then his fingers fell open and his hands become empty cups. 'Just like that. Mum, Dad, four children. All gone.'

Desolate, he repeated 'Gone' in a whisper.

CHAPTER FOURTEEN

'Right, come on down to the station and ask for me, Constable Scott Hart.' He concluded his phone call and stared at his mate. 'You were harsh on Sam before.'

Franklin held up a finger, wrote himself a note and turned back to Harty. 'Nuh, doing it for her own good –'

'*Really?*' Harty's one word dripped sarcasm.

'You answered the phone and missed when I explained the realities to her. All the bits of overtime we don't bother putting in for and getting called into work at the worst possible times.'

'True enough.'

'I said, "Take it from me, make the most of your rest days".'

'Fair enough. But tell me her little crush on you had nothing to do with it?'

Franklin's cheeks flared. He shook his head, not trusting himself to speak.

'She looks at you with doe eyes.'

He exploded. 'Doe eyes? Where do you get this crap, Harty? Melissa got you reading romance novels these days?'

It was Harty's turn to blush.

But Franklin was frowning, wondering if there was anything to it. 'Sam's a newbie with a touch of hero worship going on, that's all it is.'

'You think?' Harty looked at him with pity. 'Mate, it might've started with that, but she's definitely got the hots for you. We've all noticed.'

'Shit.' Franklin wasn't sure if him being the subject of station gossip or Sam's awe veering towards a crush annoyed him more.

'I don't get you.' Harty lifted his hands. 'You said yourself, nothing's ever going to happen with Georgie, then you ran away from Talitha the other night and now pretend you haven't noticed Sam, apart from as a proby.'

Then Slam said from the doorway, 'You better let the snake out of your pants soon or it's going to forget how to do it.'

Harty hooted.

'Fellas, if I need your help with my love life, I'll let you know.' Franklin pivoted to his computer.

Slam roared. 'Your love life?'

'What love life?' his other so-called mate queried. He was also pissing himself with laughter.

Franklin ignored them and plucked out Mr-fucking-iceberg-Defective's list per the Galassi case. He resisted the urge to screw it into a tight ball and lob it into the bin and instead folded it so sharply he severed the page.

He slid the bits under his keyboard.

My way.

The boys were still talking and laughing as he pulled a hunk of blank paper out of the printer and dropped onto his chair again.

'If you two are planning to do anything at all

constructive today, why not put our heads together on this spate of burgs?'

Harty asked, 'And the graffiti?' The uni graduate already had a notebook in hand. He made no bones of wanting to tap into the skill-set acquired on the job by his two closest colleagues, admitting his degree only went so far.

Despite being the joker in their group, Slam matched stripes with Franklin. And he could switch from clown to formidable investigator in seconds.

He did it now. 'Let's go over what we've got. Do they all involve burgs and vandalism? What tags are common? What's been stolen? Does the MO ring any bells?'

———

Over an hour later, Franklin pulled at his bottom lip, gazing at his sheets of paper. The sparsity of notes coming out of their confab left him embarrassed and frustrated. 'What're we missing?'

We're country cops. We're supposed to know everyone and what they're up to on our patch.

In the past, that would've been true, but a glut of Melburnians relocating to the mineral springs area had changed everything.

When he'd arrived in Daylesford nearly seventeen years ago, it didn't take him long to work out who the troublemakers were, along with the powerbrokers, gossips, and desperado women who threw themselves at any male in uniform, regardless of whether the bloke had a wife and child.

These days, he admitted the distinction between local and incomer blurred. Besides the retirees and tree-changers who'd moved here, a good proportion of their population flitted between postcodes. They owned B&Bs, let out their places part of the year and lived here for the remainder. Some were rich enough that their country retreats were for their exclusive use.

Then there were the kids, who were as transient as the wannabe good-lifers who discovered in their first winter that the reality of growing their produce and knitting their clothes was far from romantic. Too many kids and maybe not enough of the wannabes succumbed to the lure of the big smoke. There were only so many shops and cafés in town, after all.

If he referred to the old classification system—you weren't a local until you'd lived here at least thirty years— then he still knew most of the locals.

Franklin pouted. On that definition, he and Kat were yet to crack the status of local.

I'm going around in circles.

Harty and Slam were engrossed now in other work and hadn't answered his question.

Franklin shrugged, pulled up computerised records, dragged out folders and files. He decided to spend until afternoon patrol re-checking tags and photos and trying to expand the list of suspects.

He ploughed the records, his aggravation mounting.

Where are our crime scene results? That ripper of a handprint had to spring a match, surely.

He shook his head. It sucked being flagged low priority because their case was crime against property as opposed to crime against person. That didn't help the Galassis and other vics, who would continue to feel violated until the crooks were caught and dealt with. And it sure didn't help their team nab the band before they struck next.

'Well, fuck me.'

Franklin's ears went weird, like pressing empty conch shells on them and hearing the ocean. His hearing still whooshing, he squeezed his eyelids shut, focusing on yesterday.

Eyes open again, he drew the mug shot closer.

In the pic, the person was broad and stocky; he had ruddy checks and so many freckles on his face that they blended to a tan. But it was definitely a much healthier version of the same kid he'd spotted on the street with the older bloke.

Luke Duffy, now aged twenty-three, with one arrest four years prior for car theft, but the kid had shown remorse and caused no damage to the vehicle. The owner, who was also Duffy's neighbour, had happily accepted the kid's apology and cash to the value of a tank of fuel for his recovered car. And the magistrate had given the kid another shot with a good-behaviour bond.

Duffy had apparently kept clean or flown under the radar since because there was nothing current.

'That's right,' Franklin muttered, recalling that as a juvie, Duffy had fallen in with a bad crowd and dropped out of high school. He'd dabbled with weed, but besides that and nicking his neighbour's car, he really wasn't a bad egg, and yet his parents had written him off.

Franklin tapped his pen against his front tooth.

Hmm. And wasn't there a time the sarge caught Duffy stuffing a can of spray paint down his pants? Lunny couldn't prove he'd been chroming—inhaling the fumes to get high—or vandalising and had let the kid go with a warning.

Franklin sat up so straight his spine cracked.

Was it coincidental that he'd spotted Duffy acting

dodgy yesterday while they were dealing with a graffiti spree?

He didn't believe in coincidence, although what he had was circumstantial and thin. A chat with the kid would sort it out soon enough.

He checked Duffy's last known address. 'Bugger.' The kid's previous address matched a derelict farmhouse recently demolished for a row of factories.

Dead end.

He grinned.

Nuh, a challenge.

ONE WEEK TO CHRISTMAS

CHAPTER FIFTEEN

'WHERE DO YOU WANT TO START TODAY?' GEORGIE WAS struck by how much like her counsellor she'd just sounded. At a guess, she'd had about ten counselling sessions since her initial discharge from hospital, and around half of those had kicked off with that very question.

Sit down. There's the water and tissues. Help yourself. Take off your shoes if you'd be more comfy. Where do you want to start today, Georgie? Don't feel like talking? Did you do your homework this week? How have you been sleeping? Have you cut back on the drinking?

But in this bizarre role reversal, Georgie was the one asking the questions. And it was the teen sitting opposite whose bloodshot eyes eclipsed a pallid face.

She added, 'You said you want to do this, but remember there's no pressure, Ally, and you call the shots. If you need a breather, say.'

The teenager nodded solemnly. She plucked at the boxing mouse charm on her neck.

Georgie willed her body to relax into the sofa, hard because she was wound up with tension and excitement.

Ally finally spoke. 'Dad took up two seats on a plane.'

It was so left-field that Georgie chuckled.

'But because he was so big, he had twice as much room for his heart, you know? He was really kind. If someone was sick, especially a kid, he'd go around to their house, make balloon animals, read to them, anything to cheer them up.'

Ally drifted. Georgie gave her space.

'He was the world's biggest joker – he could have done a stand-up routine in clubs if he wanted. He pulled practical jokes on Mum and me *all* the time, and he'd crack up his customers too.'

'Customers?' Georgie bluffed. She'd extracted basic background on Warren Goyne and knew what Ally meant. But she often initiated interviews by allowing the subject to feel in control of the ebb and flow of information.

'He owned Bullock Realty. There was just him and a casual who helped out, like, seasonally. They did house and land sales, but managing holiday rentals kept them busier most of the time.'

Ally disappeared into her memories.

After a few minutes, she went on. 'Mum used to say Dad put on a happy fat man act to make everyone else comfortable. But I don't think you can *fake* happy without it showing.' She locked eyes with Georgie. 'Do you?'

Georgie had faked it at times, but it wasn't her place to disillusion Ally. She shook her head, implying agreement.

Ally's bottom lip quivered. 'Well, maybe.' She gulped. 'Maybe he did act happy after Clare...' She broke off.

'After Clare what?'

'Nothing,' Ally retorted.

Clare. The name kept arising. Eventually, so would the significance.

'I could murder a smoke.' Georgie waggled her cigarettes. 'Do you mind?'

Ally wrinkled her nose and lifted her shoulders. 'Whatever. But we'd better go outside or Mum will murder *me*.'

She led the way to the al fresco area, and Georgie perched on the edge of the planter box, lit up and inhaled. Nicotine hit her bloodstream and smoothed the edges. She sighed.

'You shouldn't smoke. It'll kill you.'

Ally's disappointed expression cut deep and sent Georgie into a coughing fit.

'*See.*'

Georgie held the cigarette between thumb and index finger. Suddenly repulsed by it, she ground it against the planter. 'You're right.' She shrugged. 'But I'm hooked.'

While they were being so direct with each other, she might as well keep going.

'Would you usually be mucking around with your mates or playing sport or something on a Saturday? I feel guilty that you're talking about all this tragic stuff instead.'

She felt worse when a tear leaked from Ally's eye and rolled down her cheek. Georgie liked Ally and hated upsetting her. What she wrote for the magazine had better be worth it.

'It *is* hard to talk about Dad, but it feels kinda good at the same time.' Ally's face screwed up, as if she were frustrated by what she wanted to say. 'It's like when you feel sick and make it to the toilet before you vomit.'

Georgie tilted her head and thought about the strange comparison.

'It's like when I got Dad's voicemail.' The teen stopped.

'What's that, Ally?'

'Dad left me a message – probably just before he died. I kept it. I listen to it when I'm scared that I've forgotten his voice or I can't sleep. It's really sad but somehow helps too.'

She fumbled in her pockets and pulled out a mobile phone. A few clicks later, a robotic female voice said, *'Message received 31 January at 7.12pm.'*

Then a male spoke over chaotic noise. *'Ally, it's me, Dad.'*

His voice spooked Georgie. She was hearing a dead man's last words, and his fear and desperation were palpable.

'I'm sorry, baby [distortion] *oh God* [distortion] *something...something really bad* [background crash] *terrible fire. I just wanted to say...goodbye.'*

They sat in silence after the message terminated. Georgie was stuck for what to say and sensed Ally didn't want comforting.

'Follow me.' Ally stashed her phone and gestured.

As she walked behind the teen, Georgie noted the tautness in the back of her neck. They stopped outside the garage. After a glimpse over her shoulder, Ally opened the door and entered.

Georgie followed and her mouth dropped open. She'd expected a bench or two, garden and handyman paraphernalia, pushbikes, a car, but that only filled half the shed. The other side held a small kiln, potter's wheel, steel sink, huge plastic-covered slab of clay, jars of glazes, tools pin-boarded to the wall, a row of drying undecorated mugs and a half-metre high mound shrouded in a damp cloth.

'This is what I like to do on weekends.' Ally waved one hand, pivoting and grinning.

'Cool. How did you get into pot throwing?'

'Ceramics,' Ally corrected, still smiling. 'Clare showed me what to do. She taught me to love it.' Her smile faded.

Clare said. Clare showed. Clare taught. Every reference is past tense.

Georgie asked gently, 'Who is Clare?'

'Dad's friend.'

'And Clare is…'

'Dead.'

With that, Ally's face slammed shut as impenetrably as a teller's screen during a hold-up.

———

'Well, what do you think?' Franklin turned to see Kat shrug.

Embarrassed, he glanced at the woman on the front porch. Hopefully she couldn't hear them or read their body language. Her toddler chose that instant to scream – for no apparent reason.

Bloody kids.

'What's your problem?' he hissed.

'Nothing. It's all right.'

'But?'

Franklin was annoyed and his voice showed it, but frankly, he didn't give a flying fuck. His ex-wife, Donna, had given their daughter jack shit since she'd walked out on them, and this occasion was no exception. He'd saved like buggery to buy a decent first car for Kat. He thought that was the Lancer and wanted her to love it, but she seemed lukewarm about it.

'Well, it's up to you. It drives well, it's in good nick. I think it suits you, but if you don't want it, that's fine. Get a part-time job and start saving for whatever you do want.'

'Dad, it's cool. I love it –'

107

'You do?'

'Yeah.' Kat looked at him like he was an idiot. 'But –'

'But what?'

'Can we afford it? Should we get something a bit older or not so flash?'

Franklin hooted. 'You're certainly not the average kid.' He shook his head. 'And that's why you deserve this car.'

With a wave in the owner's direction, he called, 'Let's talk.'

———

Clive entertained a gaggle of seniors at the library front counter but nodded to Georgie as she entered.

She immediately set up a computer, did a search and scanned the results. *Damn.* She dropped her elbows onto the desk, then had a fresh idea and hurried to the reference section. She ran a finger along the titles, recognising most of the spines from her previous visit. She backtracked by one volume.

That's it.

She pulled it off the shelf. Back at the cubicle, she re-checked the list.

Forty-six lives lost in this town alone through the Red Victoria wildfires. Forty-six out of 177 state-wide fatalities, making it the second-worst hit region.

She had to take a brief timeout before reading on.

The number was shocking enough for a small town, but it was sickening to see several uncommon surnames repeated through the death roll, with a breadth of ages that indicated two or three generations of the same families had died. Maybe that was for the best?

Georgie thought about the little girl and her mum that

Clive had warned her off. Would it have been better if the family all died together? Mum would've wished it sometimes.

Norman was right the other day; this was terrible shit. Maybe she should give the assignment up. Let someone else write her editor's story.

She held her head in her hands. Even if she did bail out, another stranger would drive into Bullock and start the intrusion on Ally, Deb, Clive, Kelly, the Pooles, and others all over again. Georgie had uncovered their wounds, promising she'd write a feature that was thoughtful and sympathetic. She was no quitter and she wouldn't let them down, but the only way she'd get through would be to focus on relevant facts.

She skimmed through the list of men and boys. It included two volunteers: a firie from the Country Fire Authority and a State Emergency Service crewman.

The final listing there was orphaned from the rest: 'Goyne, Warren Anthony, 45 (presumed dead)'. It made her stop and chew her lip for a moment.

Then she moved on to the females. Now, she slowed right down. One newborn, two other infants, five teenagers and seven adult women. The pad of Georgie's index finger hovered under a footnote, that the newborn lived for nineteen days in intensive care. *The poor mum.* Of the women, none was named Clare. The same went for the teens.

Georgie pursed her lips, thinking. Perhaps Clare wasn't the woman's first name. Some people adopt their middle names.

She examined the list again. Three women had middle names or middle initials other than C. Two were merely listed with a given and surname but that could be a deficiency in the records. One of those was eighty-four years old. Not Warren's contemporary, yet she could still have been his friend. The other was a thirty-year-old.

She added two teens with no recorded middle initial, too, but knew she could be on the wrong track. Clare could have resided nearby but not in Bullock and be listed somewhere else.

This exercise was a time-waster without local knowledge, and she groaned.

'Need help there, Georgie?' Clive folded his legs and sat on the seat adjacent. He lifted his eyebrows.

Hesitant, she rubbed her chin. She knew Clare was Warren and Ally's friend, and Warren was Clive's best mate. So this could be traumatic for the librarian. Unfortunately, there didn't seem a way around it.

Softly, she asked, 'Who was Clare?'

He took a sharp breath that whistled up his nose. 'Clare? You mean Clare Finney.' He looked through Georgie, saying, 'She was one of the most elegant and kind people you'd have the good fortune to meet.'

Finally getting the inside on Clare, Georgie's pulse quickened.

'She generally taught ceramics some ten or so hours each week.' Clive stopped, dropping his gaze as he fiddled with a button on his jacket.

'Go on.'

She waited, on edge until he continued. 'Kids' and open classes. She was an exquisite potter – no one could mix glazes better than Clare.' He sounded miserable and reverent at once. 'She sold her work from her home studio.'

'Where?'

'Here in Bullock.'

Georgie gestured to the reference book in front of her. 'But she's not on the list.'

'Oh, her death and Red Victoria aren't connected.' Clive gave a surprised headshake and double-blinked. 'She was already dead by then.'

Georgie masked her reaction. She hadn't expected that.

'No, Clare died the year prior. On her birthday.' He sniffed, then clarified, 'She suicided on her birthday.'

'Oh.'

'Oh, yes, oh.' Clive tugged down his sleeves. 'You see, Clare was one of my closest chums.'

She'd guessed as much. 'I'm so sorry,' stumbled out.

He waved off the platitude. 'Warren and Ally and myself. We all loved Clare. And she loved us. But we weren't enough for her.'

So much sadness in those words. 'Why?'

'In her teens, they labelled people like her with manic depression. Years later, in their wisdom, thanks to research, enlightenment and political correctness,' Clive's tone dripped with sarcasm, 'they called it bipolar disorder.'

His right foot tapped as he talked. His accent thickened, and Georgie strained to comprehend.

'God knows they have plenty of labels, but it's basically a cycling between mania and melancholia, or extreme highs and extreme lows.'

He rocked forward and back, clearly distressed. 'As Clare aged, she spent more time depressed than manic; the episodes lasted longer, were more extreme and separated by far less normal spells.'

He went still.

'We saw it, but we could stop it about as well as they could stop the bushfires.'

Georgie started to speak, but Clive continued. 'When

she was up, Clare was highly productive, created the most beautiful and unique ceramic pieces and won several competitions.' His eyes glistened. 'And then she'd crash down, couldn't concentrate, eat, sleep or work...and we couldn't reach her.'

The librarian broke off to say goodbye to an elderly library patron, faced back to Georgie and continued one octave lower and quieter. 'And then there's the social stigma and prejudices. Adults, who should know better, plus kids calling her the *crazy lady* during her bad periods.'

Georgie felt as grim as Clive looked.

'Do you think she meant to kill herself, or was she crying out for help?'

He scoffed. 'She took a massive overdose of her medications washed down with a half-bottle of brandy. She seldom drank alcohol because of her meds and her condition and never drank spirits neat. It was no cry for help. Trust me, she meant it.'

She saw strain etched around his eyes. Tangible grief, and she felt culpable.

'Please go.' Clive sounded drained. 'I'm shutting shop shortly—we're only open ten 'til twelve on Saturdays—and there's plenty to do, preparation for a fresh start Wednesday afternoon.'

'Clive, I –'

He held up a flat palm. 'I'm happy to talk later, but let me deal with this alone for now. Tomorrow, next week...'

Two for two. Two interviews terminated on the subject of Clare. *Nice going, Harvey.*

CHAPTER SIXTEEN

'FROWNING PREMATURELY AGES US, LOVE.'

Startled out of her daydream, Georgie said, 'Huh?'

'I said, "Frowning prematurely ages us." You're sitting there glaring at your coffee like it's offended you. It's not your most attractive look.'

Deb Goyne calls a spade a spade. Clive had said that on the quiet, right at the beginning.

Georgie noted nobody waited in the bakery queue, and few other customers were inside or outside. She waved to the seat opposite. 'Can you take a few minutes?'

Deb sank onto the bench. 'That feels better.' She grinned her buck-toothed smile. 'How's the story going?'

She obviously hadn't spoken to her daughter this morning.

'Yeah, getting there.'

Georgie hesitated, considering Deb's upfront nature, as she watched another staff member sticky tape tinsel to the front counter while wearing a morose expression.

Deb followed her gaze and commented, 'The boss wasn't going to put up decorations in case it offends. But I said, "What's Chrissie without lots of bling?" and I guess they figured if I can get on with it, they can *try* to go through the motions.'

It seemed like an invitation for Georgie to jump in, so she said, 'I'm keen to chat with you about Warren, to picture him from your perspective and see how...*this* has impacted on you.'

'This? His death, you mean?'

Yep, a spade's a spade. Georgie nodded. She plucked her mini-recorder from her handbag and lifted her eyebrows. At the woman's go-ahead, she pressed record.

'Warren was an old softie. A bit of a charmer too. He'd flirt with anyone, any age, any gender if it helped him.'

'Helped him?'

Deb did a *you know* shrug. 'Make a sale. Sometimes even charm an extra five grand out of purchasers, which made him a real hit with his vendors.'

'So, you mean business-wise?'

'Nah, not just in the real estate world. He'd do anything to be liked. He sponsored local clubs and events even when business was slow. Played Santa each Christmas.'

'So, Warren was a kind person.'

The other woman tilted her head. 'Yeah, kind. He took on lots of lame ducks.'

'Lame ducks?'

'He often visited old dears who moved from here into geriatric homes. And he helped out with the support groups.' Deb screwed up her face. 'He made cakes.' She scoffed. 'And served teas and coffees.'

Georgie didn't understand what was wrong with that. 'Support groups?'

'Bereavement sessions. AA and gambling meetings.

Kids' bullying talks. They used to have the lot in the old hall. It burned down, along with most of the town.'

So matter-of-fact: *It burned down. Along with most of the town.* No fluff. Ally's more sensitive approach to life and death would go a treat with Sheridan Judd and the readers, but her mother would be a major liability. Georgie made a mental note to roll with Clive's recommendation, to focus on the daughter and use the mum selectively.

'Anna Shaw is one of the part-timers.'

'Part-time what?' Georgie interrupted, confused by Deb's jump.

'Oh, a "weekender".' She made a finger-hook gesture and wrinkled her nose. 'Anna had a little place next to us. She's a counsellor, supplied her services "gratis",' again the derogatory finger-hook, 'but got a little funding for brochures and that sort of thing. Warren provided the refreshments and twisted a few arms to get free use of the hall and Bob's your uncle, Bullock had its own shrink sessions.'

'You weren't a fan?'

Deb sniffed and twisted her lipsticked mouth. 'It's all in here.' She tapped her skull.

Well, that's the whole point of mental illness, isn't it? Georgie knew better than to say it.

'We don't need to sit around hanging out our dirty laundry. You take a knock in life, you pick yourself up, dust yourself off and get on with it.'

'Some people –'

'Some people are too soft.' Deb made a scathing noise that hissed through her protruding teeth. 'Mental illness is a cop-out. I mean, we all get stressed out now and then, and we all take hard knocks, but do we look for labels or sympathy or say "Oh, poor me, I can't cope"? Look at Clare Finney.'

Georgie's eyes widened at yet another reference to Clare.

'She was as crazy as crazy gets and topped herself. Coward.' Deb almost snarled.

'You believe suicide is cowardly?'

'Of course. It takes more strength to live through it and get better.'

Deliberately moderating her tone, Georgie changed tack slightly. 'So when you lost Warren, you didn't see the benefit in counselling?'

'*Pity sessions.* Ask Anna or another goody-two-shoes to help me through the five stages of grief?' Deb sneered. '*No-sir-ee,* that's not for me. Don't get me wrong; I loved Warren to pieces and I miss him every day, but I don't need to be told how to live without him.'

'What happened to Anna after the fire?'

'She's rebuilding her cottage. You noticed the caravan next door to us? The part-built place?'

Georgie nodded.

'That's hers.'

'And the counselling sessions?'

Deb eye-rolled, managing the equivalent of one of Georgie's best efforts. 'She's in more demand than ever. *God.* They line up like they're going to the circus.'

Her expression triggered the opening riff of Bob Dylan's *Everybody Must Get Stoned* inside Georgie's mind. Raucous carnival music; creepy, jaded. Even worse, the dumpy woman rose and mocked a penguin waddle.

Georgie watched, disgusted.

CHAPTER SEVENTEEN

AFTER THE COP CLOCKED THEM, THEY COULDN'T RISK staying behind the church. So they'd shifted again, this time to an empty shed at the old railway station. There was a public toilet twenty metres away and running water. Only cold water, though. The shed was watertight and clean, and they were further from the cop shop, so it might be good to stay here a while.

They were both sick of moving.

Living as he and the kid did, they had no concept of time – other than they had too much of it to kill, dwelling on bad things. Weekday, weekend, it was all meaningless in their world. But when he heard a car horn, voices and clangs, he suddenly realised it must be Sunday. Market day.

He said to the kid, 'Hurry up, bud. We gotta get out of here.'

But his mate was crook again, so he had to help him get up. Sounds outside were increasing every minute, so he grabbed their packs.

'If we're quiet, they won't even know we're here.'

'Can't, mate.'

'Aw, Waz.'

'Don't. Nobody calls me that.' *Not anymore.*

'But –'

'Lean on me, bud. We gotta go.'

———

'Remind me again how I pulled the twilight yesterday, backed up by the day shift today?' Franklin grumbled.

'Nobody likes a whinger.' Slam held up his hands, box-framing his face. He looked bright-eyed and bushy-tailed after his day off yesterday. 'Winner.' He pushed the hand-frame close to Franklin's face. 'Loser.' He chuckled.

They scuffed behind tourists and hippies, passing a handful of stalls lined up in the car park, and climbed the concrete steps to the main part of the Sunday market. Their boots crunched on gravel until they turned into the entrance of the old railway station. They walked through the ticket office as instructed, to the Station Master's office.

Franklin shifted the cumbersome belt on his hips as he rapped on the glossy panelled door. He felt Slam's breath on the back of his neck. 'Back up there, mate. Bit of space.'

A voice called, 'Enter.'

They did, and a young bloke jumped up and reached out a hand. 'Welcome! I'm Manjot Singh.'

Singh led them along the platform, giving a potted version of his role as station master and volunteer coordinator here, when not bogged down with his PhD in mechanical engineering, and a history of the tourist railway.

He paused outside a shed and the three men watched the approach of a red locomotive with silver V-striping on her pug-nose. Singh grinned as kids jumped off, jabbering to their parents.

He turned solemn. 'Now, we have no wish to make trouble for anyone, but we found this today. We decided we were obliged to bring it to your notice but, well, we believe it's people a little down on their luck?'

He indicated a broken padlock and pushed open the door. They peered inside before stepping over the threshold.

Franklin took in a grey blanket in one corner, then debris in the middle of the room. *Well, well. A squatter's kitchen.*

'Anything stolen?' he queried.

'No, we'd cleared the shed last week, as it's next on our list of minor maintenance jobs.'

'Graffiti?'

'None. It's really a fuss about nothing.' Singh looked flustered. 'We should have tidied away the rubbish and bought a new lock.'

Franklin reassured him, although the bloke had hit the mark.

'I'll leave you to it.' Singh moved outside.

'Nothing like the Galassi MO, is it?' Slam said.

'Nah.' Apart from litter and a wrecked padlock, the squatters had been well-behaved, and the matter was too trivial to call in crime scene. 'This one's just kids or druggies. It could've been a lot worse.'

He and Slam poked through the rubbish with gloved hands. Empty baked beans and tuna cans, a compacted milk carton and soft drink bottle, along with a crushed packet of paracetamol, all the blisters popped.

Franklin found a lighter when he dragged the blanket off the ground. Silver, engraved 'Waz YF Clare', it was fancy, maybe vintage. *Whoever Waz is, he won't be happy losing this.*

He pocketed it, took a few pics of the scene while Slam jotted notes, but both knew nothing would come of the callout.

———

After a few bangs, a voice called, 'Housekeeping.'

Georgie groaned, hoping they'd go away.

No such luck. 'Hello? Anyone in?'

She lifted her head off the mattress and forced her eyes open to see a woman gaping at her from the doorway. She held a bundle of folded towels and obviously hadn't expected to find Georgie in bed.

'Sorry, miss. Will I come back later on?'

'I'm...' Georgie tried to make saliva to moisten her mouth, so she could finish the sentence. 'I'm leaving today.'

'You've missed checkout by over an hour. And the boss is a stickler.'

Georgie's eyes were already fluttering closed when she said, 'Then, yes, please come back later.'

Just as she closed her eyes, a rotary telephone rang somewhere in long, high notes. Georgie tensed, trying to connect the noise.

So used to the *Flight of the Bumblebee*, which she'd had

on her old mobile, she belatedly recognised the generic ringtone of her new one. 'Shit.'

She untangled from the bedclothes and hunted her phone. *Cold, colder, warm, warmer, hot.* It had silenced before she grasped the handset. One missed call: AJ.

'Double shit.'

As she hit speed dial, her toe nudged something on the floor. Distracted, she ended the call. She picked up a mug and added it to the stash on the small table: two tumblers, a chip bag, squashed Benson & Hedges packet (her preferred smokes), empty scotch bottle, twin-pack cookie wrappers and an old-style round travel lolly tin, tartan design over gold, complete with butterscotch aroma, same brand as Grandma Harvey used to favour, except she'd loved the fruit drops. Clive's lolly tin.

Her head thumped, regretting the scotch, although it'd seemed a good idea at the time. She pictured her exit from the supermarket liquor shop carrying the bag-wrapped bottle. She'd heard her name and turned to Kelly from the info centre.

They'd ended up in Georgie's motel room. Kelly called Clive. The three of them knocked off the scotch and chips. By then too late to order a meal, they'd raided the complimentary cookies.

Loosened by alcohol, hours had disappeared. The earlier awkward interviews were kind of taboo, then forgiven. Georgie remembered rubbing her gut because it ached from laughing while thinking that she'd never expected them both to be so funny. Eventually, the irate manager had hammered on Georgie's door and yelled, *Keep the noise down! It's after three!* which spurred the others to scoot off. Before much longer, Georgie had crashed.

The same sensation that followed the first mouthful of

coffee for the day flowed through her body, softening her muscles, and she hit redial again.

'*George.*' He didn't say anything else.

Her warm, relaxed feeling dissolved. It was impossible to read his tone, but considering Sunday was halfway over, she guessed AJ wasn't happy with her. Then again, it was just as likely that he was in his office, up to his eyeballs in case preparation, and had rung before to explain he wouldn't be home until late.

The harder Georgie tried to figure out AJ and what they had, the more it felt like holding onto slime. Impossible.

She rushed to fill the silence. 'I have one important interview this afternoon and then I'll be straight home.' She hated sounding so insecure but added, 'Promise.'

————

Cheese, tomato sauce, onion, mustard, smoky flavoured frankfurter bursting its seam, all in a soft white roll. Franklin eyed the hot dog appreciatively and inhaled, took a big bite and savoured the burst of flavours.

Hey, it's better to cave in to a food craving than light up a smoke.

He felt better when he saw Slam repeatedly nod as he chomped on his own dog.

Midday, the Sunday before Christmas and a brilliant sun high in a clear blue sky equated to a bustling marketplace. There were more vendors than usual as they cashed in on the season of excess, and stacks of visitors, which boded well for business.

With portable radios and mobiles on hand, and things quiet so far, they called their stroll of the market 'surveillance work' and turned a blind eye while the other bargained on personal purchases.

Franklin scored a cute cap to add to Kat's already bulging Chrissie stocking. Well, he thought it was cute; time would tell if she agreed. Slam bought his mum a hideous cactus plant and swore she'd love it.

They heard a train's long hoot signalling its return from Musk and watched it slink into the station.

'I remember taking Kat on the train when she was so high.' Franklin held his palm two feet from the ground. 'She giggled and pointed the whole way to Bullarto and back. No sooner had we jumped off, she begged to have another go. You know me,' he shot Slam a grin, 'I couldn't say no to my little grasshopper.'

'Ah, those were the days, huh?' His mate sighed.

Franklin sensed a sting.

'Hey, I've an idea.' Slam held up an index finger.

'And what would that bright spark idea be?' Franklin asked dryly.

'Why don't you,' Slam dropped into a Tom Jones voice, *'ride the tour-ist train with Sam!'*

He gyrated his hips, looking bloody stupid.

'You're kidding, right?' Franklin rolled his eyes. 'Like I'd be one of the fucking creeps in blue.'

A bad taste filled his mouth and he wanted to spit but wouldn't in public. Nothing to do with his hotdog and all to do with senior cops who abused their positions.

Slam gave his shoulder a light punch, 'Fair enough.'

To change the subject, Franklin snatched a fistful of Slam's hot chips and chewed loudly over his mate's protests.

CHAPTER EIGHTEEN

As THE CLEANER HAD FOREWARNED, THE MOTEL manager charged a full extra day for Georgie's two-and-a-half-hour sleep-in. At least her magazine gig meant she could claim it back on tax. She tucked her credit card away as she exited the motel.

One look at the electric blue cloudless sky made her forget the penalty she'd paid for late checkout. The weather god had finally remembered it was summer.

A hot dry breeze rippled over her skin, and Georgie couldn't wait to head off and snake through the Black Spur with the soft-top down on the Spider, enjoying the warmth and wind in her hair. The 'Best of the Eagles' playing on her car stereo would make it perfect. But as she'd told AJ, she had to talk to someone first.

It felt urgent.

Within minutes, the Goynes' property loomed, although it wasn't her aim this time.

———

'Georgie! Wait up. Please.'

She swivelled towards Ally's voice, while she heard a motorised roller door activate. The kid waved from the verandah, then bolted down the driveway ahead of a VW sedan pulling out of the garage.

Ally grabbed Georgie's arm and squeezed it. 'I'm sorry about yesterday. You're not mad, are you?'

'Of course not.' Georgie patted Ally's hand, plagued with guilt. She'd intended to call the teen this morning to apologise but had forgotten.

'I'm so glad. It just gets hard to talk about it sometimes.' A horn tooted and Ally flicked her eyes to the idling car. 'Mum and I are going out.'

Georgie wanted to ask if they could continue their interview another time but hesitated. Considering her prickly conversation with Deb yesterday, the mum might put a stop to their talks anyway.

The engine died and Ally cast rapid glances between Georgie and the VW, and as Deb jumped out, leaving the door ajar, she whispered, 'I want to keep going, okay?'

'Are you sure?'

Deb drowned out Ally's yes with, 'Who's your next victim then, love?'

Georgie winced. 'I'm hoping to catch your neighbour, Anna.'

'Oh?' Deb arched her eyebrows. 'For counselling or an interview?'

Georgie searched for a relatively non-divisive topic. Flustered, she started, 'For another point of view on rebuilding. I'll ask you both the same thing as I'll put to her.' She inclined her head towards next door and continued to improvise. 'How do you feel about experts saying Bullock should never have been allowed to rebuild?'

Non-divisive? Hardly. Ally's eyes widened and her mother's cheeks flushed.

Georgie ploughed on. 'That they say the likelihood of another wildfire disaster is considered so great that even with new stringent bushfire building regulations, permitting the re-establishment of Bullock amounts to, at a minimum, gross negligence?'

The mother and daughter exchanged a glance.

'How do you think we feel? It's rubbish!' Deb snarled. 'What're we supposed to do? Abandon the area? And where's safe anyway? Most of this country's bushfire prone. Can you see us living in some high-rise in town?'

Ally cut in. 'What would they do? Drown Bullock in a man-made dam to make sure it couldn't be rebuilt? Because that's what it would take to stop what's left of our community –'

'Besides, it didn't burn of its own accord,' Deb interrupted. 'A person set up a bonfire. *Deliberately.* Then they lit it and did nothing to stop it. They should be shot when they get caught.'

'Mum, how's shooting them going to help?'

'They have to pay.'

Ally and Deb stared at each other.

Georgie drew a deep breath and asked, 'What do you think would be the right outcome, Ally?'

'I don't know.' The teen's eyes welled. 'Nothing's going to bring Dad back. Maybe the person's suffering every day because of what they did. Maybe that's enough.' Her slender shoulders drooped.

Georgie scuffed the paving. Every question dug her in deeper, but if she was going to write about the Goynes, she had to press on. 'But wasn't it difficult for you to rebuild *here*? The site of your original home.'

'Difficult? Of course it was bloody difficult,' the older woman retorted.

When she didn't elaborate, Georgie pressed, 'I'm not sure I could've done the same.'

Deb groaned. A guttural noise.

'We rebuilt because that's what a community does. It sticks together,' Ally said in a fierce whisper. 'It rebuilds together.'

'Yes, but people would understand if you couldn't face rebuilding, particularly where Warren actually died.'

'Of course they would've understood,' the mother answered. 'Well, most of them anyway. But what if he comes home and we're not here?'

Ally shot her a stunned look. 'Mum, Dad's dead!'

'Officially, theoretically, but a small part of me clings to the fact that they didn't find a body because he was hurt, somehow escaped but can't remember who he is or where he lives.'

'I can't believe –'

Deb insisted, 'If he has amnesia, one day he'll get his memory back and he'll come looking for us.'

Tears streamed down Ally's cheeks. 'You're cruel. You're crazy.'

'It happens.' Deb reached to stroke Ally's hair. Her daughter twisted away, leaving her with a hand in mid-air, looking desolate. 'Oh, love. I realise he's probably gone, but a tiny little part needs to believe there's a remote chance… it's how I get through. Let me hold onto that spark of hope a little longer?'

Ally's face crumpled and she fell into her mum's arms.

Georgie swiped at her own wet eyes and recalled telling Clive, *I'm not here to hurt anyone or set back their healing.* She felt like an ugly hypocrite. Her best intentions were shattering with every interview. She'd torn off so many scabs; Bullock would need a truckload of band-aids.

She staggered back a few steps. 'I'm sorry –'

Deb looked over Ally's shoulder. She sniffed hard, then cleared her throat. 'You're still here.'

Gutted, Georgie lifted her hands. 'I'm really sorry.'

'Don't be.' Deb must've seen the surprise on her face because she added, 'It's better out than in, isn't it, Ally-love?'

Her daughter nodded.

Ally had said all along how difficult it was to talk about her father and the fire, while it also helped. It still shocked Georgie when she said in a strangled voice, 'Georgie. Later, huh?'

CHAPTER NINETEEN

GEORGIE FANNED HER FACE TO SOOTHE HER PUFFY EYES
as she turned into the next property. The gravel driveway
led to a house-in-progress with a Smart Car in the
foreground. She grimaced, having met a few greenies more
motivated by attention-seeking than carbon footprints. She
also struggled to imagine the Smart Car tackling the hilly
Black Spur and would never choose one herself, but she was
here with an open mind.

But for the car and a radio burbling softly, Georgie
might have assumed she was alone on the building site.
Then she heard a faint noise and aimed for it, not hurrying
because she was grateful for extra moments before she faced
another witness.

She skirted to the rear, by two giant water tanks and a
garden shed, calling, 'Hello?'

After a series of thuds and corresponding sways within
the pop-top caravan, a female around her own age swung
open the door and stepped down.

Georgie assessed the woman. She had a high forehead,
thin eyebrows over close-set brown eyes, dark hair pulled

into a messy ponytail that escaped in wild wisps. Her wide smile transformed a plain face into something striking.

Now a metre away, she clearly topped Georgie's five-foot-seven by several inches, only in part credited to the small heels on her Blundstones. Her lean but squarish build was clothed in well-worn and stained denim overalls with a red T-shirt underneath. Georgie liked her air of unpretentiousness; it augured well for a frank conversation. Blitzing her smile was the woman's intense gaze; a dead ringer for Georgie's shrink.

They shook hands and exchanged introductions.

'Georgie Harvey.'

'Anna Shaw.'

'I'm a journalist –'

'Don't worry, I know. Word travels fast in country towns. Even us incomers-slash-outsiders-slash-part-timers or whatever else the long-termers want to call us eventually get the goss.'

Still, those eyes drilled Georgie, and she itched under the forceful scrutiny.

———

Anna and Georgie sat in camp chairs shaded by the caravan awning, gnawing on slabs of fresh bread topped with chunks of bitey cheese.

The counsellor didn't need prompting, jumping in with, 'I stayed away that day. Remember, the Premier told us conditions were as bad as they could get for bushfires?'

'Yeah, but unfortunately most people didn't pay attention.'

'Well, I'd been here the weekend before and the place was tinder-dry. No exaggeration.' Anna gestured. 'As wet and green as it is now, it's difficult to believe that we were in drought for over a decade.'

'And now floods are the new bushfires,' Georgie mused, frowning at her own tangent.

'Yes. Well, they predicted stinking hot with gale-force winds that day. Apart from the pool and river, there's not much to do here during a scorcher. Besides, the drive down would've been a nightmare; the roads in parts were literally melting under tyres. So I decided to visit friends in Elwood instead.'

'Lucky.'

Anna pulled her mouth sideways. 'Yes. Yet I feel like the captain who deserted her ship.'

'You should've been here with the other villagers?'

'Of course.'

Survivor guilt. Georgie took a slug of mineral water, remembering Clive saying *I was grateful but racked with guilt.*

'But what could you have done?'

'About as little as anyone else not trained in these things, I suppose,' Anna said. 'But then I'd made myself responsible for pastoral care of the community and in the moment of greatest need—'

'Was it that?'

Anna looked puzzled, so Georgie reframed the question. 'But was that the moment of greatest need or did it come later? When the reality of the devastation became clearer? The next day, when you knew who lived, who died?'

'It wasn't clearer the next day.'

Georgie sat forward, encouraging Anna on.

'Every report contradicted an earlier one. We heard the

whole town went. Every building. Initial body count: the entire population.'

Anna's mouth moved but nothing came out. She turned pained eyes on Georgie, again drilling into her soul. Georgie recalled the confusion, dramatic 24-7 coverage and emotional overload of even city-dwellers in the days and weeks after Red Victoria.

'Can you conceive what it felt like to believe everybody here had perished in the fire?'

Georgie flinched before nodding.

'The loss of buildings, infrastructure, industry, whatever...that's insignificant compared with human mortality.'

'Were you able to contact anyone who could clarify what'd really happened?'

Anna shook her head. 'It was chaotic. The Red Cross, bushfire hotlines and police, everyone was in meltdown, along with their phone lines and websites. That Saturday was the worst fire event in Australia's history, but it didn't stop there. It wasn't one day of horrific bushfires; it went on for weeks and weeks in many areas.'

As she told the story, the expression on Anna's face continually changed. Wonder, horror, disbelief, anger, emptiness and grief added to the tapestry she stitched with her words.

'The majority of people didn't have a practiced emergency plan. Communities that are prone to earthquakes or tornados click into action when an event happens. We *fragmented*.'

She waved her hands.

'Because of the suddenness of the fire here, those who escaped had what they stood up in. No wallets, handbags, ID, money, phones. But they were lucky. The ones who stopped to pack died in their driveways or on the road.' Anna stopped and took a long breath. 'Of the survivors who fled Bullock, some went to official shelters, others stayed with friends or relatives. Lots of people took a week or more to register with the Red Cross.'

With a grim smile, Anna said, 'I guess that was the long answer to your question, Georgie. In short, during the initial pandemonium, we relied on ABC Radio for updates, same as the rest of the state.'

Her eyes were far away, as she said, 'The town was in lockdown. People were furious because police stopped everyone attempting to come in. But they had to.' Anna ticked off fingers. 'Because of the danger—trees, roads, buildings were all damaged, could go at any time—and risk of disease, as we didn't have fresh water or services. They had to prevent the additional trauma in civilians stumbling over bodies. And to stop looting. But also because the whole town was a major crime scene, the site of mass murder.'

'Arson.'

The counsellor nodded. Holding up two fingers, she said, 'Two different locations and different methods, merging into one calamitous event. Possibly two arsonists, whether they worked together or not.'

'How can a human do that to another human?' Georgie didn't expect an answer.

Anna's face crumpled, then she yanked herself upright.

'I'm a psychologist, have seen and heard and studied numerous disturbing cases, and *intellectually* I grasp that the offenders are almost certainly pyromaniacs incapable of fighting the impulse to light fires. They have a morbid fascination with the excitement and spontaneity of fire.'

She glanced at Georgie, who nodded to show she was following.

'Some patients are aware of right and wrong and can't resist anyway,' Anna went on. 'Others are more complicated cases, suffering from a combination of psychoses. They are mentally incompetent and don't connect consequences. Either way, we're dealing with mental disorders, and thus, these people can be helped by committal and psychiatric care, with a view of rehabilitating them back into the community, if possible.'

'They can't be let out!' Georgie cut in, appalled.

'Perhaps so, perhaps not, after treatment. Regardless, that's my intellectual assessment. My *emotional* assessment is that *I* still can't cope either. But at least I'm trying to help the people here cope. And I'm doing my bit rebuilding. A community sticks together. A community rebuilds.'

She said it as a mantra she'd repeated countless times but didn't necessarily buy into.

'A community rebuilds?' It struck Georgie as almost identical to what Ally had said earlier. 'That's what you tell your patients?'

Flustered, perhaps hearing an accusatory tone Georgie hadn't intended, Anna said, 'No. I tell them they have choices. We talk about those choices and what's right for the person, the family, the situation.'

Georgie redirected the conversation to the Goynes. 'Did you counsel Ally and Deb after the fire?' She was already aware the negative applied to the mum.

'Not formally. But Ally is a friend, and I'm always here for her. Officially or unofficially.'

'How has she coped with Warren's death?'

'You mean, how has she coped with Warren's *disappearance*?' Anna clarified.

That echoed what Clive had said at the start.

'But he's a listed victim?'

'Yes, look, I'm not by any means saying he didn't die in the fire but merely analysing it from his family's perspective.'

Georgie's brow furrowed as she focused so completely on Anna that their surroundings and all peripheral noise receded.

'The seat of the second fire was close to here.' Anna pointed across the yard and through the skeleton of her building towards the mutual boundary between her and the Goynes. 'And, with the intensity of conditions and ferociousness of the fire, the authorities concluded that Warren perished in the fire, leaving little in the way of forensic evidence.'

Georgie said, 'In those instances, they traced witnesses who saw or spoke to the deceased around the crucial time and, or, relied on circumstantial facts, like it was Bob Taylor's house and he lived alone, so the body in the bath was that of Bob Taylor?'

'I guess that's simplistic but essentially correct,' Anna agreed.

'So, in Warren's case, they couldn't even find enough to be sure they had a body but through the facts that: A, he's remained missing, B, he was last seen and heard from prior to the fire, and C, the intensity of the fire was so great that a body could have been obliterated, the coroner ruled he died in the fire?'

Anna nodded.

'How did Deb get out unscathed?'

'Luck? On par with why the bakery was the single surviving building on that stretch of the main street. Why one sole house was untouched along this entire road.'

'So, Deb took her migraine meds?' Georgie prompted, to get her head around the sequence of events.

'And "slept like the dead", her words, "until a terrible noise" woke her. That was the fire, bearing down on our houses.'

'And Warren?'

'She couldn't find him.' Anna's eyes fluttered. 'She yelled for him but could only see a few metres in front of her; it was so dark, hot and thick with smoke. Eventually, she had to make a run for it or stay and hide in the house. She had to save herself.'

Georgie thought about Deb, who was sometimes cringingly blunt, now understanding that might be how she coped with her unbearable decision to save herself and desert Warren. It also explained her need to cling to the irrational hope that he'd survived.

Anna added, 'A lot of people went missing. Most of them have been accounted for. Some, including Warren, have left their families in limbo...and they are facing yet another Christmas.' She sighed. 'It's a tough time for them.'

They both sat still and silent for several minutes.

Then the counsellor muttered, 'The *what ifs* will inevitably be on their minds until they bury him.'

Impossible according to the coroner's ruling. There is nothing left to bury.

CHAPTER TWENTY

'*CROW STREET, DAYLESFORD.*'

'Shush, please.' Franklin held a finger to his lips to mute the chatty stallholder, giving a half-smile apology. While listening to his portable radio, he forked out cash for the antique fishing reel, no time to bargain. Lunny would love it; that's all that mattered.

'*Altercation between one male, one female. The female is injured, the extent of injuries unknown.*'

He called, 'Slam,' pointing at his radio. 'That's ours.'

Franklin grabbed his purchase, sprinted for the patrol car, fumbled for the keys as he ran.

'*Ambulance has dispatched. ETA twelve minutes. Approach with care. Witnesses are unsure if the offender is armed...*'

His partner responded to the operator as they jumped into the car. Franklin flicked on strobes and cursed the bottleneck of Sunday drivers at the nearest exit. He dodged a man pushing a double stroller, pulled a deft U-turn, and they bumped along the rough track to the rear gate. Slam braced as they cornered and wove through the back streets.

'This your love triangle?'

'Yep.'

Seconds later, Franklin roared, 'Idiot,' at a car that reversed out in front of them. He swerved and planted his foot. 'Fuck!'

'What?' Slam leaned forward, stabilising with a hand on the dashboard.

'I took my eyes off Hudson and Jones. I knew there'd be trouble.'

Franklin pulled up outside the Hudson place.

'Do we wait for backup?'

'No.' He dropped his long legs out of the car and scoped the scene as he strode towards the cream-and-green cottage.

'Neil. *Please* let me in.' The tiny woman had her back to them, thumping the front door with both fists.

'Piss off, Monica.' Hudson's voice came from inside the house.

The couple gave no indication they knew the cops were there, so Franklin said, 'Mr and Mrs Hudson – Senior Constables Franklin and Sprague.'

'Neil. I want to come home,' Monica begged.

'Don't talk to me, woman.'

'We're police. We've received a report of a disturbance here,' Slam called. 'We need to talk with you both.'

Caught up in their family drama, the Hudsons continued to ignore them.

'Neil, please. I made a terrible mistake.'

'Yes.' It sounded like *yeesh* making Franklin think Hudson was drunk. 'You did.'

'You drink too much and you can be nasty when you drink.'

Franklin wondered how physical Hudson got with his wife, how nasty he'd gotten this afternoon. He'd find out.

He and Slam held back at three metres from Monica. Right now, no one appeared to be in imminent danger, but it could change in a second.

'I know.' Neil groaned. 'And I hate myself when I do it.'

'I went next door that night because you were being horrible, and Marc's always been nice. He said to come over anytime I needed.'

'I'll bet he did. Jones, *nice*! He's a slimy prick.'

Intent on making her confession, Monica went on. 'We had a drink. And one thing led to another. Honey, I guess I was mad and hurt and I wanted you to hurt.'

Silence. Then, 'Well, you got your wish.' Hudson's words slurred. 'Now piss off back to your new man. Or should I say, toy boy?'

Monica started head-butting the door.

'Ma'am.' Franklin moved in and took the distraught woman by the shoulders to restrain her.

She faced him. Tears and blood intermingled on her cheeks. Nothing like the popular, happy girl that many of her friends had tried to emulate.

'Come away, Monica. Let's have a talk.' Franklin guided her from the house to the back seat of the patrol car.

He heard Slam say, 'Mr Hudson. Open up; I need a word please.'

With a half-turn over his shoulder, Franklin saw Slam rap on the front door, then step back. He looked as wary as Franklin felt. Domestics were the great unknown. They could fizzle to nothing as quickly as they could explode into the worst kind of violence.

With one eye on his partner, Franklin said to Monica, 'An ambulance is on its way.'

'Don't need an ambulance. I just want to go home.' She grabbed his hand and gripped hard. 'He changed the locks.'

She pleaded, 'John, make him open up and let me come home.'

Franklin extracted his hand but gave her a little pat as he did it.

'First, the ambulance is already on its way and you're obviously hurt, so they'll check you over and take it from there. Okay? Second, well, we can't make him take you back. That's up to the two of you to sort out.'

Neil Hudson staggered onto the verandah. Face beetroot red, he wielded a beer bottle above his head.

'Mr Hudson, put down the bottle,' Slam bellowed, bracing.

'Stay there,' Franklin said and shut the car door; kiddie locks would keep Monica out of the picture.

'Neil Hudson.' Franklin flanked his mate but kept his tone placatory. 'Don't make matters worse, mate. You don't want to add assault police to your troubles.'

The drunken man looked bewildered. He wagged his head, then circled it upwards, taking in the beer bottle. Astonished, he dropped it, smashing and splashing glass and beer over the verandah. The brickie moaned and wrung his hands.

―――――

While Slam interviewed Hudson inside the house, Franklin attempted to get a coherent story from Monica.

'You have nasty cuts on your face there. You may need stitches. How did it happen?'

She shrugged.

'C'mon, you know me, Monica. You can tell me.'

'It was an accident.'

Franklin heard the wail of an ambulance and knew she

was unlikely to say in front of the crew what she hesitated to tell him one-on-one. 'Did Neil hurt you accidentally?'

'I've got nothing bad to say against Neil. It's all my fault.'

The ambos were fifty metres away. *Last chance.* 'It's your fault that he struck you, you mean?'

The little woman glowered. 'I mean, I've got nothing bad to say against Neil. This,' she pointed to her face, 'was an accident. And I banged my head.'

She jabbed a finger at Franklin's chest, 'You leave my husband alone. He's a good man.'

He had to back off but feared he'd regret it later.

CHAPTER TWENTY-ONE

GEORGIE LAY STARING AT THE SHADOWY CEILING. AJ muttered in his sleep and resettled.

She chewed over Anna Shaw's words: *The what ifs will inevitably be on their minds until they bury him.*

She felt achingly alert, but in the middle of the night, not much could be achieved.

Soon three questions filled her thoughts. They were improbable and yet made her blood tingle, simultaneously excited and troubled.

What if Warren Goyne wasn't a victim of the fire?

What if he did have amnesia and hadn't yet regained his memory?

Her heartbeat raced.

What if he'd disappeared on purpose?

Lou Reed's classic *Walk on the Wild Side* switched on in her head.

Whenever Georgie had trouble sleeping, she heard parts of songs on repeat in her mind. Sometimes they were tunes she'd sung along to on the radio that day. Occasionally, the music came from a deeper place.

Questions or problems scratching for answers pulled up a weird choice from the jukebox of Georgie's eclectic music brain. It could be annoying, but she'd learned to go with it because the harder she fought it, the louder it got. But more importantly, if she didn't resist, the subliminal messaging just might hit pay dirt.

Now, her foot twitched in time with Reed's talk-sing voice, until Phoebe pounced on her toes playfully.

'Go to sleep,' AJ grumbled.

'Can't sleep. How did you know I was awake?'

'I felt it,' he complained. 'And then the cat joined in.'

'Roll over, babe.' She nestled behind him, spooning. It usually made her sleepy, but she couldn't relax and soon flipped to her back.

Then she turned onto her left side as the acoustics resumed in her head.

With a soft groan, she curled to the right. At that, Phoebe jumped off the bed and stalked up the hallway.

Reed's lyrics continued. It made her think about hes that were shes and vice versa.

Did she really care in the middle of the night?

The song restarted. Music. Then music and lyrics.

It stuck again. A fat man could disguise himself twice as well being skinny and in drag. But could Goyne—in any guise—have hitchhiked his way across Victoria?

Not impossible to think that a person could have snuck away in the chaos of mass evacuation, then begged lifts.

Perhaps he didn't need to hitchhike. Although he didn't have his car, cash buys cheap rides on public transport, which linked most places in the state. If his wallet was in his pocket when he escaped, he probably had some money. A decent stash, if he'd *planned* to depart.

Could he have resettled elsewhere and taken a fresh identity? *People do it every day.* But if he did, where?

Hell, it needn't be limited to Victoria. Goyne could have travelled interstate, or even overseas if he'd managed to get a false passport.

———

At just after five, Georgie slipped from bed and tiptoed to her study.

She cranked her computer and pulled out her ever-expanding research notes. But she looked at neither, instead gazed into space.

What had led to the wild jump in her subconscious?

One: Anna's infamous *what if* comment.

Two: Clive saying, *Where there's smoke, there's fire. Where there's doubt, there's dumb hope.*

Three: Lou Reed's reminder that people fake their disappearance. Frequently.

Four: Goyne's message to Ally. Granted he loved his kid, but would he abandon his wife and risk his own safety to make a telephone call?

Five: It was the weakest of the lot but had to be considered. Goyne's wife still held hope.

None of these points was singularly persuasive, yet another old-school tune played in Georgie's mind. This time *Signs* by the Five Man Electrical Band, equally catchy as *Wild Side*. Apart from when she wanted to sleep, she'd dig both.

She needed a sign, a plan and a lot more information because this was going to be one massive story, Georgie could smell it.

'What are you doing?'

She glanced from her messy desktop to AJ's mussed hair. 'Work.'

He came closer and plucked up her notepad.

Georgie felt a little prick of annoyance because she wouldn't do that to him. But then she nestled back in her chair, happy that he was trying to help.

In the top margin of the sheet, she'd captioned a circle 'Warren Goyne' and bullet-pointed each major fact she knew about the man underneath. She watched AJ's eyes start there.

'He was forty-five?'

'Yep.'

He continued skimming down and read bits aloud, 'He was a self-employed real estate agent. "Family man: daughter (Ally), wife (Deb). Closest friends: Clare (deceased), Clive, check other. Personality: generous, funny, kind, big-hearted, but faking happy?" What's that last part mean?' AJ frowned.

'Something Ally said. Her mum reckoned Warren put on a happy fat man act. Ally didn't think you can fake happy.' Georgie gazed away.

'And?' AJ prompted.

'It reminded me of another thing Ally said. Something like, he did *act* happy after Clare.'

'After Clare what?'

She pulled him close and gave his nose a long kiss. '*That* I don't know!'

He frowned again, puzzled. 'And you're happy about that?'

'Put it on the list!' She threw him a pen.

'What do you mean by "check with P re: driver's licence"?' His forehead puckered.

She explained, 'I thought the cops could tell me if it's current or had any hits since he fell off the radar.'

'Where's this going, George? Your man's dead.'

'Ah-ha! But is he?'

Their eyes locked. AJ fell into the visitor's chair and eventually said, 'It'll be a big story if he's not dead.'

She laughed. 'Yep!'

AJ read on, 'Next points, "Credit cards/bank accounts: check. Email account: check." Who will you ask?'

'I guess Deb...but it'll be tricky,' she confessed.

His eyes moved further down the page, where she'd described Goyne, based on Ally's sketch, then she saw AJ shift left. There, under 'Dead,' she'd drawn two sub-headings, 'perished in fire' and 'died subsequent' with dot points: reports, trace evidence, police/coroner, John Doe.

Georgie explained, 'I need all the background facts, including the missing person and inquest reports for Goyne. I got the gist of things from Anna Shaw, but it seems tenuous proof that he died in the fire. If he died later, somehow, without ID, he'd be in the morgue as a John Doe.'

AJ nodded.

She clicked her tongue. 'But they'd have found a match with dental records, et cetera, so we wouldn't be having this discussion.'

'What about your other list: "MIA – involuntary (amnesia)"?'

'I don't even want to *think* that he has amnesia or can't get home or make contact for another reason. It's too random and broad. Where would I begin?'

AJ leaned forward, seeming to match her excitement. 'Leaving, voluntary disappearance. How, though? And where?'

Georgie finished for him, 'And most importantly, why?'

He sat very still, then shook his head. 'No way.' He tossed her notepad onto the desk. 'Find another story.'

'What?'

'You heard me.' He stood, looming over the top of her. 'If this Goyne did disappear by choice, he could be a dangerous adversary. It's not worth it. Not after what happened in Daylesford. We're not going through that again.'

Georgie stared at him, white noise buzzing in her head. When she'd questioned her assignment a week or so ago, he'd reminded her of its importance. And now he'd backflipped.

She muttered, 'What happened to *you're doing your job?*'

'You're not paid danger money.'

Still dazed, she said, 'It's not about money.'

'It never is, with you.'

AJ's comment was so barbed, it physically hurt inside her chest. What did he mean? That she wasn't pulling her weight financially? That he saw her as lacking ambition? That she didn't fit into his material world?

She staggered from her chair. As she backed towards the doorway, he grabbed her hand.

'George. That didn't sound right.'

She shook her head and tried to pull away. With another stab of shock, she saw his eyes fill.

His words rushed. 'What I meant was, you never put yourself first.' He begged. 'Please, George. Stop putting the story, or the people in it, above your safety.'

She quit fighting AJ and stepped towards him, moved by his words, his care.

'Drop the Goyne story, find a new angle. For me.' It

wasn't what he'd said, it was his tone. A command, not a plea.

She felt confused. Which AJ did she believe? The one who'd teared up, apparently worried about her. Or the one who treated her like his lapdog?

Then he completely lost her by adding, 'It's just a story. Not important.'

CHAPTER TWENTY-TWO

HE WET PAPER TOWELLING UNDER THE TAP AND WIPED his armpits. They stank because he and the kid rarely had safe access to running water and almost never hot water. Even what he was doing now wouldn't help much. He didn't have clean clothes to put on.

Gone were the suits and chinos. Now he possessed a small bunch of clothes, stolen or passed on from others, and they could only risk using the laundromat about once a month, so a scuff with soap and cold water had to do in between. But possessions, hygiene, and appearance meant nothing in the scheme of things.

They lived in squats to avoid being caught and because they couldn't afford rent, let alone risk applications for properties. When they moved, they slinked around in the early hours, when most people were in bed or working shifts. Out of supplies, they hunted for scraps or whatever they could nick. They tried to pick easy targets and commit good-old 'victimless crimes'. That was a joke. Surely, someone got hurt in any crime, even if they weren't actually walloped over the skull. But 'needs must' was the way they had to live.

Had to live?

No one ever held a gun to either of their heads and said, 'You must mess up your life so completely that you can't go home, can't get a job, can't exist as you used to anymore. You'll live in squalor and die early if you're lucky. If not, look forward to turning into a druggie or wino because after a while you won't be able to live with yourself sober.'

I made my choices. And now I have to live with them.

———

Raindrops suddenly splattered the windscreen and soft-top, falling faster than the Spider's wipers could deal with, and Georgie swerved onto a verge. She needed time to think anyway.

With one story, she'd please her editor and readers. It could be her best yet. But a bunch of people wouldn't be happy if she broke the story she imagined.

Yanking on the handbrake, Georgie tabled Warren Goyne after AJ at the top of the list. She couldn't foresee any *good* motive for Goyne to flee, for him to vacate his family, home, mates and identity. She curbed her imagination while admitting AJ was right. She could be heading into dangerous territory.

But he was wrong to think she could back off.

In the next second, her resolve buckled. *Poor Ally.* The kid had been to hell and back already. Her home was burned to the ground, and dozens of her friends and neighbours and purportedly her dad were killed or injured, by the fire. Her town, her world, continued to reel in the aftermath.

Georgie may be about to unearth something that would hurt the kid afresh.

Can I do it?

———

Yesterday's events had kept Franklin awake for hours, and when he'd finally fallen asleep, merged into exhausting dreams that flit between the railway shed, market and Crow Street.

In one part he was staring at a grey blanket on the floor that moved, re-shaping into Monica Hudson, as she'd looked when she was Monica McKinnon. Then her face turned sad and haggard, and blood gushed from a massive head wound, and she shrieked, *Didn't you know it was a cry for help?*

After that, Franklin had downed a beer, hoping it would relax him enough to sleep. Post-beer, getting back to sleep had proven easy but falling into a peaceful slumber, impossible.

That time he dreamt about District Inspector Knight tearing shreds off him. *She banged her head? We have to deal with a double homicide because of your incompetence, Senior Constable. Forget detective training. You'll be lucky to be assigned traffic duty in Ballarat after this.* The scene shifted to Crow Street. DI Knight saying, *Monica Hudson has done in her old man and her lover. You didn't see that coming, did you, Franklin?*

After the second nightmare, he didn't attempt sleep again and spent hours thinking. He decided the dreams didn't make sense, except to flag how disturbed he was about the Hudson case. He'd do a follow-up call on tonight's shift.

Half-nine now, Franklin lurched out of bed feeling run over by a truck. Today was supposed to be a good day. His not-so-baby girl was on school holidays. They were to pick up her new Lancer later this morning and take it on its first family outing before he kicked-off the twilight shift.

No way he'd ruin today for Kat. If push came to shove, he'd fake happy until his face hurt from smiling. Even all these years later, he remembered that feeling from his wedding day. He and Donna smiled and smiled for the camera until their jaws ached. But then they went on smiling right through the reception because they were so rapt to be hitched.

Today would be a good one, despite the rough start.

———

As suddenly as the rainstorm started, it stopped. To the side of the Spider's shiny flank, Georgie saw a pair of randomly spared mountain ash, the towering trees offset by acres of hazy grey droves of still-standing but dead neighbours. Even stranger, ahead of the lay-by, hundreds of bare tree trunks as black as her car pointed straight to the sky wearing new growth that wisped their lengths.

She'd passed piles of charred trees presumably felled for safety, considered too close to the road, too weakened to trust. Wide gravel fire tracks with even wider firebreaks cleared either side. Hillsides covered in plastic-sleeved seedlings. She and her Spider were diminutive in the scarred surroundings. As much as she wanted to save Ally from more hurt, and even if the outcome conflicted with Georgie's motives for accepting the assignment, she was obligated to the reveal the truth, and rightly or wrongly, excited by the chase.

She flipped the blinker on and gunned the accelerator.

———

He crossed his arms, left shoulder angled forward, presenting the three stripes on the epaulette of his immaculate uniform in Georgie's direction. Everything about him was a tad too perfect, except for his lazy left eye.

Sergeant Ian Boulder was not a happy man. 'You want to know *what*?'

She repeated, 'The status of Warren Goyne's driver's licence. If it's still current, whether any vehicles have been registered in his name or he's incurred demerit points or other driving offences.' She winced at her use of present tense and quickly added, 'For completion of my research.'

Boulder stooped over the counter, his nose so close to hers that he must be on tiptoe. 'Are you pulling some kind of stunt? You got a hidden camera? Recorder in your handbag? Huh?'

She squirmed. His reaction was overly hostile, but she understood where he came from. She'd glossed over her reasons for asking, couching it as standard research for a feature, but her bluffing seemed to intensify rather than downplay her controversial questions.

'Mr Goyne was a greatly respected member of this community.' The sergeant glared.

Georgie regretted coming to the Bullock cop shop and upsetting Boulder, but she wouldn't back down yet. He might let something slip.

She met his gaze. His lazy eye made him look even angrier, so she fixed on his right ear.

'Mr Goyne died in the fire. Along with too many of our community, including *my best mate* – he was best man at my wedding and a police member here too.'

Georgie cringed. She should've anticipated how intensely personal this would be for Boulder.

'They died heroically. Horrifically.'

She said nothing, copping it on the chin.

'And you have the gall to waltz into my station and ask ridiculous questions...' He pointed a finger. 'What's your game?'

Her face pinched with remorse. 'I've explained –'

'And what does it prove that his licence has expired? The man's dead.'

Boulder had answered one question, but she didn't feel any sense of satisfaction; hurting people wasn't right.

'How could he register a vehicle or commit offences from the grave?'

And that answered questions two and three. Still Georgie's conscience was heavy and now she wanted to escape.

'Turn out your handbag and pockets.'

What? Thanks to her dumb mistake, Boulder was losing it. 'Look, I'm sorry for –'

He overrode her. 'Empty them.'

'Why?'

'On the grounds that I don't trust you. And I don't like you. But I want to be damn sure you're not recording this conversation before I tell you just how much I don't like you.'

'I'm not recording –'

Boulder narrowed his gaze. 'Are you implying we're incompetent?'

Georgie backed towards the exit.

'Is that what you're doing? You watch yourself, Mizz Harvey.'

She bit back an answering retort and escaped onto the street. The automatic door snapped closed and light drizzle sizzled on her skin, cooling her head.

It'd be fair to say that Sergeant Boulder would feature high on the list of people who wouldn't necessarily be happy if Goyne returned from the dead. Or with her, for breaking the story.

CHAPTER TWENTY-THREE

THE LIBRARY'S LIGHTS WERE OFF AND THE DOOR locked. Georgie shouldn't be surprised. Most places with a similar population sufficed with a weekly mobile service, if that. Bullock was lucky to have its own library branch open for two short shifts and two longer ones.

None of those being on Mondays.

She tried Clive's mobile, left a voicemail message. She was grumbling under her breath when the sky opened. Rain fell in driving sheets and drenched her immediately.

'For fuck's sake. And this is supposed to be summer!'

A female passer-by stopped. Shrouded in a full-length raincoat and holding a black golf umbrella, she was cosy and dry and shooting daggers.

'Give us a wet summer anytime, young lady.' She dropped the umbrella sideways and let the rain flatten her neat grey curls. 'If it means we don't have to lie awake every night worrying about bushfires, it can rain every day.'

Georgie cringed, mumbling, 'I'm sorry.'

Despite her apology, the stranger added, 'And wash your mouth out. Ladies do not swear.'

She swooped up her umbrella and sloshed through the puddles.

'What day is it?'

Georgie recognised the question and voice. She turned away from the library, smiling. 'Hi, Norman, Dawn. Monday.'

'Bugger.' He patted his wife's arm. 'I messed up our days, darl. We'll have to come back after lunch on Wednesday.'

Dawn didn't respond and Georgie saw her shut down a flicker of animation. Her discipline in acting up during their walks was impressive, in a very sad way. Then again, she may not have forgiven Georgie for the other day.

'Why don't you come to our place for early morning tea, lassie?'

Georgie pictured her to-do list. She'd promised herself major progress on the feature and Clive topped her action plan. But the olive branch from the Pooles was touching.

'That'd be lovely –'

Norman beamed.

'– but I'm not sure I'll be able to get there today. I'll call you if I can't make it.'

He nodded, and already thinking about her next move, Georgie missed what he added as the old couple trundled away.

———

Georgie's day was going pear-shaped. 'Clive is *Christmas* shopping?'

Kelly's eyebrows shot up. 'Yeah, it's that big event on 25 December for which most of the world stops each year. In five days from now.'

'Really?' Georgie quipped, then let out a laugh. 'I'm familiar with what and when Christmas is but my headspace is all about work at this point.' That made Kelly look even more worried, so Georgie assured her, 'Don't worry, I have some ideas for my family and will sort out my friends before Chrissie. Too easy.'

Her companion skimmed over the info centre, empty apart from them. 'I have plenty of time to think here. But far fewer friends to buy for these days.'

Georgie saw her face darken.

'You know, at first I thought convicting the people who did this would help us heal. I'll admit I supported the burn 'em at the stake mob for a while there. But now I realise, it won't make an iota of difference.' She sighed. 'Our friends will still be dead, and we'll still have our nightmares.'

Strike three for the day. Boulder, the stranger in the rain, and now Kelly. Georgie couldn't have played the outsider with foot-in-mouth disease better if she'd tried.

Desperate to lighten the mood, she waved towards the wet and deserted street. 'At least the drought's a thing of the past.'

'Shush!' Kelly's eyes popped behind her square glasses. 'You might jinx us.'

Georgie remembered the recent Father's Day floods. She'd figured that signified the end of the drought, particularly capped off by the almost monsoonal December conditions. Apparently, country people disagreed, and she and other city dwellers were clueless.

Strike four. Can I buy a lifeline? 'Where's your kettle? I owe you a cuppa.'

They didn't speak while Georgie made drinks. But as she put a mug in front of Kelly, she said, 'Getting back to Warren.'

'Were we talking about him?'

'We are now.'

Georgie watched the woman sip from her cup. They got along well, but she couldn't forget Kelly's face shutting down when she'd first discovered Georgie's assignment. It was probably best to keep her suspicions about Goyne to herself for the time being.

'I'm filling in gaps.' She was happy with the way that sounded; thorough, yet downplaying how important her questions were. 'Besides Clive, who would you say was his closest friend?'

Kelly rubbed her brow for a few moments, looking thoughtful. 'I would've said Clare, before she died. Clare and Warren were like this.' She crossed the first two fingers on her right hand and fell introspective again.

Georgie gave a gentle prod with, 'So Clare and Warren – ?'

'Oh.' Kelly's eyes widened, then she recovered. 'Well, you'd often see the big guy and Clare walking and chatting. Sometimes with Clive and Ally, sometimes Anna Shaw tagged along too. He had lots of mates; everybody loved him, but I guess they were his closest friends.'

'Do you think there was more to Warren and Clare than companionship?'

Kelly drummed her slender fingers, clearly uncomfortable. 'I'm closer to Clive than I was with Warren. But the guys were tight, so I suggest you ask Clive that question.'

She'd intended to, except that the librarian was inconveniently Christmas shopping with his mobile switched off, but Georgie didn't respond. Most people feel compelled to fill silences. Perhaps Kelly would.

She filled the silence, all right. She gathered their mugs

and rinsed them in the small kitchenette, straightened brochures on the wall and checked a diary notation.

But eventually, she retook her seat, facing Georgie. Then she picked up the thread of their conversation from over five minutes ago as if there'd been no gap. 'Oh, there was gossip. But I never saw them act as other than good friends. Okay?'

Georgie shrugged lightly. The gesture triggered a zip of pain through her shoulder that joined with a frisson of anticipation. She was onto something.

'Her death devastated him, though.' Kelly did another frustrating pause. 'He wasn't himself after she died.'

'That would be understandable for anyone who suddenly lost their best mate.'

Kelly added baldly, 'Even more so when that person killed themselves.'

They exchanged a grimace.

'How would you say he wasn't himself?' Georgie asked.

'Geez. You often just intuit these things. You want specifics?'

Georgie bobbed her head.

Kelly squirmed, then clicked her fingers. 'Here's one example. He didn't play Santa that last Christmas. He always played Santa. Another guy jumped in, but the kids didn't get into it, and Warren didn't seem to care.'

Annoyingly, Georgie's phone vibrated on the counter between them. She spotted the name of her caller and pulled an apologetic expression. 'I need to get this –'

Kelly waved. 'That's fine.'

Georgie rued the timing, moving out of Kelly's earshot to answer. Things were heating up here, and finally she was getting a call back from a publicist she'd been campaigning for an exclusive interview.

'*Developments.*' The publicist spoke quickly. '*Caro will see you.*'

'Oh –' Georgie didn't get another word in.

'*Only you. But there's a catch.*'

'What?'

'*It has to be 1.30pm today.*'

She checked her watch. Three and a bit hours, less an hour and a half to get from Bullock to Richmond. She only needed a fresh shirt and boots, a quick pull of a brush through her hair. She could plan while she drove.

'Done. Thanks –' Georgie trailed off. She was talking to air.

She bolted from the info centre, then rushed back, promised to call Kelly later, and searched for her car keys as she jogged out again.

———

Franklin adjusted his collar and smoothed his hair. He did an automatic check of his duty belt, remembered using his spare disposable gloves at the Hudson incident yesterday and restocked. That reminded him to fit in a follow-up with the Hudsons tonight, if possible. With a pat to his gun, he hitched the belt to avoid it grinding his hipbones and dragging on his lumbar.

Finally, he sank his butt down and exhaled. Sam pulled up a swivel chair next to his desk.

'Just made it, boyo,' Slam announced.

After taking the new Lancer for a spin with Kat, the afternoon flew so fast that Franklin shaved it fine on the changeover. He threw Slam a dirty look. 'And how often have I covered your arse, mate?'

Slam chuckled and leaned in to give him a backhander,

just as Tim Lunny ducked around the corner, clad in tracksuit and runners.

'This isn't one of those when the cat's away, the mice do play occasions, is it, people?'

'No, Sarge,' they chorused back.

Slam grinned and added, 'We don't wait until the cat's away to play, boss.'

They all laughed, including Lunny.

'I just ducked across,' the sarge thumbed over his shoulder to the station house next door where he and Maeve lived, 'to grab my reel. Must've left it here.' He rubbed his hands. 'I'm off fishing.'

'In the rain?' Sam asked.

He regarded her with a grave expression. 'The fish don't mind getting wet, Sam.' He spluttered at his own joke and disappeared into his office.

'They bite better in the rain,' Franklin told the probationary constable, realising she was young and green in many things, not limited to policing.

She blushed.

He gave her a moment to recover, turning to Slam. 'Any progress on the burgs?'

'Nah, no time.'

'What about our CI bloke? Heard from him?' Franklin held no expectations of the lead detective on this case – nothing positive, at any rate.

Slam grunted. 'Yeah, had your Mr Defective on the blower earlier. Pretty much blowing it out his arse.'

'Have you come up with any ideas?'

His mate shed his belt and undid a button on his shirt, ready for the switch to his civvies. 'It feels like two groups. Two sets of cases.'

'That's my guess too.' Franklin scratched his chin.

Sam had been listening intently and nodded.

'Our railway case, that's more a needs thing I reckon, don't you, Slam?'

'Yep.'

'But at the party warehouse, the offenders took their time to do all that graffiti,' Sam contributed.

Franklin agreed. 'Yep. Blatant vandalism –'

'Versus forcing into a shed for shelter,' Slam finished.

'Two sets of crooks.'

'One would've been more than enough.'

'Yeah, well, that's why they pay us the big bucks.' Franklin laughed at his own joke.

They fell quiet until Sam piped up. 'Can I ask something?'

Both men scrutinised her.

She looked at Sprague. 'Why do they call you Slam?'

'Guess,' he teased.

Sam screwed her mouth. 'Because you like to slam crooks away?'

'Good one,' he said. 'But no.'

'You slam down the beers?'

Franklin laughed. 'Nice try but no cigar.'

'Your style, er, prowess with the ladies?'

With a groan, Franklin said, 'Don't give him a bigger head than he's already got.' He glanced at Slam. 'Do you want to put her out of her misery?'

His mate leaned back in his chair. He spread his legs and arms wide in his story-telling mode.

'My first day here, despite just getting my second stripe, I felt a bit of a basket case – no offence, Sam, but like a green proby.'

She giggled. 'Oh, I can relate to that.'

'I walked in the front door and saw his ugly mug,' he nodded at Franklin, 'and the then-sergeant, Bill Noonan.'

Sam sat forward, transfixed.

'Anyway, I walked in and the door slammed, mashing my fingers. I extracted my hand, turned to Franklin and Noonan, put out my other mitt and said, "Hi, I'm the newbie, Senior Constable Mick Sprague. But you can call me Slam!"'

'Oh!' Sam covered her mouth. She laughed until she clutched her ribs and fanned her face. Eventually, she managed to say, 'Can I call you Slam too?'

'Good to see you all working so hard,' Lunny commented. 'Hope you're not planning on putting in for overtime...Slam.'

The sergeant hoisted his rod, waved and departed with a smile quirking his lips.

'The boss is right. We'd better hit the road, Sam, and let Slam go home.'

On cue, the latter saluted and loped out the door.

Sam rose, asking, 'What are we going to do about the case? The cases.'

'The burgs and vandalism?' Franklin screwed his nose, thinking before he replied. 'Patrol first, then we'll try to find the buggers whose tags we recognised at the warehouse. They've proved slippery so far, but we're due to strike it lucky. And we'll see if we can find Luke Duffy.'

'Duffy?'

'A local kid with a prior for car theft and question mark for past vandalism. He used to hang with a bunch of bad eggs.'

Sam looked understandably puzzled. Franklin hadn't

mentioned Duffy in their team briefings and he felt cross with himself for failing to follow up on the kid earlier.

'Duffy might link in,' he said. 'And later on, we'll hit the files again and pull names for similar jobs.'

'And the railway break-in?'

'That's the one that's got me buggered. And bothered.'

CHAPTER TWENTY-FOUR

Franklin yawned and stretched.

After dealing with a back-to-back series of tedious and trivial complaints, they'd just been to see Charlie Banks. He'd reported a prowler, but even as Franklin put down the phone, he knew they'd find no one besides the old codger, along with an open packet of Butternut Snap biscuits on the kitchen table and the kettle a moment ago boiled.

Sam puffed out her cheeks. 'Wish I'd stopped at two bickies, but he looked so disappointed, I had to have more. Poor old man. He's lonely, isn't he?'

'Yep. He calls when he wants to chew the fat.' Franklin dropped the car keys onto their hook.

'And makes up a story?'

'Every time.'

'At least he rings the station directly.'

'Yep,' Franklin said again, extracting a bundle of paperwork. 'And it always seems to be about two-point-five minutes behind me pulling into work.'

'Living near the station's kinda handy for Mr Banks.'

'Hmm,' Franklin replied, preoccupied. He studied the

pics from the Galassi party warehouse, holding the photos close. He examined and threw them onto the desk in turn, then picked up the last one again and pumped a fist.

'Gotcha.'

'Boss, we have an urgent callout!'

Sam's tone made Franklin dash behind her to the front door. She hurled him the keys.

'Crow Street. Marc Jones's address.' Stress and the impact from her foot-strike made Sam's words judder as they descended the steps and crossed the car park. 'Violent altercation. Ambos are on their way.'

Franklin dove into the police four-wheel drive, slammed his door. 'Anything else?' He fired the engine.

'There's a gang of men involved, and they're hostile and possibly armed. The neighbour hung up after saying he'd done his civic duty and he was taking his family somewhere safe and staying right out of it from here on.'

Franklin's guts wrenched and the tyres of the truck squealed in sync. The love triangle had turned ugly. But how ugly?

At the address, they saw a male youth holding his head in hands, seated on Jones's step, dry-heaving.

Franklin said, 'Sam, this doesn't look good.'

'Should we wait for backup?'

'The ambos will be here before backup. We have to suss it out.'

She looked reluctant as they got out of the truck. Same as part of him felt, but he needed her 100 per cent committed. 'Constable.' They might still be able to avert disaster. 'Stay with me, do as I say.'

She met his gaze and nodded.

Franklin ran his eyes over the bloke on the step. 'Are you hurt?'

The boy moaned but shook his head.

'What's the story in there?'

The youth flapped his hands, then wrapped his arms around himself and shivered. They stepped past.

Positioned at the gaping front door, Franklin bellowed, 'POLICE! COME OUT!'

Pause.

He added, 'Or we're coming in!'

They heard voices inside the house.

Suddenly, there were loud footsteps, and they saw a tall, brawny male tearing up the dim hallway. He cast away a broken rake and came at them with his palms raised.

Franklin gestured Sam to cover the rear. 'Hold it! Police!' Then he recognised the man. 'Damo, it's me, John Franklin.'

The bloke's face was tear-streaked. 'Kitchen. You have to get in there. An accident. Terrible. In the kitchen,' he stammered.

'Right, wait outside.' Franklin gestured. 'Don't go anywhere, touch anything or talk to anyone.'

He stepped over the threshold. 'Police. We're coming in!'

'Noooo.'

Franklin paused to isolate the sound. Just a single voice, pained beyond recognition.

He and Sam raced down the hall towards the kitchen. At the threshold, he scoped the trashed room.

Up-ended table. Broken crockery. Busted chair. Spade near the fridge. Its broad head bent. One yellow brick in the centre of the floor and another shattered at the foot of the table.

Marc Jones was propped against the stove, with the jellified appearance of a person in deep shock. His ashen face was offset by blood streaming from his nose. He seemed to be unarmed.

No sign of Monica.

Franklin skipped back to the figure hunched over a body. At that moment, the distraught man lifted his face.

'Please.' He fixed them with pleading eyes, still cradling the body. 'Please help my brother. I don't think he's breathing.'

Now Franklin could see the casualty's face: Neil Hudson. Inert, but unconscious or dead?

Franklin approached the men on the floor. 'Neil Hudson's your brother?' He kept his tone calm, his actions fast and sure.

'Yeah.' The bloke clutched the limp body harder.

'What's your name?' Franklin asked, squatting alongside.

'Shane.'

'Okay, Shane, I need you to please put Neil on the ground. That's right, mate. Now I need you to go with the constable here and take some air outside.'

'I can't leave my brother.' Shane knelt over the top of the body, hands on one side, knees the other.

'Move away, please. Your brother needs urgent medical attention.'

'But –'

'Shane, I don't have time to argue.' Franklin switched to a more authoritative manner. 'Every second we waste could cost him...'

His life?

While addressing Shane Hudson, Franklin saw Marc Jones stir, nudging one of the bricks with his toe.

'Jones, watch your step. Go with Constable Tesorino outside.'

Franklin glanced sideways when no one moved, desperate for help but the probationary constable's olive skin had turned a sickly green as she gawked at Neil Hudson. The angle of Hudson's neck and a contusion on his temple didn't bode well. Franklin felt for Sam, but he needed six sets of hands to their two.

She still hadn't roused.

'Constable.'

She remained stunned.

'Tesorino, down here.'

Sam turned her eyes on him, a little glazed but finally listening.

She crouched next to him and Franklin whispered, 'Sam, you gotta snap out of it. I need to tend the casualty. You need to help me preserve the scene. First, get the witnesses out of here. Make sure they don't do a runner or talk to each other. Second, check ETAs for the ambos and backup. Then get back in here with an update.'

She nodded, moved to the younger Hudson's side and touched his arm. 'Shane. Please let us help your brother.'

Relieved that Sam was functioning and dealing with the shocked witnesses, Franklin blocked their voices. The instant Shane moved away, he swooped to the body. 'Neil, can you hear me? Squeeze my fingers if you can.'

He pressed his fingers to both of Neil's palms. And felt nothing.

Franklin tweaked the trigger point on the man's upper trapezius, the muscle between the neck and collarbone. That would startle a conscious person, they may even lash out. But Neil continued to lay mute and motionless. His limbs flopped.

He still could be with us, just unconscious.

Franklin checked Neil's airway: clear. Breathing: no.

Shit. Just compressions? Nah. Poor bastard needs all the help I can give him.

He extracted a face shield from his equipment belt, fitted it to Neil and started CPR, silently talking himself through the process.

Thirty compressions. Two effective breaths. No stopping until the ambos arrive.

But even doing those first two exhales, Franklin knew he was breathing into the lungs of a dead man. He kept at it, intent on his actions and Neil, only vaguely hearing, 'Boss?' after he'd run through seven cycles of CPR. Franklin turned his cheek between breaths and saw Sam step into the kitchen.

'Stay there; we don't want to disturb the evidence more than we already have.' He caught a guilty expression on her face.

He couldn't stop to reassure her. Blew again and watched Neil's chest expand. Automatically, not a sign of life.

He returned his hands to Neil's sternum and pumped. His neck muscles had begun to burn. Partly from the effort of the compressions, mainly tension. 'Talk to me, Sam.'

'The four witnesses are all outside. I've told them not to speak to each other. There's a crowd gathering out there, boss.'

'Bloody rubberneckers,' Franklin muttered as he mentally counted *ten, eleven*. 'Get the tape up. Block the driveway.' He continued to thrust at Neil's chest. 'Nobody comes in without a badge or an ambo uniform. Note their details in your book. Put on your toughest voice.' *Twenty-two*. 'And instruct the ghouls to disperse.'

'Got it.'

Twenty-five, twenty-six.

Franklin was struggling to think, talk, count, do effective compressions and monitor Neil all at once. 'See any joker with a mobile phone, threaten to confiscate it.'

'Yes, boss.'

Thirty.

It wasn't working. Had Neil been alive when they arrived? He'd have a hard time living with himself if his delay in starting CPR let the man slip away.

'ETA on the others?' Franklin checked.

'Ambos approximately ten minutes.'

Dread and panic made his palms damp. He pushed down the feelings.

Keep going. Gotta give him a chance.

Sam added, 'Nearest car is more than thirty minutes away.'

Half an hour for backup. Franklin's heart thudded hard. He needed help here. Fast.

'We're going to need help with the crowd and witnesses. Get onto the sarge; tell him we need some bodies urgently.'

Sam pulled her radio, saying, 'We'll need crime scene and a team from CIU too, yes?'

'Spot on.' Franklin nodded, then blocked her voice.

A couple more thumps and he exhaled into Neil's mouth again, but still no signs of life.

But he was neither God nor a paramedic, so he kept going and watched Neil's chest rise and fall.

Rather than lose it, he distanced himself emotionally. He mentally coached himself, imagining a CPR dummy on the floor, not a man.

Position the heel of the hand and push down. Firm and smooth. One-third of chest depth. One, two, three…

CHAPTER TWENTY-FIVE

THERE ARE ALWAYS CHOICES.

He hated it when the nasty voice in his mind said everything he tried to forget.

Yes, he had choices.

He'd made a choice *that day* which dictated everything that'd come after.

His stomach burned. The kid was edgy, feeling good, desperate to go out now it was dark. But he just wanted to curl up in a corner and think. It hurt to remember what he'd left behind. But without thinking about the two best people in his old life, nothing had meaning.

His fingers dug into his pocket, automatically searching for the lighter. But he'd lost it somewhere. Maybe in the leaky shed behind the church, or at the old railway where he forgot one of the blankets, although they'd been to a few other places since he last remembered using it.

'All right, Luke.' He shrugged on his jacket and watched his buddy's face brighten. 'But be careful.'

They'd go out, keeping his mate happy, and search for his lighter, although he knew it'd be pointless. It was gone, just like everything that mattered in his life.

———

'Are you two the first responders?'

Franklin viewed the speaker, a wrinkled, portly and balding detective. He'd missed the fellow's name. At least it wasn't Mr Defective, who he'd spotted with the crime scene techies. But he didn't know this bloke; he must be a recent transfer to Bacchus Marsh.

Franklin answered with a wary nod and positioned himself so he could see both the detective and Sam.

She held her coffee beaker in both hands. Sallow. Fragile. Her eyes flicked from the detective to Lunny and Harty, who'd taken over crowd control when the CI bloke issued his summons.

Franklin saw her gaze veer to the ambos who were conversing with Slam. There was an obvious lack of urgency in their actions.

Slam had joined the throng of personnel well after the others, thankfully armed with paper cups and flasks of hot and strong coffee for the paramedics and the local crew on the outer of the investigation now that the Ds had landed.

Franklin sipped his. He realised that his offsider merely clutched hers.

Sam swivelled back to the detective, as the bloke said, 'You're aware our vic is dead?'

It was no surprise, but Franklin's gut jolted. His sorrow over Neil Hudson compounded when he noticed Sam pale further. Second week in the job and her first death. Poor kid.

'What did you disturb in there, Constable?' The detective drilled his eyes into Sam.

She stuttered and Franklin arced up. By the look of him, the older bloke could be marking time until retirement. He didn't give a fuck about that, providing the bloke didn't take it out on his crew, particularly their junior member.

'Hold on.' Franklin reined in his anger. 'We had limited intelligence and an emergency situation. We did what we had to. I suspected Hudson wouldn't make it but busted my arse giving him CPR. And Sam dealt with the rest. *Under my instruction.*'

The detective raised a palm. 'Hold your horses, mate. Nobody's accusing anybody of anything, right? We're all tired and this is a shit situation. Let's start again. Martin Howell. Marty.'

They did intros with handshakes, then Howell patted his pockets until he located a cigarette pack. He offered it around, and Franklin resisted temptation. If he could get through a death on a job without a smoke, he could really quit this time. Sam shook her head vigorously.

With an inquiring eyebrow, the detective checked their okay to light up, then continued. 'Talk me through it. What you touched and where you walked. Where was this...' he consulted his notepad, 'Marc Jones placed when you arrived and same with the others? That way, the techies can factor that in. Cool?'

Nothing about tonight was *cool,* but Franklin shrugged.

'Did you speak to the witnesses, Franklin?'

He assessed the detective puffing on his smoke and saw no hostility. He recognised they were on the same side. 'Yes, independently and briefly.' He indicated the flask and cups. 'Want one, Marty?'

'Lifesaver.' Grimness tinged Howell's smile.

The three officers huddled away from the chaos and onlookers and slugged coffee. Howell ground out his butt and Franklin released a breath and with it, the layer of tension triggered by the tobacco aroma. His neck and shoulder muscles were still knotted from working on Neil's body though.

He summarised, trying to keep emotion out of it and be methodical. 'Shane Hudson, his son, and his brother's mate, Damo, had been drinking with the deceased, Neil Hudson, earlier this evening. They were all "pretty blotto".' Franklin hooked his fingers in quote marks. 'Neil got "more and more het up" as the night wore on. He jumped up, saying, "I'm going next door and bringing my wife back," and the others all rallied with him.' He flashed on Monica, and his stomach pitted.

The detective groaned. 'Alcohol and testosterone do not mix.'

Sam flinched. At least her colour had slightly improved.

Franklin went on. 'Damo stupidly thought it was a smart idea to pick up a few bricks on the way. Seeing he had these, Shane and his son plucked tools off Marc Jones's trailer. Ironically, only Neil went in unarmed.'

'Then how –'

'Jones answered the door. Neil demanded his wife come

out. Jones laughed and said, "She's not here." Neil didn't believe it. He said she wanted to come home; she told him yesterday and Jones couldn't make her stay. Jones repeated that she wasn't there.'

'So Hudson and his cronies forced their way in?'

'You got it.' Franklin pointed his thumb and finger like a gun. 'They burst in, yelling and searching for Mrs Hudson. They ended up in the kitchen and Jones sat down at the table, mocking them, according to the boy. He said Monica "took off yesterday afternoon, tail between her legs, to Mummy in Creswick."'

'God blimey,' the detective muttered. He looked older than before.

Franklin snorted, sickened. 'Yep. That set Neil off all the more. He raged that Jones should show his wife some respect. Jones said, "Sluts don't deserve respect."'

Howell said, 'He called her a slut to her old man? Dickhead.'

Dread sat more heavily in Franklin's gut as he closed in on the end of the story. 'Next thing, Neil grabbed the bricks off Damo. He threw one full pelt at Jones's nose and ran towards him holding the other above his head and screaming, "I'll have you." Jones flew back in his chair when he took the hit, his legs overturning the table. He dodged Hudson, grabbed the spade from the kid and waved it blindly, by chance whacking Neil.'

'How many blows?'

'One.' Franklin let out a hefty sigh.

Howell widened his eyes. 'One?'

'That's all it took. One to the side of the head.' Franklin pointed to his temple. 'Hudson dropped like a sack of potatoes. And we came in moments after.'

'Self-defence?'

'Nobody's saying anything different.'

They fell silent for a minute or two.

'What a waste.'

Just what the detective meant, Franklin could only guess. But he chewed over the waste of Neil Hudson's life and the effect on Marc Jones – he should've kept his dick in his pants but didn't deserve blood on his hands. And there'd be fallout for Hudson's brother and cronies who all contributed to the firecracker situation. But mostly he felt for Monica – the one that every girl wanted to be and every bloke wanted to date was now the downtrodden wife who slept with her neighbour. And she would have to live forever with her affair, her husband's forgiveness and the way he died.

What a fucked up waste, indeed.

CHAPTER TWENTY-SIX

'I'M SORRY.' ILLUMINATED BY THE MOON, SAM BURIED her head in her hands. Hunched forward she was dwarfed by the four-wheel drive and its paraphernalia.

If she were one of the boys, Franklin would give her a hearty slap on the back; they'd crack some black humour, down a few coldies after shift and everything would be fine in the world.

Because she was a she, he grappled with the right response. As a dad, he wanted to hug her. As a fellow cop, he wanted to say, *The first is the most memorable, but it isn't likely to be your worst or last, so hang in there.*

The complication of her apparent crush made him sit impotently.

After a minute of fingernail-scratching silence, he managed, 'What are you sorry for? This was your first death in the job, yes?'

She nodded, still clutching her head.

'So then, besides freezing for that moment there, you did an all right job.'

'All right?' She lifted her head and frowned.

He rolled his eyes, annoyed with himself. He remembered blues with his ex, Donna, making it clear women consider *nice* or *all right* an insult. He was a bloke. Words weren't his thing.

'You did *good*, Sam. You handled everything I asked. You didn't throw up. Did you?'

Her mouth twitched. 'Nuh, I didn't throw up.'

'There you go, then. Nothing to be sorry about.'

She cracked a smile now. Then she leaned in, about to kiss him, and Franklin pulled back, hoping he'd misread the signals, but certain he hadn't. His sympathy didn't change things. Colleagues were off limits, especially a young proby under his wing. Even taking out the sleazebag senior cop angle, getting involved with a teammate generally led to a hell of a mess, that'd eventuate in one of them taking a sideways or backward transfer. He knew a couple that worked the van together to this day and had been happily married for years, but they were the exception. Besides that, Sam failed the twelve-year rule; partners can't be younger or older by more than that because of generational differences. His thirty-seven to her twenty-three made her technically young enough to be his daughter.

He pretended not to see her lip quiver and decided never to say anything to anyone about what she'd just done. Gently, he said, 'You go home. I'll get onto the paperwork after I make the call.'

'No, I'm coming with you.'

Franklin's head spun. Sam's fragility had disappeared. Resilience would serve her well in the job, but she didn't need to prove it by doing this.

He reached across and threw open her door. 'Sam. Get to bed.'

She pulled the door shut. 'I'm coming with you.'

'There's no need. I've gotta see this through, but you've dealt with enough today.'

'Boss, if you're doing it, I am too.'

Quiet, yet adamant; he admired her for that.

'It's part of the job,' she said.

'Sure it is, but Rome wasn't built in a day, true? You can do your first death knock another time.'

She reasoned, 'We usually do it in twos.'

He sighed softly, sensing he'd lost the argument. 'Yes, but it seems this case is all over bar the shouting.'

He gave convincing her one last shot. 'The Ds will dot their i's and cross their t's, but there won't be any charges laid. You know what happened. A bunch of armed, drunken men forced themselves into Jones's home. He was then physically assaulted and threatened by a pissed man in a wild rage and used reasonable force in self-defence. They won't waste resources prosecuting this one. And even if I'm wrong, any which way it falls for Jones, Hudson's wife is not a suspect.'

'Yeah,' Sam countered, 'but you could do with moral support, so I'm going to Creswick with you.'

———

Franklin eventually conceded defeat. So they drove out of Daylesford on the all but deserted Midland Highway. They went through the blink-and-you'll-miss-it town of Newlyn and reached Creswick in record time. Along the way, the moonlight winked on low-lying paddocks that'd become sprawling dams, fences disappeared into the water, and trees and sheds were marooned. Torrential rain earlier this month, on top of the September floods, had also swelled several creeks over their banks. The roads were passable, especially in their sturdy four-wheel drive.

A minute or so off the main drag, Franklin pulled up in front of a Victorian cottage behind a champagne-coloured Camry. He exchanged a glance with Sam before they left the truck's cocoon, neither speaking as they moved to the front door, their footsteps heavy.

They smoothed their uniforms and held their hats as they waited for an answer to Franklin's knock. With each second, the knot in his throat grew bigger. When he cleared it, Sam gave him a nervous look.

The door opened enough for an eyeball.

'Yes?' A woman's voice, with an anxious quiver.

Franklin recognised her fear. Police don't drop by after midnight unless something bad has happened. 'Ma'am. We're sorry for the late call.'

She dropped the security chain and allowed the door to swing wider. She had donned a floral dressing gown, high-buttoned at the neck, and fluffy pink slippers but forgotten to comb her hair, which stuck out in grey tufts. Her tousled, vulnerable appearance made Franklin sadder about what he had to do.

He presented his ID, and his colleague followed suit.

'Ruth.'

Her hand trembled as they did handshakes. 'I remember you,' she said to Franklin. 'You were with Donna.'

He nodded, but it wasn't the time or place for reminiscences. 'May we speak with Monica please, Ruth? We understand she's here at present.'

'Monica?' The woman covered her mouth. 'What do you want with her?'

'Please, ma'am.' Franklin used a kind but insistent tone. 'Can we come inside and speak with your daughter?'

He'd done several notifications in his time, but they never grew easier – and nor should they, because someone's demise left at least one other person shattered. And that crushed person was usually the one the cops called on to deliver the news. The centre of their world, no matter how flawed or ordinary, was gone. Forever. And if the cops were involved, it wasn't a gentle parting, rather something that was sudden, violent, tragic, or all of the above.

Franklin ignored the voice in his head saying, *Christ, I hate death knocks* and focused on his mum and Kat and how he'd wish bad news be delivered to them if the worst ever happened. It was the only way he knew how to cope.

The wrinkles outlining the mother's eyes deepened. She guessed something, maybe correctly, but it was Monica they'd come to speak with. She deserved to hear it first.

At that moment, Monica emerged. She came to a halt, facing the trio. Franklin saw her process police uniforms, hats in hand, the late visit and her mother's shocked state. He tensed because here was where experience meant jack shit. Every victim's loved ones reacted differently. The woman could freeze, collapse, abuse them or even turn violent – possibly the whole lot in a mêlée of emotion.

'No!' She grabbed fistfuls of hair and buckled.

Ruth reached out and tried to move to her daughter but stumbled. She fell back against Sam.

Franklin approached slowly. 'Monica. Here, take a seat.'

He helped her sit, but she clung to his hand and elbow, obliging him to kneel in front. He met her eyes, panic underscored by the sutures and purple bruises she'd sustained a few days ago.

'We're sorry to tell you that we have very bad news concerning your husband, Neil Hudson.'

He saw her expression hollow. Her skin blanched to a grey-white.

'No, it's not true. I'm dreaming this.'

I wish you were. Franklin remembered his nightmare last night. Premonition or copper's instinct? He'd known things would go haywire. *But you didn't see this coming, did you? You got it wrong, Franklin.*

He gazed at Monica. He should have prevented this or at least tried harder to defuse the situation.

She begged, 'Please tell me it's not true.'

Thankfully, Ruth rallied then. She gathered her daughter into her arms and stroked and soothed. And after five or so minutes, Monica released a heartrending howl.

Sam and Franklin stood. Silent, drained, respectfully watching. Superfluous for now because the women had each other and their shock and pain excluded outsiders.

Soon, they would answer questions, make cuppas, and provide whatever comfort they could. Then they'd leave the women to grieve.

Sometimes the job sucks.

CHAPTER TWENTY-SEVEN

Back at the station, Franklin considered sticking around to deal with the paperwork but reckoned Lunny would cut him slack until the morning. He knocked out a message on his mobile and waited.

He rocked sideways in the swivel chair. He breathed loud and deep and craved a smoke. His body was beyond weary. It ached with exhaustion.

Beep.

Franklin reached for his phone. One new message: 'Come over.'

It only took a few minutes to drive across and the door opened as soon as he lumbered onto the step.

Without a word between them, Talitha took his hand and drew him inside. Her shiny black tresses swayed as she navigated furniture in the softly lit hallway. Her short nightie showed a lot of tanned skin.

After a small hesitation, she led him to the living room. She had been confident at the door but standing in front of him now seemed nervous.

They gazed at each other for a moment. Then she asked, 'Like a drink?'

As she gestured, one strap of her wine-coloured nightie slid down her arm, tugging the lace trim low over her breast. Fabric covered her nipple but not the blushing half-moon over the top.

Talitha didn't pull up the strap but dropped her eyes shyly, waiting for his move. He'd thrown enough mixed signals in the past that she was rightfully confused. In all honesty, Franklin was confused himself. Tonight's tragedy had left him reeling. He was an emotional wreck and needed physical comfort and a release. The kind that his male mates or daughter couldn't give.

But in all the ten-plus years of their friendship, he and Talitha had never gone past matey, with a little flirting on her part. That'd included a degree of accidental contact, and some more blatant, like at the pub the other Sunday.

She'd always shown she was keen on him. They had friendship as a good basis. Maybe what his heart needed was right here.

He reached out and they linked fingers. In fact, he didn't want to think, or a drink.

Franklin drew Talitha close and they exchanged a mute *are we sure we're going to cross this line?* Then her gaze fired with the same lust that warmed his groin.

Her throat stretched and eyes closed. He kept his open to drink her in. Girl next door she may be, but Talitha looked pure woman right now.

Their lips parted and tongues met. Talitha gave a small growl and his body responded.

Franklin nuzzled into her neck, struck for an instant by the shape of her collarbones and the fragrance behind her ears. Both were so different to Georgie's.

He blocked her from his mind, thinking only of the woman in front of him.

Talitha's fingers freed his pants button and zip. He slid the straps of her nightie down her arms and watched it slither over her full breasts, further to expose a sparkling diamante belly ring, then over her smooth pubis. And finally, past hips to floor and she stood naked in a puddle of satin.

She popped his shirt buttons as he cupped her breasts, then covered one with his mouth, with a hand gliding over her back and buttocks.

Both moaned, as they fell onto the couch.

No thoughts. No complications. Complete release.

———

Talitha slept with her head burrowed into his neck and knee draped over his thigh, having been in the same position since they'd made love. Franklin had dozed, then lay for the next hour and a bit, staring at the ceiling, wide-awake.

Made love? Be honest, Franklin. You had sex.

His chest was heavy with shame and regret. He liked Talitha. A lot. But he didn't love her. For some sad fuck reason, he loved Georgie, although he couldn't have her, and going to bed with Talitha only made that more obvious. And he hated himself for using his friend to relieve his emotional chaos.

He didn't know how to repair this mess. But he did know he needed to get out of her bed.

Gently moving Talitha's leg and wriggling free of her head, he swung his feet to the floor and rubbed his nape in a weary gesture.

'John?' she murmured.

Franklin whispered, 'Sorry. I need to get home. Kat...'

'Oh. Stay.'

'I can't. But –'

But what? You bastard, Franklin. Leave before you make it worse.

———

Georgie checked the peephole, then threw the front door open wide. 'Bron!'

'Yes, it is I, in the flesh.' Bron fluffed her carrot-red bobbed hair, then flung out her arms. 'I figured if Mohamed won't come to the mountain, the mountain will come to Mohamed.'

As they hugged, Georgie asked, 'Have I neglected you badly?'

'On a scale of one to ten, with one being *horribly neglected*? Hmm.'

Georgie punched her mate's bicep.

Bron grinned broadly. 'All right. So it's only been a few days, but I missed you.'

'Aw, ain't she sweet?' Georgie said to Molly, who pushed against her leg to get to Bron. 'Coffee?'

'Is this what you want?' Bron scratched between the dog's ears, then answered, 'Finally, she offers coffee. Thought I'd die of thirst waiting.'

'My, you are full of attitude today,' Georgie quipped and waved towards the kitchen, letting Bron lead the way up the narrow hallway. The dog and cat bounded behind the two women, their toenails scratching on floorboards. They adored Bron.

But then who in their right mind wouldn't?

Georgie filled the kettle and flicked the switch, then scrutinised her mate. 'You look good.'

'I'm great, Georgie Girl. Jo's received another all clear from her cancer.'

Relief slithered down Georgie's spine. Cancer was a bastard. And every time Bron's girlfriend was due for a check-up, she put on a brave face, dreading the worst news. 'I'm so glad.'

Bron's eyes misted. 'I know. Thanks.' Upbeat again, she added, 'So we're going to celebrate with a posh room at the Hyatt. Spa, king size bed, the works. *Ooh lá lá.* The only thing ruining my mood is that I haven't seen my best buddy.' She thumbed towards Georgie. 'So here I am. Give me the latest.'

Georgie skipped her complicated personal life and launched into work talk as she poured their coffees. She finished her update as they drained their mugs.

'So you were making headway on your hunch about this dead-or-maybe-fugitive redneck, then you had to abandon everything for an interview?'

'Yes. It was a one-time opportunity and I'm glad I took it, but still, I wish it hadn't happened right then. It felt like I was onto something, but now I can't remember what.'

'Short memory,' Bron sang.

Georgie groaned, then clicked her fingers. 'You've reminded me!'

'Huh?'

'Norman Poole, the old guy I told you about who lives in Bullock. The one with the wife in a wheelchair because of her injuries from the fire? Yeah, well, he has terrible short-term memory and writes things in his notepad –'

'And?' Bron screwed her nose.

'I was going to drop by after seeing Kelly, and then

Caro's publicist rang.' Georgie squirmed. 'Damn, I feel awful. I said I'd call if I couldn't make it but totally forgot.'

'You're going back there, aren't you?'

She'd already risen. 'Yep. I need to catch up with Norman.' She counted the points with her thumb and fingers. 'I want to see Ally. I've a few questions for her mum. And I have to see Clive; we've been playing phone tag since yesterday.' Georgie fanned her hand. 'Something's still missing, or I'm missing something. Anyway, there's plenty to follow through on, especially where Goyne would go if he went into hiding.'

Bron pointed a long crimson fingernail at her. 'And I thought I'd take you Christmas shopping.'

'We've still got plenty of time.'

'A whole three days,' Bron countered. In her sanguine way, she added, 'Tomorrow then.'

Georgie shook her head and shrugged but couldn't help smiling.

Bron returned the grin. 'I can be your sounding board again. I'll even buy you a coffee if you behave.'

———

The sound of a door shutting made Franklin jolt. He listened to the approaching footsteps and knew they belonged to Harty. Though tall and lanky, he walked quietly compared to the others, even in steel-capped boots.

'You look wrecked. Isn't it your rest day?'

He felt wrecked and nodded in answer.

'Did you pull an all-nighter?'

'Nah. I had trouble sleeping and came in around four. Thought I'd make my way through the reports on the Hudson death.'

Harty gave his shoulder a sympathetic smack. 'Cuppa?'

'I've sunk ten already, but yeah, that'd be good.'

As Harty bashed about in the lunchroom, Franklin's head drooped. He thought, *I'll just rest my eyes for a tick*, but must have fallen asleep because his mate gave him a gentle shake, saying, 'Wakey-wakey. Coffee's getting cold.'

Some of the other boys clunked into the station simultaneously with Franklin putting his lips to his mug. He sighed inwardly, wishing he'd finished up before day shift arrived.

'Can't keep away on your day off?' Slam commented, dropping into the nearest chair.

One of the fellows who hadn't been involved last night perched on the desk next to Slam. 'Tell us what happened.'

Harty passed Franklin a muesli bar and sat on his other side, asking, 'How was Sam with the widow?'

There's not much worse than a bunch of coppers bombarding you with questions. They are skilled in what to ask. They have the knack for memorising what you say and seize onto what you don't say. The thing working for him at present was that they hadn't let him get a word in edgeways. Otherwise he would have spilled the lot – how he'd stuffed up and let an explosive situation detonate, costing a man's life and a whole bunch of people endless grief. That he now knew for certain that the proby under his wing had a crush on him, and he'd gone to bed with another woman but shouldn't have. And with the shame of it all, he couldn't sleep and crawled in here. But his brain wouldn't function, and what would usually take an hour or so was only half-done.

And now I'm facing the Spanish Inquisition.

Instead of confessing he was one big fuck-up, he peeled the wrapper off the muesli bar and took a bite. Then he pictured Georgie. Another reminder that what he'd done to Talitha was wrong on every level.

Slam asked, 'Have the hommies come in?'

The energy hit greased Franklin's brain cogs into a slow churn. He reckoned on just enough cognitive function to trust himself with a few sentences.

'CI's finishing the prelims but it's doubtful it'll go to homicide. Sam did a stellar job; she'll cut the grade. If Lunny comes asking, I'll be done with the paperwork in another half hour. I'm going to put my head down and bum up here to wrap it up.'

Franklin gave them a tight smile and swivelled to his computer. Conversation closed.

CHAPTER TWENTY-EIGHT

'I'M PASSING THE BLACK SPUR ROADHOUSE.' GEORGIE realised she was competing with road noise and lifted her mouth closer to the Bluetooth mic on her sun visor. 'Can we hook up?'

'I have a shift driving the mobile library later, but I'm free until then.' Clive's voice sounded tinny.

Georgie snaked a bend and reception dropped out. She swore, kept one eye on the phone's service bars, the other on the winding road ahead.

One bar popped up and faded. Two corners on, she gained full service and redialled Clive. 'Me again. Whereabouts are you?'

'Home. But it's rather hard to find. Let's meet at the bakery in around quarter of an hour.'

She agreed, they disconnected and Georgie made a fresh call.

The landline number rang and eventually rang out, not even picked up by a machine.

She tried a mobile and reached voicemail.

'Hi, this is Ally. Do your thing and I'll get back to you

soonaz.'

Frustrated, Georgie left a message. 'Ally, this is Georgie. I'm coming into Bullock soon. Can we get together? I know you're on school holidays...anyway, phone me, please.'

She drove one-handed, flicking through her notebook. 'Damn.' She didn't have a phone number for the Pooles. So much for calling them if she couldn't make it yesterday. Hopefully she'd catch them at home.

She mulled over her conversation with Bron and decided to hold Deb, her neighbour Anna Shaw, and Kelly Lavestone from the info centre in reserve, depending on what she learned during the other interviews. She had sufficient background on the fires and the rebuilding process for the town, providing the focus remained on the Goyne family, but still didn't have a clear angle aside from Warren Goyne as the undead.

It felt vital to move the story forward today.

Georgie zoned out, listening to Muse's *Resistance*. She read double meanings in the lyrics, finding links to Goyne in the words about secrets, hiding places, the truth.

A reflector post on the road edge loomed. She panicked, steering sharp right.

She had to think—but concentrate on driving—and muted the radio.

Assuming Goyne's alive, what do I need to find out?

She drummed her fingertips on the steering wheel, working through the obvious questions.

Why would he sham death and sever contact with his closest allies, including, or especially, his daughter?

How did he pull it off? *Where* would Goyne escape?

She clicked her tongue against the roof of her mouth. *And how do I get answers without off-siding or hurting the people who matter?*

———

'You're a mind-reader, Clive.' Georgie sank her teeth into a blueberry Danish and tiny snowflakes of pastry sprinkled over the timber-slatted bench. She brushed the crumbs to the footpath, hoping the little sparrow from her first visit would find them, and inhaled the steaming brew before taking a gulp.

The tall Welshman opposite her scooped froth from his cappuccino, swallowed and licked his lips, then both sides of his spoon, before sipping his coffee, while she dragged on her ciggie.

Clive took a third of his Danish in one bite, then said, 'Fire away, Georgie. What was so pressing yesterday?'

Georgie tapped her temple with a fingertip. 'I've got way too much going on in here. Can I put a heap of questions to you?'

He nodded.

'Can you just spurt back the answers?' she asked, knowing it wasn't really fair without clueing him up about the content. But Clive agreed.

'You said without a body, there's hope. Do you think Warren's alive?'

'I'd like to. But no.'

She nodded. 'Who would you say comprised his circle of friends?'

'Me, Ally, Anna, Clare,' Clive rattled off. 'Why?'

She held a finger to her lips. 'Let me get my flow and ask your questions later, okay?'

He looked bemused but didn't argue.

She narrowed in on his response. 'Why didn't you mention Deb?'

Clive stilled. 'You've got me there.' His eyes slid

SANDI WALLACE

sideways and up.

Thinking or inventing?

'To me, a circle of friends doesn't generally include family,' he added.

'Yet you mentioned Ally without blinking,' Georgie pointed out.

'Yes, but how is this relevant?'

'I need to humanise Warren for readers.'

Clive pulled his lips tight, then exhaled. 'Well, I'll grant you that.'

'So, trust me with these questions, please.' Georgie squirmed. She wasn't being honest with him yet expected him to be open with her. When he didn't answer, she wondered if she'd lost him. She stubbed out her ciggie, then met Clive's eyes.

The slight lift of his chin must've meant he'd go along with it—for a little longer, at least—because he then said, 'Ally and Clare were near on as close as Warren was with Clare. So it felt natural that Ally joined us in nigh on everything. And once we came to know Anna, she complemented the rest of us oddballs too.' He half-smiled at the bittersweet memories.

She gave him a moment thinking about better times, then said, 'But Deb never palled up with you all?'

'Not us as a group. Myself, yes, I spent many a weekend with the family. We were chummy then, but Deb, Ally and I have grown much closer since Warren died.'

'Why didn't Deb fit into the group?'

His answering headshake was unconvincing. He seemed too stiff.

Interesting. But she'd beaten that bush enough. 'Where was his favourite place?'

'Hereabouts?'

When she nodded, he twitched his mouth down and tapped a finger on his cup. This time she interpreted the signs as Clive over-thinking rather than being evasive, so she prompted, 'Just say whatever springs to mind.'

She allowed that to sink in.

'Where was Warren's favourite place locally?'

'Clare's studio.'

'Outside of Bullock?'

'Kine Falls.'

Closed questions were working, so Georgie stuck with them. 'More than twenty Ks away?'

'God knows. Pass.'

'How much did family mean to Warren?'

She searched his face and saw melancholy shadow his features.

'Ally was his world.'

Ally wasn't his whole family.

In time with her thought, Clive choked on a piece of his Danish and reached for his coffee. He gulped the remnants.

Now she could ask, 'What did Warren think of his wife?'

Clive's jaw tensed. 'When?'

Odd reply. 'Immediately before his death.'

'Mother of Ally.' His lips thinned.

Georgie couldn't help screwing her face. Deb was a nonentity apart from being Ally's mother. *Really?* She tried again. 'Deb?'

'His wife.'

Her head tilted. *Not his lover? Not his best mate?* She reflected on Clive's earlier response *when?* and backtracked. 'Deb and Warren at the time you became friends?'

'Peas and potatoes. Happy.'

Ah. The changed Goyne rears his head. 'Would he leave

Deb?'

Clive didn't hesitate. 'Not without Ally.'

She skipped on, hoping it wouldn't reveal her hand. 'Is there any circumstance you can imagine where he could be parted from Ally?'

'To save her life. To protect her.'

Georgie nodded; she thought that too. She moved to the next point. 'Clare Finney.'

'Notwithstanding our mateship, surely his closest chum.'

'More than a friend?'

His head jerked. 'I don't think so.'

'But you're not certain?'

'I fail to –'

'Clive, I'll only use what's pertinent.' That wasn't a lie. But the chasm between what Georgie needed to include and what Warren's friends and family wanted in print could be vast. 'I've only got a few more questions, okay?'

He gestured defeat.

'Were Warren and Clare more than friends?'

'I'm not certain.'

'Warren after Clare's death?'

'Destroyed man.'

Georgie sat taller, suspense making her breaths shallow. 'Did Warren contribute to Clare's death?'

'What?' he yelped. 'Are you insinuating euthanasia? Or worse? Codswallop.'

Georgie touched his arm. 'Please, Clive, I'm not suggesting anything in particular. But, various times, in various ways, it's been mentioned that Warren changed following her death, understandable considering he suddenly lost someone special. But did he blame himself?'

'No. He blamed Deb.'

CHAPTER TWENTY-NINE

FRANKLIN STARED AT THE PHONE FOR A MINUTE, maybe longer. It'd be a miracle if he'd made sense to the lead detective on the Hudson case. Then he wondered if Marty Howell was running on empty too.

His yawn cracked his jaw and made his eyes water. Exhausted and strained didn't make for good bedfellows, especially on top of excessive caffeine. He may as well test a few theories and try to sleep later.

Yesterday, he'd finally caught a line on the burgs, then they'd received the urgent callout to Crow Street. He couldn't reverse time to change the outcome of that, but he could break the back of these burgs. One win wouldn't offset the enormity of his failure, but it would go a long way in restoring his sense of self.

He used to think that his self was largely the blue uniform and silver badge. He'd thought he could do more for the community trading the uniform for plain clothes. This morning, he questioned if he deserved the badge and uniform, let alone promotion to detective.

Franklin stood up so abruptly his knees crunched. He

stuffed his crumpled shirt into his pants, hoisted the weighty belt off his desk and buckled it. After checking the pouches, he nodded, while unconsciously rasping a hand across the stubble on his chin.

Despite having told Sam to make the most of rest days, he didn't give a flying fuck if he wasn't rostered on. Being a copper didn't start and end with set shifts. Being a good copper meant working as many unpaid hours as it took to do the job right, then enjoying R&R with a clear conscience.

He'd start with another go at tracking Luke Duffy and following the lead he'd spotted yesterday. Then he'd deal with whether, or how, Duffy's older companion connected to the burgs.

———

'Hello, anyone home?' Georgie rapped her knuckles on the door for a second time. The sound rebounded and faded. She dialled the landline from her mobile and listened to it ring through her handset and the door. There was still no response.

She scouted the perimeter of the house, in case Deb and Ally were in the yard and hadn't heard the door or phone. No success either, so at the back door, she tapped hard. Again, uselessly.

Next, she knocked on the access door to the garage and deflated when all she heard was an empty echo. She tried the handle and, not expecting the door to open, stumbled inside.

At the doorway, she scanned the room, noting the kiln with its door ajar, the mound covered with a cloth, clean potter's wheel, diminished slab of clay, hanging tools all aligned and the previously unfinished mugs now glazed in an amazing red and black design.

Georgie's eyes returned to the mound. No one would know if she took a quick peek, so she lifted a corner of the cover. What she saw made her reel, accidentally tugging the material. The cloth hit the floor. She watched horrified as the thing teetered on its stand and just managed to catch it before momentum took over.

She righted it but didn't let go until her heart stopped hammering. Then she checked she hadn't left evidence of the close call, any bits squashed or broken, still not retrieving the shroud.

She stared and Goyne returned the look.

His mouth was open in laughter, and his various chins formed rippling shadows of the smile. But did the smile reach the eyes behind his thin-framed glasses?

Georgie leaned in to examine the clay bust. To her, Goyne appeared secretive and sinister, instead of jolly and kind. Or was she reading everything into nothing with not just Ally's sculpture but also her theories about Goyne?

She replayed the last part of her conversation with Clive, thinking that Ally's sculpture made it all the more monumental.

No. He blamed Deb.

Just four little words, yet massive.

'Why?' she'd asked, shocked.

'Why? Because Deb calls a spade a spade,' he'd repeated his earlier advice. 'Don't misunderstand; I love Deb. She's always been a good chum to me, and we're closer than ever since Warren died.'

'But?'

'She's not sympathetic to mental illness.'

Georgie recalled Deb performing the hideous penguin waddle.

Clive had continued. 'On top of that, I believe she felt threatened by Warren and Clare's relationship.'

Softly, Georgie had prompted, 'And?'

'Clare was barely functioning, but it suddenly became vital for her to buy a birthday cake and throw a tea party. She summonsed us—Warren, Ally, Anna and me—to her place at five o'clock and trundled off to the bakery in the morning. Still wearing her pyjamas. Deb served her and made a typical Deb remark, possibly not meaning to be cruel. But in Clare's precarious state, it tipped her over the edge. Or that's what Warren presumed.'

He took a bleak expression. 'Perhaps we all did, truth be told.'

A few minutes ticked by, then Clive had finished with, 'You see, Clare bought her birthday cake. Went home, tossed down an overdose of her meds with straight brandy. And left a note taped to the cake box saying, "Sorry".'

———

The sky clouded over as Franklin looped through to Crow Street. Chequered police tape restricted access to Marc Jones's property, and there were a couple of units parked in front: a police truck and the unmarked CIU station wagon Howell had been in last night. So the poor bugger was still at it.

Franklin was curious about what was happening at the crime scene but rode on. This mission didn't concern Hudson and Jones.

He'd last seen Duffy with his older mate near the creek. So it was a good place to start. He favoured the Kawasaki for this type of job because he could take it off-road and access places his Commodore didn't like to go. On the downside, the motorbike turned heads with its blue-over-white duco and panther growl. With its rider donning a blue monkey suit, with a leather jacket and helmet thrown on top, it didn't make for an unobtrusive surveillance machine. But Franklin's inquiries were police business despite him being off the clock, so the uniform had to stay.

The bike chewed and spat out the steep, narrow street and cut through the gravel cul-de-sac. Franklin's gaze constantly raked the roadway, paths and gardens, but he caught no sight of the two men.

Wouldn't it have been peachy to be that easy? He hadn't expected an immediate payoff.

He circled up Stanhope Street and entered the drive weaving through the botanic gardens, past massive conifers and elms, lawns and flowering shrubs, up to the peak of Wombat Hill. Franklin checked the toilet block and picnic shelter. Then he climbed the steps to the top of the tower and paused to take in the panoramic view of the town before focusing on the interior. Vagrants sometimes spent a night or two up here, particularly in these milder months, but apart from a vague piss smell, his efforts came up with zero.

He next checked with staff in the works area, but the other structures and nurseries were undisturbed too.

Now, he pulled up at Duffy's last known address. Fair enough, the dilapidated building had been bulldozed for redevelopment, and his drive-by last week had yielded no indication of squatters. But the new factories at the address were unoccupied. In fact, they were advertising for squatters with the number of *For Lease* stickers on the windows and street-fronted signs, and Duffy could've gravitated back to his old stomping ground since Franklin last checked.

––––––

Georgie's mobile beeped with an incoming SMS and she thumbed it open without stopping.

'Hi G. Mum said I need to take a rest from all this. Away until NYE or longer. Sorry :(Ally'

'What?' Georgie stumbled to a halt and re-read the message. 'New Year's Eve?'

Her phone beeped again with another text from Ally. 'Mum said don't ring any more. A'

Georgie bet Deb was vetting the messages. She raked fingers through her hair, still glued to the spot, punch-drunk with conflicted feelings.

She did a tight exhale. 'Stopping's not an option.' She'd just have to work around Ally's absence.

She considered lighting up a smoke but decided this latest hurdle made time and other leads more crucial than ever and hastened on.

Less than a minute later, her phone gave another beep. She checked the screen.

'Really am sorry. In the loo writing this! Will try to ring later in week when sgt major not around. Happy xmas. A xoxo'

––––––

'Georgie. Come in.' Dawn wheeled herself in reverse to allow the door to swing, gesturing for her to enter.

They moved into the living area and Georgie took her previous spot on the sofa. She searched for hints of Dawn's mood while they sat in silence. The woman's facial features held a velvety softness, without visible stress, and her hands rested lightly on her wheelchair arms. They were good signs, but Georgie was determined not to upset Dawn again and waited for her to initiate a safe conversation.

'Norman's looking for his specs. He can't remember where he put them.' With a naughty grin, Dawn added, 'I told him to write down where he puts them as soon as he takes them off and he pooh-poohed me. Tell me again who the silly one is?'

Georgie broke into a chuckle, amused and relieved.

Norman rushed into the room. 'I heard that.' With a flourish, he held up his glasses. 'And I found them on the bedside table.'

He popped them on, then stepped over to Georgie and grasped her hands. 'I knew you'd come.'

'I'm sorry I didn't make it yesterday.' Her face heated. 'Or at least phone –'

He brushed off her apology. 'It doesn't matter. It's ready.'

'What's ready?'

He drew her to her feet, led the way to the dining table, pushed her down and sat adjacent. 'I have a lot of new photos and documents.'

She'd obviously missed something.

He saw her confusion. 'We've received an excellent donation for the historical society. Dawn and I are on the committee.'

'Oh, right.'

His face fell. 'I felt sure you'd be excited.'

Maybe her brain was sluggish after Clive's recent revelations, along with Ally's departure, because she still wasn't following.

Norman spoke as he would've for dim kids in his class: slow and clear. 'A gift of photos and papers. That might be helpful with your story.'

'Really?' Georgie snapped alert. 'Great!'

Dawn wheeled up and parked on her right. All settled, the old man beamed and extracted a bundle from the topmost archive box. He aligned it with a tap on the tabletop, then removed the first photograph. His fingers only touched the edges as he offered it to Georgie.

She took it carefully and inspected an image of the opening ceremony for Bullock's real estate agency. A huge Warren Goyne beamed for the camera. He wielded over-sized scissors ready to snip a red ribbon across the door.

Georgie held the photo closer and marvelled at Ally's skills. With allowances made for ageing and further ballooning of his weight, in both her sketch and sculpture she'd perfectly reproduced her father.

Dawn waved and Georgie passed the photo, handling it as Norman had done.

He gave her another. This featured Anna Shaw with a group of people seated in a ring. In the background, Goyne tended a tall urn. Only Anna, Goyne, and another woman were in full view; the rest were caught in profile or from behind.

'Was this one of Anna's group therapy sessions?'

'Yes, indeed,' Norman replied, bouncing in his seat. 'In the old building.'

'Clare Finney wouldn't be in this photo, would she?'

'Absolutely.'

Georgie's heart beat faster as Norman leaned across and used the nail on his pinkie finger to point to the woman on Anna's left also facing the camera, her image faintly blurred as if she'd moved in that instant.

Clare's straight ash-blonde hair framed an egg-shaped face. She was smiling, making her eyes crinkle into slits and cheeks resemble shiny apples. Dressed in a long-sleeved pale grey shirt and striped scarf in pink, red and purple hues, the potter appeared so elegant and poised that Georgie's chest swelled with sadness for her. Beautiful, gifted and so ill that she ended up killing herself.

They ploughed through stacks of photos of occasions and gatherings in Bullock. Spells of silence peppered with questions and commentary, while Norman passed each image to Georgie and she handed them to Dawn. He built a smaller pile to his left, saying those pictures weren't relevant to the town and must've been accidentally mixed in.

Occasionally, Norman or Dawn paused, overcome by emotion or to recount a tale. Georgie let them stop as often as they needed, fetching tissues or glasses of water to help them recover and listening attentively.

From these photos and the old couple's stories, her players firmed in her mind as real, and Bullock reverted to the quaint, touristy town she remembered from pre-Red Victoria. But most importantly, the Warren Goyne described by her various sources took life.

As Georgie examined photos of these events long past, she knew that many of the people they featured were now dead. They had died prematurely and horribly. They were people who others loved and grieved for still.

———

Franklin kicked down the stand and propped the Ninja. The parking spaces for the shiny new factories were vacant, barring his bike. He pulled off his helmet and listened. It was quiet but not silent. He couldn't miss the annoying buzz of a fly near his ear, which he waved off. He also picked out chattering birds. But aside from faint traffic, nothing indicated any people were around.

He walked to the right boundary of the factory block, checked doors and windows as he crunched along the gravel. He kept going, until he returned to the front, disappointed that Duffy wasn't there.

———

Norman studied the next photograph with a puckered brow. 'How did this one come to be here?' Yet, he handed it across instead of adding it to his discard pile.

Goyne again, but Georgie agreed with the old man; it didn't fit with the rest. 'This isn't Bullock, is it?' She placed the photo on the table and stared. She tilted her head, recognition knocking on her memory bank.

Dawn edged in, craning her neck. 'No.'

On her other side, Norman muttered, 'Another one.'

Georgie reached for it. 'Oh, it can't be.' But she was certain. A second later, she doubted herself.

'Can't be what?' Dawn asked.

Georgie pointed to the background of the photo. 'The Sunday market at Daylesford.'

She switched back to the first picture and analysed it. 'That hat stall...yes, you can just see the big old tree on the right. So it has to be.'

She broke off to examine Goyne, who was captured trying on a red-hot fedora with black band and jaunty yellow-tipped feather.

Next, she looked at Ally. At about age eleven, the girl was a replica of her teenage self, albeit slighter, and she held up her hands in a ta-da gesture that framed her head.

Georgie recognised what Ally wore as a Greek fisherman cap, grey tweed with a black bill. She chalked that up as a benefit of having a close friend who was Greek, alongside feasts of moussaka, baklava, and ouzo.

Georgie told Norman and Dawn, 'If I'm right, I stopped at that stall when AJ and I went to the market because there were heaps of cool hats – and the tweeds made me think of Grandpa.' She zeroed in on the left edge. 'Yes, there's part of a food caravan and the cyclone fence.'

She replaced that image on the table and picked up the second one again. 'And that corner of a building behind Deb has to be the railway station.'

Norman rooted through the remaining pile of photos. 'Here's another one, lassie.'

Once again, Goyne and Ally featured. In this picture, the father reached for something that his daughter held up to show whoever took the photo. *Deb, probably.* Ally knelt on a blue tarp, surrounded by tools, chains and boxes of junk. Through squinting, Georgie could see Ally held a wooden-handled tool, something similar to those pegged in her ceramics studio.

But the most interesting thing about this photo was the sign behind the girl. Georgie could only read 'Dayl' because a stranger's figure blocked the rest. But those four letters were enough to confirm that they were in Daylesford.

Were these photos significant? Georgie's stomach clenched. Would she have to return to the spa town to find out?

CHAPTER THIRTY

After morning tea, they'd continued through the rest of the photos, but nothing else jumped out. A second mug of coffee made it five for the morning and Georgie buzzed with caffeine. She ignored protests by Norman and Dawn and washed up their plates and cups, looking through the kitchen window at grass shorn to the bare minimum above soil level for it to be green. Pool-table-felt green, thanks to all the recent rain.

She dried her hands, thinking about her next move. She didn't want to love and leave the couple, but time seemed to be passing at double speed this morning.

'You need to go.' Norman laughed. 'So go, lassie.'

Georgie impulsively hugged him, surprised at the strength in his embrace.

'Here, take this.' He slipped the hat stall photo into her hand. 'It doesn't have historical significance to Bullock, and what the duffers don't know won't hurt. It may help with your story on Ally's family.'

Dawn rolled near. 'And if it reminds you of your

grandpa or a nice day spent with your boyfriend, all the better.'

Georgie realised the woman had snuck under her skin too. She could see how local families came to adopt the Pooles. They made good quasi-grandparents, just like her neighbours Ruby and Michael Padley.

She dropped a kiss on Dawn's silky cheek, inhaling a waft of lavender scent.

'Aw.' Dawn patted her skin where Georgie had kissed her. 'Good luck. And come and see us soon, won't you?'

At the door, Georgie pulled out her mobile and confirmed she'd added their number correctly. Then she departed in a flurry of goodbyes, heart thudding. The photograph in her hand would be essential if she tracked down Goyne.

Fifty metres from the Poole house, Georgie typed a message on her phone. 'Ally, need to talk. Urgent. G'

With her bag swinging between her butt and hip, she hustled back to the Spider. She leaned against its long flat nose and chain-smoked two cigarettes, eyes never off her phone screen.

Georgie switched to sitting in the convertible, warming the engine, ready for action. She drummed the steering wheel with her left hand until it began to ache.

'C'mon, Ally. *Please.*'

Repeatedly, she flipped her wrist to check her watch. Instead of time moving at double speed as it had with the Pooles, seconds slowed to minutes, minutes slowed to hours.

Thinking she might have better luck with a phone call, she dialled Ally's number, but it connected straight to voicemail. *'Hi, this is Ally...'*

'Damn.'

'...and I'll get back to you soonaz.'

'Ally! Georgie again. I know you're not supposed to talk to me but we need to speak. Please ring me straight back. Find an excuse, go for a walk, something. Please!'

If she hung around with the car idling much longer, someone might report her to Sergeant Boulder for loitering. Or she'd go nuts. There seemed little point in staying here. Further chats with Anna or Kelly could wait, Ally was out of town, and Goyne long gone. All Georgie needed was a clue as to where he'd fled.

Ally held the clue, if anyone did.

A few minutes passed. Georgie tried redial, again reaching Ally's message. She disconnected.

For want of a good plan, she drove off. Aimlessly at first, then she steered by the Goynes' new house, past the location of Clare's old studio and up the redeveloping main street. She nosed the Spider beyond where the Pooles lived.

Finally, she found herself on the road to Kine Falls.

———

Riff-raff elements were inevitable in any area, but Franklin hated it in his hometown. He geared down as he cornered into a stretch where many of the original residents had moved out at the first signs of trouble, while others hung on until it was too late to sell, and now squatters were taking hold.

He parked the bike outside the house of a nice old couple. They'd abandoned it a few months ago, and on his last drive-by, he'd propped up their *For Sale* sign but found nothing else untoward.

The sign lay on the ground again today, uprooted and mangled, along with the garden.

Franklin fumed. He couldn't stand people who

vandalised for the joy of it or blamed it on their rough childhood. It felt personal.

He faced the front door covered in tags and profanity, the choice ones aimed at the 'pigs'. He muttered, 'Now it is personal.'

Franklin rapped on the door, yelling, 'Police, open up!' then bolted around the house to cut off whoever scarpered out the back.

'Shit.' They'd separated.

One vanished over the top of the paling fence to the rear, then Franklin spotted movement on the eastern side and sprinted after a squatter in a dark hoodie, catching a glimpse of a fair, slightly ruddy complexion when the bloke half-turned.

At the fence, the squatter ducked between wire strands and the hood of his windcheater snagged. Exposed, he paused in profile, then cleared the fence and raced away.

But that was all Franklin needed to ID him. Brown hair shaved in rows with the appearance of a bad hair-replacement job. As luck would have it, the bloke's right side was the one visible, and Franklin couldn't miss that he only had half an eyebrow.

Bingo bango. He was chasing Andrew 'Whitey' Whitehead, and he was just the bloke he was after, because although he hadn't left his tag at the party warehouse, Franklin had spotted a graphic in the photos as individual as his signature.

Spurred by his good luck so far, Franklin put on a burst of speed, took the fence and closed the gap to ten metres.

Whitey reached the next fence and ducked under. Franklin gained a metre and saw the youth throw a backward glance.

'Suck me, pig.' Whitey took a sharp right and added five metres.

Even with his chest on fire, Franklin wouldn't give up. Whitey surged down a driveway, hit the street and veered right again, heading in the direction of where they'd started, while he turned and lifted his middle finger with a sneer.

You little shit.

Franklin heard an engine rev and timber splinter and followed the sound to see a sedan screech to a stop at the old couple's crossover and Whitey dive into the back. He was still swinging the door shut as the car accelerated, aimed at Franklin.

He and the driver locked eyes until Franklin hurdled the neighbour's fence.

It'd been a close call, but that game of chicken gave him long enough to recognise the lightly-bearded male at the wheel as Reginald Redwoods.

As Franklin rubbed his bruised shin and swore over the tear in his uniform pants, he mulled the association between Redwoods and Whitey.

Redwoods more than doubled Whitey in age. Whitey possessed violent form, while the other crook tended to hit on lonely women and the elderly.

Since when did they hook up?

———

Georgie leaned on the Spider's roof, awestruck by the landscape. A few other vehicles were in the car park, but she couldn't see or hear anyone. Perhaps reverential silence was a common reaction.

Five minutes out of Bullock, this area had been razed during Red Victoria. Nearly two years on, the forest crept back among the inferno debris. Without the thick vegetation she'd seen on her previous visit with AJ, or a coating of snow, the boulders that covered the craggy hillside dominated visually.

Yet they couldn't outdo the noisy cascade of water. Victoria's wet winter and spring had correlated with a bumper snow season. Now at the start of summer, Georgie guessed thawed ice from Mount Starke blended with heavy regular rain into the waterfall.

It was spectacular.

She dragged her gaze away and scanned the surrounds. Some works were complete—the new road, car park, a viewing platform at the base of the falls that harmonised with the environs while making it safe—and more re-construction was under way.

Georgie wandered to the platform while thumbing redial on her phone. The call went straight to Ally's voice message, and she disconnected.

The falls ricocheted on the rock face, as she propped with her hips pressing on the handrail. Water particles fragmented in every direction and misted her bare skin.

This was Goyne's favourite place in the district, apart from Clare's studio and Georgie could see why. But she had to move on.

She jogged to the Alfa, keying another SMS. 'Need to know. Where was your dad's favourite place? URGENT. Thnx.'

Beep. Georgie read Ally's 'Why?' and her pulse raced.

She begged aloud as she typed, 'Just tell me.'

'Home!'

'Outside of Bullock?'

Confused face emoji. 'Not sure'

Georgie prompted: 'Favourite place for hols?'

Ally took longer to reply. 'Torquay & Daylesford'

'Which most?' Georgie shot back. She hoped the answer would be the surfie town on Victoria's west coast. Then she changed her mind.

'Dford'

'Why? Special reason?'

'Still don't get why u r asking'

'Trust me, A!' Georgie alternated between hot and cold flushes, overexcited and stressed.

'Dad loved D. Used to say we traded one hill for another. We both loved it.'

Both, as in Goyne and Ally. 'What about Deb?'

'Not so much. She prefd Torquay' Ally adjoined a surprised face.

Georgie took the icon to mean Ally wasn't keen on the beach town. It seemed irrelevant though. 'Any special place in D?'

Cyber silence. It stretched until Georgie admitted temporary defeat and decided to head home.

————

Franklin knocked in the last nail that he'd recycled from the wreckage and surveyed his work. He'd salvaged several of the longer boards from the splintered barn-style doors and criss-crossed them over the front of the garage. It was a patch job that'd hold off a flea, but the token act notched down his anger at Whitey and Redwoods.

He tossed aside the brick he'd used as a hammer and whacked on a pair of disposable gloves, striding to the open back door.

As he did a walk-through of the cottage, Franklin's blood pressure ratcheted. The squatters had trashed the place. He had expected it, judging by what he'd seen in the garden and how they'd destroyed the garage, but still fumed.

He bagged several ciggie butts, intending to get the techies to run them through and see if they matched those from the party warehouse. Even as he sealed the bag, he almost tossed it away. The CSOs would prioritise the Hudson death, meaning he'd probably still be waiting *next* Christmas for forensic results from the Galassi warehouse, let alone any new requests.

———

Franklin was an idiot for not getting the rego number for Redwoods's car, although it probably wouldn't have helped much.

He had a gut feeling it'd belong to the crook's latest mark, and if he tracked her down via the plate, she'd refuse to cooperate. Motivated by embarrassment at being duped, or because they'd enjoyed his attention, even if for the wrong reasons and for a limited duration, those Redwoods— and cockroaches like him—swindled, generally kept mum.

Franklin had already phoned the homeowners and delivered the bad news. They were resigned, which made him more determined to get the crooks who'd wrecked their place.

He did drive-bys of Redwoods's favourite haunts and even checked in with Andrew Whitehead's mother to see if he'd returned to the nest.

She served him an earful about her poor innocent good son, yada-yada-yada, and screamed, 'And if I do see my boy, you'll be the last to know. *Pig.*' She slammed the screen door, almost taking off his nose, and he cursed himself for being a stupid prick.

———

AJ dropped his briefcase next to the breakfast bar, giving Georgie a hopeful look. She wrapped him in a hug, murmuring, 'The flowers are gorgeous. The messages saying sorry, even better.'

She rested her chin on his shoulder, studying the bouquet. Flowers, apologies and make-up sex were a pattern in their relationship, but at least their fights never went beyond verbal.

Moving to the stove, she said, 'I'm making your favourite tonight.'

The prawn spaghetti was her equivalent peace offering. He'd overstepped yesterday, but she wasn't entirely blameless.

She clanged down pots as AJ poured two glasses of red. While she prepped the ingredients, Phoebe wove around her ankles purring loudly, and AJ talked to the dog, and for a moment, it was just simple, perfect. But then she retrieved her wineglass and swirled the ruby liquid without drinking. She checked her phone, disappointed and dropped it onto the table, before tossing spaghetti in boiling water and firing up the wok.

She stirred the prawns, then gravitated back to the table to glance at her mobile.

AJ propped his elbows on the bench. 'What's with the phone, George?'

'Huh?'

'You've been glued to it since I came home.'

'I went to Bullock again...' Instant regret; she'd opened the subject that'd divided them yesterday.

'I gathered that.' AJ sounded flat, then the corners of his mouth turned up. 'Sure you don't have a secret lover there?'

Norman or Clive? She chuckled. 'You have nothing to worry about in Bullock.'

'And not in Bullock?'

Why had she added *in Bullock?* Her stomach twisted with guilt.

On dangerous ground, she had to dodge that subject with another taboo, her progress on the Goyne story. 'Funny. Anyway, I'm this close,' she pressed her thumb and finger together, 'to a break. But I'm waiting on Ally. Oh, no!' Georgie rushed to the stove.

She rescued the spaghetti before it overcooked. It'd been a lucky save in two ways. She couldn't tell AJ that Deb had dragged her daughter away from Bullock and banned her from contacting Georgie, because it'd spark another fight.

Lamely, she finished with, 'I hope she gets back to me soon.'

THREE DAYS TO CHRISTMAS

CHAPTER THIRTY-ONE

GEORGIE'S MIND DRIFTED AS SHE LAY IN A SEMI-conscious state. In her dream, a church organ played a heavy rock rhythm. It sounded like *Waiting for the End* by Linkin Park.

The volume raised and Georgie clicked she wasn't dreaming. Her mobile was playing its new ringtone nearby, growing more insistent.

AJ jolted upright. 'What the –'

'Sorry. It's my phone,' Georgie murmured, easing him back to his pillow.

She felt around, strained her eyes and ears, anxious because in a few seconds the call would divert to message bank.

She glimpsed a tiny beam of coloured light and touched the mobile's smooth, cold base. Lifting it close, her bleary eyes couldn't make out the name on-screen.

'Hello?'

'Georgie, it's me. Ally.'

'Hang on.'

She tiptoed out of the bedroom in darkness and slipped

the hallway door closed to blockade the front end of the house. In the kitchen, she flicked the light switch.

'I'm back.' She grabbed notepad and pen.

'I can't talk long and have to be really quiet. Mum took my phone after she sprung me texting. So I had to wait until she fell deep asleep to steal it from her bedroom.'

'Ally, don't get in trouble.'

'It's okay if it's important to you. But if I suddenly shush you, it's because Mum snores like a jet fighter but stops every so often. Normally she's just skipped a breath, but occasionally she jumps out of bed, wide-awake.'

After a micro-pause, Ally said, *'Where were we earlier? Mum deleted our messages.'*

Georgie recapped, 'I asked about your dad's favourite holiday place.'

'And I said Torquay and Daylesford.'

'Then you said Daylesford in particular.'

'Yeah, well, Dad wasn't all that into the beach, being big.'

'And your mum?'

'Mum loves Torquay, so Dad and I got dragged along so she could have her fix, but once we arrived we had fun too. Growing up, she spent lots of summers with her cousins and uncles and aunties and friends who live here.'

'Here?'

'Yeah, we're in Torquay. For Christmas.'

Georgie nodded and made a note. 'So, here's the question you didn't see. Did you and your dad have a special place in Daylesford?'

'Special place, as in – ?'

'Favourite place you stayed or visited?'

Ally took a moment to answer. *'Well, we're all market-lovers, so I remember going to one near the old railway.'*

No surprise there; Georgie had seen photo evidence. She waited to see if Ally would add more.

She did. *'And the Convent Gallery. Do you know it?'*

'Yes.'

'It had awesome art stuff, but Dad kinda got bored.'

Ally stopped, so Georgie asked, 'How often did you go to Daylesford?'

'We saw Uncle Ken heaps when I was really little, but less later on.'

Georgie wrote Uncle Ken on her pad and circled it. 'Uncle Ken?'

'Yeah. He died about three years ago. He was, like, ancient.'

Sure, a teenager would consider forties or fifties old, but *ancient*? 'Was he your mum or your dad's brother?'

'Neither. He was Dad's dad's brother.'

Georgie clarified, 'Warren's uncle, your great uncle.'

'Yeah.'

Ally hadn't exaggerated, then. He would've been old, if not ancient.

'Have you returned since Uncle Ken died?'

'We all went to the funeral. Dad travelled up a few times to sort out his will and stuff. His solicitor was in Castlemaine – Mum said 'cos the old coot, as she called him, didn't want the locals knowing his business.' Ally added, *'Mum can be a bit mean,'* seeming apologetic.

'You used to stay with Uncle Ken when you went to Daylesford?'

'Yeah...and Mum complained about it. He didn't worry about housework, and we always ate eggs and lamb 'cos Uncle Ken kept chooks and sheep. She reckoned if his house was dirty and his sheds were dirty, the animals would be dirty, too, and we'd get salmonella poisoning.'

Georgie wrote farm, sheep, chooks and underlined them.

Ally breathed hard down the receiver. *'Mum also used to go on about Uncle Ken being a hermit because he never saw his neighbours or socialised and only shopped once in a blue moon. Even the postie didn't come up to the farm.'*

'Uncle Ken used a roadside mailbox?' Georgie guessed.

'Yeah, a rusty old milk can on a pole at the intersection with the main road, with a bunch of other mailboxes. Not that it was a real main road.' Ally laughed. *'Not even by Bullock standards.'*

Georgie doodled on her pad, then heard a muffled noise. 'Are you okay?'

'Yeah, I'm in bed with my doona over the top of me and I needed air.' Ally giggled and continued. *'Anyway, whenever we went to Uncle Ken's, about all we did was stay on the farm, which I thought was great, but Mum hated it.'*

'And your dad?'

'He loved the old guy and wanted to keep the place after he died, but Mum said uh-uh.'

'And your mum got her way?'

'Mum usually does. She nags until everyone else gives in.' Ally sounded like she was smiling, though.

'I loved Uncle Ken's farm.'

A smile definitely in her voice.

'Uncle Ken used to go to the tip and recycle people's rubbish into the coolest things. He made me a rocking chair when I was little and an awesome scooter, better than what you buy in the shops. He built a garden edger – you know, for cutting lawn edges into straight lines? He gave it to Mum for her birthday. She was not impressed.'

Georgie added handyman to the pad. Ally went on. *'Uncle Ken and Dad made a sign for the gate from reclaimed wood, chains, and a sheep's skull. It said Bella Bonza Vista. Mum reckoned the name was pretentious, but according to Dad, it was tongue-in-cheek 'cos Uncle Ken was so ocker-Aussie and the old stone house so Swiss-Italian.'* She laughed softly.

Georgie liked hearing the teenager chat happily and smiled.

'Oh, and he fixed his truck out of junk from the tip. Although, Dad's theory was rust held it together.'

After noting those points, Georgie felt disgusted with herself for exploiting Ally's memories.

'Shush,' Ally hissed and paused. *'Phew. Mum's still asleep, but better be quick.'*

'So the spot you visited and loved most in Daylesford was Uncle Ken's farm?'

'Yeah, but it wasn't in Daylesford, although we'd always stop there before driving to Uncle Ken's, 'cos after two and a half hours on the road Mum busted for the loo and Dad was desperate for a snack. From there, it took fifteen minutes or so to reach his farm. He lived on the outskirts of this weird place in the middle of nowhere. Yandoit. Oh, no…gotta go.'

———

Franklin's phone beeped and he jerked to instant alertness, well trained by years on the force. In reaching for his mobile, he rolled on his grazed leg and groaned. His tumble over the fence yesterday had resulted in a whopper bruise.

One message. He clicked it open.

'Hope things r better. Why don't U come over? Lonely.'

'God, I need a license to operate this thing.' He twisted his phone, trying to decipher the icons she'd added, muttering, 'We're the same age, so how come Talitha's at home with these emoji-thingummies and I'm stuck in the dark ages?'

Regardless, he knew what she implied. He rubbed his forehead and sighed. He should've done the right thing by her and been in touch before now. But he still didn't know how to let her down gently.

Franklin considered the proverb that went something like act in haste, repent at leisure. Well, he certainly regretted hurting Talitha and wished he could turn back time to the moment he thought texting her from the station was a good idea, while still reeling from the Hudson death.

He should have lit up a smoke instead. That way, the only person hurt would be him.

He heard Kat shuffle up the hallway to the toilet and stuffed his mobile under the pillow in case it went off again. Easy fix, unlike how to put things right with Talitha. But responding to her tonight or beating himself up over what ifs weren't going to help. Better to deal with it in the morning.

———

'George, what are you doing? It's the middle of the night.'

She turned towards AJ's voice. He leaned on the mantelpiece and scratched his scalp.

'I have a meeting with the partners first thing.'

Georgie waved at him. 'Then go back to bed. I'll be quiet.'

He sat at the table. 'I won't be able to sleep until you come too.' He yawned widely, picking up her notepad before she could stop him. 'What's all this?'

Seconds later, his eyes bugged. 'You think this Warren Goyne left Bullock and went to Daylesford.'

'Yandoit. It's near Daylesford.'

'Because of a farm named Bonza View?'

'Bella Bonza Vista,' she corrected.

'I'm too tired for this.'

Still, he didn't make moves to go back to bed and Georgie gambled that was a tacit offer to help. 'If you went on the run –'

'Why?'

'*Just because.*' She eye-rolled. 'So, if for *some reason* you needed to leave, where would you go?'

'Matty's.' Interesting that he said his brother first. 'Or Mum and Dad's. A friend's.'

'Say it can't be an obvious place.'

He huffed.

'Work with me.'

'All right.' He held up a finger. 'I'd go to Darwin.'

She frowned. 'Why Darwin?'

'Because it's the other side of the country.'

It made annoying sense but raised infinite possibilities, and Georgie screwed her nose. Aware it was a leading question, she said, 'Okay. You can't be conspicuous, don't have a passport or access to much cash and won't be able to return home – where would you go?'

'All right,' he repeated, drawling the words. 'In that case, it wouldn't be Darwin. It would have to be in Victoria.'

'Uh-huh!'

'I'd have to know the area well.'

'Right.' She grinned.

He stilled, looking as if he'd nudged a tripwire.

A moment later, he disappeared into the courtyard, supposedly to retrieve something from his car. Georgie recognised it as a timeout and read over her notes until he returned, poured two fingers of scotch for both of them and sipped his, watching her.

She stared into the fiery ochre in her glass and swished the liquid while organising her hypothesis on Goyne.

She lifted her gaze. 'So, assuming that Goyne went on the run, I reckon he chose somewhere he's familiar with, might even have fond memories of, although it's likely to be a location where he interacted with very few people.'

Georgie sniffed her glass, then replaced it on the table. After too much scotch the other day, she didn't want it. Or anything that blunted her thinking.

'I asked Ally where her dad's favourite places were aside from Bullock. One was Torquay, but they have friends and relations in the area, so Goyne could be exposed. Deb and Ally are actually staying in Torquay for Christmas.'

AJ remained silent. She couldn't read him, except that he was wide awake. Her fault.

'Number two was Daylesford. But it turns out that they spent ninety-nine per cent of their visits on Ally's reclusive, since deceased, great-uncle's farm outside of Yandoit, which itself is fifteen or so minutes from Daylesford. They didn't even speak to the neighbours and rarely went off the property.'

'But that one per cent makes all the difference?'

'Yep. They spent a minuscule amount of their Yandoit holidays exploring Daylesford, which was enough to build an overview of the area, yet too little for Goyne to fear recognition.'

'I sense an "and"...'

'And Daylesford is accessible via bus, if Goyne didn't, say, hitchhike.'

'A fairly compelling argument –'

'Spoken like a lawyer.'

'So, you're going back.' AJ said it as a statement, not a question, and sadness flicked over his face before he masked it. He squeezed her hand, the scarred one, although it didn't hurt, physically. Emotionally, he reached into her chest and squeezed her heart.

'To Yandoit,' Georgie agreed. 'As a starter.'

He didn't say anything.

'I have to go. It's gone beyond the story now.'

'So what's new?' His words held a touch of bitterness.

'It's Ally –'

'And last time, it was Pam and Susan and Roly, and who else?'

She stiffened. 'Take it or leave it, it's who I am.'

He tossed back the last of his scotch. 'So, are you finally going to tell me about it?'

'Huh?'

Georgie shot AJ a confused glance and saw it in the blaze of his eyes. Although they'd never discussed the sparks between her and the man who'd saved her life, or their one kiss, and she was positive no one else had told him, AJ knew. He'd probably like to blame all their troubles on it, but if he were truthful with himself, he'd realise it was a symptom of problems pre-existing the happenings in Daylesford last autumn.

She couldn't say there was nothing to tell; she'd cheated on AJ with that kiss and given away a little of her heart. So, she raised a hand and said wearily, 'Stop. Before we push to a place we can't come back from.'

CHAPTER THIRTY-TWO

'SORRY TO RING SO EARLY ON YOUR DAY OFF BUT MAEVE *asked me to phone,'* Tim Lunny apologised.

Frustrated by his restless slumber, more than an hour ago Franklin had traded bed for a run on the treadmill.

He was halfway through and grateful for the breather. 'No probs.'

'Good, good. Now, you and Kat are coming over for Chrissie dinner?'

Franklin smiled. 'Well, we plan to. But with my prick of a boss, I might end up getting called in to work.'

Lunny chuckled.

'Of course we'll be there. Thanks for asking us.'

'You're part of the family; you know that.'

'Yeah.' Franklin rubbed his chin, uncomfortable with the touchy-feely talk. He cleared his throat and changed the subject. 'I've organised bread, meat, and plenty of beer for our station bash on Friday night.'

'Reckon we'll need some rabbit food, too, with Sam on the team?'

Give him a barbecued sausage in a white bread blanket

with plenty of tomato sauce and a frothy on the side and Franklin was content, as were the rest of the boys in blue. But Sam changed things. *Women love their salad.*

He agreed with Lunny. 'Yep. We'd better get a ready-made from the supermarket.'

'Have you heard the latest?'

Franklin could tell Lunny had switched to shop talk. 'What?'

'The Ds pulled Marc Jones in here for a few hours yesterday, but he's been released without charge.'

'I'm not surprised.' Franklin felt relieved for the man, nonetheless.

'We had a bunch of Neil Hudson's sympathisers picketing the station while that went on.'

Franklin's eyebrows shot up. 'But –'

Lunny cut him off. *'Hudson lived here his whole life and had a tonne of local connections. In death, he's become a top bloke in his friends' eyes. They knew he was a drunk who verbally abused his wife, but now he's dead, they're tempering the memory.'*

Franklin groaned.

'Now Jones was born here but spent most of his life away, so he's considered an incomer. He's young and good looking, to add insult to injury.'

'Let me guess; everything is his fault?' Franklin groaned again.

'Yep, that about covers it.' Lunny sounded weary. *'I have a sinking feeling trouble's not going away – even if and when the coroner's inquest backs up Jones's story and finds for accidental.'*

––––––

'And where do you think you're going?'

'Bronnie!' In the act of pulling the front door shut, Georgie had missed Bron's approach. She checked the lock with a tug, then greeted her friend properly.

Bron eyed the folder in her hand and frowned. 'I'm here to take you Christmas shopping.'

Georgie slapped her forehead.

'You forgot.'

She cringed. 'Completely. Sorry.'

'C'mon, girlfriend. The shops are waiting.'

'I can't. Tomorrow...maybe.'

Bron reached out, clasped Georgie's shoulders and drew her face-to-face. 'What's with the badger look?'

Georgie shook free.

'I haven't seen rings that dark around your eyes in months, GG. Are you and AJ fighting?'

'Why do you always assume that?'

'Because I'm generally right.'

By digging in her sports bag for something she didn't want, Georgie dodged Bron's intuitive stare. 'Hey, I'll catch you later, okay? I have to get my car.' She waved towards Ruby and Michael's yard, where the Spider was parked.

Bron snapped her fingers in front of Georgie. 'Neither of us is going anywhere until you answer me.'

Her redheaded friend could match her in pig-headedness, so Georgie sighed. 'We're having a bit of a cold war. He's not happy that I have to go to Daylesford.'

'Daylesford?'

'Yep, to follow a lead in the Goyne story.'

Bron's green eyes gleamed. 'And that's all you guys are fighting about?'

Georgie winced and again evaded her mate's gaze. She hadn't told a soul about what happened with Franklin, either time, not even her best friend or counsellor. And she'd denied, ducked and weaved Pam Stewart's warning about danger acting as an aphrodisiac, just as effectively as she'd shut down AJ this morning, which got her a cold front from him in return.

'It's sweet, Bron. You know how AJ and I are. We fight, we make up. It'll blow over.' Her tone was light, while doubt coiled on the inside. Would this time be the exception?

And she kept telling herself: *It was one kiss. Nothing else can ever happen. End of story.* Yet she didn't feel any relief.

———

Franklin chuckled. 'The Thing emerges.'

Kat poked out her tongue, adding a nice touch to yesterday's makeup ringed eyes and a fountain of tangled blonde hair. 'How could I sleep with you thudding around?'

'Ah, payback for when I'm on nights and trying to sleep during the day and you put on your music.'

He shrugged into his leather jacket.

'Can I come?' She ran her fingers through her hair, pulling a begging expression. 'We haven't taken a ride together in weeks.'

She was right. Between their schedules, they hadn't had time to tinker with the Ninja.

Distracted, he peered closer at her. 'Have you put purple stripes in your hair?'

'Blue, Dad. You're colour-blind.'

'That's as may be, but old women do the blue-tint thing.'

Kat swiped at him and Franklin ducked, laughing.

She looped back to the earlier subject. 'So, can I come out on the bike with you?'

'Maybe later. I'm doing work stuff this morning.'

'Aw, but it's your day off.'

He tapped her nose. 'Give me this morning and I'm yours later, okay?'

———

Franklin jostled through the coloured plastic strips on the front door, then held them aside for an elderly woman to exit.

'Thanks, dear. Are you going to call in for a cuppa soon?'

'Sure thing.' He grinned and added, 'You wouldn't need a light bulb replaced while I'm at it, by any chance?'

She giggled and waved.

'John? What are you doing here?' Talitha smoothed her black apron front, smiling broadly.

With such trust and pleasure in her expression, he had to look away. He ran his eyes over the café. The tables were empty, ready for the next flow of customers, and another staff member glanced at them while she stacked cups by the coffee machine.

His gaze landed back on Talitha. 'Can you spare a minute?' He twitched his head to indicate outside.

He saw her draw back, then shrink, all within seconds. She nodded.

As he'd done for the old woman, Franklin spread the PVC strips and Talitha ducked through. He pulled out a chair for her but she moved to the other side of the table. After hesitating, he slid onto the seat he'd intended for his friend. He perched on the hard chair and almost immediately shifted the ashtray.

Quitting sucks.

His elbows dug into the laminate top, so he dropped his hands onto his lap. Still uncomfortable, he let them hang by his sides. A moment later, he placed them back on the tabletop. And Talitha sat rigidly, surveying his jittery display.

'Um…'

She didn't help him out.

He tried again. 'The other night…'

She blinked. Her mouth pulled into a straight line.

'I. Er…'

Finally, she spoke. 'You want me to make it easy for you?'

He flushed, ashamed because he wished she'd do just that. *God, I'm a prick.*

'You don't do casual, do you?'

Casual relationships. Casual sex. Honesty is the best policy. 'No.'

'Well, I don't either,' she said.

I totally suck.

'But you needed comfort the other night and I gave it to you.'

Franklin chafed his chin, nodding.

Talitha swayed a finger. 'We're mates and it won't happen again. Right?'

He locked eyes with her, and promised, 'Talitha, I wouldn't dream of trying that.'

She nodded.

He reached over to give her forearm a squeeze. She pulled away but curled her lips to soften the rejection. It might've been better if she'd blown up at him. Her poise highlighted more than ever what a low-life he was. He folded his face into a mute apology.

Mute was cowardly, so he spoke it. 'Talitha, I really am sorry for hurting you.'

Her reply came with a soft sigh. 'I know that.' She rose, stepped around the table and slapped between Franklin's shoulders so heartily, the breath whooshed from his mouth.

She smiled. 'Ring me later and we'll get the gang together at the pub.'

Then Talitha lifted her chin and stalked into the café. Her dignity made him feel better and worse.

CHAPTER THIRTY-THREE

HE TOLD THE KID YESTERDAY THAT NEVER GOING BACK to the squat the same way twice wasn't enough; they had to keep moving every day or so too. They might be able to rotate through their favourites, but staying still was complacent, and complacency got you caught.

The kid was okay with that, and he'd said, 'Waz – Warren, can we go back to the lake?'

Though his mate was feeling pretty good at the moment, there was something feverish in his eyes. It made him think the kid sensed it too. That they didn't have long until things were going to change, and as hard as it was to imagine, it'd be even worse for that.

So he'd said, 'Why not?' happy when the kid's face broke into a big grin.

But when they set themselves up for the night, it struck him how strange it was coming back to the start, where they'd met nearly two years ago. He'd arrived in Daylesford without thinking much further than getting here, then remembered the swimming shelter and decided to stay there a night and come up with a better idea the next day. He'd woken with the kid staring at him. Luke hadn't said anything but handed him a can of cold baked beans and the dregs of his coke, and they'd looked out for each other since.

But this morning, the kid was stuffing around. The later it got, the riskier. Too likely someone would come across them. He'd lost it with Luke, something he never did, and left him having a wash. They'd meet up later, but soon after he walked away, he felt guilty. He was supposed to be looking out for the kid, not taking a walk in the bush.

––––––

After seeing Talitha, Franklin felt a small part relieved and a larger part vexed that he'd relied on her to do the talking. He lowered his helmet visor and revved the Ninja.

Not pretty. But done. One item ticked off today's to-do list.

Vincent Street was a logjam of tourist and local vehicles, unusual for a Wednesday except for it being school holidays, and people in holiday mode and others in a hurry combined as oil and water. Franklin bypassed an inept attempt at parallel parking and a driver reversing from a space from which he should have exited forward. Today, he hadn't donned the monkey suit and had bigger fish to fry than knucklehead drivers on the main drag.

A minute later, he turned into Central Springs Road and left the traffic behind. He accelerated up Wombat Hill past several old churches and turned right. He geared down and approached at a cruise.

Shreds of the blue and white police tape dangled on the driveway. Monica's champagne Camry was absent and the same went for Jones's ute.

His tipping trailer sat alone in the carport.

Then Franklin groaned, noting its signwriting had been over-sprayed with 'Mr Garden: gets away with murder'.

Blood-red paint, of course.

He parked the bike and approached, alert for onlookers, although the place felt empty. The garden equipment not confiscated by the crime scene crew had been strewn behind the carport. Handles snapped, hessian bags sliced, hand mower upturned and dented. The crooks had left the ride-on in place but painted a large red cross over the sides, bonnet, and seat.

It was the work of some very angry units.

Franklin skirted the house and checked all the windows and doors. He gazed into the distance and shook his head sadly.

For form's sake, he went to the Hudsons' place and rapped on the door. He called out to Monica, his voice ricocheting. He sensed she wasn't home nor was responsible for the mess next door. The graffiti, at any rate.

He extracted his mobile and speed-dialled the station while walking to his bike. 'Harty, I'm at Jones's place on Crow Street.'

'*Why?*'

'I figured it worth doing a drive-by considering the

controversy. And unfortunately, I was right. Some hot heads have been busy here with spray paint and playing scratch-and-dent.'

'Our friends from the factory burgs?'

'Nah, mate. This is personal.' Eyes flitting between the two empty houses, Franklin hurried on. 'The damage seems to be contained to Jones's trailer and garden gear. I've done a quick scout and the house appears okay. But you'd better get down and have a proper go-over.'

———

Another job ticked off the to-do list and another bitter taste in Franklin's mouth. While not involving bloodshed, the carnage against Jones's property may well be a precursor.

He rode in circles that matched his thinking and ended up in the cop shop car park, next to the boys' personal rides. As he didn't spot a marked vehicle, he assumed they'd crossed over, the team arriving at Crow Street, while he'd taken his circuitous route to the station.

Gritty wind whipped up as he removed his helmet, making him duck and squint while he used his key and code to enter the station.

He strode into the muster room. Harty's desk chair still held warmth and as he'd hoped, the computer hadn't hibernated, so it took just minutes to run the checks.

Licence and vehicle checks for Andrew Whitehead and Reginald Redwoods revealed nothing overtly useful, just as earlier ones on Duffy had drawn blanks. They had no current warrants or flags, except for those in his head.

Franklin jotted associates for each while at it and tapped his teeth with a pen when he spotted a familiar name: Daniel Stephenson.

Stephenson was into drugs and burgs. Aggressive bloke who fancied a bit of fisticuff action but wasn't averse to using whatever weapons lay handy too; fence palings one of his favourites.

Stephenson was a mate of Whitey, probably attracted to a matching obnoxious personality.

Interestingly, Franklin remembered he had something in common with Redwoods too. One of Redwoods's first victims was Stephenson's sister, and rather than side with his sister, Stephenson had helped the conman steal her car. They'd both done a stretch in jail courtesy of that irate sibling.

Chances they've stayed bosom buddies? A sure bet.

He leaned back in his chair, startled when the phone rang.

'John Franklin, Daylesford Police.'

'Ah, the man I wanted.'

On the line was the crime scene techie who'd gone over the ropes with him at the Galassi warehouse. They exchanged chitchat, then the bloke said, *'Look we're snowed at the mo, but I wanted to shoot you a quick verbal.'*

'Great, thanks –'

'Don't thank me.' His apologetic tone set off warning bells.

'But we had stacks of prints.'

The tech replied, *'No matches for the fingerprints. Several perfect specimens, but their body isn't on record. Yet. Hopefully, you'll rectify that during this case. A few of the partials point one way but not good enough for court.'*

'We struck out on the handprint too?'

'Eleven million palms on NAFIS but no hits for yours.'

'What –'

The CSO went on, oblivious to Franklin's interruption.

'The sneaker tread's size ten male ASICS Gels. If you pull in a suspect with their runners, we may be able to match wear in the shoe tread. Ditto the ciggie butts. It's wish-list versus reality, as you well know.'

Despite his intense frustration, Franklin understood.

'We just don't have the resources to run all the DNA checks you'd like. We can't justify processing butts from the periphery of the crime scene. Tighten things up and we'll be more than happy to help, though.'

Finally, the bloke breathed. 'That's it.'

Franklin fixed on one of the points, sparking up. 'The partials?'

'Without boring you to tears, I'd be happy to say, between you and me, that a certain Daniel Stephenson was at your warehouse.'

Stephenson's in on it. 'Well, well.' Franklin chuckled.

'I take it you know who I'm talking about.' The techie sounded pleased. His tone regretful again, he added, 'But it's not much use to you because six points of minutiae aren't going to stand up in court.'

CHAPTER THIRTY-FOUR

GEORGIE CUT LEFT OVER A SHORT CAUSEWAY CROSSING the lake and hooked right. Unusually, there were plenty of parking spaces, and she nosed the Spider into one facing the water.

She tugged the key from the ignition yet lingered, listening to the tick of the engine. It smoothed the edges, allowing her heartbeat and breathing to fall into steadier rhythms.

She hadn't been able to drive straight through to Yandoit as she'd planned. The intense reaction she'd had coming into Daylesford only a few weeks after she'd left it behind for good, added with her sleep deficit and angst about AJ, necessitated a break.

Georgie exited, lighting up a smoke, and the knots in her muscles quickly slackened. Hot wind whipped up her hair and she laughed in surprise, startling a team of ducks that scattered with flapping wings.

The ducks eased more of her tension, and with another smoke, Georgie's brain-fuzz ebbed. But as the ciggie encroached on its filter, a cloud blocked the sun and her mood dimmed too.

She binned the butt and returned to the Spider to retrieve her notes. She read as she walked and fumbled her file when a couple of kids sprang from nowhere, perhaps as cosmic payback for her alarming the ducks. While her heart still tap-danced, she smiled at the little girl who chased a slightly bigger boy, giggling. The kids dodged past and their footsteps and laughter diminished.

Georgie strode on, her mind crowded by random thoughts of Ally, Goyne and AJ, but determinedly, not Franklin.

Next thing she realised, she was in deep shadow thrown by lofty old gums and cypress trees, in the picnic area at the cul-de-sac of the lake. With no one else in sight, she tramped the pathway, her body more purposeful than her mind.

She looked around. On her left was a white art deco mansion behind a high picket fence. To the right, a stone amphitheatre and timber jetty. Farther ahead, a stone pavilion atop a steep bleacher-type wall of stairs in the same random patterned paving filled her view. Georgie imagined people armed with towels, tote bags and inflatables swarming here on hot days and nights. Then the picture faded, leaving her alone and contemplative again.

Distant voices drew her gaze to the picket fence. She saw the boy and girl duck through the gate and scamper up an external staircase, then disappear. Somehow it seemed like an omen, that her chase to Daylesford and Yandoit would be anti-climactic.

She felt pulled to the pavilion. She and AJ had once lapped the lake and on a separate occasion continued along the track to sample the mineral springs, which must be an acquired taste. Both days they'd overlooked this spot.

The other-worldliness won today.

Georgie skirted the building with her hand stroking the stone. *If only these walls could talk.* She came to the front and the first of three doorways beckoned. To what? A barbecue, table, and chairs? Quaint historic relics? Or a boring empty shell?

She crossed the threshold, collided with a young guy who rushed out, and her notes scattered.

Georgie took in his shorn wet hair, and yellow-tinged skin stretched over his facial bones before she ducked to grab her papers. He stooped at the same time and gathered some sheets.

A breeze ruffled the documents still strewn over the ground, and Georgie dived on escaping pages. She turned back to the wet-haired guy, frowning when she saw he was staring at something clasped in his hand. Her unease increased when she spotted that his jaundiced face had paled.

What the hell?

She plucked the photograph of Goyne that Norman had pressed upon her from the guy's shaky right hand, then pulled the Whereis.com printout from his other fist. The page held a map and directions from Daylesford to Yandoit, the route committed to her memory. She would've been devastated to lose her photo of Goyne—her sum total of physical evidence so far—but was also glad the printout hadn't gusted into the lake.

'Thanks for saving them.'

He looked at her blankly.

Georgie retrieved the rest of her papers and all the

while, his stare was a thorn in the back of her neck. Weird, but she thanked him again.

He grunted, yanked his hoodie over his head and plunged back into the building, leaving her to notice a weathered sign blending into the wall.

'Shit.'

Heat scorched her face. If she'd missed the wet-haired guy by even seconds, she would've barged into the men's toilet, making her double-check the plaque outside the ladies' before entering it. Inside, she breathed deeply.

'Right, Harvey.' She spoke aloud to refocus. 'Use the loo, take five to blow off a few more cobwebs, then get out of here.' She took the Goyne file with her.

———

Franklin stared at the computer screen and rubbed the furrows on his brow. The police radio crackled in the background. He subconsciously listened and dismissed the communication. It had nothing to do with him, and he wasn't officially here.

He grabbed his mobile, cutting off *Telephone* by the weirdo Lady Gaga, Kat's choice of ringtone linked to her VIP number on his phone. 'I have no idea how you talked me into having Gaga as your ringtone, kid. But when I get home, you're changing it.'

'*Hello, Kat, lovely to hear from you,*' she replied sarcastically.

'Okay. Hi, Kat. Now, when I get home, can you set a real song for me?'

'*Speaking of when you get home...are you on your way?*'

'Soon.'

'*You said –*'

'All right, yes.' He cracked a smile. He was lucky; Kat actually wanted to spend time with her dad, not like some kids. He'd hit a brick wall with his inquiries anyway, so why not take a ride on the Ninja together and shoot the breeze?

———

Georgie stared at the café across the lake, muttering, 'I don't have time for this.' But she'd travelled too far for a U-turn, being halfway around the waterway. She should have been in Yandoit, on the chase for Goyne. What had she been thinking, setting off on a walk like a tourist?

Three primary-coloured paddleboats were out on the water. A dad and kid were in the one nearest the jetty, two teens in the middle one and a sole occupant in the boat closest to Georgie. She waved, just as the paddleboat arced away.

Index finger and thumb together, she held them to her mouth and let out a whistle. No reaction from those on the water. No chance of catching a ride.

Georgie took off at a fast pace. Until this point, she'd been mulling over AJ, unmindful to all else. Now she observed her surroundings, hearing rustles in the undergrowth and inhaling fresh air with a whiff of eucalyptus. She passed an impressive house, another jetty and a couple walking the opposite way with a tri-coloured spaniel.

A different sound came from behind and she glanced back. The pathway was clear and she pushed on, now thinking about the incident with the wet-haired guy.

She might've put his bad complexion and undernourished appearance down to illness. But the shakes and his strange manner could indicate drugs. And what was with his wet hair?

There were no showers in the female washroom, so it followed there wouldn't be any in the men's, and although the water looked pretty with its sunlit ripples, it would take a strong heart to swim in the lake. From Georgie's experience and the various signs dotted near the water's edge, she knew cold currents lurked. Lethal in winter and unbearable even in December unless the temperature climbed another ten degrees.

So maybe he'd washed in the basin. It was odd, but she shrugged, not really caring. Then Georgie heard a stone skittle across the path and plop in the water. No one was ahead of her, so she did a half-turn, and tensed when she saw a figure dart into the shrubbery.

Panic surged inside her, as her legs pumped out a walk so fast it was almost a jog. She knew she was overreacting but couldn't help it. Her body was flashing back to autumn. She'd never seen her attackers clearly and they'd pulverised her in ways she'd only witnessed on movies. The person behind her could be harmless. But her instincts said otherwise.

Georgie heard a swoosh of shrubbery, then feet on gravel, drawing in. They barely faltered after a skid on loose rubble. As the steps thudded closer, she heard the rasp of breath and knew the person wasn't out for a jog but chasing her.

She didn't turn or hesitate, just followed the urge to run. With her file hugged to chest, Georgie sprinted, her foot strikes frantic. The path became a curving, natural tunnel, overhung by clumps of dead trees and rambling shrubs. Her fear ramped up; no one could see her from any direction, except her pursuer.

She threw a quick glimpse over her shoulder, saw a person only metres away, gasping when she recognised the guy she'd collided with at the pavilion. His mouth was a determined slash and his eyes held a manic look.

Georgie's breathing rattled with exertion and fear. Galvanised, she chopped her elbows harder to increase speed, fighting a burn in her lungs and legs, and scanned for an alternative exit. They were close to the road but surrounded by bush, hidden from across the lake and the road. He'd grab her before she could scramble through.

'Help!' she yelled, then remembered the self-defence adage: don't waste your breath calling for help as most bystanders won't get involved. 'Fire! Fire!'

Too late.

He yanked a fistful of hair and flipped her onto the ground. Her teeth rattled when she hit the dirt.

'Who are you?' He panted into her face, his breath pungently sweet. His elbow pressed on her larynx, all his weight driving her down, as sharp rock jabbed the back of Georgie's skull. His legs pinned her arms. She could scarcely breathe and with him crushing her voice box, couldn't answer. She squirmed for leverage. Gravel sprayed under her sandalled feet. She skinned her heels, twisting and thrusting.

Her attacker may be sick or undernourished, but he possessed wiry power. He trapped her right arm and partially her left. Georgie clawed the skin where his T-shirt had ridden up, rueing the loss of strength in her left hand, the one damaged in March.

He didn't flinch, repeating, 'Who are you?' He rammed her against the ground with each word.

Georgie's eyes watered. Her head had twisted and rock chiselled against her left ear now. Her pulse sounded loud, then faded, in waves.

She didn't understand why her mugger wanted to know her identity.

'Tell me.' His words were a frenzied hiss. He punched the side of Georgie's face, knuckles jarring her cheekbone and jaw. She bit the inside of her cheek and tasted the warm, metallic tang of blood.

It hurt like hell, but his weight had shifted off her throat when he hit her, so she could breathe freely again and think. *What does he want?* The only things with her were car keys and the Goyne file. He'd lucked out if he wanted mobile phone or money unless he raided the Spider after he finished with her.

After he's finished with me. Her heart rate spiked as her chest contracted. *Is he going to rape me?* She'd lived through one violent attack and yet rape seemed far worse. She would not let that happen.

Georgie went limp, pretending to be out of it. She waited, felt his grip slacken marginally, then inhaled, exhaled and bucked, bringing her right knee up hard.

The air blew out of his lungs and he let go of her to grab his groin. She twisted out from under him, rolled into a crouch and pushed to her feet, wresting her file from under his shoulder. He threw out an arm and clutched her jeans, making her stumble. She swivelled, backhanding him across the face, and bolted.

CHAPTER THIRTY-FIVE

Georgie sat half-in, half-out of the Spider, a little woozy, head throbbing and fighting down nausea. She massaged tender spots and dusted off grit stuck to her skinned feet, then leaned towards the mirror, angled her face and inspected her jaw. She'd have a huge bruise for Christmas, which would make AJ blow up and his stick-in-the-mud parents say, *We told you she's too common for you, son.*

She tried to get a grip, reminding herself that he hadn't raped her. But the valve on her anger opened wider. *The shithead's got my file.*

All her general research into Bullock and the wildfires. Gone. Grabbed from her hand as she'd raced away. Fortunately, not the audio file interviews on her computer or her notes on the main players in her story including Goyne; all that was in the notepad she'd fortunately left in the Spider. And luckiest of all, she still had her photograph of Goyne. Georgie lifted it off her lap reverently, thankful that she'd stuffed it into her jeans' waist back at the loo.

She inspected the crumpled photo: Goyne in red-hot

fedora, with Ally in her fisherman tweed. It'd fascinated her mugger so much, he'd gotten the shakes.

What other motive could the guy have for attacking her and stealing the Goyne dossier, apart from that he knew (or thought he knew) the man?

Now, she felt even more certain that the coroner had been wrong about Goyne. And more determined to trace the ex-realtor.

As she started the ignition, Georgie made another resolve – to join a gym once this was over and get more real with her physio exercises. She would fix her damn body. No more spasmodic efforts, as she'd been guilty of since April. No Dawn Poole-like cop-outs. She'd saved herself this time but might have avoided another beating and kept her file if she'd outrun her attacker.

Before taking off, she extracted nail scissors and a zip lock baggie from the compact first-aid kit in the glovebox and clipped the nails on her left hand close to the skin, capturing the cuttings in the bag.

She'd scratched her mugger; his DNA was on those fingernails. But what she'd just done was a complete waste of time because she wouldn't report the attack. She couldn't go to the local police because she might see Franklin. For both their sakes, she needed to avoid him, but it still felt good to have that little bag of clippings.

Georgie gripped the steering wheel, cleared her head. She was ready for Yandoit, but during the drive there, she decided it was like breaking the seal in a booze session. By telling herself she had to avoid Franklin, she'd let him into her head, and she couldn't switch off as she traversed through Hepburn Springs and turned onto the Newstead Road. It got worse when she drove through Franklinford.

Franklinford, unbelievable.

With her head tumbling memories involving Franklin, she steered the Spider on autopilot, then found herself heading towards an isolated strip of buildings, set among hills and pastures, grazing sheep and dry-stone walls, with the odd farmhouse here and there. The signpost confirmed she'd reached Yandoit.

Georgie trawled the main street in search of a general store, pub or post office. Her first impression was that the town looked ramshackle in a sepia monochrome. Rundown and deserted.

On second thought, the buildings with their red-bricked walls, rust-striped galvanised iron, and peeling paint on weathered cladding made her think of an abandoned movie set. That idea leapt to her imagining she'd entered the Twilight Zone so vividly she heard the theme music.

From one end to the other, she saw about six houses, a tiny school and Mechanics Institute Hall, but no pub or shops. In not much more than a blink, she passed through the whole town and all she could see left or right were roadside mailboxes, farms, junk and a sign for a church.

Georgie figured she'd missed at least one store on her first sweep and drove the Spider slowly on a return trip, spotting some weathered people parked on rickety seats on the porches of their weary houses, who surveyed the Alfa's approach, locked suspicious eyes on Georgie through the car window and turned their heads to follow her trek.

It was a little spooky, so she thought twice about pulling over and asking for directions to Bella Bonza Vista. What actually stopped her was fear that they might know Goyne and tip him off. Instead, she'd try to find the intersection Ally had described.

Georgie threw the Spider into a U-turn. Maybe Uncle Ken's mailbox was one of those she'd passed minutes ago.

She pulled up at the roadside boxes. How many rusty old milk cans on poles could there be? *How about seven, here alone?*

She pressed her temples. *Think, Harvey. What else did Ally say?*

She'd mentioned an intersection with a main road, that wasn't a real main road, not even by Bullock standards. This spot qualified yet was little help because each mailbox bore a set of numbers; one or two displayed a surname also, but none gave a property name.

On the bright side, assuming Georgie had stumbled upon the right milk-can-slash-mailbox among these seven, as there were few roads to choose from at this intersection, she might chance across a wood, chain and sheep skull sign for Bella Bonza Vista after a few tries. That's if the current owners hadn't redecorated or renamed the farm.

———

Kat yanked Franklin onto the floor and linked ankles. He groaned. His abs already burned and would cane like buggery tomorrow. *What do you want to do now?* hadn't seemed dangerous twenty minutes ago.

'Hey, Mr F,' distracted Franklin. His guard dropped too low and Kat tapped his chin instead of fists.

'Enough.' He surrendered and after a quick clutch of his belly, faced the little group of kids, returning their greeting.

His youth liaison portfolio was the roundabout reason he and Kat were here at the boxing studio. When his two old footy mates opened it in October, he'd convinced them to give local kids a discounted off-peak rate, which encouraged troves of youngsters to join. Good for the establishing business, and good for Franklin because it kept kids occupied, although he had to be careful to point out he encouraged exercise, not fighting.

'Mr F,' young Drew said. 'Can you spar with us?'

The others said, 'Yeah, *please.*'

He and Kat had sparred since she was a little tyke, playfully at first and later more seriously testing her self-defence skills. If it was okay for his daughter, the same applied for other youths, but Franklin milked the moment, enjoying the enthusiasm of the four primary schoolers. He didn't require begging, or a motive beyond that he loved it. He glimpsed Kat in animated discussion with her best friend, Lisa Cantrell. They'd be content for ages.

'Put 'em up,' he said, jumping to his feet.

The smallest, blond-haired Kayla, slit her baby-blues and giggled, then pointed out, 'You need your focus pads.'

He held up his gloves, looked at them cross-eyed, then knocked his temples, as if to say, *I'm a dumbo.*

The kids laughed. It bloody helped that there was a lighter side to his work.

———

Georgie found Uncle Ken's old property; she wasn't sure she wanted to be here.

A sense of déjà vu made her queasy. Months ago she'd made the huge mistake of jumping in without consideration of the consequences. And look where that got her.

She U-turned and passed the skull a second time and a further layer added to her trepidation. Her mugger at the lake had picked up Goyne's photo and her Whereis.com printout for Yandoit. He'd reacted so strongly to the photo that he *had* to know Goyne, and her map gave away that she'd found a connection to this area.

If she'd joined the dots correctly, he'd know what she wanted in Yandoit. He could've returned here while she was pulling herself together at the lake. But would he lie in wait to have another go at her? It made more sense that her delay gave him and Goyne a chance to escape.

Georgie circled by the property again. Farther on, she dialled a number on her phone – someone needed to know where she'd gone and why, just in case.

The one person who sometimes judged yet always supported her was Bron. Unfortunately, the call went straight to message bank. Georgie swore again and left a message.

No more procrastinating. I need to know if Goyne's here or if he's been and gone.

She vaulted the gate and felt a chill incompatible with the hot, muggy wind that ruffled her singlet top. Her stomach flipped. *Be alert but not afraid* repeated in her mind.

The driveway left her exposed. In darting for the cover of two-metre high thickets of gorse, she skirted three rusty vehicles nestled into the waist-high grass. As the truck in the middle loomed, its massive grill looked menacing, like it would bite. She cleared it, then came to a rock-edged dam filled with muddy sludge, rubbish bags, and bald tyres.

The thought of dams leapt to snakes; snakes love to bask on rocks around dams or skulk in long grass. She ran faster and didn't stop when she reached the gorse clumps, not even when the thorny weed snatched at her bare arm, drawing blood.

Georgie sprinted on with her lungs burning until she reached a dilapidated barn. One of its two lean-tos had collapsed into a heap of iron and broken timber. The rest of the building remained standing, albeit at a slant and pocked with holes.

She took a few seconds to control her breathing and wiped the sticky perspiration off her palms and brow.

Let's do it. She ducked through the surviving lean-to and wrenched ajar one of the barn doors. Powdery dirt rained down, and she almost popped ribs suppressing a sneeze. No one could've recently preceded her through that doorway, but there might be other ways in, so her senses stayed on high alert while she searched the ground floor.

Odours of hay mould and rat or possum poo made her nose and eyes itch. She heard a scratchy rustle and expected to face off with a set of beady eyes any minute.

No evidence of human presence, but there was still the loft. She gingerly scaled the rickety ladder. Incredibly, the rungs held out, and she let out a thankful sigh as she pulled herself onto the mezzanine. A floorboard ruptured as she moved to check behind smelly hay bales and she dropped to hands and knees, crawling the rest of the way with her heart racing.

All of that was for zilch too.

Georgie backtracked through the barn and outside again, eyed the two-storey Swiss-Italian building of stone, timber and corrugated iron. It matched Ally's description, just as everything else had so far. She calculated the distance to the house. *Seventy metres?* Every one of them out in the open, so once she left the cover of the barn, she had to move fast.

She dashed for the nearest door of the house. She hugged the walls, stepping over a pile of red bricks, remnants of a tumbledown chimney.

Now facing the door, she realised she hadn't thought this through. If Goyne and his mugger friend were hiding inside, they were hardly going to answer a knock on the door. So, she had to hope she could enter with stealth and see or hear them before they spotted her.

Georgie pushed gently at the solid timber door. Nothing happened.

She turned the knob and tried again. It moved a centimetre and re-stuck. She rammed it and burst into the kitchen in a cloud of dust. *Hardly stealth, Harvey.* She let out a nervous laugh that turned into a cough. If anyone were inside, they'd have to be deaf to have missed her entry. So, after recovering, she called, 'Hello?'

The word echoed. And her antennae twitched. *Because someone's here? Only one way to find out.*

Top to bottom, the sparse furnishings tallied with what a resourceful scrounger would find or make, and everything was old and filthy. Perhaps it'd been this way since Uncle Ken died. It crossed Georgie's mind that Goyne might've hung onto the place behind his wife's back.

The power wasn't connected. Pipes for gas bottles dangled. And a turn of the kitchen tap produced a lump of gunk with a dribble of brown water. Georgie recalled the rubbish-filled dam and wondered if that constituted the water supply to the property.

The bedroom robe, shaving cabinet over a rust-stained basin in the bathroom, and rudimentary kitchen cupboards were empty.

It was clear that no person had been here for a long time, not even living rough.

She exhaled. 'Now what?'

She couldn't shake the instinct that Goyne and his mugger mate were close.

CHAPTER THIRTY-SIX

THE KID WAS IN BAD SHAPE WHEN THEY CAUGHT UP IN the afternoon. All shaky and sweaty and they had to find somewhere quiet for him to have a lie down before heading to their next squat.

Luke wouldn't talk about it until he suddenly blurted out, 'Some girl had a photo of you today.' He looked at him strangely, like he didn't know him all of a sudden. 'Why would she have that, Waz?'

He let the *Waz* go, his mind too busy going crazy.

A girl? Ally?

'What'd she look like?' He grabbed the kid's shoulder, must've pressed too hard, because he saw Luke wince.

'I dunno.' The kid shrugged out of his grasp. 'Tallish, long hair.'

He couldn't breathe.

'Older than me. Maybe around thirty?'

Not Ally. **He felt relieved and disappointed.** *So who's the girl and what does she want?* **His stomach burned.**

'What'd she want?'

'I dunno.' The kid lifted his shoulders. 'But she had all this stuff on those bad bushfires we had a few years back.'

Maybe not personal then, just someone with a strange interest in the fires, not specifically what he'd done. He hoped.

———

'That's not your girlfriend's car, is it?' Harty said.

Franklin frowned. *Talitha?* Harty knew she drove a late model gunmetal Mazda3 hatch, but how did he hear about their one-nighter? 'Huh?'

Harty pointed through the side window. 'It's a pretty distinctive frog nose.'

Franklin's stomach pitted even before he saw it himself.

He parked his SS Commodore a few spaces from the black Alfa. His thoughts were erratic, like his heartbeat. He never stopped thinking about Georgie, all the while believing he'd never see her again after what she'd said a few weeks ago. Faced with the chance now, he wasn't sure if he wanted to run inside or run away. He would've much preferred to be staring at Talitha's little hatchback.

His mate chortled. 'When did Georgie Harvey get back in town?'

'Your guess would be as good as mine,' Franklin replied.

'Wanna go to my place instead?' Did he want to let this chance slip? *Yes, no, maybe...no.*

'What and miss the Franklin and Harvey show?' His mate grinned, pulling his mobile. 'Slam'll never forgive me if I don't give him a hoy.'

———

Georgie was darkly contemplative because her day couldn't have gone much worse.

Conflict was nothing new for her and AJ, but despite her bluff and bravado with Bron this morning, Georgie realised they'd plunged into unchartered waters. He knew something about her and Franklin.

But what 'something'? Did what she feel for Franklin run deeper than attraction? Was it just the allure of opposites, the pull of surviving peril, even the taste of forbidden fruit? How could she open up to AJ, if she wasn't sure what she was opening up about?

She'd shunned the Wombat Arms tonight to avoid bumping into Franklin. Although their last chance encounter at a pub had been at the Wombat, it didn't mean she was safe at Burke's Hotel, just that the risk was lower. And she could get drinks, honest pub food, and a bed for the night here.

She really had to stop thinking about AJ and Franklin. On cue, her mind skipped to what she'd said to Bron when they finally stopped playing phone tag tonight. *Who gets mugged at Daylesford Lake?*

Only you, mate, Bron had drawled. How true. But the final straw had been her trek to Yandoit. All that build-up, to just fizz out. And she still didn't know if Goyne had sold Uncle Ken's property.

Georgie had been on a roll with that, having snapped pictures of the neighbouring farm, which was for sale. With her prepaid WiFi playing up, she went to Daylesford Library and tapped into theirs to locate the corresponding online ad. It didn't include the full address, so she'd called the listing agent and obtained address and title specs. Then she continued using the skills she'd picked up as a commercial litigation clerk at AJ's firm in her previous life, jumping onto the Landata website to run a land title search on Uncle Ken's property. But Landata had crashed, and now she had to wait until tomorrow.

Damn you, Fat Man. She checked herself over the Fat Man slip, then thought, *Hell yes, I'm pissed off with Goyne.* He deserved the epithet, this man who had allowed his family and friends to grieve over his horrific sham death.

She looked around the pub. Most of the people congregating had the air of regulars. The bartender, a good-looking guy of European descent, conversed from behind the beer tap, chatted at each table and gave tips to the aspirant pool sharks. He was chummy with everyone else, but while he'd been friendly when he served Georgie, he'd left her alone since.

She finished her beer and brooded over a comment that Deb Goyne made, seemingly ages ago. *With your eyes darting all over the place, scribbling lots of notes, chugging on the ciggies and coffee like there's no tomorrow, you certainly come across as a writer, love.*

Deb had sized her up accurately. While she had many friendly acquaintances, Georgie's group of real friends was small, select and much like a blended family. Not everyone got her. They often liked her but saw her as self-sufficient, leaving her to take part but involved on the outer. Mainly watching, recording, asking questions but not giving much of herself away.

Here on her stool, elbows on the bar, sucking on her beer, was the perfect example.

———

'Georgie?'

Her heart knocked in her chest when she recognised the voice. She twisted, grazing her empty beer bottle. Pinned by the intensity in his eyes, she froze.

Franklin righted the bottle. 'Can I get you another?' A blush crept over his skin.

She nodded and he called, 'Manny, can we have a couple more?' without breaking their gaze.

'Why are you here?' *What a lame thing to say.* Georgie's face flushed now.

'Wouldn't you know? This is our regular.' Franklin gestured in the direction of two guys who stood at a distance.

One she recognised as Scott Hart, who'd helped her back in autumn. The second guy rang a bell as another of the local cops. They were both staring and waved. She returned the wave and the men drifted to the pool table.

For some reason, she and Franklin laughed. Both sounded strained.

'My turn,' he said. 'Why are you here?'

His expression was hard to fathom. By profession he was an expert at hiding his thoughts and emotions, she supposed. But when she gave a hazy answer about an article she was working on, he looked a bit dejected.

Or is that wishful thinking?

She held her body tightly, wanting him to stay longer.

Then he thumbed towards a wine barrel table flanked by beer keg stools. 'Might be quieter.' His voice had taken a deeper tone.

They transferred spots and then sat in awkward silence. She busied herself with peeling the label off her beer bottle, while Franklin rocked on his stool, watching her.

She felt his tension but was shocked when he abruptly leaned forward. She jolted at the light pressure of his fingertips on her skin as he touched her puffy, bruised jaw and tilted her chin.

'Did your boyfriend do this?' His touch was gentle, but anger simmered.

'What?' she stammered, never anticipating people thinking AJ had hurt her. Not physically.

'No, of course not.' She drew back slightly, sad when a flash of hurt crossed his face. 'I had a little accident, but everything's cool.' *What a dumb answer. It's battered-partner stuff.*

'Georgie.' His deep voice made her name sound exotic. 'You would tell me if he'd hurt you, wouldn't you?'

She nodded, meeting Franklin's eyes. She laid a hand on his for a moment. 'I would tell you, but he really didn't.'

They fell silent again. Then, Georgie and Franklin both took slugs of their beers. They gradually unwound as the jukebox played an assortment of old and new tunes, chiefly rock, a bit of country. The pub was crowded, and all the tables were full. Franklin's mates had caught up with others and again hovered next to the pool table waiting for a game. The stools that had been in front of the long bar when Georgie had arrived were now arranged into circles and occupied, while other patrons propped on the counter or mantelpiece or stood with arms crossed, their elbow crooks becoming stubby rests.

Before long, Georgie couldn't remember a night when she'd felt so good, yet drunk so little. In a second of sentimentality, she likened it to tripping into a corny musical. Luckily, she kept that to herself.

They sat close; the volume of the bar made conversation tricky, but she knew they'd inched a little nearer than necessary. The almost-touch of their thighs and occasional brush of arms or hands as they reached for their drinks was electric. So wrong but so right.

A woman leaned against the bar. She faced Georgie, sending daggers.

'Do you know her?'

Franklin half-turned and rubbed his ear as he settled back. 'Yeah, she's a mate. Talitha.'

Georgie suspected there was more to the subject but let it drop. It was probably best not to know.

Their bottles were empty, but getting up would breach their connection. She ran a moistened finger over the foil of the chip bag to savour every spicy speck, watching him talk, as she licked her finger.

They bounced over an array of topics – except for her exact purpose in town, AJ, and Franklin's love life. She ribbed him for barracking for the Tigers, the league's wooden spooners bar one that season. He snorted over her footy team, labelling her *one of those feral Pies supporters*. He chuckled. So much character in that angular face.

Later, a young woman joined Franklin's buddies at the pool table. Petite, with long dark hair and olive skin, she stared at Georgie. Her attitude was harder to fathom than Talitha's.

'Another of your groupies, Franklin?'

He turned, waved and chafed his chin, rasping his five o'clock shadow. 'That's Sam, our probationary connie.'

'Oh?' She lifted a brow, pulling it down quickly. She had no right to be jealous.

Franklin said, 'Nice girl, smart. She'll make a good cop.'

Georgie relaxed. They fell back into conversation as if they'd known each other for years.

Too soon, last drinks was called. They stretched their final beers and Georgie felt Franklin battling with himself over what to say.

Manny was packing up chairs, wiping counters, and had turned off a few lights. They had to say goodnight.

'I, er.' Franklin faltered. 'It was really good to see you.' He looked pained.

Georgie gently pressed her fingertips on his. She tried to say goodnight. Goodnight rather than what could be, really should be, their last goodbye. The words choked.

Finally, she managed, 'If I don't see you, have a nice Christmas.' Immediately, she despised her lameness but Franklin's nod made it clear he was struggling too.

He leaned in as if to kiss her and she held her breath, body still with shock and desire, mind in a silent battle over tipping her face so that their lips didn't meet, making it a kiss between friends, not another lie to keep from AJ. She felt his soft warm breath on her skin that already tingled with electricity. Then he veered away at the last second and her breath escaped in a long, silent sigh.

The spell of the past few hours shattered and they parted.

Georgie drifted towards the room she'd booked for the night, then felt lured to the window, like a moth to light. She watched Franklin chat to his mates and drive away.

Long after they'd gone, she still stood there, her breath whispering on the glass.

CHAPTER THIRTY-SEVEN

LAST NIGHT'S HAD BEEN ANOTHER RESTLESS, PATCHY sleep as Georgie's brain was overbusy. Songs, snippets of conversations, and wistful thoughts competed with her plans for finding Goyne and the two stories she owed Bullock. One was on Goyne, if her instincts proved right and she could track him and the truth down; the second was the feature she'd been assigned in the first place, and she hoped Ally would still be at its centre.

Tired but fuelled by adrenaline, she tried her wireless – it was still cactus, so her first task today would be a return to Daylesford Library to complete the title searches on the Yandoit property.

Then she'd hang around places everyone had to go some time or other, on the slim chance of sighting her mugger or Goyne.

Her only other idea was revisiting the lake, again hoping she might stumble across signs of Goyne or his mate. Then, it'd be home, unless she cracked a lead.

Meanwhile, she put Franklin and last night out of her

mind. Ditto for AJ and the second Bullock story. For now, she could only think about Goyne.

———

Franklin viewed the café façade, stifling a yawn. Full of regrets, sleep had eluded him. He should've asked Georgie about her boyfriend – although he sensed things might be rocky, she hadn't said anything directly and he was too gutless to ask, in case she was wildly happy; he should've suggested they meet up again while she was still in town; and, he wished he'd kissed her. If he'd done that, maybe he'd be wiser as to how she really felt about him. And maybe shattered.

Behind him, the proprietor set up tables and chairs on the sloped pavement. Franklin noticed that Benji's movements were hectic as he went through the motions of business as usual, except for the graffiti defiling the bow window and twin-panelled entrance doors of his shop.

Franklin asked, 'No break-in?'

'No,' Benji confirmed, propping menus behind salt and pepper shakers, and sprigs of fresh holly into squat vases.

'Nothing taken, either?'

'Nuh-uh.'

'And you came in this morning to open up and found that?'

'Yes.' Benji sounded tetchy.

Sam spoke softly from Franklin's side, '"Killer-lovers – enter at risk". Same MO as the mower, boss.'

Franklin had reached that conclusion too. Similar reference to murder, style of lettering, blood red paint. This was aimed at Jones and his supporters. But he needed the owner to fill in the gaps.

Benji put hands on his hips and looked directly at them for the first time. His eyes were red-veined and swollen underneath.

'What are you –' His demand dwindled as a voice cut in.

'He needs coffee. Can't you see how upset he is?' The speaker rushed past, threw a protective arm around Benji and squeezed.

Franklin nodded, saying, 'Sam, move the crowd back. I'll take this inside.'

The young constable faced the throng and lifted her palms like stop signs. 'Let's make some room. Any of you folks see anything helpful?'

'I won't take too much of your time,' Franklin promised.

'Can I get you a coffee?' Benji offered. Without waiting for an answer, he added, 'Sit! Sit!' He waved Franklin to an old church pew. 'Van,' he beckoned to his partner, 'come help.'

Franklin chose a spot where he could observe the street and most of the narrow shop's interior, while the two blokes fussed behind the counter. The hissing coffee machine obscured their exchange.

Minutes later, they pulled up chairs opposite him at the long wooden table.

Franklin inhaled and sipped the brew. 'Good coffee.' He opened with, 'This attack appears personal, fellas.'

They traded a glance.

'Wanna tell me about it?'

Benji leaned on his elbows, tucking tight knuckles under his nose. Franklin studied his face, as he took another swallow of coffee.

Next, he eyed Van, seeing him grow apoplectic.

Within the minute, Van exploded. 'Well! If you're not going to tell him!'

'Of course I'm going to tell him,' Benji bickered.

Franklin rubbed a hand over mouth and chin, secreting the tickle of a smile.

Still observing the blokes, he became aware of Sam's voice, authoritative even from a distance. 'Step back. You are encroaching on a crime scene.'

She had things in hand outside. More than he could claim here. Frustrated, he asked, 'Do I need to hazard a guess?'

Benji squeezed his eyes shut. He exhaled and gazed at Franklin. 'Marc Jones is my cousin.'

'Go on.'

'We lost touch after he shifted to Warrnambool with my uncle after his parents divorced, but when he returned to town, he re-inherited a whole tribe. Family.' Benji tilted his head. 'Isn't that what matters? What everything's about?'

Franklin had twenty-plus years of professional experience dealing with the most dysfunctional of families, along with seeing ordinary ones shatter in the domino effect of tragic events, but it wouldn't pay to disagree. He nodded.

'So when he became entangled in the Hudson mess –'

Entangled? Causative more like it.

'And you police arrested him.'

'Questioned yes, arrested no,' Franklin said mildly.

Van shot him a glare.

With another slow head-tilt, Benji continued. 'Fine. After the police *questioned* Marc and released him of any wrongdoing, naturally the family felt a celebration in order.'

'A celebration?'

Benji flushed. 'Yes, a private dinner party.'

'Just family?'

'Uh-huh.'

Franklin put two and two together. 'Here, by chance?'

'Yes.'

His brow creased as he reversed the last bits of the conversation. *Uh-huh* hadn't been convincing. 'Just family?' he repeated.

'*We-ll.*' Benji sounded like Elizabeth Montgomery in her *Bewitched* days. He sideways-glanced to his partner. 'And a few friends. We, er, may have put it on our Facebook page.'

Franklin repressed his groan. 'May have?'

'We only posted to our friends.'

'Of course,' Franklin said, thinking that plenty of Kat's schoolmates had thousands of Facebook friends. Friend was a much looser term than when he'd been a kid. 'So, you held a party for Marc Jones. Here. Which you invited your family and friends to via a social networking site, so potentially a large number of people were aware of it.'

The blokes nodded. One was glum; the other blushed.

'And the writer of the paint job outside, do you know who it is?'

'We wish,' Van answered for them both, but Franklin figured Benji was right when he said it's all about family and that the rational place to start would be Neil Hudson's nearest and dearest.

———

Three thousand years later, the Landata home page opened. Georgie navigated to the next screen and rubbed her hands together, muttering, 'Promising so far.'

She registered on the Victorian land search service and

waited as the computer whirred. She began to sweat on whether the site would crash again.

It didn't. She typed in the property information for Uncle Ken's neighbour and waited, then followed a few more steps, made payment and finally printed a copy of the subdivision plan.

She worked out which plot was Uncle Ken's and, armed with those specs, completed a fresh search. The computer did its sluggish grind again. She wondered if it'd show Ken, Goyne or a stranger as the current owner.

The screen changed, and Georgie skimmed down it.

CHAPTER THIRTY-EIGHT

MONICA STAGGERED AND LEANED AGAINST THE doorjamb. 'Yes?' She looked at Franklin with dead eyes. No recognition, no curiosity.

'Can we come in for a quick chat?'

She did a sparrow-like twitch as something infiltrated her consciousness. 'About Neil?' she slurred.

Alcohol fumes wafted up Franklin's nostrils. How much had she drunk?

Monica's legs sagged. Sam reacted instantly, supporting the frail woman and leading her to the couch.

Franklin let his offsider settle the widow, fuss with a cushion and make a cup of coffee.

Monica sipped her cuppa. 'A drop of rum?' She pushed her mug towards Sam, spilling liquid.

Sam cut her eyes to Franklin and he cut to the rum bottle on the coffee table. It was empty. He wouldn't give it to the widow in her state anyway.

'Here you go, Mrs Hudson.' Sam pretended to add a drop and passed the mug back. 'Drink up.'

Monica gulped obediently.

Franklin watched her, pity stirring his guts. She shouldn't be alone. He wondered why she'd left her mother's home in Creswick.

She answered his unspoken question, mumbling, 'I had to come home. Mum's great but I felt suffocated. I need to be here. With Neil.'

He knew she meant it figuratively because Neil was in the morgue, but he shuddered. 'Have your friends been supporting you?' seemed an innocuous segue into the café graffiti.

Her head wavered and chin dropped to her chest. A pill bottle slipped from her sleeve.

Alarmed, Franklin patted her arm. 'Monica?'

No response. How many pills had she ingested with straight alcohol?

'Monica. Open your eyes.' He squeezed her shoulder. 'Sam, call the –' He shut up, realising she was already on the blower, requesting an ambulance.

———

While Georgie scouted out the chemist, newsagency and banks on Vincent Street, she made calls using the information she'd gleaned from the title search.

She'd lucked out on spotting Goyne or her mugger so far, but finally reached the new owner of the Yandoit property.

After he had identified himself, she said, 'Thanks for calling back. I'm trying to get in touch with the family of Uncle Ken.' She ran through her spiel, thinking it was only a stretch of the truth.

'*I'm sorry.*' He sounded it too. '*But I'm not related and never met them. My purchase was all done through the real estate agent and my solicitor.'*

So another dead end. Damn shame.

Likewise for the TAB betting agency and supermarkets, although she didn't linger long at each point. Then, Georgie found herself at the lake about twenty-two hours after her previous visit, one parking space to the right and clenching the Spider's steering wheel.

I really don't want to do this. But I really have to.

She dropped her feet to the ground and twisted out of the convertible. After checking the lock twice, Georgie gave the door a pat.

She couldn't leave Daylesford without doing this but was admittedly fearful of running into her mugger again here. On the busy main street would've been safer. But the feeling that she'd missed something yesterday was overwhelming.

———

Franklin called to Sam, 'How long are they saying for the ambos?'

She glared at him, clearly straining to hear the other person. She spoke into the mobile and threw her spare hand skyward.

'Hold, please.' She addressed Franklin, 'Still another ten minutes. At best.'

The district prided itself on a ten to fifteen-minute response time. Due to a heart attack, tractor accident and an imminent birthing, the paramedics were stretched to capacity and more than twenty minutes had gone since Monica Hudson's collapse.

In the last few minutes, Monica's lips and skin had lost

colour, her breathing turned shallow and irregular. Franklin feared another ten minutes could be fatal.

He weighed the stakes of moving an unconscious casualty. She'd been walking earlier, or rather, staggering. So there was significantly less spinal danger transporting her than someone they'd discovered out cold on the floor and an exorbitant risk in doing nothing but wait and observe.

Franklin gathered the small woman into a fireman's lift.

'Sam, get the door. We're taking her to A&E.'

———

Georgie skirted the stone pavilion with her mind on Goyne and his mate. She continually turned, searching the scene, determined not to be ambushed.

She started with the women's toilet, which wasn't really warranted, but she'd hate to wonder later. Of course, it was empty, with no signs of recent use. The middle room was unoccupied too.

Next, she stood where she'd collided with the wet-haired guy. Someone might be inside, who may or may not be Goyne or her mugger. Either way, she couldn't enter the men's toilet without warning.

'Hello?' Her call bounced off the walls, while her inner voice chanted *Are you ready, Harvey? Damn straight I am.*

Georgie went in.

———

North, then up Stanley Street, left onto Central Springs, right at Camp Street, past the cop shop. Franklin cut off a sedan and zipped over Raglan. Up Jamieson and left into

Hospital Street. A little under two kilometres and three minutes later, he pulled the truck into the accident and emergency bay.

Sam had given the hospital a heads-up and a team stood-by. They had the passenger rear door open before Franklin turned off the ignition and offloaded the inert woman onto a hydraulic stretcher. They drew an oxygen mask over Monica's face, rattled questions at him while they hastened for the automatic doors, and took the pill bottle from Sam.

Franklin could breathe properly now. Monica was in safe hands, already getting treatment. And if she needed more specialist help, ambos would transfer her to Ballarat or Melbourne.

As the trauma entourage sped inside, he started to follow, but Sam cried, 'Boss, callout.'

———

Unless someone was behind one of the cubicle doors, the room was vacant. Georgie kept her back to the wall, and an eye on the doorway in case Goyne, his mate or some unsuspecting male entered, and started her inspection of the men's toilet block.

She wanted to be out of here but needed a lead. *Think.* She frowned. *There's something about this place. I feel it.*

But she'd thought that about the Yandoit farm too. And it seemed she'd struck out there.

She did another full scan of the room. It was a mirror image of the ladies' washroom with a vast central space, couple of toilet cubicles, single basin and one rubbish bin. She did a double-take to the bin, stepped closer and peered inside.

The ladies' bin had been virtually empty; this was almost full. She tipped the contents onto the concrete floor and raked through the debris with her hand swathed in clean paper towel.

Lots of crumpled towelling, a bunch of scrunched tissues, but among the crap, gold: yesterday's newspaper, a crushed milk carton, paracetamol blister sheet, baked beans tins and a blunt razor.

Georgie fist-pumped, taking it as proof that at least one male had used the pavilion, either to sleep here or for toilet and washing facilities. Goyne and his mate, she bet.

———

'You've got to be joking,' Franklin grumbled.

The young constable glanced at him sharply. Her face looked like a giant question mark. He read fear that she'd stuffed up her rare opportunity of driving, even though she'd babied the truck from go to whoa.

'Not you, Sam. The garage wall.'

She followed his finger up the driveway and groaned too.

Same scarlet paint, written in the same style, this time: 'Kill and run: Mr Murder hides here.'

'I guess we've worked out where Marc Jones has been staying since the incident,' Franklin remarked.

They exited the truck, as a woman erupted from the house, screaming and her arms flailing.

She was covered in blood.

Franklin ran his gaze over her as she raced towards him, looking for obvious injuries or weapons, automatically evaluating danger. 'Ma'am. Are you hurt?'

He noted details. Her lilac T-shirt was spattered red,

and she was flicking blood off her hands. He didn't have the full picture yet. Was she the victim or offender? Did she have a concealed weapon?

'You have to come!'

'Ma'am, please calm down.' Franklin raised his palms.

The woman gulped a breath.

Franklin noticed that Sam had fanned out three metres. Smart position for backup if the situation turned nasty.

The woman started to pant. 'Come! Inside!' Each word held a rising inflection. She took choking breaths. 'Look what they've done!'

They?

Franklin needed to assess what they'd encounter inside the house. In a moderated tone, he said, 'I'm Senior Constable John Franklin and this is Constable Sam Tesorino. What's your name?'

'Lorraine.' Her gaze held puzzlement but at least she'd stopped jumping around.

'Okay, Lorraine. Who's hurt?'

'Come and look what they've done!' She was worked up again.

He tried asking a different way. 'Can you tell us what the story is here?'

She nodded and inhaled more steadily than before. 'They spray-painted my garage.'

'They? Do you know who?'

'No, they were already gone when I came back from the shops.'

Lorraine paused and Franklin waved for her continue.

'They got inside somehow. I'm not quite sure I locked up,' she admitted.

Franklin wanted to shake her, but he'd give her a safety lecture later. 'And once they got in?'

'They sprayed an outline on the kitchen floor.'

'An outline, Lorraine?'

She leaned in and whispered, 'Like they do on tellie crime scenes.' Wide-eyed, she added, 'Of a body. A homicide.'

American TV shows have a lot to answer for.

With Lorraine now in close range, Franklin examined the spatter on her clothing and sticky mess on her skin and picked up a distinctive odour.

'That's paint, isn't it, Lorraine?'

She looked at her palms and frowned at Franklin. 'Yes. I tried to wipe it off the floor. Wasn't thinking.'

Paint, not blood. If the Hudson death weren't such a tragedy and messing with so many people's lives, he would've laughed at his fuck-up.

CHAPTER THIRTY-NINE

GEORGIE SQUATTED BESIDE HER REAR LEFT TYRE. 'Shit!' She leaned her forehead against the Spider's quarter panel and shut her eyes. After a deep sigh, she inspected the tyre and the bitumen around it, but couldn't see an offending spike, broken glass or similar cause for the flat, although it could be stuck between the compound and tarred road.

Was she just unlucky? Instinct told her to check the other tyres. She skimmed forward and saw another flat on the front passenger wheel.

She swore again but it didn't help, especially when she walked around the other side of the convertible and saw those tyres were pancakes.

Someone had declared war.

———

Franklin strained through the windscreen. 'Sam, slow down.'

Their callout had been to Creek Street, and they were

returning to the station via Leggatt Street. What he saw in the lake car park set off butterflies in his stomach.

'Don't turn. Go straight up and grab a park,' he told the constable.

She nosed into a space and waited.

'I need a minute. Stay in the truck or grab some air but don't go too far in case we get another job. I suspect it's going to be one of those days.'

Sam lifted her chin and gave a solemn nod. He sensed her gaze as he approached the sporty black car.

First, he noticed it was empty. Then he spotted two flats. 'Bloody hell.' He circled the other side and realised all four were punctured.

He found Georgie sitting on the ground several metres from her convertible, sight fixed in the distance.

'Got yourself a spot of bother, Georgie?'

She jumped. 'Shit.' She gave him a dirty look. 'You shouldn't sneak up on a person.'

He laughed and after a few seconds, she joined in.

———

Georgie watched Franklin confer with his female partner, happy to see him but wishing it wasn't because she was in another mess. One tyre, she'd have fixed it with the spare; four was an expensive pain in the butt.

He gestured to her car, explaining something. His partner nodded and waved as Franklin walked back to Georgie.

He crouched down, slid off his sunglasses and peered at her. 'Four deliberate punctures is extreme.'

She replied with lifted shoulders and a wry smile. 'This would never happen in Melbourne.'

He chuckled, yet looked unconvinced. 'It seems aggressive, personal. You're sure you don't know who did this?'

She shook her head.

'Have you had other troubles? Is it connected with those bruises?'

Georgie dodged both questions, answering honestly, 'I didn't see anything and don't know who did it.'

Franklin's eyes narrowed. 'Sam's making inquiries. Someone may've seen something.'

So few people were nearby that Georgie doubted it.

Franklin asked a couple more questions, then reclined beside her on the lawn, propped on an elbow facing the lake. The scene felt so surreal that she gave herself a pinch on the thigh.

It's real.

She peeked sideways and did a covert inspection. One leg extended, the other bent, his blue work trousers puckered at the knee. The leather belt on his hips was bulky with a daunting array of gear. She tilted; yes, pistol in the holster and all. His short-sleeved work shirt stretched across defined pecs and biceps, and a little wispy chest hair escaped at the collar. He wore a small closed-mouth smile, but the lines around his eyes scored deeper than usual.

'Tough day so far?'

With a whistling sigh, Franklin answered, 'Yeah, you could say that.'

'Can you talk about it?' She wasn't sure if he was allowed to or would want to.

He didn't speak but shifted to lay long, fingers clasped behind his head and eyes shut. Georgie breathed with the rise and fall of his chest, wondering if he'd answer.

Franklin's eyes flicked open. 'I shouldn't. But I'm struggling.'

She guessed he didn't admit that too often.

'A few days ago, a love triangle situation blew up...and we came in to find the hubby lying on the floor, not looking good.'

'Oh, no.'

He nodded. 'I tried to revive him, Georgie.' He turned miserable eyes on her. 'I couldn't bring him back.'

She touched his shoulder lightly.

'So now, the wife is suddenly a widow, and I know her —well, I did back when she was friends with my ex—which always makes it worse, somehow. She's shattered and either deliberately or accidentally OD'd on a sedative and alcohol cocktail this morning. We got her to the hospital before our last job. Meanwhile, the dead bloke's mates or relos are persecuting the lover via a spate of ugly vandalism.'

Franklin stopped and sighed.

Her chest constricted.

'I don't know how far they'll go. Jesus, all this fallout from one affair could only happen in the country.' He broke off.

Georgie couldn't think what to say. She heard distant children's giggles and a car engine fire. All too happy and innocent, considering what Franklin had just shared.

She glanced down, clueless how to help. 'The paint on your boots. Is that from the vandalism?'

Franklin sat up to examine them and muttered as he scraped off the red paint with a stubby fingernail. 'Uh-huh. And you know what?' He stopped scraping. 'That isn't all. We've also had a run of break-ins and graffiti. It'd be convenient to think it's all related, but it's looking like we have at least two distinct groups of vandals, actually three including the fallout from Neil's death.'

'An awful lot for a small town.'

'Yeah, things are usually quiet around here.' His lips twitched as he said, 'It must be you, Harvey. You attract trouble.'

Georgie whacked him. 'Huh.' She huffed but smiled, then lay next to him, covering her face with crossed forearms.

He said, 'Your turn.'

Georgie wiggled her toes in her sandals, thinking, until Franklin prodded her ribs.

'What? Is the tyre guy here?'

'Ha ha.' He clearly didn't buy her confusion. 'C'mon, tell me. Why are you back, and what gives with that black-and-blue jaw and the four punctures on your Alfa?'

She attached a proviso before starting. 'Promise this won't end up in a lecture?'

He blew out his lips. 'I don't think I can promise that, but I'll try. How's that?'

Georgie considered it. *What the hell?* She was keen to pitch her theories to him.

She sketched him the story of Ally…that her father was believed dead but no body found.

'It got me thinking, what if he didn't die? What if he copped amnesia and can't remember who he is and how to get home?' Georgie paused. 'And *then* I got to thinking.' She whispered, 'What if he didn't die and wasn't injured but deserted his life?'

With a doubting frown, Franklin said, 'But why would he do that?'

She shrugged.

'And what proof have you got that he's alive?'

'As much proof as they have to say he's dead. Up until this.' She pointed to her cheek. 'And that.' She pointed to her car.

'Holy shit.'

She nodded, smiling grimly.

———

After Georgie finished her story, Franklin absolutely wanted to give her a lecture about getting into dangerous situations. And he wanted to nail the bastard for hurting her.

Then her mobile rang. He eavesdropped on her side of the conversation, trying not to make it obvious.

'At the moment...yes, later today...not sure when I'll be home yet.'

Her eyes cut towards her disabled convertible but she didn't explain to the caller, who he presumed to be her boyfriend at the mention of *home*.

'Don't be like that. What's your problem?'

Now Georgie pinned her gaze on him, and he wondered why. She turned away and clutched the phone to her ear. Franklin strained so he could still listen.

'I'm here on a story; you know that...no, there's nothing else going on. Oh, piss off, AJ.'

She disconnected.

———

Franklin's mouth hung open, but to Georgie's amusement, he didn't have a chance to say anything, because the tyre guy arrived.

The middle-aged truckie jumped down from his cabin, waving. 'Hey, I'm Pete.'

He trotted the perimeter of her car, then regarded her with a seen-it-all-before-but-what-a-beauty expression. 'Geez, you've done a top job of it, love.'

Georgie felt her eyes wince at the *love*.

Still chuckling, the guy plucked a phone from his shirt pocket and speed-dialled. 'Hey, boss. Yep. Full set. Hang on.' Pete bent over and recited the specs from one of the tyres.

He listened, nodded, then said, 'Yep. Ya-huh. Okey-dokey. I'll get Jay to give her a tow.'

He disconnected and dialled again, speaking before Georgie could cut in. 'Jay, buddy...yeah, good, good. Need a tow, from the lake. Classic Alfa convertible with four flats.'

Georgie waved, trying to get Pete's attention.

Oblivious, he continued, 'Ya-huh. Back to Phil's. Cheers, mate.' He hung up. 'Bad news, love. We don't have four of these in stock.' He nudged a tyre with his toe.

She tried to cut in. 'But I need –'

'So, I've got Jay coming across. He's one of the mechanics in town. He'll load her up and take her to Phil's.' He patted the Spider's black flank.

'Should be able to get you sorted tomorrow.' Pete wrinkled his nose. 'Providing we can get a set in from Melbourne. If we can't get 'em by tomorrow, geez, you'll be out of luck then.'

He counted on his fingers. 'Christmas Day Saturday, Boxing Day Sunday and then Monday and Tuesday are public holidays in lieu, so it'd probably be next Wednesday if it's not tomorrow.' He screwed his face. 'Sorry, love. But Phil'll do his best to see you right.'

Georgie's stomach pitted. *What the hell am I going to do?*

———

Towards the end of the shift, Franklin hooked the four-wheel drive keys onto the board and trailed Sam into the muster room. She busied herself with paperwork.

Despite the rough beginning to their day, his worries that the Hudson-Jones saga would escalate further hadn't eventuated. They'd been busy, with no opportunity to progress the various vandalism, property damage, and theft cases, but it'd all been pretty routine after he'd seen Georgie off in his old-faithful SS Commodore.

Sam had been too quiet since, and he guessed why. He still had sympathy for her hero worship-turned-crush but was also frustrated. That stuff didn't belong on the job, and he thought he'd made it clear the other night they weren't getting involved. Not in words, but he'd hoped pulling away was a kind yet blatant rebuff.

Sam had to get over it and get on with the job because there'd never be anything between them.

He sighed, thinking the same could probably be said for him and Georgie. At least he'd get to see her one more time when she returned for her Spider and handed back the Commodore.

CHRISTMAS EVE

CHAPTER FORTY

GEORGIE'S BRAIN POUNDED. 'I NEED A TIME-OUT, Bron.'

'You're soft,' her mate retorted. 'This is the woman who trundles off to the country, gets mugged, her tyres ruined and wants to return ASAP for more trouble. Yet she can't hack shopping?'

'The same Christmas songs over and over are doing my head in.' Georgie frowned.

'Did we have too much fun with Mr Champagne last night? Have you got a sore head? Boo-hoo.' Bron dug a knuckle into the corner of her eye in a mock sook.

'It was all work.' Georgie groaned. 'And I only had three glasses. Now I remember why I don't drink bubbly.' She moaned again. 'There are people *everywhere.*'

'What do you expect, leaving it to the day before Chrissie?'

'I used to think you were a nice person.'

Bron chucked her under the chin. 'You still do, GG. But you need tough love.'

With an exaggerated sigh, Georgie replied, 'Coffee break?'

———

The night before Christmas, a time to sip eggnog, sing along to *Carols by Candlelight* and wrap pressies. In the Disney world, not the real one. In reality, Franklin had drawn the Christmas Eve twilight shift and the festive season wasn't bringing out the best in everyone. Rostered on with him was Sam, who swung between warm to cool, continuing from yesterday.

They were ducking in and out of the station Chrissie party between callouts, the last being a brawl between two teenagers and they'd just picked up a doozy apparently involving alcohol, aggression, and cars.

They shot through town, then up Ajax Road, which stretched between Daylesford and Hepburn. Apart from a reference to *near Jimmy's Track,* the anonymous triple zero caller had been vague.

'Drag racing?' Sam asked.

Franklin focused ahead. 'Could be.'

They passed the rubbish tip on the left and he eased off the accelerator as bitumen merged with purple-red gravel. Sam swayed against the passenger door as he cornered. They whipped through a forest of lanky gum trees and the speedo edged towards ninety Ks.

Franklin said, 'We're not far now. Another curve and we might be able to see...'

He leaned forward, dropping a little speed to take the bend. Then he slammed on the brakes and shot an arm across Sam.

The patrol car skidded to a stop mere metres from a

roadblock formed by two sedans and a ute. Empty, stationary with doors wide open. A bunch of people were punching the crap out of each other in the middle of the road.

Merry Christmas. Peace on earth and goodwill to all mankind.

Franklin reversed back to the bend and parked across the road with strobes on so that other drivers would have ample warning. He swung out of the car, annoyed at the idiots involved.

'Sam, set up flashers to secure the road on the other side but give these brawlers a wide berth.'

She nodded and followed his instructions.

'Cut it out!' Franklin yelled.

The brawlers ignored him, and his blood pressure hiked.

'Stop! Now!' He approached the fray. 'Police! If you hadn't noticed.'

Not that bells and fairy lights on the cop car aren't pretty fucking obvious.

One blood-spattered face turned towards him. *Damo.*

Damo's opponent also spun around. *Marc Jones, again.*

The others halted too, lacerated knuckles held in mid-air, frozen in street-fighting stance. A female included. Franklin scanned the crowd. He recognised Shane Hudson, brother of the deceased. Two others rang a bell, but he couldn't place them. The woman might be Lorraine from yesterday's bloody-paint job, but he couldn't be sure because her face was a mess.

'Right. This will go much better for you all if you do as I say.'

He stopped to let it sink in. Sam came alongside him.

'Separate. Each of you step away five metres. Don't look. Don't touch. Don't talk to anybody else. Got it?'

To his amazement, they complied.

'Now. Does anyone require an ambulance?'

Nobody replied.

'Sam, I think that's Lorraine from yesterday over there. It may not be as bad as it seems. Glove up, check it out and call it in if you think an ambo is warranted.'

The constable approached the injured woman, and Franklin returned his attention to the mass. 'We're going to talk to you individually. That's going to take a while. But we can't leave the road blocked; it's dangerous. So, I'm going to take your names. After that, the owner of each vehicle is going to make them safe and then wait until I'm ready to speak with you. Got it?'

They all gazed at him, mute and unmoving.

He glared back at them. *I'm missing Christmas Eve with my daughter to deal with you knuckleheads.*

———

Franklin looked at each person seated around the table. Cuts had been cleaned, drunks had sobered, and even Lorraine resembled a human again.

The café proprietor and his partner owned this place. A twenty-five-acre hideaway near the corner of Jimmy's Track and Ajax Road, the intended destination of Marc Jones and a couple of his other cousins before he'd been intercepted by the emotionally frayed Shane Hudson and his cohorts.

In character, the two hosts served their unexpected guests with fancy coffees and teas, mince pies and Christmas tree-shaped shortbread. Monica Hudson perched in the middle, having been collected by her brother-in-law and Sam a little earlier. Supporters of both camps saw that the listless widow had a cup of tea and something to eat and fretted over her.

Franklin was bothered by one thing – that Sam was shooting him wonderstruck looks again. But truth be told, he was quietly chuffed with himself too.

———

Later, Franklin rode the Ninja home, thinking over what he'd said to Sam: 'We've got five minutes to end of shift to get the rest of the barbecue bash cleaned up. Then we're out of here.'

She'd clapped, making the pompom on her Santa hat bounce, then slid a plate of leftover sausages into the fridge.

After more than twenty years in the job, Franklin knew if shit hit the fan, it happened at Christmas. It was one of the worst times for suicide attempts, family brawls, and accidents fuelled by alcohol, speeding, or both. He and Sam had gotten off relatively lightly, but whoever worked the day shift would cop the full chaos of Christmas.

He snuck in the front door but as always after a late finish felt knackered, and yet too wired to go to bed. He tiptoed into the lounge room and shucked off his boots.

Kat had left the side lamp on. In the subtle light, tinsel on the Christmas tree twinkled, and a light breeze from the window fluttered the strings of cards over the mantel.

Franklin sank into his favourite armchair, spied a covered plate on the coffee table and reached for the note alongside.

'Dear Santa-Dad, Merry Xmas! Your beer's in the fridge. What Santa needs after a long hard night? See you soon. Luv K xx'

He chuckled, retrieved the stubby from the fridge and took a long draught. Then he lifted the cover and dived into the plate of White Christmas, a treat he and Kat began making together for Santa in the era of her inaugural tourist train ride. After one of the neighbourhood boys had disenchanted her about the jolly, red-suited fat man, she had taken over. Every year she tried a different recipe, and tonight's might be her best yet.

He sighed again and closed his eyes with his beer resting on the chair arm. A small smile crinkled his features. Images flitted through his mind. Of his daughter arranging the fresh White Christmas for his return. Of the Hudson and Jones clans all around one table, a truce drawn, and young Sam's impressed expression. Of the fun at the station Chrissie bash.

Overall, the upsides of the past few days far outshone the negatives.

Inevitably, he drifted to the taboo. The person he'd like to see on Christmas morning or, more truthfully, wake up next to.

Franklin drained his stubby and moodily dumped the empty into the recycling bin. He cringed at the noise and sent a silent apology to Kat.

CHAPTER FORTY-ONE

RAUCOUS KNOCKING AT NINE O'CLOCK ROUSED GEORGIE from the sofa. She flung open the front door, and hugs from Bron and her partner, Jo Holt, practically sent her sprawling.

The next few minutes went in a confusion of Christmas greetings, inbound parcels and an esky of foodstuffs for their brekkie feast, with the excited cat and dog underfoot, and cheers after popping the cork of the real champers, a perk of Georgie's recent interview with Mr Champagne.

As Georgie poured and handed out flutes, Bron frowned under her corkscrew fringe. 'Where's AJ?'

Georgie took a long moment to answer. 'He asked me last night if I genuinely wanted to go to his parents' for lunch today. I hesitated. He knows his olds and I are chalk and cheese, but he blew up. He said, "don't bother" and packed a bag.'

She stared at the parcel that sat apart from the others under the pine Christmas tree. The red and green foil tied with gold ribbon held her lie. Everyone thought she'd started and finished her shopping yesterday, but she'd purchased this one after much research and with great secrecy two months ago.

She said, 'He left last night.'

Bron plonked her flute onto the coffee table and rushed to hug her. She asked gently, 'Have you broken up?'

Jo pushed her glasses up the bridge of her nose.

Georgie's eyes pooled. She blinked hard. 'I honestly don't know.' Her stomach was in knots. 'It was only a minor hesitation. He knew I'd go to his parents' lunch.'

Bron looked at her sadly, then over to Jo, who pulled at her mottled hair.

'There shouldn't have been any hesitation. And it's not a matter of *going* to a family event. You have to *be* part of the family,' Jo said.

Georgie couldn't dispute that. 'I know.' She lifted a hand. 'I've always been detached from AJ's family, while he fits right in with mine.' She glanced at Bron, then Jo, admitting, 'Except lately. Little things...' She couldn't finish the thought.

Her best friend clasped Georgie's hand and gave it a kiss. 'You poor thing, GG. It hasn't been right for a long while, has it?'

They went through the motions of Christmas, alternately drifting back to AJ and veering away from the subject.

Bron and Jo were due at Nana Holt's home for lunch for not just each generation of Jo's family, but also a full contingent of the Silvers clan. They'd invited her to join them, then offered to stay with her. Although kindly meant, Georgie thought that highlighted even more how dysfunctional she was and pushed them out the door.

Lonely, she nestled into the sofa and stared at the

champagne bottle. Her cat jumped onto the coffee table and regarded her solemnly.

Then *Waiting for the End* pierced the quietness and Georgie jumped up. She raced to locate her mobile and checked the screen. One part of her deflated; the other did a mental fist pump.

———

Kat wore the cap he'd bought at the market. It looked pretty darned cute on her, and Franklin felt chuffed. He'd got it right, which was no mean feat with a teenage daughter.

'You're wearing the tee I bought you, Dad.'

She grinned and Franklin smoothed his hands over the new cotton shirt. She'd got it right too.

The landline rang and Kat shot the telephone a hopeful glance but didn't move.

Franklin covered the room in a couple of lopes. 'Hey-llo?'

A voice yelled, *'Merry Christmas, Frankie!'*

'Vinnie!' he replied, noting Kat's shoulders slump. It was the fourth call this morning, and each time he'd seen her spark up, then shrink.

Every Christmas and birthday, he witnessed the same bloody thing. Her desperate fucking wish for her selfish mother to remember to ring on the day.

How could that be too much to ask?

———

'Ally! Merry Christmas!'

'Georgie! Merry Christmas to you, too.'

'I didn't expect to –'

301

'Hear from me until after New Year's? I know! Mum mellowed. Isn't it great?'

They exchanged small talk and Georgie's spirits lifted a little. Ally sounded relaxed. Maybe Deb had been right to take her away from Bullock.

While they chatted, Molly trotted into the room and lay on Georgie's feet. Phoebe stepped on the dog to climb into her lap, then made a nest, purring. Mixed emotions swamped Georgie as she stroked Phoebe and listened to the teen rave about Torquay, talking little herself.

'You sound sad today.'

Caught off-guard, Georgie verged on admitting it but swallowed it down. 'I'm fine.'

Her words hung for a moment, then Ally said, 'We're going to my aunt and uncle's place for lunch. We'll need to leave soon. What about you?'

Georgie pictured a long table set with fine crystal, china, and linen. A traditional roast turkey feast, with plum pudding and brandy sauce after, and a different wine served with each course. The Gunnerson family lunch she was no longer going to.

'Nothing for lunch, but I'll be seeing my family tonight.'

What was meant to sound nonchalant came across melancholy.

'Oh, that's sad.'

Georgie didn't want Ally to dwell on it. 'When will you be going home?'

'Day after New Year's probably.'

Georgie massaged her bruised jaw. She had to ask, and there was no subtle way to put it. 'Did your dad know other people in Yandoit or Daylesford?'

Ally's pause was agonising.

Finally, she said, 'I s'pose. A few to wave to.'

'No special or close friends?' Georgie pictured her mugger. 'A younger relative?' She gripped the phone, hanging on Ally's answer.

'No, no relatives. And I can't think of any young friends. My age?'

'A bit older?' Georgie tried to act casual.

Ally asked, *'What's this about?'* Her tone was high, thin.

'Loose ends for my story. That's all.' The veins in Georgie's temple thumped. She felt terrible for lying and had to ask another hard question. 'Ally.'

She heard a muffled noise, then, *'Okay, Mum.'* Ally's voice sounded clearer when she said, *'I've gotta go, we're heading off to lunch.'*

'Could I –'

'I'll try to ring you tomorrow. Hope you have a nice night with your family, Georgie. Merry Christmas!'

Defeated for the time being, she returned, 'Merry Christmas, Ally.'

Georgie put the phone down and looked around the room. The house was too quiet. She raided the fridge and nibbled on a marinated chicken wing left over from the morning. She tossed the bones onto her plate and sighed.

She listened to Molly softly snoring and considered her choices.

One was to continue wallowing. Her second option was to contact AJ. The third included anything but one and two.

She had an open invitation to join Ruby and Michael's Christmas party next door, and although they'd come with her to her family do later, right now she wanted to be where a horde of people would be talking loudly, and it'd be impossible to feel lonely or not fit in. She left the house, letting the door slam.

———

Despite being lean like her husband, over a foot shorter and more than a decade older than Franklin, Maeve squashed his ribs as she hugged him. She pulled away, studied his face and embraced him again. 'We don't see enough of you, John.'

He bent and kissed her forehead. 'You see me plenty. My daughter virtually lives here.'

She tweaked his cheek. 'That's Kat, not you. How can I be your second mum if you don't come over?'

Ages ago he'd admitted she was like his second mum. It had clearly tickled her.

They laughed, then she adopted a stern expression. 'Have you phoned your mother?'

'He has, we have,' Kat assured. She flung herself into Maeve's arms. 'Nan and Pop are caravanning up the east coast. They've only got from Nowa Nowa to Mallacoota so far, so it looks like we won't see them for ages.' She stretched *ages*.

'Yep, they've travelled a whole two hours in two weeks and are loving it, by all accounts,' Franklin inserted.

Maeve smiled broadly, nodding. Then she ushered them inside the stationhouse, gesturing at the full living room. 'You know everybody. Get yourselves a drink.' She took the basket from Franklin. 'Thanks for bringing this, but you didn't need to – we have plenty.'

Kat dashed away and Franklin greeted the throng. He noted all the familiar culprits. An equal ratio of relatives of the Lunnys, to strays from the station, him and Kat included, along with Harty and Slam.

Minutes later, Maeve called, 'Lunch is up, folks!'

Franklin couldn't help himself and piled his plate. *So what? It's Christmas.* He dug in.

Slam jabbed his elbow into Franklin's side. 'So, tell us how you got the Hudson case sorted.'

He managed to silence the room.

Franklin's cheeks fired. 'We just did our job, Sam and me.' He loaded his fork with pumpkin and peas and hoped his friends would leave it there. *No chance.*

Slam coughed. 'Ahem, too modest, mate. Spit it out.'

Franklin rubbed his jaw, hesitant. 'Well, we split them up and took our time getting their stories while they sobered up.' He sighed. 'Every one of them was hurting.'

A murmur of sympathy rolled around the Christmas table.

Kat rose and moved behind Franklin. She laid a hand on his shoulder. 'Go on, Dad.'

'Well, I figured the worst outcome for everyone involved, would be to take the official road.'

'It's called being a rogue cop.'

'A maverick cop.'

Franklin ignored his mates' interruptions. 'That would've just fuelled the problem and ended up in an all-out war. Leave that sort of stuff for Melbourne. We have better ways.'

'Hear, hear!' cheered Maeve, clinking her wine goblet against her husband's beer glass.

'So I got them to agree – to not press charges, and more importantly, to drop the conflict. Hudson's clan will clean up their graffiti. Jones's lot will cater for Neil's funeral and organise his headstone, and everyone will do their bit to support Monica.'

His daughter's arms snaked around his neck, as she said, 'And *that's* why I'm joining up as soon as I can.'

Everyone talked at once, some cheered.

Kat had alluded to it before. Now she sounded determined. *My daughter, a cop.* Franklin felt proud and terrified.

———

On their return from her family's Christmas dinner, the taxi dropped off Georgie, Ruby, and Michael, and she saw the couple inside, before going home. With a heavy heart, she turned her key in the lock and pushed the door.

Phoebe greeted her with a meow. Georgie heard the retriever's toenails tap across the floorboards, and Molly's wet nose nuzzled her hand seconds later.

She walked up the long narrow hallway to the dark living room, trailed by cat and dog. Georgie knew the red and green parcel would still be unopened. And that she would spend another night alone in their bed.

She sighed and considered a cigarette. Instead, she dropped onto the sofa and tucked her knees under her chin, hugging them into her body. She kept the lights off.

'George.'

She jumped. 'Shit!'

'Sorry, I didn't mean to frighten you.'

She traced his voice to the deepest shadows. 'AJ.'

'Yeah.' Then, an awkward void.

CHAPTER FORTY-TWO

GEORGIE CLEARED THE OUTCROPPING OPEN FIREPLACE and rounded the dining table. AJ was sitting on the sofa beside a pile of bedding. His hair ruffled, face creased, he looked tired, beaten.

She hadn't slept either, and fatigue weighed her body. 'Is this where I say sorry? Because I am.'

His mouth curved into an unhappy smile.

'How about I give you your Christmas present?' Georgie said.

'George –'

'I'll get it.'

He stood, watching awkwardly, as she retrieved it and thrust it at him. She leaned in to kiss him but ended up giving an air-kiss and stumbling.

AJ had been her friend for over six years and live-in lover for more than three of those. *And it ends like this?*

He stared at the package.

'Open it.' Her voice failed.

AJ looked from the gift to her, and his shoulders sagged.

Minutely, but she knew him so well that she saw it and felt it replicate in her body.

'Go on.' Her legs went to jelly. She sank onto the sofa.

Eventually, AJ sat, too, tugging at the gold ribbon, releasing the bow. He placed it aside, then peeled the wrapping away.

'Oh, George. You shouldn't have.'

His hands caressed the old rosewood timber grip in the centre of the U-bend handle, tracing its swirls. Georgie knew the original patina glided silkily under fingertip.

AJ's fingers crept to the brass mounts. He lifted the piece, angling it so he could read the maker's marks on the antique woodworking brace. 'Sheffield. England. It's beautiful.'

His eyes shone with awe, overshadowed by something else.

'It's too good to use,' he said. 'It's too much.'

'No, you're worth it.' She felt a little thrill, which couldn't override her dread. The months of searching for his perfect gift had paid off. It was just right.

AJ laid the brace over his knees. His hands rested on top. 'Oh, George. We have to talk.'

And yet, neither spoke for minutes, while Georgie fought nausea and AJ seemed to be struggling with what to say. She tried to think of a way to change the outcome.

Something, anything, nothing.

'I've been offered a secondment to our sister firm in Hong Kong.'

Her eyes widened. This wasn't what she'd expected. 'But what about moving into chambers?'

'I can join the Bar when I come back.'

'But I can't go...'

AJ did a long blink, then sighed. 'I'm not asking you to

come.' Gentle, yet harsh.

'You're splitting up with me?'

He looked away, to the window and back to her. 'I think we need to give our relationship a rest. We could try dating again when I return.'

There was no certainty in his last sentence. More like a dangling question.

He sighed again. She saw resignation in his face. 'I lost a bit of you when we lost our baby.'

Georgie's throat tightened.

'It wasn't until much later that I realised it wasn't just the miscarriage, it's how much I pushed you for what wasn't right. It was for me, but not you. Then you went to Daylesford earlier this year and came back shattered. Understandably.'

'But –'

He held up a hand. 'We've both hung on, but lately.' He shrugged. 'And then, two nights before Christmas you came back from *another* trip to Daylesford, covered in cuts and bruises, driving that cop's car, then went out on the town with a champagne magnate. I know it was all to do with your job, but...'

His headshake was sad, not judgmental. He drew a small parcel from his pocket.

Georgie recognised a jewellery case and her stomach flipped. *So he isn't breaking up. He's toying with me about Hong Kong.*

AJ placed the box in her palm. He fixed mournful eyes on her. 'It's a charm bracelet. I chose ones for good luck, safety, wisdom, happiness, a few others. I hope you find all that and more, George. I really do. I don't think you understand how much I've worried about you. So much it's making me sick.'

'He's been back.' Charlie Banks rubbed his hands together. 'I told you someone'd been sneaking in and poking about. Didn't I tell you, the other day?'

Oh sure, Charlie. Now pull my other leg. Franklin suppressed his grin and nodded as he stepped over the threshold. He and Sam had found no evidence of forced entry two weeks ago and chalked it up as another of Charlie's colourful pretexts for a visit. Same as today's call would be.

'Like I told you on the phone, he stole me two favourite jumpers.' The old man ducked his head outside the front door, turning left and right. 'You didn't bring your team?'

Two jumpers didn't require Slam joining him while there were other tasks pending at the station. Nor did it necessitate a crew from crime scene. That's if anything had actually been stolen.

Nonetheless, Franklin would humour his buddy. Hopefully, somebody would return the favour when he was a lonely old bloke.

'No, we're a bit light on at the station today, mate. I should be able to manage it.'

Charlie trotted down the hallway to his kitchen. He flicked the kettle on, which took a jiffy to re-boil. He poured water into prepared mugs and handed one to Franklin with a shaky hand.

'A snowdropper, that's what we have.' Charlie pushed a plate of shortbread towards his guest.

'So he stole your jumpers off the clothesline, hey?' Franklin took a bickie and munched, enjoying the change from Butternut Snaps.

Charlie hesitated, then said, 'Well, I can't say that. It

could have been the clothesline. Or it could have been from the basket. Or it could have been from me chest of drawers.'

The old man took a slug from his mug, then wiped his chin.

'I can't help you with details. But I'm telling you, he definitely stole me two favourites.'

Gently, Franklin asked, 'Are you positive you haven't misplaced them, mate? Sure it's been a bit strange in the weather department lately but not so cold that you need your winter woollies.'

Even saying it, he realised that Charlie wore a long-sleeved flannelette shirt with brown trousers, vest, socks and shoes. Maybe the old fella felt the cold.

Charlie dropped his chin and peered over the top of his glasses with his rheumy eyes. 'I may have told a fib or two to get you to drop by in the past. Just once or twice, mind. But *this* time, I'm telling you the truth.'

Franklin found himself believing Charlie. But then his mobile pealed. He answered the call and heard Slam say, '*Déjà vu, mate. Get your arse back here ASAP. More trouble at the market.*'

———

Manjot Singh stood on the platform near his office. His face split into a wide smile before he brushed a hand over his close-shaved head in an anxious gesture.

'Sorry to trouble you on Boxing Day,' he said.

Slam spoke. 'That's all right, mate. We're rostered on, so we might as well be busy.'

The station master nodded, then led them to a small room. 'I think our friends have returned.'

'What makes you think that?' Franklin queried, curious as to what Singh sensed.

'Well, as did the previous occasion,' Singh grinned self-consciously, pointing at the jimmied door, 'this incident involves the minimum of fuss and damage.'

He indicated to the white cabinet painted with a green cross. 'They've raided our first-aid supplies. Taken paracetamol, band-aids, antiseptic spray, saline solution and the shock blankets. Yet they left the rest neatly and shut the door. But for that band-aid on the floor there, I may not have checked the cupboard until much later.'

Franklin nodded as his offsider jotted notes.

'It's little more than nuisance value and barely worth reporting to you, I know.' The station master sighed. 'The committee insisted I bring it to your attention, but personally, I'd prefer the person or people responsible get the help they clearly need,' he waved at the first-aid cabinet, 'than to see them in trouble.'

Franklin appreciated Singh's concise briefing and fair assessment. Pity more people didn't show humanity.

While his partner proceeded to take photos and details from Singh, Franklin raked the small room for clues. He paused, studying the splintered wood on the door frame. 'You wouldn't have a set of tweezers handy, would you?'

Singh rooted through the first-aid gear and handed over a pair.

Franklin plucked a wad of strands and angled them to the light. Next, he pulled from his pocket the photos that old Charlie Banks provided as exhibits in the stolen jumper case.

Bingo. The coloured strands looked remarkably similar to the wool in Charlie's number one favourite jumper.

CHAPTER FORTY-THREE

SIX MONTHS. TWELVE MONTHS. HONG KONG. FREE TO *see other people. Leave Molly here for now. We'll sort out what's best for her later.*

Georgie had shadowed AJ, mutely watching him extricate his life from hers. Lastly, he went into their bedroom and did a sweep through the wardrobe, saying he'd return for the rest.

Her body a dead weight, she'd sunk to the end of their unmade bed. AJ had hugged her, then left. She'd heard the door close, his car fire and accelerate away.

The writing had been on the wall for their relationship for a long time, but now that it had ended, cold grief over the loss of their love, and possibly their friendship, had taken a grip, and she'd been rooted to the spot for hours with his voice swirling in her mind. Meanwhile, the landline shrilled and rang out, and her mobile rang and beeped several times. But Georgie had disconnected from the world.

On afternoon foot patrol, Franklin and Slam clomped along Vincent Street, suffering in the intense mugginess. An acquaintance shouted hello, waving, and they returned the greeting.

'Not much open today,' Slam commented.

Franklin swatted a fly buzzing at his ear. 'Not everybody's been suckered into working on Boxing Day.'

A handful of businesses had opened for the tourist trade, and the two cops entered a shop at the low end of the street filled with the smoky aroma of chicken and chips.

After a round of handshakes, Franklin asked, 'And how're things going?'

The owner replied, 'All right, *now. But,*' and launched into a talk about patchy trade. After a bit, the man leaned in. 'Heard about the graffiti at the café around the corner. Heard it was backlash over the married woman who had an affair with her neighbour – *whose poor hubby died.* Shocking stuff.'

Franklin's skin prickled. The bloody thing about country towns: everyone knows everything but nothing's as simple as gossipmongers make it.

'We've sorted that out.' He briskly changed the topic. 'Speaking of graffiti. Heard anything about the recent break-ins and vandalism?'

The owner shook his head, clearly regretful that he didn't have the gossip on that.

Franklin smothered a sigh. 'Right.'

———

A blast of music roused Georgie from the sofa where she'd dragged herself after leaving the bedroom, but the call rang out before she located the phone.

She checked the screen. 'Nine missed calls.' Incredulous, she re-checked. In fact, she had nine missed calls and seven new messages.

She listened to the messages. The first was from Livia, but Georgie didn't have the strength to talk with her mum, who'd know something was wrong at one word, especially after AJ's absence from their Chrissie do last night. Ditto for Bron, who'd left a voicemail with cricket noise in the background. She heard old Pam Stewart's voice wishing her a Happy Christmas and New Year, and her skin infused with a warm buzz.

She'd call each of them back when she wasn't such a mess.

Her stomach contracted at a message from AJ, and it knotted more painfully when he sighed after saying her name and hung up.

Then Georgie reached the final three messages, and with each one, her heart took a wilder beat. They were all from Ally.

———

With two hours left on shift, Franklin's sense of urgency prompted him to do a runner on Slam while he was busy on the computer. He preferred to work this alone anyway, although chances were, it'd be another dead end.

'Do you think I'd want anything to do with those two?' Stephenson's sister screwed up her mouth. 'I haven't seen Daniel and Reggie since court.'

Franklin would've written them off, too, in her shoes. But Daniel was family, so he checked, 'Not even for Christmas?'

'We never worried much about Christmas in our house.'

He saw her guard drop marginally. 'We didn't have money for toys or special food when we were little unless our dad'd been lucky on the horses or he'd had a good find.'

As Stephenson senior had more form than his son for theft, Franklin suspected she meant stolen loot by *a good find*.

'Has your brother been in touch?'

'Why would I have anything to do with him after he helped Reggie rip me off?'

'People forgive and forget all the time.' *Especially women*.

'I'm not a dumb chick that's going to make the same mistake twice,' she snapped.

He responded 'Good' and meant it.

———

Georgie called Ally back immediately but got message bank. She left a voicemail. As she silently urged the phone to ring, a sliver of purposefulness broke through her numbness. And although her movements were sluggish, her brain and limbs rallied while she retrieved her laptop, the dog-eared photo of Goyne, and the new file she'd constructed after her mugging in Daylesford.

Another fifteen minutes later, Georgie's mobile pealed and she checked the screen. 'Yes!' She tapped connect. 'Ally!'

'No. Her mother.'

That didn't bode well and Georgie stiffened. 'Deb. Happy Christmas.'

They chatted idly for several minutes without Deb passing the phone over to her daughter or explaining the call, before Georgie asked, 'Is Ally there? I'd love a word.'

There was a long pause. *'She is.'* Deb hesitated again. *'But I think it may not be a good idea for you to stay in touch.'*

Through an even longer gap, Georgie's throat tightened.

'I don't think you should write your story about us. There are other people you could write about. More interesting people, even.'

'You *are* interesting. And Ally has worked with me intensely, and while she's admitted it's been difficult, she's also said it has helped her, so I think she'd be disappointed not to finish what we started.'

'Oh.'

Silence hung, while Georgie panicked, sending vibes to Deb not to hang up while suffering for the lies by omission she was keeping from the Goynes. Besides her original assignment, she needed Ally's help to test her theories about Warren.

'Oh,' Deb finally repeated. *'I hadn't looked at it that way.'*

'Can you put Ally on now please?'

A second later came, *'Georgie!'* then Ally barely let her say hi before talking non-stop.

Finally, there was a gap and Georgie said, 'Ally. Tell me about your dad and Clare.'

A whisper of soft breaths meant she was still on the line.

When Georgie heard a seagull squawk then fade away over the phone, she urged, 'Please, Ally.'

'What about them?' The teen sounded as distant as the seagull.

Don't hang up. I need you. Gently, 'Were they more than friends?'

'No.' Ally was sharp, defensive, telling Georgie plenty.

'What tipped Clare over the edge?'

'*Do we have to do this?*' Ally's voice strained.

'It seems significant.' Georgie's memory replayed Clive's words. *No. He blamed Deb.*

Eventually, in a tiny voice, Ally said, '*Clare bought a birthday cake.*'

'That's right.'

'*She hadn't been well leading up to her birthday.*'

Georgie panged, hearing Ally's voice crack.

'*She went to the bakery in her jammies.*' Ally moaned. '*Mum served her and said something mean.*'

Clive had admitted: *In Clare's precarious state, it tipped her over the edge. Or that's what Warren presumed. Perhaps we all did, truth be told.* Did he mean that Ally believed it too?

Softly, Georgie said, 'And you think that was the final straw for Clare?'

'*Yes. I love Mum, but yes.*'

'As your dad did?'

'*Yes.*' Monosyllabic. Bald. A world of pain.

Georgie knew it was now or never. 'Your dad and Clare, they had feelings for each other beyond friendship?'

'*Yes.*'

'And after Clare died, your dad changed?'

'*Yes.*'

'How did he treat your mum from then?'

Ally dropped into a hoarse whisper. '*Like he hated her, mostly.*'

'And a few months later –'

'*He died.*'

Georgie thought *Did he?*

CHAPTER FORTY-FOUR

GEORGIE BROUGHT HER OTHER WORK UP TO DATE, THEN revised the facts and theories concerning Goyne, dwelt on her mugger and how he fitted in, and reviewed every detail of her Daylesford and Yandoit trips.

While the fresh information from Ally supported her theory that Goyne's actions revolved around his relationships with Clare and Deb, that didn't tell Georgie where he'd gone, or clarify her differing hunches as to why. And she was clueless where to go from here.

———

Tim Lunny ducked his head around his office door, saying, 'You and Harty are taking out the unmarked this arvo.'

Damn. Franklin had been itching for headway on tracking down Whitey, Stephenson and Redwoods, or the Terrible Three, as he'd started thinking of them.

He was sure he hadn't sworn aloud but his boss said, 'Non-negotiable, Senior.'

'What's the job?'

'Your favourite: the old hairdryer.'

Great, pointing the radar always led to arguments from pissed off speeders about revenue raising versus safety. And his open cases would have to wait.

―――――

'Georgie? Phil here, about your tyres.'

She returned the greeting, dreading another delay.

'Sorry again for the hold-up,' he apologised. *'We tried hard to get your set in before Christmas.'*

'I know, Phil. Thanks anyway.'

'Anyhow, your car'll be ready tomorrow.'

'Really? I didn't expect you'd be back at work until Wednesday.'

'We're not, officially. But I managed to arrange a special delivery for your Alfa, and it'll be in first thing. So, I'll fix you up, then enjoy the rest of my day off.'

That went well beyond friendly service, so Georgie asked, 'What do you drink, Phil? I'm bringing you a thank you.'

―――――

Harty leaned forward. 'Got a customer.' He lifted the radar, then lowered it to his lap, muttering.

'You need specs, mate?' Franklin ribbed.

'I thought I saw –'

He heard a beep, glanced at Harty, then realised it'd come from his pocket. He pulled his mobile and saw one message waiting. His thumb shook when he noted the sender, and it took two attempts to pick it up.

'My car will be ready tomorrow. Would 10am at Phil's Tyres suit you for swap?'

Rostered on for the twilight shift, he had the day free. But with Harty throwing him strange glances, it took Franklin ages to construct an answer that didn't give away his nerves at seeing Georgie again.

He ended up with: 'Sure.'

CHAPTER FORTY-FIVE

HE'D BEEN THINKING ABOUT *THAT DAY* ALMOST constantly since the girl turned up. It'd been easy to do the most heinous thing imaginable. Too easy. Conditions were primed. He had a fully kitted-out man cave, everything he needed right on hand. It worked better than he'd expected, never having practised or even planned such a thing.

He'd acted and then reacted.

He'd had everything he needed, and now he had nothing.

He'd tried to kill himself last year but couldn't go through with it. Just as he wouldn't give himself up. Not because of his buddy; at the end of the day he wasn't flesh and blood. No, it was because he'd sunk to be the scum of the earth, capable of everything and anything,

except hurt her any more than his actions had already done.

The truth would come out if he turned himself in. Same if he died, unless his body was never discovered.

His only choice left was to live this way. For Ally, he had to not exist.

———

Franklin wore the T-shirt that Kat gave him for Christmas with his favourite jeans fresh from the wash and should have felt good. Instead, he jittered, inside and out, and had walked to the tyre shop so fast that he arrived early.

He leaned against the wall and pretended to be engrossed in his mobile until he recognised the rumble of his Commodore's V8 motor. He told himself to settle and raised his head, feigning casual.

He lifted a hand in a brief wave. She lifted three fingers in reply.

———

Georgie strolled towards him. 'All done.'

'Good.'

It was hard to read his tone.

When she handed over his keys, their fingers brushed and she jolted. There was a light stammer to her, 'Thanks again for helping out with the loaner.'

'No problem.'

She glanced sideways at him and saw his Adam's apple

slide up and down in an awkward looking swallow. It struck her that whatever it was that they felt confused her as much as the rawness of her break-up with AJ, despite its inevitability.

Georgie indicated to the Commodore. 'It drives pretty well.'

Franklin nodded in reply, doing another swallow.

'No comparison to my Spider though.' She smiled, and they finally held a look. His eyes bore an unusual brightness. She couldn't leave him then, not like that.

He began to say, 'You wouldn't want to go to the lake for –'

As she said, 'Wanna grab a coffee?'

———

'I could stay here all day.' Georgie sounded dreamy.

Franklin eyed her, sprawled on the lawn, forearm shielding her face from the sun, with empty takeaway cups between them.

'You could.' He didn't want her to leave. A duck waddled from the water's edge to his feet, giving him an idea. 'We could have a go on that.'

She lifted her head and followed his finger to the bright red paddleboat waiting on the dock.

———

Their legs pumped hard in trying to outdo each other. Eventually, Georgie raised her feet and told him he could do it alone if he wanted.

He laughed and took a rest too. They bobbed midway between the boathouse and far bank. Georgie trailed a hand in the water until the coldness allayed the muddle in her

DEAD AGAIN: WILL SOMEONE KILL TO KEEP THEIR SECR...

mind.

'I didn't have an accident.' She scrunched her nose and pointed. 'I took a beating over there.'

Franklin looked to the bank, then skimmed over her face. 'The bruising's subsided.'

She gently pushed at the bumps. They felt less puffy and tender, but suddenly she needed to share the details she'd withheld or fibbed about.

'Remember that Bullock story I'm working on?'

'With the dead-man-walking angle?' He grinned.

He was watching her intently, so she assumed he wasn't mocking her.

'The guy that mugged me...well, earlier, before he did it, I ran into him.' She gestured to the distant stone building. 'Literally ran into him outside the men's.'

Franklin's eyebrows hiked.

'My research scattered and he helped pick it up. He saw a photo of my subject—Goyne—and acted weird.'

He frowned. 'How?'

'He stared and got the shakes. I think he recognised Goyne. Then I went for a walk.'

'And he attacked you?' The words rasped.

'Yes. And the strange thing is, he kept asking who I am.'

'You think because he's protecting his mate, Goyne?'

'Yes.'

Franklin grunted and paddled at an easy pace, steering away from the reeds.

Georgie joined in, resuming the story. 'So then I went to Yandoit.'

'Why?'

'To check out a place that Goyne often visited with his family. His uncle used to own it.'

'Dead end?'

'Yep. Well, I think so. There were no signs anyone's been there recently. But something's niggling at me.' Georgie sighed. 'Anyway, the next day, I came back and sussed out the men's.' She indicated the pavilion again.

Franklin said, *You did what?*

'I found food scraps, a newspaper, and other stuff indicating it's been used as a base.'

He wore a thoughtful expression. 'I've had two strange cases intersect. A nice old fella's two missing jumpers and a couple of soft break-ins at the railway.'

'Soft?'

'They raided the first-aid supplies but otherwise just crashed there.'

Georgie pictured her mugger. Sick or junkie, after he'd mugged her she'd fixated on only his connection to Goyne. She grabbed Franklin's arm.

His legs stopped and the little boat teetered.

She said, 'We're thinking the same thing.'

He nodded. 'What's Goyne's first name?'

'Warren,' Georgie answered.

Franklin murmured, 'Waz.'

'What's that?'

'I found a lighter at the first railway break-in engraved "Waz YF Clare".'

Clare again. 'It's him.'

Franklin's eyes widened. 'Maybe, probably. But someone else could've gotten hold of his lighter.'

———

Franklin watched Kat's eyes flick from Georgie to him. Then she peered at the dining table and back to them, saying, 'Oh.'

He rose, feeling awkward. 'Kat, you remember Georgie?'

His daughter bobbed her head and greeted their guest, then scanned the room again, openly curious. He saw her process the table covered in sticky notes, printouts, unfamiliar laptop, photographs, crumb-coated plates and used mugs.

Her gaze rested on Georgie, then him again. Kat smiled. Franklin recognised that smile; mischievous and knowing.

'I think I'll go to Lisa's, Dad.' His daughter smiled again. 'All right with you if I sleep over? It'll give you two some space to do whatever you're doing.'

He tried, but couldn't stop his blush.

———

Georgie checked the clock, then began to gather her notes.

'What are you doing?'

'You start your shift soon, so I'd best get out the way.'

Franklin touched her hand. 'Stay.' *Why did I say that?*

She gave a startled blink, then blurted, 'I've broken up with AJ.'

'I'm sorry.' And he was sorry if she was hurting. He also felt guilty for being pleased.

He collected the dirty crockery and moved into the kitchen. She'd frozen.

After a strained silence while he stacked the dishwasher, Franklin cleared his throat. 'I meant, stay here. In our spare room. That way, we can continue this later.'

She stared at him. He couldn't work out what she was thinking and the longer her answer took, the more he shrivelled with embarrassment. And disappointment.

She's trying to work out a nice way to let me down.

Face still unreadable, Georgie finally said, 'I could ask Ruby and Michael to feed the cat and dog while I'm gone.'

———

Franklin convinced Harty to do the patrol one-up, allowing him to dabble with the graffiti cases.

Fifteen minutes into his window of alone-time, he'd hit the wall on a few possibilities and exhaled loudly, frustrated. It was too late to catch the hardware manager today and check if he'd seen Whitey's gang recently. They'd purchased or stolen their spray paint from somewhere.

He pulled out his daybook and made notes for tomorrow, then headed for the station.

———

A gentle breeze brushed Georgie's skin, giving respite to the humidity as she sat on the stone steps leading to the verandah. But despite the relaxed setting, a montage of faces, together with a thousand fragmented notions, filled her mind.

She willed herself to sit in the quiet and chill, but her brain soon rebelled and swirled again. Even lighting up and dragging on a ciggie didn't calm her. It wasn't until she consciously focused on the present, instead of the blanks in the past and future, that it occurred to her that Franklin didn't have much of a garden.

Georgie chuckled, as she smoked and daydreamed.

He appeared more domesticated than she'd have expected. She squirmed, remembering their initial encounter in the tiny police station while she attempted to report a missing person back in autumn. On that first day, nothing figured further from her imagination than Franklin as a single dad in his civilian life. She'd found that out later, making it four hard facts that clouded whatever their first reaction had been. He was a country cop and had a teenaged daughter, and she was a city writer in a relationship.

When they'd arrived here earlier today, she hadn't expected the inside of his home to tend towards modern with its new kitchen and neutral tones; masculine but softened by fluffy cushions and artwork. The latter was possibly courtesy of Kat, but then again, the more she learned of Franklin, the more he surprised her.

In contrast to the cosy feel inside, while neatly mowed lush green grass surrounded the cottage, aside from several shrubs and fruit trees, the yard lacked design.

Georgie frowned, as her thoughts scraped at raw scars. AJ had been her first love and their breakup cut deep. She sighed into the night, admitting it came with relief too. He'd made the decision she'd struggled with that what they had wasn't enough.

Now, her life spread like the blank canvas of Franklin's garden. She had responsibilities—Molly and Phoebe, family and friends, her job—but overall, the page that'd just turned was yet to be written. Did that scare the hell out of her or excite her? She decided both, in equal parts.

For some reason, Georgie pictured the lake and her at the edge with one foot poised. Should she dip in a toe? Jump in? Or run?

CHAPTER FORTY-SIX

Franklin locked the door, gave it an automatic check before he waved to Harty, and mounted his bike.

As he kicked over the engine and pulled on his helmet, his gut flipped. He'd had few girlfriends since divorcing Donna and none live-in. It'd been a long time since someone apart from his daughter waited at home for his return. But tonight, Georgie did.

He laughed, a strange chortled noise inside his helmet.

———

A truck rumbled past, then the roadway dropped into quietness so different to what Georgie was used to because Richmond was never still or silent. A few minutes later, her ears pricked at a sound that grew into a distinctive roar. Near the cottage, the vehicle geared down into a growl.

Her chest burned with adrenaline as her insecurities came to a boil.

Georgie's feet barely brushed the timber decking and same for the floorboards as she dashed into the cottage.

Inside the guest bedroom, she pulled the door behind her, and her heart thudded as she pressed her forehead and palms against the panelled door.

Outside, the motorbike silenced, and moments later, she heard boots stride across the front verandah and the sound take a slight echoey tone as Franklin entered the house and closed the door. He took a few steps, then paused before resuming at a slower pace up the hallway.

He stopped again outside her room. Part of her hoped he would speak. Or knock.

After what felt like many minutes but may've been just one, he let out a soft sigh and walked away, leaving Georgie touching the door and wishing it was him.

———

Georgie entered the kitchen, her hair still wet from the shower, although it wouldn't take long to air-dry. Whereas yesterday and last night had been muggy, today dawned with the instant heat that heralds a stinker.

While she'd had the foresight to pack an overnight bag, it hadn't crossed her mind that accommodation would be scarce in the Christmas to New Year week, making Franklin's offer to stay in the spare room welcome, yet disturbing. She had feared the strange bed on top of everything else might trigger nightmares, so while desperately craving rest, she had taken hours to unwind.

But then she'd slept right through until she was woken by Franklin moving around the cottage about fifteen minutes ago. Now he stood leaning against the kitchen bench, following her with his gaze.

They exchanged *good mornings* while the air charged

with awkward tension. Not the void she and AJ fell into on Christmas night, yet still full of things unsaid.

She gestured to the kettle. 'Can I make you a cuppa?'

Franklin looked like he was holding himself in so tightly he couldn't answer, so she went ahead.

Eventually, he asked, 'Sleep well?'

She nodded and stretched, feeling his eyes watching. When the coffee was ready, they sat together at the table.

He rubbed his face with his free hand. His hair was damp from showering but he hadn't shaved, and his skin made a light rasp. He stared into his drink lost in thought and Georgie drank in silence, her swallows sounding loud.

After a while, he said, 'We'd better report your assault.' He pulled out a notebook and pen. 'I'll knock this up formally at the station but tell me what you remember.'

She did, right down to her little baggie of nail clippings.

Franklin laughed, then frowned, reviewing his notes. Georgie placed her mug on the table, sensing he was onto something.

'I think we have another hit.' He met her look, with a lively glint in his eyes. 'I think I know who your assailant is.'

She whooped.

'And if I'm right, I saw him with an older fellow.'

Georgie felt a zip of excitement. 'Goyne?'

Franklin hesitated, then shook his head. 'Nah.' He drummed his fingertips. 'The fellow I saw was approximately fifty. Long skinny face, mo and beard, beanie covering most of a buzz cut. Scruffy.'

His description didn't match and she deflated.

'Your man was heavily overweight, clean-shaven and wore glasses, right?'

Georgie retrieved her photo of Goyne and showed him.

He drew her gaze, and that glint was back. Maybe he was onto something after all.

Her eyes widened. Back when she couldn't shut down the lyrics of *Walk on the Wild Side*, she'd brushed on the idea that a fat man could disguise himself skinny and in drag. Make that skinny and living rough, could it have been Goyne that Franklin saw?

Georgie said, 'Could it be the same guy –'

Just as Franklin remarked, 'Dropping a heap of weight ages people, yeah?'

They stood at the same time, meeting hands in a high-five. Shocked by the electric contact, she belatedly dropped her hand, as he lowered his own, their eyes still connected.

Franklin massaged his temple where Georgie could see a vein tick, and she lifted his hand away, overturned it and kissed his palm softly. She circled a finger lightly over his temple to soothe it, then combed through his short hair, and like a cat accepting a stroke, his neck arched.

Now she traced over his angular cheekbones and jaw and outlined his mouth with her fingertips. His lips parted, but aside from that tiny movement, he'd frozen, with his eyes pleading. She sensed that he'd wanted another chance to kiss her so much, and for so long, that he needed to be sure it was what she wanted too.

Although she did, completely, she twinged with faint guilt when she reached both hands to his face. She drank in his features, her heart telling her this couldn't be wrong.

Franklin moaned, and she felt the deep vibration in her body. 'Jesus, Georgie.'

Hesitantly, he cradled her cheeks, too, easing closer, and slowly, softly, their lips met – gentle and tentative, the first touch of tongues shy. The kiss deepened, and his light stubble made her mouth throb with the thud of her heart.

Franklin drew back, studying her face. 'You're so beautiful.'

She wanted to say *so are you* but couldn't speak. She hoped her eyes told him.

They entwined, with their hipbones skimming, as their lips met again. Georgie stroked lean muscle shaping down the vee of his back, while Franklin's lips grazed from hers, down her neck, hovered over the puckered scar at the dip between her neck and shoulder, then caressed it with soft, fluttering kisses.

Georgie floated in sensory overload from his spicy soap and apple shampoo, the sting of his whiskers and hot breath on her skin, the hard beat of his heart when she laid a hand on his chest, knowing this was special.

Released from the final shadows of guilt, her body softened and her mouth searched for his. Desire flashed in his eyes, but this kiss was long and slow and sensual. And when Franklin swung Georgie into his arms, she looped his neck, with her gaze lost in his as he carried her to the bedroom.

CHAPTER FORTY-SEVEN

F RANKLIN TOOK A BITE OF AN APRICOT, FRESH FROM the tree they sat under. Conscious of her thigh lightly touching his, he worked hard to stop grinning like an idiot. Just a few days ago, he'd thought being with Georgie was an impossible wish. And now it'd come true.

He just had to ignore the prickle of fear that she'd return to Melbourne, her ex-boyfriend, and her life and that somehow he'd have to forget all about Georgie Harvey. Again.

She suddenly said, 'I can't figure out what to call you.'

'Huh?'

'You've always been *Franklin* but that doesn't seem right – now.' Her cheeks tinted with pink. 'I don't think of you as John, Johnny or Jonno.'

He laughed.

'You certainly can't be Jacko. But I haven't made my mind up about Jack yet.'

Jack sounded good when she said it.

Georgie didn't say anything more, just contemplated him with those dark eyes.

———

Franklin paced next to the dining table, causing their notes on the overlapping cases to flutter. 'Let's kill two birds.'

Georgie threw him a curious look.

'Grab your photo of Goyne; I've got an idea.' Eyes twinkling, he added, 'Want to take a spin on the bike?'

'Hell, yeah.'

Hot or not, she grabbed her leather jacket and met him at the weatherboard shed, where he was rummaging inside. She decided he looked good in uniform, better in leathers.

'You and Kat are around the same size and she wouldn't mind.' He tossed her a pair of boots.

She remembered Kat's secretive smile yesterday and thought she'd happily lend Georgie the boots if it aided and abetted her dad's love life.

'Have you ridden pillion before?'

'On trail bikes and quad bikes.' That dated back to her fruit picking days with Bron. 'Not on-road, though.'

'It's much the same.' He ran through instructions while Georgie fidgeted.

Eventually, she extended her right leg over the seat, slid up and put her feet on the pegs. Her knees hugged Franklin and she held his waist. She patted his ribs twice. Ready.

He replied with a tap on her thigh and took off in a steady, smooth acceleration, but Georgie still felt a backward thrust. She inhaled the thrill. Even at moderate speed, by all of 200 metres down the road, she loved the power and the sense that she, Franklin and the Ninja were in perfect synergy.

They entered Vincent Street and to Georgie's disappointment, took a vacant spot in the centre-parking strip.

She gave him a confused glance as he led her to a craft shop. Her surprise increased when the plump, cheery woman inside greeted Franklin with a peck on the cheek, then gave Georgie one, after he said, 'Sunnie, this is my friend, Georgie.'

———

'I need a favour.' Franklin grinned.

Sunnie's eyes shone with curiosity. 'Of course.'

'Show Sunnie your photo please, Georgie.'

He pinned his eyes on his old friend. 'Real long shot. Have you seen this bloke?'

Sunnie's glasses hung from a chain around her neck. She perched them on her nose and scrutinised the picture. 'I don't think so.'

Shame but no surprise. 'I thought as much. Are your sketching skills as brilliant as ever?'

'Aw, shucks.' Sunnie flapped a hand, chuckling. 'I haven't completely lost it.'

Georgie looked mystified, and Franklin enjoyed building the tension.

'Do you think you could sketch him?' He tapped Goyne's image.

'Of course.' Sunnie gathered a pad, pencil, and eraser.

Franklin watched Georgie, as he added, 'Think you could age him a couple of years, drop sixty or seventy kilos, lose the glasses, add a beard and give him a buzz cut?'

Georgie's eyes opened wide. 'Ohhh.'

And Sunnie answered, 'Does a sausage need sauce?'

A little while later, they had the sketch and jumped on the bike again. Franklin headed to the station to kill the second bird. He and Georgie dismounted, leaving helmets with the bike and entered the station, shucking off their leather jackets.

Lunny placed a folder on the front counter, watching them enter while maintaining a perfect poker expression, aside from a gleam in his eyes.

'Ah, Georgie. It's been a long while.' He did the double-handed shake he reserved for people he liked, and she smiled broadly. 'Haven't seen you since the ruckus earlier this year.'

Georgie's smile faded, as her face darkened. Perhaps ghosts of last autumn continued to haunt her, as they did Franklin on regular occasions.

He ushered her up the hallway to the muster room, feeling the sarge watch his hand find the small of her back. He broke contact, then let his hand drift back, enjoying the way her body undulated beneath his palm, through her T-shirt.

She wandered around the room talking, while he typed her assault up in the legalise format of an official statement.

Next, he pulled Luke Duffy's mug shot and laid it out with a bunch of others. 'See your fellow in this lot?'

She pointed to Duffy's photograph. 'Thinner, paler, looking crap, but that's him.'

Cha-ching.

CHAPTER FORTY-EIGHT

AFTER TWO DEFINITE HITS—SUNNIE'S SKETCH OF THE now-older, not-so-fat-Goyne matching with Franklin's recollection of the guy who'd been with Duffy, the kid who was her mugger—Georgie had been anxious not to lose momentum. So she canvassed the streets with her pic and Sunnie's sketch when Franklin started his shift at 4.00pm.

The first hour was productive, while the shops that'd opened that day still traded. But most of them closed at 5.00pm sharp. Some would straggle on for another half-hour and she deliberately left the later-trading takeaways, supermarkets and pubs for after that.

Two hours later, she was shattered – no one had definitively recognised Goyne. She lingered at Burke's Hotel over a beer, considering a pub special for tea.

She felt a nudge to her upper arm and swivelled on her stool, as a person in a hoodie ducked around the corner. In that glimpse, she judged it was a male from gait and build, although she wasn't certain. Nobody else had moved or appeared to be paying her any attention, and the contact could only have been deliberate, so she instinctively followed the figure, pausing before the exit to wonder if it was a trap.

The pub was bustling, which gave Georgie a sense of security, and the hooded person might have information on Goyne that he wanted to pass on privately. Adrenaline coursed through Georgie at the prospect of cracking a solid lead.

She approached the open doorway, peered out, seeing nothing but kegs, wheelie bins, a shed, cars. No people, which surprised her. She checked the nearby beer garden. It was deserted too. Her warning bells went off, just as her head was wrenched sideways, a hunk of her hair tearing from the roots.

She cried out and her assailant threw an arm over her chest, twisting her at a painful angle, bringing his hand up to cover her mouth. Beyond a smidgeon of his clothing and skin, she couldn't see him.

He punched at her kidney and she exhaled in a whoosh behind his hand. The pain which shafted through her spurred her instincts of flight and fight. She bit his hand, squirmed, threw wild punches and yelled.

But he swept her legs out from under her, dropping her to the ground, then kicked with sneakered feet. She curled into foetal position, still calling out, hoping someone would hear from the street or inside the pub.

Was it Duffy again, another cohort, or Goyne himself? It definitely felt personal.

'Get off her!' a man shouted.

She saw someone behind her attacker, just before he staggered back mid-kick, as if her good Samaritan had pulled him away. Georgie rolled out from the men's scuffling, circling feet and crawled behind a keg, her head in a sickening spin, unable to process what to do.

Grunts, skids in gravel, punches, the sound of someone winded, and curses rang in her ears, along with the thump of her pulse. She breathed, clearing some of the brain fog, tested her sight and it came into focus as one man heaved a punch into the other's stomach. His hoodie fell back slightly, revealing a fraction of a lightly-bearded, bony face.

Goyne.

―――――

'Burglary in progress. 51 Echidna Drive, Daylesford. Daylesford Medical Centre.'

'Sam, call it in.' Franklin triggered lights and siren. 'We're a minute away.'

'Got it, boss.'

As the police truck cornered from Raglan Street into Echidna, he tensed. No matter how many years in the job, it never paid to become complacent.

General duties didn't necessarily mean mundane—or safe—even in the good old sticks of Daylesford. In the real world of cops on any beat, they could interrupt a drug or alcohol loaded gang on a short fuse. The offenders could be armed with anything from broken bottles or blood-filled syringes to semi-autos. They'd need to keep their wits about them. It went doubly for him as the supervisor.

In their stationary vehicle, Franklin cautioned his offsider. 'Stay close. Listen sharp. Don't play the hero. The clinic's alarm is going hell for leather, so we'll leave the fairy lights on.' He pointed to the roof, indicating the red and blue strobes. 'Chances are, they've already scarpered but we're not leaving things to chance.' He paused. 'Ready?'

'Yes,' Sam answered tightly.

'Turn down your radio. We don't want it to squawk at

the wrong moment.' Franklin did the same and silenced his mobile too.

————

The boxers' dance revolved, and Georgie realised her good Samaritan was Manny, the bartender, as he did a soccer-style manoeuvre, throwing Goyne off balance.

While Manny had the upper hand, Georgie dialled triple zero and reported the emergency. She spoke quickly, anxious to go to the bartender's aid.

'We'll have a unit out there as soon as possible,' the operator promised.

Georgie disconnected, belatedly realising the woman was still talking, then emerged from cover intending to help Manny, just as Goyne pounded his chin. Manny staggered, fell backwards, then lay groaning.

Goyne sprinted straight at Georgie, slamming her into a stack of crates, then raced through the gateway in the tall picket fence. Georgie threw off the crates and darted after him. It took seconds. But that was all Goyne needed to vanish.

————

'Confirm cold burg at the address,' Franklin called in, meaning the crooks had gone before they arrived.

The D24 operator thanked him and added, *'We've had another job not far from you. Burke's Hotel.'*

'What's the go?' He pictured his favourite pub and wondered which of the usual suspects were involved.

'Initial report was patchy; some sort of altercation. The update is two assault vics; one male, one female. No serious

injuries. *Offender decamped area on foot, although he may have had an accomplice in a vehicle.'*

'Who's attending?'

'We have a unit on its way from Trentham.'

Franklin asked to be kept posted and clicked off the mike. He said to Sam, 'Let's do another sweep.'

They completed their second run through the medical centre, with him jotting notes and Sam taking digital photos, and stepped outside as a white panel van with amber flashers arrived with a sharp U-turn and squeal of tyres.

After Franklin had updated the security guard, he dialled a number that was answered with, *'Marty Howell, crime investigation unit.'*

Franklin blew out a breath. By good luck, he'd drawn the new bloke from Bacchus Marsh, not Mr Defective. He gave the other cop a sketch of the recent spate of burgs and vandalism and similarities between this and the party hire warehouse break-in.

He told him, 'It's a definite escalation.'

'How's that?'

'They've broken into the drugs supply. We won't have an inventory until we interview staff, but that ups the ante. Plus they've nicked computers and probably all the cash on hand. They left the safe open and empty.'

Howell groaned. *'So, you think it's the same gang?'*

'For some of the jobs. We have a match for several tags.'

'It's a bit brazen, isn't it? It's still light. Plenty of people out and about.'

Franklin had thought that through, too. 'I think it's become about fun for them, as much as whatever they nick. They took their time at the Galassi place and this time went even bolder, forcing entry not long after the staff've left but while the sun's shining. Targeting a premises liable to be alarmed.'

Howell was quiet.

'What do you think, Marty? Secure the scene and get the CSOs and you suits in?'

'Sounds good, mate.'

A couple of door knocks later, Franklin walked away from the latest house, answering his mobile.

'How's it going, Franklin?' His counterpart at Trentham then switched to business with, *'I have a friend of yours here who's been in a spot of bother.'*

Franklin clicked. 'The pub fight?'

'Yeah.'

'Who?'

'Georgina Harvey, from the city.'

King-hit, he gripped the receiver, spluttering.

'Hold on; she's fine. A bit stunned and a few bruises – by the way, is this woman a sucker for trouble? She's wearing a bunch of older contusions too.'

Franklin's mouth twitched in a grim smile. *You could say that.* 'She's definitely okay?'

'Definitely.'

'Good.' Franklin rubbed the back of his head. 'I can't get there straightaway. We're on a break-in around the corner and have another door to knock. What's your status?'

'We need to head off, so I'd like to handover to you for the statements.'

Franklin recalled there were two victims, Georgie and a male. 'Who's the other vic?'

'The barman, Manny. He's a little worse for wear than your friend, but wouldn't stay away from his bar for more than five minutes.'

'Can Manny keep tabs on Georgie until we arrive?'

———

A flash of light blue caught Georgie's gaze, but a stranger blocked her view. She craned, hoping it was Franklin, not the Trentham cops again. It was, but the young female officer walked with him. That, and the curious stares from around the pub since the attack, restrained Georgie's reaction to a brief wave.

Franklin sat next to her. She gave him a sideways look, careful to shield the fresh bruise, spotting the tautness of his posture, although his expression seemed deliberately composed.

He turned her chin with the lightest touch, concern etching his features. 'Judging by that shiner, I think you found Duffy again.'

'Second-chance shot?'

Both his eyebrows hiked. 'Not Goyne?'

———

'You think the trail's gone cold, boss?' Sam asked Franklin.

From the back seat, Georgie grimaced, staring out her window, seeing houses and vacant blocks, then paddocks flick past as raindrops slapped the glass. Goyne had shot away, and although she and Manny had split into different directions, checking vehicles and yards, stopping passers-by to ask if they'd seen their man, he'd vanished.

Georgie shifted in her seat, freaked out that she'd been oblivious to being on Goyne's radar, angry with herself for losing him.

'Why attack Georgie?' Sam asked.

'To stop her finding him.' Franklin sounded sure.

'Why not do another runner?'

345

'Can't for some reason?' Georgie hazarded.

They tossed around theories and fell into contemplation.

Minutes later, Franklin glanced at Georgie via the rear-view mirror and broke the silence. 'I think you're still in his sights.'

Sam seconded the motion.

'Maybe, so I'll be more careful, okay?'

'And keep me in the loop.'

Georgie met Franklin's eyes in the mirror and nodded, while Sam said, 'Good.'

Her mind flicked away from Goyne to the one upside to tonight: Sam appeared to be thawing to her, which somehow seemed important considering she had an obvious crush on Franklin and was his colleague and friend. If Georgie and Franklin made a go of whatever it was they'd launched into, his friends would become her friends, so it would be bloody awkward if the other woman held a grudge.

That was all a little weird, so Georgie was relieved when Franklin cut into her thoughts.

'Could Ally know?'

'No way. She sculptured a shrine to her dead dad. She bit her mum's head off for suggesting he didn't die in the fire.'

'You haven't known her long,' Franklin countered.

'Long enough.' Georgie tried to explain. 'You have a copper's instincts. Credit me with the same as a writer because our jobs aren't that dissimilar.'

She sat forward, reached between the bucket seats to touch Franklin's shoulder. 'Ally's an honest, grieving kid.'

He nodded, accepting her theory. Happy with that, she

returned to what gnawed in her gut. 'So where are Goyne and Duffy now?'

———

Franklin stopped pacing and smacked his forehead. Georgie ceased swivelling in her chair and watched him.

He dug out his mobile and hit a speed-dial number. After a few beats, he said, 'It's me…sorry but it's important. I'll remind you of that.'

Georgie leaned closer to hear the voice at the other end. No chance.

'Look, I realise it's late, but pack a bag.' He shook his head. 'I'm on shift but we'll be there shortly. Give Lisa a bell.'

Ah-ha, he's talking to Kat.

'Give her a heads-up that I'll be phoning her mum…Kat, quit it. Tell her you need to stay with them a while. That's no hardship, is it?'

He laughed and disconnected. As he crooked his finger at Georgie, he yelled to Sam that they'd be out for a bit.

———

Kat inspected Georgie, her eyes growing by the second. 'What happened to you? You've got more bruises.'

Franklin said, 'That's why you're going to Lisa's. It's all clear with Mrs Cantrell.'

The tension between the three of them heightened.

'No offence to Georgie,' Kat shot her an apologetic glance, 'but I've got nothing to do with whatever she's been stirring up.'

'Yes, true. But she may've been followed here, and the

347

person responsible for that,' Franklin pointed to Georgie's face, 'might've clocked you, Kat. If he has and he gets desperate enough, you could be next.'

A punch of guilt winded Georgie. She'd never intended to flag herself, let alone endanger Kat. She would hate herself if anything happened to the teen because of her. 'Sorry, Kat, please go to Lisa's.'

Kat hedged.

Franklin hammered home the danger with, 'There'll be times Georgie and I need to be someplace else, and you're not to be alone while she's being hunted. Deal?'

'Deal,' Kat agreed. 'But Dad?'

'But what?' His forehead puckered.

'Promise me you'll get him before he hurts Georgie again.'

Franklin's face crumpled, and Georgie swallowed a lump in her throat.

They all exchanged a glance and Franklin nodded. Grimly.

CHAPTER FORTY-NINE

HE STILL DIDN'T KNOW WHO SHE WAS AND WHAT SHE wanted, but the girl wasn't just a random interested in the fires. She was trying to find him and knew he was in town.

He rubbed his eyes, looking into the distance, trying to clear the blur. He'd only risked keeping two things from his old life, his glasses and the lighter Clare gave him, but didn't have either now. Whitey had stepped on his glasses one night while he was dozing at the squat. He suspected he'd meant to do it too. And the lighter, well, he'd lost that, which hurt a lot more than the glasses.

His vision was okay for getting by the way they did. But he was blind as a bat when it came to long distance, especially at night, so nicking a car and taking off was out. Luke could drive,

but he was having one of his bad days, so he couldn't drive them either.

They needed to get away but how and to where? And how much did that girl already know?

———

'Shoot from the shoulder,' Franklin told her.

Georgie cringed as her blows made a *thud, bang, thud, bang*.

'What's with the patty cake, patty cake on your left?' he taunted.

She tried harder, ignoring the nerves stabbing down her left arm. *Bang, bang, bang, bang*.

'Better. Now, focus on follow-through. Good. Fast rips!'

Georgie growled, pummelling the bag while picturing Goyne's kidneys under her gloved knuckles.

'Five, four, three, three, three –'

'No one likes a smartarse, Franklin.'

He laughed. 'Franklin again, huh? What happened to Jack?'

She shot him a glare.

'Who told you to stop? Start again.'

He counted from ten to one and Georgie clouted the heavy bag twice more for measure, then grumbled, 'We've stuff all to show for today.'

Franklin grabbed her fists and held them under her chin. 'Not true. You're not punching like a pansy anymore.'

'A pansy?'

'Yes. And besides, a watched kettle never boils. So, we're letting things simmer.'

At the start of shift, Sam called, 'Boss! Some kids here to see you.'

Franklin moved to the front counter, spotted his visitors, and beamed with genuine pleasure. 'Hey, kids, how're you doing?'

Lined in a row were Drew, Chelsea, Liam and Kayla; his favourites from the boxing studio, their expressions unusually intense.

'Hi, Mr F,' Drew answered.

Franklin leaned on the counter. 'You all look very serious. What can I do for you?'

Liam could never keep a secret. So naturally, he dropped the bombshell. 'We've solved a crime for you.'

Franklin's eyebrows hit the ceiling.

'We came earlier today,' Drew said.

'But you weren't in yet,' Chelsea added.

Kayla put her bit in. 'And Sergeant Lunny said you started at four.'

The interview looked to be a tag-team event.

Franklin interlinked his fingers. 'You said you'd solved a crime?'

'Yes, Mr F,' Chelsea agreed, bobbing her side ponytail.

Drew glanced at his girlfriend. They exchanged the barest of nods and he admitted, 'We were riding our bikes last night. It was light but *technically* we weren't supposed to be out on the street that late.'

'That's okay, kids.' Franklin smiled. 'Get to the crime-solving bit.'

'We were riding on Echidna Drive.'

Franklin's eyes turned into saucers. *Jesus, what're these kids onto?*

Drew continued, 'And Chelsea spotted something funny going on at the medical centre. So we dumped our bikes and hid in the bushes.'

Kayla piped up, 'And we saw three men do bad stuff.'

'You saw them? Could you describe them?'

Liam and Kayla grinned. He said, 'We can do better than that,' and the little girl pulled a few sheets of paper from her backpack.

'I drew them,' she announced.

Franklin flicked through three sketches, recognising the trio. *Holy shit. Kayla should be put on the payroll. She'd make a bloody good police sketch artist.*

Chelsea said, 'And we can do even better than that.'

'How?'

'We can tell you where they are now.'

These kids deserve a medal.

———

They'd done a recce in the unmarked earlier and set up backup. Now, Franklin called, 'Go!' clicked off the mike and pointed, seeing the gesture replicated in a chain reaction.

He thumped on the front door. 'POLICE! Open up!'

A distant voice called the same from the rear of the house.

Franklin heard pounding footsteps inside, as he twisted the doorknob and lurched through the doorway, with Sam covering him as they moved stealthily, keeping the wall close. They heard a loud, explicit exclamation. *One caught, hopefully.*

Sam and Franklin checked the living area and a bedroom. Both a tip but empty.

They advanced up the hallway, stepping over rubbish, including spray cans. A muffled sound made Franklin pause and he held up his hand to warn Sam. Then came splintering glass, some thumps, a commanding voice and a sharp cry. *Two down, one to go?* Which of the bastards was he going to nab?

Outside the next closed door, Franklin motioned for Sam to stand opposite him. Ready, their weapons in hand, he held up fingers mouthing *three, two, one.*

He threw open the door and entered with Sam following, and glimpsed heels as someone dived under the bed.

'Police! Come out! Show your hands!'

He heard an answering scuffle and his spine prickled. They were overexposed. If their man was armed, he could use them for target practice.

Franklin pointed to Sam, indicating she move the other way, then vaulted the bed. He landed on top of a huddled body, but an elbow or knee caught him in the abdomen knocking the wind out of him.

The bloke grunted on impact, too, but was apparently unhurt because he thrashed about underneath, kicking out and flinging his arms, walloping Franklin in the balls.

Franklin swore, his eyes watered, but he didn't relent. Instead, he pressed all his weight down, grinding the bloke's cheek into the grungy carpet.

'Gotcha, Redwoods.'

He grinned and slapped a pair of bracelets on Redwoods's wrists.

———

Franklin had been home for less than an hour after his shift, still on a high after bagging the Terrible Three, as he kept calling the crooks who'd obviously gotten under his skin. Georgie was happy for him but contemplative. She tried not to dampen his good mood, but he must've sensed a vibe.

'What's up?'

She sighed. 'Should I tell Ally that her dad's alive?'

'We've talked about this.' He looked at her sadly.

'Yeah, but –'

He silenced her by pressing his lips to hers. Then murmured, 'No, Georgie. You can't tell her. What you have so far is inconclusive.'

'But I'm *sure* I saw Goyne.'

'Yes, but you saw your attacker in glimpses, and you're comparing your memory with an aged likeness by an untrained artist–'

'But–'

'It's too soon. Wait until we catch him, formally ID him, and *then* tell Ally and her mum.'

Georgie felt sick. 'But I'm keeping this horrible secret from them.'

Franklin watched her, with an expression she couldn't read. 'I thought you people didn't have scruples.'

You people? Had they slipped back to autumn when he told her that he couldn't stand journalists? 'Are you kidding me?'

'Yes.' He chuckled, running a finger down the side of her face. 'It's just my dumb way of reminding you that scruples go both ways. We both know it's Goyne, but you can't act without proof.'

Georgie nodded, then admitted something she'd never told anyone. 'Maybe I'm not cut out to be a journo.'

Franklin's smile fell. 'There's room for a heart in your

job. Just be careful.' He pointed to her chest and then his. 'You nailed it when you said our jobs aren't that dissimilar. Some things are really shitty, and bits'll sneak through the cracks and get to us. But it's time to hang up the police badge or journo ID if we don't do our best job or become heartless or don't care about the truth, yeah?'

Touched, she didn't answer.

Franklin wrapped her fingers in his. 'We'll find Goyne. And if he doesn't 'fess up, his fingerprints or DNA or our fancy iFace facial recognition technology will catch him out. Don't worry. We'll get him.'

She held up a bunch of papers. 'If we don't find him soon, he'll hit the road again.'

A flash of something crossed Franklin's face. Maybe the first sign of doubt that they'd catch Goyne.

She whispered, 'We can't think that we've already lost him.'

NEW YEAR'S EVE

CHAPTER FIFTY

THE RINGS AROUND HER EYES WORRIED FRANKLIN. So did her working through without breaks and running on caffeine alone. 'Georgie, you can't operate without food.'

'I'm not stopping, but you can. Throw me a banana.'

He aimed the fruit at her and chuckled when she intercepted it without glancing up.

'Wise guy, Franklin.'

Franklin again, huh?

She lifted her head, running her gaze over his face. 'You've got a heavy shift later. You should take a rest.'

He shook his head. 'We're in this together.'

Georgie's eyes took a distant look. 'That lighter. *YF.*'

'Could mean "your friend", "yours faithfully".'

She said, 'I'll bet it's "yours forever".'

'So this is all about Clare?'

'I think so. Let's go through it.'

She flicked to a fresh sheet on her notepad and they recapped all the facts in chronological order, starting with Clare's suicide.

Franklin mused, 'So Goyne blamed his wife for her suicide –'

'And that anger escalated to the point that he went through the motions but wasn't functioning normally.'

'Then came Red Victoria.'

Georgie nodded. 'Deb and Warren were caught near the seat of one of the fires. She escaped. He was presumed dead. But we know–'

Franklin finished, 'He faked his death and escaped.'

Georgie skipped to, 'And at some stage afterwards, he turned up in the Daylesford area, hooked up with Duffy.' She frowned. 'Why stay after Duffy realised I was tracking his mate?'

'Because Duffy's too ill to travel? Or because they're familiar with this area and can blend in, while they'd stand out as strangers elsewhere?'

'You're good at this.' With a wink, Georgie added, 'You should be a detective.'

'Ha ha.' Red fired over Franklin's skin. Then, serious again, he said, 'Goyne's played dead since he ran from Bullock.' All trace of his smile disappeared. 'And you've become a threat to that.'

'And put you and Kat at risk by association with me.'

———

Franklin rose and stood behind Georgie, planting his lips into her hair, inhaling the faint scents of fruity shampoo and musky perfume. 'I'll be off in a minute. Special early start at four today.'

He rubbed her shoulders, his fingers finding a knot that made her gasp before letting out a long sigh. She flopped her left arm and fingers as if he'd found a magic trigger point releasing pent-up pain.

'That feels good.'

Franklin kept massaging until she twisted around.

'I could try to draw out Goyne.'

'What?' His gut balled.

'Go to the lake, make myself visible and see if Goyne or Duffy takes the bait.'

'Georgie, don't. Please. It's too dangerous.' He tried to catch her hand, but she was out of her chair, pacing, clearly frustrated. 'You need backup for something like that. It's New Year's, so I'll be flat out all night, even if most of it's trivial. Wait until tomorrow, when I can help.'

She sighed, sounding unconvinced.

He tried another angle. 'Anyway, Goyne and his mate moved on from the lake, remember? It seems they went via Charlie Banks's place to grab a couple of jumpers, then shacked up back at the railway station.'

She argued, 'Yeah, but they moved on again after the station master called you in the second time.'

'True. But would they go back to the lake?' Franklin doubted it.

'*Where* then?' Georgie persisted.

He shrugged.

'We know they've been at the lake and pub. If they're short on options, they might go back. Or they might go to the Yandoit property.'

Her eyes begged, deepening from brown to ink, and Franklin almost went to putty.

He puffed his lips. He wanted to nab Goyne, too, but shook his head. 'I'll do some checking tonight and work with you on it tomorrow. Okay?'

Georgie blew out a deep breath.

———

Georgie's instinct that Goyne had done more than fake his death was solidifying, but she wouldn't share it. Not until certain. She felt hungry, not for food, but to prove her theories and nail the story, and grabbed at her phone when it rang.

The caller's ID was blocked but when he said *'Georgie?'* she immediately recognised the voice and smiled.

'Great to hear from you, Norman.'

'Merry Christmas, lassie.'

A tad late, but it was sweet of him anyway. 'And to you and Dawn.'

'Dawn reminded me that you rang while we were out on Christmas Day. I forgot to return your call.' He sounded sheepish.

'That's okay. I just rang to wish you both a happy day.'

'That's lovely.'

Norman rattled on for several minutes, losing track and repeating himself, while his gentle convoluted dialogue gave Georgie a respite from her obsessed thoughts.

'Oh!' he said excitedly. *'There's something special I wanted to tell you.'*

Her pulse surged. *Something about Goyne?*

'My MG is making a stab at independence from her wheelchair.'

His voice drummed with pride, and although it wasn't the revelation she needed, Georgie was thrilled. 'That's great.'

'She had me make a physio appointment and one for a dietitian.' Two beats, then, *'But if it goes wrong, she could easily slip back into depression.'* Norman's tone had changed, giving Georgie the impression he'd cupped the

phone's handset and lost his smile. *'Almost a new year and another anniversary so much closer.'*

Sympathy and remorse took a double-edged stab at her, followed by shock when he added, *'Can you talk to her, lassie? You've been through your own physical trauma. You could help.'*

'Me?' Georgie doubted she measured up as a role model, but said, 'Sure.'

CHAPTER FIFTY-ONE

Franklin gazed along the town's main drag, marvelling at the transformation ahead of the New Year's Eve parade.

Already in place were temporary stages, PA systems and musical apparatus. Stands and a hefty supply of stacked logs for the woodchopping competition were ready, and the axes would come just before the event. The petting zoo awaited the arrival of its star citizens. And barricades blocked traffic, although these would later admit an array of floats that would crawl along Vincent Street.

Everything seemed neat, calm and festive, and Sam had just confirmed peaceful preparations at the other end of the street too.

———

Georgie drove down Raglan Street in the Spider, spied barricades blocking Vincent Street and swore. She tried to visualise an alternative route.

After pulling a U-turn, she backtracked up Wombat

Hill, made a couple of unsuccessful attempts, then wound through, coming out at the intersection of the Ballan-Daylesford Road and the little overpass to the lake. Which was exactly where she wanted to be.

'Way to go, Harvey.'

Her grin turned to a frown. She hoped Franklin didn't spot her because he'd assume she still intended to bait Goyne, whereas although prone towards stubborn and impatient she wasn't—or tried not to be—altogether stupid.

Her amended plan was to suss out the lake but play it cautiously. There would be heaps of people around celebrating New Year's Eve, so if she stayed in the open and with the crowd, she'd be safe.

At worst, she'd kill time. At best, she might just crack a lead on Goyne's whereabouts.

———

It was unusually early for New Year's Eve shenanigans, but Franklin and Sam were checking out reports of firecrackers in the state forest.

Despite being inundated with a record amount of rain lately, explosives and a forest were always a volatile mix.

Franklin found a blackened patch and discarded packaging but the firecracker bandits had vanished. They'd probably been spooked by the witness who'd called it in.

Whatever, their next call was to the lake, to look into reports of a stranger behaving oddly.

It could turn out to be a fizzer too, but it was all part of the job.

———

Georgie muttered, 'Bloody hell.'

Picnicking families and couples crammed onto every inch of lawn, as well as the space in front of the old bathing house, amphitheatre, bridge, and jetties. She had no hope of spotting Goyne and Duffy if they were there. If the mass hadn't scared them off.

Even so, she'd hovered at the pavilion, strolled around the lake and loitered for close to an hour. All the while, she felt suspicious eyes upon her. Maybe people thought she was a pickpocket.

It was time to move on.

———

More people piled into the pub each minute, while Georgie leaned on the mantelpiece and savoured what would be her only beer for the night. It'd be standing room only by midnight.

At a vibration against her hip, she pulled out her phone, noted the caller with a jolt, and moved to the back door where it would be quieter. A couple was entwined a metre or so away, and a throng of mates guzzled beers where she and Manny had brawled with Goyne two nights ago. There was safety in numbers and from her post in the doorway. History wouldn't repeat.

'Ally?'

'Hi, Georgie.' The teenager sounded upbeat. Surprising after their last conversation.

'What's new?'

'We're home! Mum decided we should be home with our friends for New Year's. We're at a barbecue party at Clive's place.'

Georgie tensed, hearing a clatter. A fat tabby cat slinked by and she released her breath.

'I just wanted to say hi.' Then Ally said, *'Georgie, can you visit soon? It would be awesome.'*

Would it?

After her conversation with Ally, Georgie finished her beer and Manny cleared the empty bottle. Without that to occupy her, she grew self-conscious standing alone, not drinking, in a pub on New Year's Eve, so she returned to Franklin's house to regroup.

———

Sam and Franklin were scoffing hot chicken rolls; dinner on the go, while milling with the crowd. Numbers were swelling by the minute, as the kick-off for the parade drew nearer.

Franklin's eyes continually raked the street, upper windows and balconies, taking in couples, families and larger groups of locals and tourists, happily entertained by buskers, comics and the petting zoo, or just chatting.

No trouble. At the moment. Experience told him this was the lull before the storm and it'd be a different story in an hour or two.

———

Distant music and an excited voice on a PA system wafted through the dining window. The main street parade was underway and Georgie considered joining in, then immediately dismissed the idea. She had to locate Goyne before he absconded.

She scanned her notes again; then her gaze drifted to

the window. At the height of summer, the sun wouldn't bed down for another three-quarters of an hour.

She was suddenly very aware of being alone. New Year's was about fun, happy times with friends or family, whether that be mellow get-togethers or pumping parties. All of Franklin's neighbours could be at the parade or other events, doing those normal things. She may be the lone person on the block.

And Goyne could be stalking her right this moment.

———

A motley crew of floats had done their proud procession and dissipated. But other celebrations were in full swing. Face-painters transformed kids into aliens, animals and superheroes. Mums and dads were getting among the wood-chopping. The restaurants all appeared to be managing the currently cheerful and peaceful crowd.

Franklin decided it was time to move on. They had a host of locations to patrol over the night, in addition to responding to callouts. Fortunately, Harty and Slam were also on the road in the patrol car or they'd have Buckley's of coping.

———

Georgie sat outside, chain-smoking, thinking back to her earlier conversation with Franklin.

Why did Goyne pretend to die? Why did he run? He'd hated Deb, but couldn't he have divorced her? That way he'd still be part of Ally's life, instead of tossing that away with his legal identity and having to live as a fugitive.

Georgie blew out a stream of smoke.

———

'Mind if I check your bottle?' Franklin asked.

Two young teens blushed. Their buddy retorted, 'Don't you need a warrant?'

Sam smiled. 'You wouldn't have something to hide, would you?'

Franklin flashed the young constable a discreet grin. 'Tell you what,' he said conspiratorially. 'Say there's a little more than coke in those two-litre bottles, and you water those shrubs over there with the contents, my colleague and I'll leave you to enjoy the rest of your night.'

The arrogant kid crossed his arms.

Franklin pulled his sternest expression. 'But ignore this friendly advice and you'll find yourselves in big trouble.'

Sam added, 'It'll ruin your New Year's.'

The kids jumped up and rushed to the shrubs.

The two cops chuckled and continued mingling with locals and tourists, watchful for anything that could mean trouble.

———

After half an hour, Georgie stamped out pins and needles and cut a line across the deck, trying to make sense of her thoughts.

She murmured, 'Could Goyne have set the fire between his and Anna's place?'

Revolting. Scary. Plausible.

For as long as she'd been trying to fathom why he'd faked his death, she'd resisted this possibility because it was too despicable. And because rather than hurt Ally, it would shatter the teen.

But now Georgie surrendered to her gut instinct and aloud wondered, 'So if he did it, why?'

He might be one of Anna's pyromaniacs. But wouldn't there be whispers of gossip attached to Goyne then, a history of fire-lighting or strange behaviour?

Her mind jumped to murder-suicide. Perhaps Goyne had reached his limits and wanted both him and Deb dead. She squeezed her head with the heels of her hands and resumed pacing, already doubting the idea. If murder-suicide had been Goyne's intention, he'd have stayed with his wife after starting the fire.

'It's all about Clare.'

Goyne hated Deb for causing Clare's suicide. He might've intended to kill her to avenge his girlfriend's death and, after playing the grieving widower for a period, enjoy a Deb-free life with Ally. *But it all fucked up.*

He may've seen he'd botched his efforts and, fearing Deb knew what he'd done, absconded. Alternatively, he lit the fire and freaked out. Unable to face their daughter, regardless of whether her mother survived, he did a runner.

Georgie heard Franklin's voice in her head. *All this fallout from one affair could only happen in the country.*

Her breath escaped in a sharp hiss, as her arms dropped in limp shock, sure now that Goyne had done it all to kill his wife. But had he plotted it, or taken advantage of the fierce conditions and the umbrella of other arsonists' work?

CHAPTER FIFTY-TWO

Franklin slapped his forehead. 'Shit.' He'd forgotten his promise to Georgie that he'd monitor for signs of Goyne.

Even the callout to the lake about a suspicious woman hadn't earned more than a cursory scan for the fugitives while he worked the job, which itself turned out to be a non-starter. Witnesses had provided wildly different descriptions of the stranger and nothing concrete as to why she'd raised their hackles. Merely that she'd been acting strangely and lurking. Finding bugger all, they moved on.

Franklin figured they had time for a quick recce and phone call to Georgie.

———

A blast of rock music broke Georgie's trance.

As soon as she answered, the caller said, '*Where are you?*' No preliminaries. Franklin.

She mumbled, 'Your place.'

'*Good.*'

She heard happy shrieks and music. Other people were having fun. Other people weren't fixated on arson or attempted homicide. They weren't trying to track a killer.

Franklin said, *'Sam and I have done a recce at the lake and pub – nothing.'* He kept talking. *'And there's a gig happening on the railway platform so they won't go there either.'*

Georgie's brain felt dull. Shock will do that.

But they have to be somewhere. Have they gone to Uncle Ken's place?

'Georgie?' Franklin sounded uneasy.

'Yes.'

'Is anything wrong?'

'I've figured –'

'Hang on.' She heard Sam's voice in the background, then Franklin said, *'Sorry, I have to go. Job coming through.'*

And the call ended.

———

'Noise disturbance, boss.'

Franklin shook his head, exhaling loudly through his nostrils. Neighbours could cut each other a bit of slack on New Year's, surely. The occasion deserved cranking music and kicking up heels.

'Where?'

'Macadam Street.'

'Confirm we're on our way.'

———

Georgie's sense of urgency was a scream inside her head. She felt sure Goyne would be long gone by morning. He and his mate had sent her a couple of warnings, but rather than scare her off, she'd gone harder and enlisted the cops, which left them no choice but to run.

She prodded at tender spots from her encounters with Goyne and his mate, pushing until her eyes watered. She'd made plenty of mistakes in the past and would probably make more in the future. But one she hoped never to replicate was to jump into the ring without backup.

Goyne was a cornered man. He'd already killed, although not who he'd intended. Georgie suspected he'd do it again if she got in her way or looked about to expose his dirty secret.

———

The woman with a stick so far up her arse that it came out her nostrils would not calm down about the noise from next door. Franklin's immediate assessment was that the Macadam Street party was tame. And after a brief walk-through, he decided the gravest offence they were committing was playing the top 100 worst-ever pop songs; the cranky neighbour a bigger pest than those in the party house.

———

Georgie plonked down on the verandah steps, tossing up between a smoke and going out again to search for Goyne among the New Year's Eve revellers. He couldn't hurt her in a crowd.

Anxiety pumped her calf muscles of their own accord so that her sandal heels clacked on the step. Her head followed the thump of her feet, and she shut her eyes, zoning into the beat.

Something wrapped around her throat and she cried out as her fingers flew to her neck. She grappled to pull away from the coil that compressed her skin, her fingertips digging at twisted strands. Rope about the width of her index finger grated the necklace of lacerations from Duffy's attack last week.

A grunt from close behind came with a yank. 'Why couldn't you leave me alone?'

Georgie recognised the voice from the distorted message saved on Ally's phone. Goyne sounded as frantic now as he had then.

He wrenched the rope harder, forcing her upright. She stumbled into the verandah post, making the structure reverberate. Goyne jabbed what felt like a metal pipe behind her ear. The pipe was cold with blunted edges, and she desperately hoped it wasn't a gun muzzle.

Georgie struggled, but pinned by the rope and pipe, couldn't match his strength. He half pushed-half pulled her down the stairs. The pressure on her throat prevented her from yelling.

At the bottom of the stairs, Goyne thrust his face against hers. His breath smelled fetid.

'Who've you told?' His voice was quiet but full of fury.

The rope bit too hard for her to answer. And she didn't know what the right answer was. Her heart pounded. If she said no one, he'd do a runner, getting away with his crimes again. And he'd kill her so that she wouldn't expose his story.

A firecracker went off, accompanied by distant shrieks of laughter, and Goyne jumped, swore, and jabbed the pipe harder into Georgie's neck. It hurt, but she took his jitters as a tiny positive. He wouldn't risk killing her here. Too worried about interruptions, witnesses, evidence, he'd take her somewhere else. Then kill her.

He released slight pressure on her throat and repeated, 'Who've you told?'

Hoarsely, she bluffed. 'No one.'

'Don't bullshit me.'

'Not.'

He yanked the rope.

'Told.' Georgie gasped for air. 'No one.'

Goyne pulled her noose tighter so her nose pointed to the sky, moved the pipe and shoved it under her chin, forcing her breaths into scraping gasps. He didn't speak for a few moments and seemed to be thinking. She hoped he'd bought her lie. That she'd just bought some time.

He said, 'See this gun?'

It is *a gun*. Georgie's hearing tunnelled in on his heavy breathing and the remnants of a country drawl.

'Do as I say or...' He jabbed the gun under her chin. '*Bang.* Get it?'

'Yes.'

Goyne thrust her forward. 'Hurry.'

He pushed, as Georgie dragged her heels.

'Move it!' He propelled her towards the Spider.

Georgie wasn't going anywhere with Goyne. He intended to shoot her, just not here, so she would do her damnedest to get away.

Thirty seconds later, she saw her chance while Goyne had both hands full between gun, tether and trying to manoeuvre her into the Spider.

She slumped into a dead weight and the noose bit deeper, then slackened fractionally as Goyne tried to fight her momentum. She instantly pivoted, ignoring the pain as the rope scalded her skin. She drove a knee into his nuts, brought her left elbow into his chin when he sagged, and twisted to bring her right fist up into the same spot with her body weight behind the punch. Goyne struck her with the gun and her jaw sheared with pain, snapped closed. She bit her tongue and her mouth filled with warm blood.

He pulled the rope, bending her backwards. He glared down at her with no sign of the funny, kind, fat man Ally had known. 'Get in the car.'

Her feet barely touched the ground as he manipulated her into the driver's seat, looped the rope around her neck and headrest and pulled it taut.

The gun stayed jammed into her temple.

Her right leg quaked as she pressed on the accelerator. She felt hot and cold all at once. Blood mingled with bile in a sour coating on her throat, and her tongue didn't seem to fit in her mouth.

As she turned left into the Castlemaine road, the Alfa's headlights picked up a group of revellers. Hope and excitement made the shaky leg quiver harder. Georgie's teeth chattered as she plotted a last-ditch effort to escape.

The metres seemed endless, but finally she neared the pedestrians. In a split-second, she flicked on the high beam and leaned on the horn.

The revellers raised their bottles and cheered, 'Happy New Year!'

Then Georgie's hopes crashed when they turned away and staggered on.

Goyne yanked the rope.

Georgie's eyes watered with pain and disappointment.

CHAPTER FIFTY-THREE

GEORGIE'S PHONE SOUNDED AND VIBRATED IN HER jeans pocket. The call rang out and a moment later, her phone beeped with a single jolt. Another message.

Goyne ignored the noises. Mostly, he seemed unaware of her presence, and if she tried hard enough, she could almost forget he was there too. He spent most of the time still and silent, blending into the darkness, with his forehead and palms pressed against the wall.

She'd tried to get out of her bindings before with no luck, but desperation made her replicate the action of pulling against the rope with all her might. Goyne didn't react as she grunted with effort, and the rattan chair wobbled but held firm. The rope around her torso and arms that'd earlier been her noose had no give. If anything, it tightened.

Her heart banged inside her chest. *Pull yourself together, Harvey.* Georgie slowed and deepened her breathing. She shut down the hysteria, then swung the other way, into self-pity.

After a while, she shifted in the seat and her whole

body screamed, the fuzzy edge to her brain leaping into painful awareness. New bruises upon fading ones. Skin scraped while being lugged up here stinging. Numbness in her feet and hands turned to shooting pins and needles. She swallowed her yelp and grimaced as the throbbing in her swollen jaw ramped up.

Georgie's eyes watered. She blinked hard to clear them, frustrated that only a weak glow from the moon breached the darkness, worse for the grimy glass and stone walls. But it was enough for her to see the menacing outline of a rifle leaning against the wall near Goyne's leg.

Her mobile rang again and she strained against the rope, breaking into a cold sweat.

I need my phone.

It dug into her hipbone, lashed inside her pocket with only a layer of cotton between it and her skin. About a classroom ruler's gap separated her hand from her mobile. But the rope wouldn't give.

When it beeped, Goyne muttered, swinging away from the wall, angry.

Georgie gasped and froze. When he went quiet, she remembered to breathe and tried to strategise. At the end of the day, what does a writer do in a crisis? Ask questions.

'Where's Luke Duffy?'

She braced, flooded with déjà vu because when she'd sprayed questions while he tethered her to the chair, his response had been, 'Shut up or I'll whack you.' He'd brandished his gun, backlit from the window and unsure if he'd meant hit or shoot her, she'd shut up.

How long ago? Minutes? Hours?

This time, Goyne surprised her by answering. 'He's sick. Leave him alone.'

'What's wrong with him?'

'Couldn't take him to the doctor.'

'Why?'

'Are you stupid? They want Medicare cards and addresses. They'd either turn him in to the cops or set a social worker onto him.'

She considered what to say next, but then Goyne said, 'He started using. Sharing sticks, as they say. He's very sick.'

Georgie flashed back to Duffy's gaunt appearance and sallow complexion, guessing, 'Hepatitis?'

He sighed. 'I think so.'

'You've lost a lot of weight. Did you get sick too?'

Goyne laughed unhappily. 'It's called the *guilt diet*. Highly recommend if you're obese – try to kill your wife and accidentally murder forty-six of your neighbours, then say welcome to a living death and watch the kilos drop off.'

Georgie's mind reeled. *Shit, he's just admitted it. He did it. He caused the carnage.* She vowed to bring him down. She took strength from that and wiggled her fingers and toes, relishing the shafts of pain that grounded her.

Keep him talking. 'How do you know Luke?'

Goyne didn't answer, just left the room.

She heard him scuttle downstairs and took the opportunity to map the layout of the Yandoit farmhouse and anything that may help her escape. She was in a room on the second storey, accessible by only a steep and narrow internal staircase.

Goyne returned while she tried to conjure up a way to lure him to the stairs and push him down.

She kept thinking while asking questions. 'So, what happens now?'

'Luke's safe. I'll move on. Thought I had more time, but you've stuffed that up.'

She cringed at the anger in his voice but couldn't stop

herself snapping, 'You'll find another squat buddy in a random town and live off what you can steal or scam?'

'We only stole what we needed,' he retorted. 'Not like some of the others.'

'The others?'

'We shared houses, here and there. Some were all right. But others acted as though the world owes them. We never wrecked stuff just for the sake of it. Luke's a good kid. Even on the speed, he's got a good heart.'

Goyne scuffed the floor, dragging something.

'I got Luke out of the last place before they caused us trouble. You just had to look at Whitey the wrong way and he'd take your head off.'

Whitey? Georgie stiffened. Franklin had recently nabbed a violent guy named Whitey. It couldn't be coincidental. 'What are you going to do with me?'

'You?' Goyne sighed as he said it, making the word quiver. 'You should've stayed out of it. If you hadn't gone around stirring up trouble, I wouldn't have had to hurt you.' Another sigh. 'There's only one way I can be sure you won't tell.'

'You'd kill again?' *You'd kill me?* Georgie's blood iced.

'What does one more body matter? I'm already a monster.'

Georgie slumped, hit with the reality that, trussed to a chair on the second floor of a deserted farmhouse in the outskirts of Yandoit, this was her end. Her time was up.

She held a flutter of hope that if she could stall Goyne, Franklin only had to open the file she'd left on his dining table to find the property searches, photos and Whereis.com map that'd lead him here.

Let's hope he puts it together soon.

While this all tossed in her mind, Georgie was

overcome by morbid curiosity. 'How're you going to do it? The gun?'

He gave a hollow laugh; the sound made her skin ripple into goosebumps. Then he lifted the weapon. 'This?' He snapped it open and ejected a handful of pellets. 'It'd sting but probably wouldn't kill you. Though it might if I did it here.'

In a few steps, he crossed the room to stand over her and pressed the muzzle against the egg on her jaw. She swore.

Goyne pulled the gun away. 'It's an air rifle. Luke used to shoot targets. Bagged us a few dinners along the way too.' He threw it down. It skittered along the floor and out of her sight.

Georgie's phone rang again, and as she waited for the inevitable beep, she heard it.

And he heard it too. He rushed to the window suddenly illuminated by bright light from outside. And for the first time since they'd faced off in Franklin's garden, she saw Goyne clearly.

Distorted with rage and alarm, he looked hideous.

She glanced above him at the window. Red and blue strobes flashed, along with beams of white. Sirens wailed their approach. Out of sync, they filled the air.

But she knew he'd kill her and flee before the vehicles even parked.

Georgie's heart thudded. She tried to shrink into herself, to curl into a protective ball, but the rope constrained her.

Goyne lunged at her, with outspread fingers and grabbed her throat. He squeezed. She bucked as far as the trusses allowed.

He pushed her harder, pressing her into the cold, stone wall. Her lungs cried for oxygen and with the strain of raw panic, she screamed against the unfairness of never seeing her family or friends again. Her air-starved body managed only croaks that seared her throat. She writhed under Goyne's hand and against her restraints, furious now, because he was going to get away with all the devastation he'd caused.

Her nails clawed at the chair, as Goyne loomed closer, his grip relentless until her vision swam.

'You shouldn't have interfered.'

Georgie struggled, her strength draining fast. She floated, distanced from her body, aware of her stifled breaths, tunnelled sight, muscles slackening, and eyes shuttering. Drifting, but not peacefully, stricken by the loss of Franklin. *All over, when we only just got started.*

Goyne released her throat, but spread his hand over her face, pulling the skin on her upper cheeks downward. 'Look at me.'

She wheezed, shallow, burning inhales, still impeded by his palm and her swollen throat but some air making it to her lungs. Fast blinks cleared spots from her eyes and she gazed into his. Bloodied squiggles over his whites, inflamed lids, watery, maybe tear-filled.

He was trying to speak to her through his stare. She didn't understand.

'Prom –' Goyne shook his head, then tried again. 'Promise me you'll tell Ally how sorry I am.' The words choked off.

Georgie stared at him, disbelieving. *Is he letting me go?*

'And tell her that I love her.'

Is he going to make a run for it?

'Tell her that I never planned what happened.' He spoke faster. 'I was messed up over Clare and made a terrible impulse decision.'

Spittle sprayed Georgie's forehead.

Goyne's voice cracked as he said, 'Tell Ally I did it all for her. Pretended to be dead. Stayed away. So she'd never have to know what I did.'

His fingers circled Georgie's neck again, pushed deep. 'Promise me!'

Her throat seared, trying to answer. Impossible to.

He pulled Georgie forward and thrust her away. She saw him grab the gun.

'Police, come out!'

Is that Franklin? Georgie twisted in the chair, straining towards the window.

'Police!'

'Police!'

More than one voice out there.

'Warren Goyne! Luke Duffy!' That was Franklin. 'Come out. Show your hands.'

Caught in a spiral, unable to stop it, Georgie's heart raced.

She saw Goyne step in front of the window. He lifted his rifle, settled it into his shoulder, with a finger on the trigger, spurring frenzied yells outside.

She screamed, 'No!' and winced at a double crack of gunfire, the splinter of glass and watched Goyne jerk and fling backward.

———

Franklin's heart pounded as he huddled with Slam and Harty. They pressed against the side of the stone building, under the second-storey window that'd just been shot out. Two shots. Could've been Franklin or one of the uniformed boys from Trentham that'd hit Goyne.

Time would tell.

Sam and the other two were covering them from behind their vehicles. The proby had already seen too much in her first month out, but he couldn't afford to think about her.

'Georgie is still inside.' Franklin had heard her scream just before Goyne went down. Everyone had. 'We saw Goyne take the hit, but that's all we know. Consider him injured, but armed and dangerous. Have to assume Duffy is armed and inside too, but not necessarily upstairs with his partner,' Franklin instructed, his voice low, edgy.

Goyne hadn't responded to demands to show himself. Neither had the young bloke. Franklin wasn't prepared to wait out a siege situation. Not with Georgie inside. Their strategy was shaky. The three cops out the front were to distract Duffy and Goyne, while he, Slam and Harty snuck in to surprise and disable the two crooks.

It was dangerous, but his two best mates had volunteered to take the risk. They had each other's backs. He knew they wanted Georgie out of the firecracker situation as much as he did.

Strobes flashed off the rugged stone wall. The colours washed over Slam and Harty, adding a sick tinge to their grim faces.

Franklin wanted to bolt upstairs and find Georgie, but they had to be systematic. If not, they'd put her at greater risk, along with themselves. His gut dropped. He'd already made a critical mistake. He pulled his radio and called through.

'*Boss?*' One word, full of static; not from the reception but Sam's nerves.

'Sam.' Franklin kept his voice low. 'Duffy could be anywhere. Can't assume he's upstairs. Don't assume he's even inside the main building. Be vigilant. Expect him to come from anywhere. And to be armed.'

They connected eyes across the overgrown yard and the bonnet of their truck. She nodded and he returned it.

Franklin glanced to the door they would enter, then to his mates. He whispered, 'Ready?'

Slam and Harty each gave a thumbs-up.

Franklin held three fingers high. Dropped one. Then a second.

Sam and the Trentham boys yelled, 'DUFFY! GOYNE! Come out! Now!'

Franklin pumped out the *go* signal.

———

Georgie struggled to breathe, only partly because of her bruised larynx. She drew rapid, shallow, useless breaths and felt light-headed too, while her pulse dragged, slow and weak. Transfixed by the spreading pool on the floor. The spatter glistening at her feet. A few wet dark spots on her jeans. Maybe blood.

She shuddered...didn't want to look at Goyne. When she did, she couldn't look away and began to quake. The thumping of her nerves reverberated through her body and the chair legs, tapping the floor.

———

They swept the ground floor with silent precision. Franklin was sweating hard. Georgie's scream could've been a warning. *Or she's been hurt. By Goyne or Duffy.* Adrenaline buzzed. Fear mixed in.

At the base of the stairs, they exchanged gestures, all on

the same page. Franklin led the way. His feet sounded loud, boots scraping the treads. Slam pounded right behind him. Beads dotted Franklin's lip. He paused, mimed soft knees to Slam, and they covered the last stretch quietly.

Two rooms up here. One door ajar. Franklin's senses heightened. He clocked the disturbed dust on the floor around both thresholds. An indistinct sound; a kind of drumming noise, hard to pinpoint what or where it came from.

Which one? He drew his shoulders back. *The door's shut for a reason.* He twitched his head at Slam, then Harty, who'd closed in the rear.

Slam took the lead. He threw open the door, stepped right, sweeping the room with his gun. Franklin followed, crouched, taking a left.

Goyne was on his back. Immobile. But it could be a ploy.

Franklin and Slam shouted over the top of each other, 'Police! Don't move!'

As Harty hammered up behind them, Franklin heard a soft moan that came from his left. Goyne remained prostrate before them, and Slam had him covered with his gun.

'Show yourself, Duffy.' Harty ringed to the right.

Franklin followed the sound of another moan, with his weapon raised.

———

Georgie flinched when the door banged open, terrified it was Duffy, slow to take in police uniforms and drawn guns. Time stretched and raced together in an impossible warp.

Even when the cops yelled, she was still numb, eyes back on Goyne, who didn't move.

He hadn't moved since those few twitches after he hit the floor. She stared at his empty fingers. Trigger finger still extended. Gun gone. Somewhere on the floor. Her gaze travelled up his body, to his head. It lolled, angled towards her. Lifeless eyes. She wished she could unsee the mess above them.

Her body trembled, then juddered with the shakes, making the chair bang on the floor again.

———

Franklin's extended arm wavered, then lowered, as he met the eyes of Georgie. She was bound to a chair, and he moved towards her, checking the area was clear of booby-traps. Dread was quicksand sucking at his body.

Closer now, he could see her skin under the fresh cuts and bruises was deathly pale, her forehead covered in beaded sweat. She was clearly in shock but had no apparent life-threatening injuries, and his limbs jellified with relief. He almost smiled when she shook her head as if trying to push through the cloak of shock.

As he rushed to free her, he thought, *That's my Georgie, never giving up.*

CHAPTER FIFTY-FOUR

FOLDED TOGETHER, CHEST TO CHEST, THEIR heartbeats matched rhythm. When they'd emerged from the stone house, Franklin pulled her away from the cluster of vehicles. They'd barely spoken since, simply held each other.

Georgie noted the arrival of a mute ambulance, travelling at a sedate pace because the emergency was over for Goyne.

Yet more cop cars followed, their occupants hyper as they alighted. The search for Duffy was still on – they wanted to know what he knew, to fill in the gaps of Goyne's last two years. But Georgie thought he was long gone, that Goyne meant that when he said the kid was safe.

After some minutes—maybe five or ten—Georgie waved off ambos who wanted to treat her injuries. She took the proffered shock blanket and draped herself in it, just to get rid of them.

Later still, Lunny joined them. But Franklin's headshake made the sergeant turn and retreat without more than a touch to each of their shoulders.

Georgie was grateful for that touch, even more so for Franklin's arms. But she needed to go. *Not allowed to. Don't want to leave Jack anyway. Not yet.*

She blocked everything, tuned into the sound of wind shimmying through the long grass they stood in. They clutched each other and more time passed.

'Senior Constable Franklin.' A barrel-shaped female cop approached. 'You can't be with this witness until she's been thoroughly debriefed. You know that.' The cop lifted her hand, beckoned Georgie by bending her fingers. 'Ms Harvey, let's start.'

The woman was so uptight that she probably starched her undies.

Another cop, this one towering over Franklin's nearly six feet, with lots of shiny bits on his epaulettes, patted Franklin on the back. 'Rough night, John.'

Franklin nodded, unsmiling. 'District Inspector.'

'I came directly from Clunes, soon as I heard.' They shook hands.

Georgie noted the DI didn't offer the use of his first name, a privilege she knew Eddie Knight gave Franklin at times, but this situation was obviously too serious.

'You know we'll need to take your weapon, John.' The DI drew breath through his teeth. 'Let ballistics do their thing.'

Georgie strained but couldn't hear more as the female cop introduced herself, name immediately forgotten, leading her to the ambulance with its back doors open.

'Let's get those injuries checked over while we talk.'

Georgie grimaced. The woman was doing it by the book. She had something to do with professional standards. That, Georgie remembered. She'd come across from Castlemaine, but whether she only acted for them in the immediate mop-up or belonged to the PS team was hazy.

Georgie submitted to photos, let the ambos poke and prod, protesting she was fine, wondering if she had a mild concussion, somehow bluffing her way through the tests. She gave the cop what she needed, as her wounds were cleaned, sutures and other dressings applied, and was close to tears with gratitude when the female ambo wiped the spots off her jeans.

Her eyes found Franklin in the crowd, still conferring with his DI. She rose from where she perched on the ambulance step and fixed the PS cop with a stare. 'I need to be somewhere urgently. I've told you everything. I have to go now.'

The cop made protests that Georgie ignored. She paused long enough for the woman to press a business card into her hand and extract a promise to make a full statement later that day.

Tangles of official vehicles and people blurred around her, as Georgie moved towards Franklin, with a hole in her heart over this conversation, yet more so about what she had to do next. Wretchedly aware it was her responsibility, not necessarily better coming from her, but the right thing to do.

————

Georgie's eyes stung, but she knew if she let go of one tear, it would turn into a torrent, forcing her to pull over and lose more precious time. Her calf muscle cramped from pressing the accelerator so hard for so long, and she dealt with the spasms in her left hand by rigidly gripping the steering wheel, pushing the ache deeper into her body. The agony in her throat was relentless, worse when she swallowed.

But for all of this, she took nothing but small sips of water, embracing her pain as a just outcome for what she'd unearthed and the hell storm to follow. She heard the ping of an incoming text message; a reply to one she'd sent before leaving Yandoit, and there was no going back now.

Despite several erratic drivers and a visible police presence via several booze buses and highway patrol cars, little traffic hindered her travel, but the trek seemed like an eternity. She cursed having to drive to the fringe of Melbourne before cutting across; no direct route could get her there faster.

Georgie counted on delays at the scene. Fatal shootings by cops meant masses of red tape. PS cops to investigate their fellow cops, along with the Coroner and Office of Police Integrity. Most would come from their beds in Melbourne, giving her time.

Goyne hadn't carried ID. He'd changed dramatically after supposedly dying two years ago. The cops would have to verify several facts beyond Georgie's story before they did a notification.

Giving me even more of a head start. But how much? I have to be the first to arrive.

Her memory jumped back to the farm, and a vice gripped her chest as she remembered their parting:

She moved to the Spider with Franklin trailing. He touched her arm, and emotion trembled through the connection and in his voice when he said, 'Wait until I've finished and we'll go together.'

'No. This is something I need to do myself. Urgently.' With a small step backward, she broke his hold, adding, 'And you'll be caught up for hours.'

He gazed at her and reached again. His palm touched

hers and their fingers entwined, their pulses combining into a heavy throb.

'I have to go, Jack.'

He swallowed heavily. 'Apart from this.' He waved at the scene, but she knew he meant it in a wider sense than the Yandoit property. 'What about us?'

'I don't know.' As she said it, Georgie winced. She saw Lunny approaching and stepped closer to Franklin. She clutched the lapel of his uniform shirt. 'Get this done...give it time...'

He looked shattered. She kissed his lips, then sprinted past Lunny and slipped into her car.

Now she'd travelled around 200 kilometres in record time.

She texted a second message to Ally, 'Almost there,' and entered the sleeping town. But then she couldn't drive on, picturing so many people whose pain hurt as her own, not least the two she was about to face. With shaky hands, she steered the Spider to the kerb and parked opposite the library.

Can't.

Georgie's breaths shuddered.

Must.

She had to stand in front of them while explaining the awful truth.

Five minutes later, Georgie turned into the bluestone driveway. As she reached to the ignition, it occurred to her that today was more than the first day of a new year. It was another black day for Bullock.

Frozen in the motion of turning off the car, in the eerie pre-sunrise Georgie saw the tall girl with straight hair silhouetted under the sloping verandah. She wore short pyjamas, which accentuated her lean, youthful build.

Ally.

Georgie's heart splintered.

They met on the verandah with a hug that lingered.

'What happened to you? You're hurt.' Before Georgie answered, Ally added, 'What's going on?' At the same time, her mother said something from within the house.

Georgie's jaw tightened, but it was only right that she told them both at the same time. 'I'll explain inside.'

She ushered Ally into the living room. It seemed like years since she'd first visited this house and entered Deb and Ally's lives. Now the teen stood in front of her, eyes imploring. Deb rose from the sofa when Georgie arrived but stayed on that side of the room, her expression a mix of emotion amid shadows of tiredness.

For once, Deb kept quiet.

Georgie urged both to sit, but they refused. She'd had over two hours to practice what to say and now couldn't remember a word of her spiel.

Clumsily, haltingly, she started to deliver the devastating news. 'I don't even know where to begin, really.'

Ally's brows pinched, her chocolate eyes were worried. Georgie reached for her hand, but she backed away, cringing.

'It's very complicated. After –' Georgie faltered, 'afterwards, I'll go back to the start and give you as much detail as you want. If you want.'

Deb was shooting her glares. She couldn't know what Georgie was about to reveal but already realised she'd hate it. She sank to the sofa.

Georgie started, 'Warren didn't die in the fire.'

His wife gasped and clutched her chest as though stabbed. 'What?' A kaleidoscope of emotions crossed her face. Hope, doubt; Georgie thought anger, too.

Ally shook her head continually, mutely. Her expression was unambiguous. *Liar. I hate you for lying to me.*

Georgie drew a breath and continued. 'He is now...he's passed away now, I'm sorry, but he was on the run –'

Deb jumped to her feet. 'Rubbish. On the run! My Warren?' She pointed towards the door. 'Get out.'

Georgie blinked away tears. She deserved their anger. 'Please.' Her tone begged. 'Let me finish.'

Ally hummed, losing it. Georgie thought about the scabs she'd promised not to rip off. The truckload of band-aids Bullock needed, thanks to her.

When you have to tear a band-aid off someone you care for, it's best to do it fast.

'Warren lit the fire in your yard on Red Victoria.'

'How dare you! Get out.' Deb's voice shrilled.

Georgie kept ripping. 'He never intended the town to go up as it did.' She bit her lip, looking at Deb. The woman was abrasive, may well have triggered Clare's suicide or contributed to it, but she didn't deserve what Goyne did or to hear about it, yet she had to know. 'He thought the fire would be contained at your place.'

Ally's hum became a deep moan.

'But I was inside, asleep. With my migraine. He knew that.' Horror drained all colour from Deb's face. She understood. She clapped a hand to her chest again.

Georgie's hand crept to cover her own mouth.

Deb fell to her knees, staring at Georgie with dry, hollow eyes. 'It's not true.' She said it on repeat.

But Ally was Georgie's focus.

She blanched, grabbed the fine silver chain around her neck and gave it a sharp yank. Georgie reached one hand to catch both of Ally's, trapping the broken necklace and its boxing mouse charm in the teen's fist. With her other hand, Georgie folded Ally into an embrace.

'Ally, don't,' she whispered. 'One day you'll be glad to have something special from your dad, from the good days. No matter what he did on the day of the fire and afterward, he loved you. He always loved you.'

Ally's slight body shuddered, and Georgie held her tighter. She murmured, 'He told me that he was messed up over Clare and made a stupid, impulsive, *terrible* mistake.'

Ally stiffened, pushing away slightly from Georgie.

'He wanted me to tell you that he was sorry and he's always loved you.'

'Then why?' Ally's voice was a rasp. 'Why did he try to kill my mum? Why did he let me think he was dead?'

Georgie couldn't attempt to answer her first question, not yet. It was too awful. She held Ally's heartbroken gaze, speaking softly. 'He stayed away so you'd never find out what he did.'

Ally searched her face. Georgie stroked the teen's long hair. 'There's more. Do you want to know now?'

Deb sobbed, broken already.

Her daughter swallowed, then mouthed yes.

'Your dad was on the run. He did this because he felt caged.' Georgie pointed to her face; Ally gasped. 'Everything was finally catching up with him. He couldn't protect you any longer.'

Ally shook her head. 'No, no...' Her fingers bit into Georgie's arms, pressing on bruises made by her father.

'He had a gun. He used it to threaten police. It was only an air rifle but they had no way of knowing. They shot him.'

'When?' Ally spoke faintly. 'Where did he die?'

Georgie held the teen's gaze. 'Tonight, today...at Uncle Ken's old farm.' She pulled Ally into her body and cheeks pressed together, arms gripping each other, their tears merged, unheeded.

She whispered, 'He didn't make it. I'm so sorry.'

THREE MONTHS LATER

CHAPTER FIFTY-FIVE

GEORGIE BROKE OFF FROM RESEARCHING HER LATEST article and listened to the sounds coming from the courtyard – the new norm after only a month: thuds, exclamations and the creak of chains on timber, as her housemate pounded a boxing bag attached to the verandah.

The dog gave a playful bark-howl, and she heard Maz say, 'You wanna see fancy?' A belly laugh, then a set of pummelling followed, punctuated by Molly's deep woofs. Apparently, Georgie wasn't the only one happy to have someone else around the house again, and the bonus of her boxing instructor living in was extra one-on-one practice; Georgie was getting better, definitely not punching like a pansy anymore.

Her mind drifted as she absently stroked a thumb across her mobile phone. She jumped when the back door banged.

'Want a coldie?' Maz trekked past to the kitchen and pulled open the fridge, extracting two beers.

Georgie almost said yes, but the phone lying in her palm silently egged her on. 'Later. There's something I've got to do first.'

She and her roomie danced around each other in the small kitchen as Georgie grabbed her pack of smokes. On second thought, she poured herself a glass of red and took that outside too.

For a moment, she simply sat on the back step, squinting against the bright sun, thankful for a light breeze that stirred the heated air, softening it. Then she took a sip of wine that was more like a gulp.

She murmured, 'Slow down, Harvey. You've waited until now, so get it right.'

In the next sip, she could taste peppery berries and oak, but when she lit a ciggie, her hand quivered with tell-tale nerves. After a long drag and equally long exhale, the phone was back in her hand and she had dialled.

'*Georgie?*' Excited and tense in that one word.

My fault, but good. He still cares. 'Yes.' She clammed up, struggling. For a wordsmith by profession, finding the right ones when it counted should be easier.

'*I'm glad you called.*' His voice deepened, adding, '*Waiting was killing me, after our last texts...*'

The connection was so clear; he could've been in front of her, not hours away.

Georgie pushed away the complications. *If I never jumped into things, life would be a whole lot safer...and bloody sad and boring.*

'So, Jack –'

'*Jack again, huh?*'

'Hmm.' A smile quirked her lips and she pictured Franklin's face, starting again, 'So, Jack. I got to thinking.'

'*Did you, now?*'

'Uh-huh. The thing is, I know my way around your house, and I know that you like your coffee strong, white with one. I've met your closest mates and your daughter, and ridden pillion on your bike. We've chatted for hours in pubs and at the lake, gone paddle boating, kissed…' Her cheeks flushed as she added, 'And we've slept together.'

His chuckle through the phone connection was as warm as the summer air.

'*But*…we've never been on an official date.' Georgie took a swallow of wine and stubbed out the cigarette she'd forgotten.

'*So,* Jack. I got to thinking, would you like to go on a real date with me? Dinner someplace dimly lit by candles, with soft music, the full monty…'

She held her breath, thinking she knew his answer.

'*Georgie.*' His voice sounded thick, and she wished she could see him. His eyes would tell her what he wanted to say.

As the pause stretched, she had to put down her wine glass, afraid she'd snap the stem.

Finally, he said, '*Sure,*' then cleared his throat. '*What are you doing tonight?*'

Dear reader,

We hope you enjoyed reading *Dead Again*. Please take a moment to leave a review, even if it's a short one. Your opinion is important to us.

Discover more books by Sandi Wallace at https://www. nextchapter.pub/authors/sandi-wallace

Want to know when one of our books is free or discounted for Kindle? Join the newsletter at http:// eepurl.com/bqqB3H

Best regards,

Sandi Wallace and the Next Chapter Team

The story continues in:
Into The Fog by Sandi Wallace

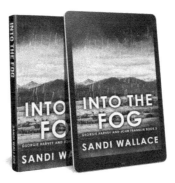

To read the first chapter for free, please head to:
https://www.nextchapter.pub/books/into-the-fog

ACKNOWLEDGMENTS

Though many readers will tragically have their own experiences of major bushfires, an event known as Black Saturday (and Black February) inspired the backstory of *Dead Again* as a way to honour those who fought, survived and died in the fires, and the lessons learned. That said, the town of Bullock, all characters and incidents are fictitious.

I am grateful to the many people who helped with this book. Any mistakes are my own.

Warm thanks, firstly, to the team at Next Chapter.

I am appreciative of the police members who assisted with my procedural questions, including David Spencer, then attached to Victoria Police Media & Corporate Communications Department, Film and Television Office, and Tessa Jenkins and Joanne Morrison.

My gratitude goes to the original publisher of *Dead Again*, Helen Goltz of Atlas Productions, along with Dr Amanda Apthorpe, Marianne Vincent, Jaye Ford, B. Michael Radburn, Vanda Symon, Monique Mulligan, Anne Buist and J.M. Peace. Thanks also to Lindy Cameron,

Ruth Wykes, Kylie Fox, Judy Elliot, Raylea O'Loughlin and Sharon Gurry.

I have been fortunate to make many wonderful connections in my writing journey. New friends in the Yandoit area, Daryl Puddick and Duncan McKinnon, introduced me to Colin Mitchell whose truck matched the one I imagined for Uncle Ken in this book, and other welcoming local families. On that day and others, I took many photographs in the area, including several of Colin's truck, along with an amazing stone house that strongly resembled my visual image of Uncle Ken's property, which was restored by its owners Dale Fuller and Marnie Ireland. My sincere thanks to all, but particularly to Colin, Marnie and Dale for permitting my use of these unique Yandoit images.

To my lovely readers, many thanks for all your wonderful messages, emails and reviews letting me know how you have enjoyed my stories. I'd love you to hear my book news first and stay in touch by joining me on Facebook or Instagram, or please follow my website.

Lastly, thanks to Glenn, who never stops believing.

ABOUT THE AUTHOR

Sandi Wallace's crime-writing apprenticeship comprised devouring as many crime stories as possible, developing her interest in policing, and working stints as banker, paralegal, cabinetmaker, office manager, executive assistant, personal trainer and journalist. She has won a host of prizes for her short crime fiction including several Scarlet Stiletto Awards and her debut novel *Tell Me Why* won the Davitt Award Readers' Choice. Sandi is currently at work on a psychological thriller. She is still an avid reader of crime and loves life in the Dandenong Ranges outside of Melbourne with her husband.

Connect with Sandi at

Website www.sandiwallace.com
Amazon www.amazon.com/author/sandiwallace
Goodreads www.goodreads.com/author/show/
8431978.Sandi_Wallace
Facebook www.facebook.com/sandi.wallace.crimewriter
Instagram www.instagram.com/sandiwallacecrime
Pinterest www.pinterest.
com.au/sandiwallace_crimewriter/

CPSIA information can be obtained
at www.ICGtesting.com
Printed in the USA
LVHW081651260521
688349LV00019B/459/J